Remembrance

Remembrance

RITA WOODS

A TOM DOHERTY ASSOCIATES BOOK

NEW YORK

REMEMBRANCE

Copyright © 2019 by Rita Woods

A Forge Book
Published by Tom Doherty Associates
120 Broadway
New York, NY 10271

www.tor-forge.com

Forge® is a registered trademark of Macmillan Publishing Group, LLC.

The Library of Congress Cataloging-in-Publication Data is available upon request.

ISBN 978-1-250-29845-4 (hardcover)
ISBN 978-1-250-29847-8 (ebook)

Our books may be purchased in bulk for promotional, educational, or business use. Please contact your local bookseller or the Macmillan Corporate and Premium Sales Department at 1–800-221-7945, extension 5442, or by email at MacmillanSpecialMarkets@macmillan.com.

First Edition: January 2020

Printed in the United States of America

0 9 8 7 6 5 4 3 2 1

To the men in my life: Kenneth, Jonathan, and Logan, who tolerated chaos, tears, and takeout for longer than I care to admit.

And to Serenity, my baby girl, who asked every morning and every night, "How's your story going?"

Remembrance

Gaelle

CURRENT DAY

"How do I look?"

Gaelle glanced up from the *mayi moulen* she was spooning into Rose's mouth. Her grandmother stood fidgeting in the kitchen doorway. Grann always looked beautiful, but this morning she looked especially stunning, the emerald green of her suit shimmering against her dark skin. She pulled at the buttons that ran down the front of the jacket.

"Grann, *yo sispann*," cried Gaelle. "You look lovely. You will get the job."

Her grandmother gave her jacket another tug. "I don't know. Maybe I am too old, *wi*?"

Gaelle sucked her teeth. "You? Old? Don't be silly." She swatted her sister's hand. "Rose, stop. You're making a mess."

There was the faint rumble of thunder.

Grann looked up and sighed. "I'm going, then."

Another rumble, this one much louder, rattled the tiny house. Gaelle felt it in her teeth. A teacup crashed to the floor. She felt the chair vibrate beneath her. And then a roar cracked the morning into a million pieces, drowning out all other sound. Gaelle leaped to her feet, reaching across the table for her sister.

"Grann?"

But her grandmother was staring up at the pale blue sky where just moments before there'd been ceiling.

"Grann," she screamed.

They locked eyes, and then her grandmother vanished beneath a mountain of wood and plaster and dust as the world ripped itself apart.

Gaelle jerked awake, gasping for breath, arms flailing, reaching for Grann.

A dream.

The same dream she'd had countless times in the more than ten years since the earthquake had destroyed her family, her island. She lay rigid under the covers, waiting for the shaking to stop, the tears rolling unheeded into her ears.

Taking a quivery breath, she turned her head and glanced at the clock: 5 a.m. The terror, the devastation of Haiti was a long time ago. A lifetime. And she had to get to work.

She moved mechanically around her apartment, turning on the coffee, ironing her scrubs. The apartment was small. The owner called it a carriage house, but it was really little more than a converted garage at the back of a decaying mansion in the middle of a long block of decaying mansions, most of which sat empty, or were occupied by squatters. She grabbed her travel mug and headed for the car, her mind thankfully blank. There was nothing in her past except pain.

It took barely a quarter of an hour to reach the Stillwater Care Facility where she worked, the streets nearly empty in the winter predawn. Stepping from her car, she stood for a moment, breathing deeply. She imagined the cold air traveling down to her lungs, layering her insides with a glaze of ice crystals, shimmering in the darkness, purifying her.

Everyone thought she was crazy. Her sister thought she was crazy; Rose said she would never live in a cold place again. But the dead of winter was Gaelle's favorite time of year. The world seemed to slow down, to grow quieter, coating everything in a layer of snow and ice, so that even the ugliest parts of Cleveland acquired a certain beauty. She held her face to the sky and felt the snowflakes melt on her lips. Smiling, she walked into work.

"You lose somethin' in there?"

Gaelle started. She turned to find Toya peeling off her thick bubble coat and stuffing it into her locker. Toya Fairfield was another nurse's aide who worked the same shift. She'd been at Stillwater even longer than Gaelle. They'd become good friends.

"You standin' there starin' in that locker like you expectin' a genie to come poppin' out."

"No." she smiled. "No genie."

"Well, if one does, then I got dibs on at least one wish. You feel me?"

"And what would you do with your one wish?"

"Girl, I'd wish for three more wishes, that's what."

Gaelle laughed lightly. It was what Toya always wished for.

"And what about you, Miss Thang? What would you wish for?"

She shrugged and closed her locker. She would wish for Grann to be alive. She would wish for her and Rose to be together again. She would wish for Haiti to be made whole. But wishes were for children. They held no real power.

"A million dollars," she said. "I would wish for a million dollars."

"I heard that. Holy Christ! It's cold as a polar bear's butt out there," cried Toya, kicking off her boots. "I'm freakin' freezing. Quick. Do that thing you do."

She thrust her hands into Gaelle's.

Gaelle gripped her fingers and squeezed. She closed her eyes and felt a prickle of heat start in her elbows and flow down her arms into her hands, felt the hard coldness of her friend's hands lessen, then disappear. She opened her eyes as Toya sighed contentedly.

"Damn, girl! You're just a little walking furnace." She slipped her badge over her head. "Should probably get your thyroid checked out or something, but appreciate if you'd wait until this weather's over. You better than a space heater."

Gaelle held up her hands. "No thyroid, just my superpower."

"Well, it ain't a bad superpower to have in the middle of December, that's for darn sure." Toya opened the lounge door into the hallway. "By the way, you get the old lady again today."

"I do not mind."

"Yeah, I know you don't. You and her got some weird kinda thing going on."

Gaelle grinned and stepped into the still-quiet nursing home hall.

From where she stood in the doorway, the old woman was barely visible, the barest suggestion of a person-shaped lump tangled in the blankets on the bed in the darkened room. The television was on and shadows flickered across the ceiling and walls.

Twice, the director of nursing had tried to switch from the twenty-four-hour news station to something she deemed more suitable, something more cheerful for a geriatric nursing home resident: *Dancing with the Stars,* or one of those Real Housewives shows, but both times, the old woman had bolted upright in her chair as if suddenly electrified, eyes blazing in her cadaverous face, shrieking and cursing until the windows rattled and the terrified assistant had gone running from the room. After the second time, the DON decided to leave her alone. Now, solemn voices intoned from the television speakers all through the day and all through the night about earthquakes and fires and drought, about the opioid crisis and far-flung wars.

From the corner of her eye, Gaelle saw Toya coming down the hall toward her, pushing the med cart ahead of her.

"Seriously, Guy, what is with you and that old lady?" she asked, stopping beside her.

"I do not know. I just feel . . ." She shrugged and pointed to her heart. "I feel a connection."

She turned and looked at her friend. "Do you not ever look at her and think: There is something . . . ?"

"Yeah," responded the other aide. She tugged at her straining scrub top. "There's somethin' alright. Somethin' freaky. All this time and still don't nobody know nothin' about her. Where she came from. Who she is. Nothin'. She just sits in that chair not sayin' a word, news playin' twenty-four/seven. She gives me the heebie-jeebies for real, girl. Like she came back from the dead or somethin'."

"Not well is not dead," said Gaelle, something she'd heard her grandmother say.

"What? What does that even mean?" Toya rolled her eyes. "Girl, you as peculiar as she is. Why'n't you go on now and hang out with your weird, not-dead friend. I got meds to pass."

Gaelle chuckled and turned back to the darkened room as the aide rolled her cart down the brightly lit hallway. Toya wasn't the only one who thought her attachment to the old woman was odd. Everybody did. The rest of the aides did the bare minimum required: changed her sheets, gave her the pill at night to help her sleep, cut the food on her tray into the tiny pieces she barely touched. Gaelle was the only one who lingered. She massaged the old gnarled hands, rubbed oil into her cracked feet. Even she didn't understand it, her affinity for this mysterious elder, but she understood that some questions had no answers. Their spirits were linked in some way, and so she accepted that as the beginning of it, and the end.

Plus, it gave her an odd measure of comfort to offer the old woman this bit of extra care. She was most likely someone's grandmother, someone's great-grandmother, yes? Maybe out there, somewhere, there were people who loved her, missed her.

She stepped into the room.

"*Bonjou,* Manman."

She often spoke to the old woman in her native Creole. Except when Rose was home from school, she almost never spoke it any other time. It felt too personal, a thing she wanted to keep just for herself. But here, in this room, there were no odd looks, no personal questions she didn't want to answer.

She glanced at the television. Onscreen, something was burning. People were marching in the streets. People that looked like her, like the old woman, in every shade of brown. Their mouths were open. They were shouting, their eyes wild, and she was thankful the sound was muted. A swastika flashed on the screen. A line of white men marched side by side, their arms locked, except for the one on the end who waved a Confederate flag high overhead. Something curdled in the pit of her stomach—so much evil in the world. She turned away, blocking the images with her body.

"Come now, Manman. That is not something to watch on an empty stomach, *wi?*" She pulled a chair close to the bed and began spooning applesauce into the woman's mouth, softly humming a lullaby. When she couldn't cajole the woman to take another bite, she pushed the tray aside and pulled a fresh nightgown from the drawer and gently eased her into it. She took her time. It was like dressing a kitten: tiny bones under soft, loose skin. There were rumors that the woman was well over a hundred, and that wasn't hard to believe. She looked every bit of it. She had simply appeared one day in their lobby two years before, bald, skinny, her clothes in rags, pale healed burn scars crisscrossing her arms.

Gaelle glanced at the clock above the door. As much as Toya fussed at her about all the time she spent in here, Gaelle knew her friend would cover for her until she was through. Carefully, she rolled the nearly weightless old woman from the bed into the chair.

"What will you do today then, Manman?" she asked.

She didn't expect an answer and she didn't get one, but deep down she was sure the woman could hear her.

"Perhaps you go to the activity room later, *wi?* It is movie day. You get out. You meet your neighbors. Watch something nice. Not these *bagay led?*" She jerked her head toward the screen.

The old woman's eyes never left the television.

Sighing, Gaelle shook her head and began stripping the bed. Fresh linen sat neatly folded on the bedside table. As she yanked back the blanket, something clattered to the floor and she bent to retrieve it.

"Ki sa nan syel la?"

What in the heavens? It was the remote. Or what was left of it. The entire controller was flattened, misshapen, the buttons fused into a single white mess in the center, as if the whole thing had somehow been melted, then put back together badly. She stared at, turning it over and over in her hands.

"What happened here?" She looked up and inhaled sharply. The old woman was staring at her, her red-rimmed eyes glittering under the fluorescent lights.

The hair on Gaelle's neck stood on end. She felt a surge of fear, an inexplicable sense that this frail, ancient woman was dangerous. They stared at each other for a long moment, and she felt her heart pounding in her ears.

"Well," she said, finally. She bit her bottom lip. "You know you're going to have to pay for this now, *wi?*"

She gave a shaky laugh and dropped the remote into the pocket of her scrubs. The director of nursing was not going to be happy. She reached to straighten the old woman's collar.

"Okay, Manman . . ."

She never saw the old woman move. The clawlike hand clamped around her wrist and Gaelle was yanked forward and off her feet before she even realized what was happening, only barely managing to not fall directly on top of the woman. She blinked, stunned. Their faces were mere inches from each other's, and this close, the sense of danger seemed even greater. She felt a roiling in her gut, as if she might throw up.

"Manman, *bondye*," she hissed and leaped to her feet. She tried to pull free, but the woman's hand held her like a vise clamp, belying both her size and her age.

The old woman held fast, her eyes locked onto hers. Gaelle felt a sudden pain in her head and once again she fought the urge to vomit.

"Kite'm ale!"

Something changed in the room. The air suddenly smelled of rain, of freshly mowed grass. As if someone had left a window open somewhere. Except that it was winter and a hard crust of ice covered any grass for miles. The pain in her head grew worse.

"Let go, Manman; I do not want to hurt you." The bones in her wrist felt like they might break.

She felt something shift deep inside her and cried out in pain, instinctively grabbing the woman's hand with her free hand. There was a sharp, white-hot pulse in her shoulder, then heat, but not the gentle prickle she'd felt earlier in the lounge with Toya. This was a blowtorch firing up, igniting her arm, her hand. The old woman's eyes widened, first in surprise and then in pain.

And then Gaelle was free.

Gripping her wrist, she staggered backward until she touched the wall behind her. She stared down at her hand. It looked unchanged, yet she still felt the hard thrum of heat echoing in her fingertips. She locked eyes with the old woman. Next to her, police cars rolled across the television screen, sirens blaring.

"What are you?" she whispered.

The old woman opened her mouth in a silent, toothless laugh, and then the world went black.

Part One

Far Water, Louisiana

1857

Margot

Margot caught a glimpse of herself in the mirror as she passed and stopped to peer at her reflection. Her sandy-colored hair had worked itself loose from its bun and lay damp and heavy against her neck. Her face shone with sweat.

The house had been closed up since the fall, and in the mid-July heat, the air was stale, the rooms like an oven. She pulled a handkerchief from her pocket and dabbed at her forehead, her cheek, then leaned forward to study herself in the glass. Though the heavy drapes were still pulled closed, enough light leaked into the big room for her to clearly see the freckles scattered across her nose and cheekbones.

She sighed and shifted the heavy linens in her arms. Mistress Hannigan and her three children would be coming down from New Orleans in less than a week, and the house needed to be in perfect order. There was only Margot, her younger sister, and their grandmother to set the house to rights before they arrived . . . and it was a big house.

If only the heat would break.

Something—a movement reflected in the mirror—caught her eye. She turned, but there was nothing in the massive dining room except the mounds of sheet-covered furniture . . . and her.

She laughed nervously. She'd been on edge ever since they'd arrived the night before. Chewing her lip, she scanned the room, squinting uneasily at the odd shadows cast against the walls.

The feeling of dread that seemed to be following her from room to room made no sense. She loved this place—had spent every summer since her birth here: wandering the gardens, reading beneath the old hickory out near the creek whenever she found a spare moment. Every year, from July until mid-October, the Hannigans closed down the mansion in the city and came here—bringing their house slaves with them—to escape the disease-ridden air of the New Orleans summers: malaria, cholera, yellow fever. Here, the air was fresh, the water clear.

But ever since they'd stepped from the carriage, Margot had been unable to shake the feeling that some dark, infected cloud had followed them out of New Orleans and was settling itself all around Far Water.

Far Water.

Named for some plantation in Haiti, lost long before Haiti had been known by that name, the estate had been in the mistress's family for over a half century.

Catherine Hannigan was French Creole but had married James Hannigan, an American. Her family might have been far more scandalized had Monsieur Hannigan had far less money.

Margot brushed aside her unease. There was furniture to be uncovered, windows to be washed, and the half-dozen fireplaces all needed to be swept clean of last season's ash. And where was Veronique?

She moved to the window and pushed aside the thick drape. The manicured lawn swept down toward the road, where it disappeared from view beyond two magnolia trees. Her little sister was supposed to be helping to clean, but Margot hadn't seen even so much as her shadow since their morning coffee, hours before.

Something rustled behind her and she spun, the hairs on her neck standing up.

"Veronique?" she called. She cocked her head and listened, but the only sound was that of the old clock out in the hallway.

"*Idiot, fille,*" she muttered.

She straightened and ran a hand across the gritty mantle. Never mind the vague threat she felt oozing from every corner. There was real work to be done and the very real Grandmere to fear.

In less than six months' time Margot would be eighteen. The Hannigans had promised her her freedom on her birthday, but until then, her grandmother could still pinch her arms until they turned blue if she caught her daydreaming instead of working. Margot smiled as she stepped into the hallway.

"Boo!"

Margot yelped and dropped the bundled sheets as her sister danced gleefully in the hallway.

"I scared you, didn't I?" crowed Veronique. "Admit it! I scared you. Did you think I was a ghost?"

Margot glared at her younger sister as she bent to pick the linens up from the floor. "I was not frightened. . . . And where have you been?"

Veronique simply laughed and grabbed her from behind in a tight embrace.

"What mischief have you been up to, *ma petite*?" Margot laughed in spite of herself, pulling away to face her sister. "Sweet Virgin, you are a mess."

She ran a thumb across the dirt smudged along Veronique's cheek, tried to smooth down the wild hair, the same sandy color as her own, except that her sister's stood in a wild tangle about her face and was matted with straw and feathers.

"I was collecting eggs."

Margot eyed the feathers. "Collecting eggs or playing with the baby chicks?"

Veronique threw out her arms and laughed. "I do one and then the other is easier, *oui*?"

Margot smiled and shook her head. She thrust a handful of the sheets at her sister to carry. "Come, silly girl. There is real work to be done."

All night she'd tossed and turned in a fitful sleep, and now, just before dawn, she lay wide awake. Groaning softly, Margot sat up. Yesterday had seemed to last forever—endless hours of scrubbing floors, beating half a year's worth of dust from the carpets, airing out the bedding. The heavy work—mending the coop, taking the shutters from the windows—that would be left to Girard when he brought the Hannigans from the city, though their work had been hard enough and Margot's body ached with fatigue.

Pale light seeped through the window of the small cabin she shared with her sister and grandmother. Wincing, she pushed herself out of bed. Veronique was still asleep, curled in a tight ball at the edge of their bed. Margot glanced across the narrow room toward the cot where their grandmother slept, and groaned softly. Grandmere was not there. The small sitting area off their bedroom was empty as well. Margot pulled a thin shawl from the hook by the door and stepped onto the porch.

"*Non*, Grandmere," she muttered. "Not again."

The day was still just beyond the horizon but the predawn air was already thick with heat. Across the damp grass, fireflies flickered in the shadows of the cypress trees.

"Grandmere?" Margot hissed into the darkness. "Grandmere, *es tu ici?*"

From somewhere deep in the gloom, where the grass dissolved into bayou, a cougar screamed. Margot flinched.

Their cabin sat on a slight rise, connected to the main house by a stone walkway, and though her grandmother was an early riser, the house was dark. In the other direction, the walkway led to the creek. Growling in frustration, Margot turned toward the creek. In the shifting light, something brushed across her face and she swatted frantically.

"*Nom de Dieu*, Margot," she murmured. "Get hold of yourself."

The walkway was cool beneath her bare feet and she moved slowly in the dim light. She rounded a bend, and there on the creek bank loomed the old hickory tree, a lantern flickering at its base. But her grandmother was nowhere to be seen.

A thick mist rose from the dew-covered grass. Moss, hanging from the tree branches that leaned far out over the creek, quivered in the slow-moving water.

"Grandmere?" Her voice bounced from tree to tree, then disappeared in the fog.

A figure moved in the shadows down at the creek's edge, and she stiffened. Moments later her grandmother stepped into the small circle of light cast by the lantern. Her nightdress was soaked and muddy all the way to the knees, her square face scratched and bloodied.

"Holy Mary, Mother of God," whispered Margot.

The old woman stared blankly into the trees and Margot rushed to her side. She flung her arms around Grandmere and tried to guide her back up the walkway toward the house. But though her grandmother was well into her seventies and a head shorter, she was strong and solidly muscled. It was like pushing against a tree.

Margot glanced at the sky. It would be light before long, and Veronique would wake and find herself alone. Her sister had an unreasoned fear of being left alone. Margot pushed harder.

"For the love of God, *chére*. What are you doing? Do I look like a wheelbarrow to you? Stop pushing on me." Her grandmother was squinting at her in irritation.

Margot dropped her arms. "What am *I* doing?" She glared at Grandmere. "What are *you* doing out here in the middle of the night, *vielle dame*? And look at you."

Grandmere glanced down and grunted, seemingly surprised by the mud caked on the hem of her nightdress. "Ah."

She picked up the lantern and turned toward the cabin.

"Grandmere!"

"Hush, *chére*," snapped Grandmere. She grabbed hold of Margot's hand. "The spirits called my name."

Margot felt the hairs stand up on her arms.

Her grandmother spoke to the spirits often—as often as she spoke to her and Veronique. Each morning, Grandmere lit a candle and whispered her prayers. Each night she did the same. On holidays, she saved a bit of the choicest meat and the richest cream as an offering to the ghosts of the ancestors. The Hannigans knew and left her to it. At least the mistress did. But the master . . . well that was a different matter.

But when she began to wander—when Margot would wake to find her grandmother gone in the middle of the night, or worse—missing for one whole day, or more—then Margot grew terrified. For it was at those times, few and far between, that Grandmere said the spirits were calling especially to her, had come to whisper their warnings.

The feeling of dread that had weighed on Margot since they'd arrived grew heavier, making it hard to catch her breath. Grandmere was watching her.

"Come," she said. "Your sister will wake soon. The fireplaces all need cleaning and the linens got to be laid in the sun to freshen." She sucked her teeth.

"And that kitchen garden's a mess. I'll get to working on that, then make us some sweet potato biscuits for supper." She smiled. "You and your sister can grow fat as me, *oui*?"

Margot resisted being pulled along. "Grandmere, you promised Master Hannigan . . ."

Her grandmother whirled. "Master Hannigan does not control the spirits, girl! He does not control the world of gods."

"But he controls this world, Grandmere. The one we live in every day. You might remind your spirits of this when they come whispering in your ear late at night."

Grandmere reared back, the air quivering hotly between them. For one long moment Margot thought her grandmother might strike her.

"Master Hannigan is spit in the ocean, Margot," said Grandmere finally. "In fifty years, a hundred, who will know his name? But the ancient ones, they will still rule the ways of the world."

The old woman turned and stomped away, leaving Margot alone in the shadows. By the time she arrived back at the cabin, her grandmother stood waiting on the tiny porch. The two stared at each other.

"*Chére*," said Grandmere finally. "I will not always be here like this for you and your sister. But when the world is black, when you think you are alone, the spirits, my spirit, will be with you, living in your heart. When you don't know the answers, just listen. Quiet. And the answers will pour into your soul."

She gazed up at the lightening sky and laughed bitterly. "They might not be the answers you want, but the spirits always answer."

She turned and walked into the cabin, leaving Margot shivering on the threshold.

3

Far Water sat on the far eastern edge of the vast Atchafalaya Basin, wedged on a narrow spit of land between seemingly endless miles of swamp and marshland. The estate was far enough away from the poisonous air of the city for safety, yet still close enough should James Hannigan have the need to rush back and attend to his business empire.

The big house was invisible from the main road. Perched at the end of a long, curving drive, it appeared suddenly to visitors—with its heavy stone walls, tall, white pillars, and ornate shutters—rising like a massive wedding cake between the trees.

Catherine Hannigan had filled Far Water's rooms with crystal chandeliers and heavy velvet tapestries. The windows and doors were trimmed in gold leaf. The bureaus and cabinets overflowed with silver. Far Water was as grand in every way as the Prytania Street mansion back in the city, thirty-five miles to the northeast. During the long, hot months of summer, the Hannigans entertained often. Those who made the trek from their plantations along the great River Road that ran beside the Mississippi or from their mansions in New Orleans or Baton Rouge were feted like the cotton, coffee, sugar, cattle, slave-holding royalty that they were.

Margot was on her hands and knees in the foyer, giving the floor of the great hall a final scrubbing before the family arrived. The marble glowed in the sunlight streaming through the tall windows on either side of the front door.

"You missed a spot."

Margot jerked, nearly overturning the water pail. She hadn't heard Veronique come down the stairs.

"What are you doing?" she asked over her shoulder, dabbing at the spilled water.

Veronique shrugged.

Margot rolled her eyes. "Well, what are you *supposed* to be doing?"

Her sister didn't answer and Margot sat back on her heels to look at her. Veronique sat with her tiny hands clenched in her lap, her lips pinched tight.

"What is wrong with you?"

Veronique reached up and began to worry the scarf knotted on her head. Grandmere had tied it there just this morning, and already most of her pale, thick curls had worked themselves free.

"Is something bad going to happen, Margot?" she asked finally.

Margot inhaled sharply through her nose. "What are you talking about, goose?" She forced a smile.

"Grandmere. I woke up. Really late. And she was gone."

Margot looked away. Sunlight danced on the gleaming marble steps. "Mar?"

She sighed. "Yes, *chére*. She went out last night."

"Then something bad is going to happen."

"Perhaps not, Vee."

Veronique fixed her with a look and Margot felt a chill spiral up her spine. She remembered the fear she'd felt hours before out by the creek with Grandmere, and she searched her memory for a time, any time, when Grandmere had wandered in the world of the spirits and the words they'd whispered in her ear had been anything other than a warning of something terrible to come. She shivered.

"Remember the flood?" asked Veronique.

Margot nodded. She'd been ten, Veronique had just turned six—but she remembered clearly how they'd woken to find Grandmere gone, the tiny room off the kitchen they all shared filled with flickering candles, the door to the outside wide open. Mistress Catherine had been frantic. She hadn't believed for a moment that the old woman had run away. Fortuna Rousse would die before she abandoned her granddaughters. And what reason would she have to leave? Weren't she and her girls treated just like family? Girard had finally found her, wandering Magazine Street in the dead of the night, her white hair wild around her face. She said she would speak only to Master Hannigan. She never shared what passed between her and her master, but James Hannigan had, suddenly and without explanation, moved a large share of his stored cotton out of his warehouses in the business district. Two days later, a levee broke upriver. Water roared down the Mississippi, flooding the district. The stench of the muddy river lay over their neighborhood for weeks, nearly paralyzing the city. But while the other white businessmen wandered the sodden Garden District with pale, pinched faces, stunned, bankrupt, the Hannigans were little more than inconvenienced by the flood. At Christmas that year, Mistress Catherine had slipped three gold coins into Grandmere's apron pocket.

And that had been a good thing, yes? Money in Grandmere's pocket? The Hannigan's fortune spared? Except that James Hannigan had become oddly distant after that, watching Grandmere from across the rooms, his expression wary, fearful.

"And the fever?" Veronique went on. A cloud seemed to pass across the golden floor. Margot nodded, her mouth dry.

"I remember," she murmured.

1853. Just four years before, winter had seemed to last forever, cold rain lashing the muddy streets of New Orleans. A dank fog hovered over the rooftops, the stink of raw sewage choking every breath.

Then suddenly, without warning, it was blazing hot, the fog burned away. The city had been joyous. People poured into the streets to warm up and dry out, everyone's spirits high in anticipation of Mardi Gras.

Everyone except Grandmere.

Once again, she began to wander. One night, then two. Fortuna Rousse moved through the house as if in a daze, lips moving in silent prayer. The bread she baked was thick and tasteless, her stews thin and bland. Margot struggled to get up earlier and earlier every day, trying to cover for her grandmother, while Veronique drifted behind her, anxious and silent.

And then, the Sunday before Mardi Gras, Grandmere had stalked into the dining room and slammed a platter of fish onto the table. Catherine Hannigan's brother, his wife, and their seventeen-year-old son were visiting from Natchez. They'd been discussing plans to have the mistress's nephew start in James Hannigan's business. They all stared in silence as the platter skidded across the tablecloth.

"New Orleans will be filled with death," declared Grandmere. She fixed her eyes on her master. "Get the mistress and the little ones to Far Water. Now."

The whites said nothing. Margot gripped a pitcher of iced wine and glanced at her master. Master Hannigan's Adam's apple bobbed wildly above his silk collar. Time seemed to stretch, then warp, like hot taffy. Margot saw her sister trembling in the doorway, a basket of biscuits in her hand. She shook her head, warning her to stay quiet.

Finally, Catherine Hannigan laughed. A short, quivery bark. "Fortuna is so superstitious. You know these Louisiana Negroes." Her voice was shrill, pleading, as she addressed her guests. "But she makes the best beignets and biscuits in all New Orleans."

"Mistress," said Grandmere, turning toward her. "It is the fever. It will come this year. . . ."

"Some fever or another comes every year to this maddening city." James Hannigan had found his voice at last. He rose slowly from his chair, and Margot read danger in his eyes. She was certain her grandmother saw it, too, and yet . . .

"This will be like no fever before, or after," insisted Grandmere, her voice hard. "Before it ends this will become a city of ghosts."

"Fortuna . . ." Hannigan growled a warning.

From the doorway, Veronique whimpered, so softly that only Margot heard. James Hannigan was a bear of a man, quick to laugh and quicker to anger. He brooked no nonsense: not from his employees, not from his wife and children, and certainly not from his slaves.

Margot stood frozen, staring at the table, shoulders hunched, waiting for the explosion. The fish lay partially off the platter, its dead eyes glazed, as if plotting its escape across the sea of lace and cutlery.

"You will all die," said Grandmere, her voice flat. "Corpses will float in the street like—"

"Enough," roared Hannigan. A fist came down on the table, sending a crystal glass crashing to the floor. "Enough of your voodoo, black magic, witchcraft! Get the hell out of here, old woman, before you make me forget you belong to my wife and not to me."

"James!" His wife was on her feet, her normally pale face as red as her hair.

Grandmere turned and left the dining room without another word, pulling Veronique with her. Margot would have followed except that she had taken root to the spot, heart racing, hands welded to the wine pitcher. Hannigan stood glowering at the door for a long moment, then he turned his great, bearlike head and caught Margot's eye. He blinked slowly, then visibly shook himself.

"Bring me some a' that wine, Margot," he called to her. He plopped in his chair and laughed. "Damn Louisiana niggers. Superstitious as hell with their curses and their ghosts."

"James," said his wife again, sinking back into her seat, her face still flushed.

Her brother and his wife sat wide-eyed and pale. Their son, Alain, looked amused. Margot managed to pour the wine without spilling it.

Hannigan raised his glass. "Ain't no saffron scourge can ever get James Hannigan." He drank from the glass and smacked his lips. "And I'm staying right here in New Orleans all summer long just to prove my point."

But he hadn't.

Catherine Rousse Hannigan may have been quiet, and skittish as a rabbit, but she believed to her core in what she called Grandmere's visions. She had made her husband's life a nightmare of tears and pleading and slammed doors. The entire Hannigan family was at Far Water by Easter.

By the end of that summer, eight thousand souls had succumbed to yellow fever, including seventeen-year-old Alain Rousse. James Hannigan would never again allow Grandmere in the same room with him.

Now, remembering, Margot tugged nervously at her hair.

"Do you remember . . . ?" began Veronique.

"Enough, *oie*," cried Margot. She'd had enough remembering. Each memory twisted the knot in her stomach tighter. "You're a goose. With all this foolishness. And if Grandmere catches you lazing about on these stairs . . ."

A movement on the landing above them caught her eye. They both looked up, and there stood their grandmother, silent, wreathed in light from the round landing window.

"I am almost done here, Grandmere," said Margot pulling the pail closer. "And Vee was just . . ."

She stopped abruptly. Grandmere was not looking at them. Her attention was riveted elsewhere. The old woman descended the stairs, stepping absently over her youngest granddaughter.

"Grandmere?"

Their grandmother strode across the still-damp marble floor as if she hadn't heard, and flung open the front door.

"Come," she snapped.

Frowning, Margot glanced at her sister, who shrugged.

The two girls sprinted after their grandmother, who stood at the edge of the wide porch staring down the drive.

"Grandmere?" Veronique reached a hand toward her grandmother, then pulled it back.

The old woman was trembling. Margot followed her gaze, but except for a wild pheasant pecking in the dirt, the drive was empty. She felt her sister's hand clutching the back of her blouse.

"It comes," whispered Fortuna Rousse. "It comes *now*."

"Grandmere. Come in," pleaded Margot. A blade of fear pressed itself between her shoulder blades. Sunlight poured onto the porch, and yet she felt frozen to the bone. "There is nothing out here. Come in now. I will put on fresh coffee."

"Shush," said Grandmere.

The three slaves stood in silence, waiting, time having seemed to slow to a standstill in the thick bayou air.

Margot couldn't bear it, the stillness, the crushing sense of dread. The beating of her own heart. She opened her mouth to say those words, to say that there was work to be done, to ask what they were doing standing there like statues in the sun. But before she could speak, she felt Veronique stiffen beside her, saw Grandmere step from the porch, her hands clasped tight over her heart.

And now, Margot could feel it—through the soles of her feet—the faintest vibration. Could feel it before she could hear it.

Horses. Moving fast.

Someone was coming.

Veronique fumbled for her hand and Margot grabbed it, holding tight.

"*Mère Vierge*," whispered Grandmere. "Sweet Virgin, help us."

And then, Catherine Hannigan's barouche hove into view.

Girard, James Hannigan's groom, valet, jack-of-all-trades, sat high in the driver's seat, his waistcoat flying wild behind him, his caramel-colored face gray with road dust. They could just barely make out the huddled figures behind him. The large carriage swung wide, and Grandmere crossed herself, muttering a prayer, as one of the back wheels caught in the gravel that marked the edge of the drive, skidding into the sloping grass on the far side. The horses, eyes wild, heads thrown back, seemed to stumble as the barouche pitched crazily from side to side. For a moment, it looked as if Girard might be hurled from his seat, as if the carriage itself might go over. But Girard fought for control until the horses finally regained their footing, and dragged the carriage back onto the drive.

"Miss Fortuna! Miss Fortuna!"

Margot heard the desperation in Girard's voice as he screamed for her grandmother. Yanking hard on the reins, he stopped the carriage less than a foot from the old woman, before tumbling from the seat.

"Miss Fortuna, hurry."

Grandmere shot her granddaughters a look, a silent command to follow. Veronique moved to her side, but Margot stood fixed at the edge of the porch, staring openmouthed at the barouche. As wide and long as a boat, the black metal carriage gleamed in the sun. It had been imported all the way from Paris as a gift from James Hannigan to his wife. Catherine Hannigan rode it to the theater, to the balls, to her grandmother's house in the Vieux Carré. It was fancy and expensive and completely unsuited for the rutted, unpaved country roads that ran between Far Water and New Orleans.

"Margot, *allez!*"

Her grandmother's voice yanked her from the porch and she hurried forward. Three feet away, she skidded to a stop once again. The oldest Hannigan child, thirteen-year-old Marie, was already standing in the drive. Thin and pale, eyes pinched closed, her mouth open in a silent scream. Inside the carriage, ten-year-old Lily lay sprawled, half on, half off the forward-facing seat, her lavender silk dress covered in black vomit. She had soiled herself as well—Margot could smell it from where she stood—but the girl was beyond caring. Her blue eyes were open and she stared unblinking, unseeing at the hot, blue sky.

But it was the sight of the mistress that froze Margot in her tracks. Catherine Hannigan had clearly gone mad. She was crouched on the floor of the barouche, her skirt up past her knees, legs spread wide, as if preparing to give birth. Her red hair was tangled, stray tendrils plastered against her forehead. Her blue eyes, so like her daughter's, were wide, crazed. She was shrieking, making high-pitched, unintelligible sounds. In her arms was her youngest child, Alexander. He was wrapped, head to toe, in a pink coverlet, but one hand had come free, and Margot could see that his skin was the color of cooked butter.

"Miss Catherine, give him to me," Grandmere was saying. "You got to give the boy to me now."

Catherine Hannigan drew back her teeth and snarled, spit flying from her chapped lips. Margot flinched. Her grandmother did not.

"Come, mistress," pleaded Grandmere. "It's going to be alright now. But I got to take that baby. Let me take him so I can tend to him, *oui?*"

The white woman blinked and seemed to see the old slave woman for the first time.

"Fortuna," she whimpered. She grabbed Grandmere's wrist. "Save my baby. Save my son."

"I make no promises, mistress. But you give him to me and I swear I try."

"No!" Catherine Hannigan screamed.

The word ricocheted off the house, the trees, fracturing the air. Veronique cried out. Marie Hannigan gripped the barouche and silently shook.

"No," screeched the mistress again. "You will promise me. You save my baby. You can do that. I know you can do that. Don't think I don't know what you are. Don't think I don't know what you can do. You save my baby. Do you hear me? You save my baby or else."

Bile rose in Margot's throat and she locked eyes with her sister.

"Mistress," said their grandmother, her voice still calm. "You give me *le petit*."

The white woman clutched the bundle that was her son to her chest, the yellowed hand flopping limply against her thigh, then, with a sob, finally released the child to Grandmere's waiting arms.

Grandmere whirled from the carriage, her face hard, the dying boy pressed against her.

"Put the carriage away and take . . . Miss Lily to the root cellar," she commanded Girard.

"Veronique, you get the mistress and Miss Marie into the house and cooled down. Margot, come with me now. I need you."

Margot tasted the bile once again climbing into her throat. Her grandmother turned to look at her.

"*Ma petite*," she said. "You come now. We must try and save this baby's life. Before it is too late."

With a last look at the dead girl in the carriage, Margot followed her grandmother into the house.

4

They carried the boy behind the main house to the small, stone building that was their kitchen and laid him on the little wooden table.

The sight of the boy laying limp and lifeless where just hours before they'd taken their coffee and biscuits caused Margot's stomach to clench. She clamped her teeth together, fighting a sudden wave of nausea.

Grandmere gently touched the girl's face. "Breathe, *chére.*"

Margot nodded, reassured by the rough feel of her grandmother's hand against her skin. Grandmere would make it alright.

"Watch him close, yes?" instructed Grandmere. "I need to gather some things."

Margot nodded once again as the old woman disappeared through the kitchen door. She gazed at the boy. He was short for his age, thin, like his mother and sisters. But while his sisters had the pale skin and red hair of their mother, Alexander was dark like his father.

He was a lighthearted, chatty child who teased his sisters, made up riddles, and loved to go riding with Girard. Now, he lay on the kitchen table, eyes closed, lips blue and crusted with the same black vomit as his dead sister, and only his fast, shallow breathing showed that he was still alive.

Margot took a hesitant step closer and swallowed hard, the sound loud in her ears. Standing over the boy, she reached out a hand, then pulled it back, not quite able to bring herself to touch him. Not yet.

Mistress Catherine had said that she'd known what they could do, known what they were. But she didn't. Not really. She believed that Grandmere had a sort of healing magic, the same magic that brought about what she called "Fortuna's visions." Mistress Hannigan had prayed about it, she said, and she didn't believe, as her husband did, that what Grandmere could do was evil. It had come to her in her prayers that Grandmere was a gift to her from God. It was part of the reason that she had agreed to free Margot and Veronique on their eighteenth birthdays: as an offering. She wouldn't free Grandmere— oh, she would never do that; Grandmere was much too valuable—but she could free the girls. It was only right, she'd said.

But the mistress had no idea.

Grandmere was a healer. But there was nothing mystical, nothing magical about what she could do. She had a way with plants: knew which ones could temper a fever, which could draw out infection.

The boy twitched on the table. A bubble of black vomit formed at the corner of his mouth, and Margot hissed in disgust.

It wasn't Grandmere that had the magic. It was her.

Most of the time, the poultices and teas Grandmere made from the plants and herbs that grew along river and deep in the bayou were enough to soothe a colicky baby or settle the mistress' nerves. But there were times—when a wagon wheel ran across Girard's foot, when a local teamster's leg wound festered and poisoned his blood—when Grandmere's herbs weren't enough.

And then Margot would use her touch.

She wasn't a healer. Not exactly. But when she laid her hand on someone, she could feel the things that were wrong inside of them, feel them deep inside herself, like a reflection in a mirror. Their pain was not her pain, any more than a reflection was actually her face, but she could feel it, study it in all its details. When Girard's foot had broken, she'd run a finger along his swollen ankle and was suddenly aware of every bone, every nerve, in her own foot. She knew the size and place of the fracture, could feel the other slave's pain vibrating deep inside her flesh. Grandmere had made a special plaster for him, and now, months later, he barely limped.

She stepped closer to the table to study the boy. She had known Alexander since the day of his birth. He was a sweet child, and she loved him in the twisted, complicated way of slave to master.

Warily, she laid a finger lightly at the boy's throat. She winced. His skin was like chilled cowhide. She felt the fever feasting on his organs, digesting the boy from the inside out. Felt the effort each breath cost him. He was far gone, and neither she nor her grandmother had the power to raise the dead. She pressed her hand against his forehead, taking shallow breaths, repulsed by the meaty stench of decay that mingled with his sweat. She forced herself to hold still, to search for the thing that was most wrong inside him. Alexander was dreaming: of hot-breathed monsters, of blood. The hallucinations twisted and warped, terrifying his fevered five-year-old mind, and Margot felt an answering vibration inside her own head. The boy had not much left in him.

"Chére?"

Margot started. Her grandmother stood in the doorway, a wooden bowl of water in one hand, herbs tied with rough twine in the other. Under the stench of vomit and rot, Margot smelled lavender. They locked eyes, her grandmother's unspoken question writ clear on her broad face. Could he be saved?

With a nearly imperceptible shrug, Margot bent over the boy and pressed her hands tightly against his shoulders. His pulse was sluggish, stuttering beneath her palm. She held herself motionless, feeling the struggling rhythm in her palm, feeling it in her own chest. Her heart searched for his, found it, grabbed hold. She felt the boy's heart spasm, then . . . beat by beat, begin to speed up, settle down, until it had matched itself to hers.

The little boy exhaled and Margot caught his breath in her mouth, tasting death on her tongue.

Grandmere whispered. "Hold now, *chére*. Keep him bound here with the living."

As if from a great distance, she felt Grandmere slip a reed down

Alexander's throat, spooning meadowsweet-laced water into him, the wintergreen scent mixing with their body odors, felt the weight of the cooling linens against her skin as they were drawn over the boy. As her grandmother worked, Margot held fast to him, riding his nightmares with him, reaching out when the linens needed changing. Time passed unnoticed until, finally, the fever had retreated to a small, hard thing in the center of the boy. She focused all her concentration there, drawing it toward her like a magnet draws a nail. She saw it, felt it: the heart strengthening, the bleeding slowed. Felt death's hold on the boy loosen, then give way.

And then Grandmere was there, easing her down against the cool brick wall, brushing cool water against her face.

"*C'est très bon, chére,*" Grandmere whispered. "It is good, child."

Turning, she went to the boy who was now whimpering on the table.

"Child, drink this tea. It will make you strong." Grandmere was pleading with the boy, trying to get him to sip from a little china teacup, but the boy pulled away, shaking his head and crying for his mother. Margot looked up. Alexander's dark hair stood in stiff spikes around his head, and though his skin still glowed a sickly yellow, his eyes were bright and he looked strong as he struggled against her grandmother.

"*Maman,*" wailed the child. "Fortuna, I want my *maman!*"

Grandmere hefted the boy into her strong arms. "Come. We take you to your mama, then to your bed, *oui?*"

Still gripping the boy, she turned to look at her granddaughter. "Rest, *petit. Tout va bien.* The mistress will be out of her mind with sorrow about Miss Lily, but seeing the boy will help some. I will come back as soon as I can and we will have our coffee, yes?" She smiled. "Everything will be alright, *chére.*"

And then she was gone, holding tight to the still-wailing Alexander.

Margot laid her head against the cool bricks and closed her eyes. She didn't have visions. Not like Grandmere. But she'd seen the monsters inside Alexander's head, felt what he felt.

She'd felt the thickness of the Hannigan's bedroom rug beneath her feet. Smelled the bittersweet smoke of her master's cigar.

And there'd been something else as well.

A smell.

A terrible smell.

She'd walked inside Alexander's head as he entered that room, dark, the drapes drawn, even though it was late morning.

Master James, laying there on the bed. Still, so still.

That smell, that bad smell, growing stronger.

Margot clenched her eyes tight, her mouth open in a silent, agonized scream.

James Hannigan lay in a pool of vomit, eyes open, his last view in this life the red velvet ceiling of the Prytania Street bedroom.

She screamed because she understood, even if little Alexander was too young to, that her master had finally been caught by the saffron scourge after all. And nothing would ever be alright again.

5

Margot stood on the oriental rug that ran the length of the back hall, listening as the house breathed around her. Deep in the walls, the old timbers creaked, as the stone foundation settled itself into the damp Louisiana soil.

The Hannigan house was in mourning.

For three days, James Hannigan had lain in the bedroom of his mansion, alone, his body swelling, bloating in the heat. There had been no one to bury him. In that hot, hellish summer, there had been too many bodies stacking up in the streets and sewers and parks of New Orleans. Too many bodies and too few gravediggers. In death, not even his money could buy him a swift burial.

A business partner—a cattleman from Texas—who owed Hannigan a favor had finally rented a dray and hired four freedmen to go to the Prytania Street mansion. There, they had wrapped the stinking, leaking corpse in an oil cloth and carried it to Lafayette Cemetery. One of the freedmen, an old, mixed-blood Indian named Cale, had dabbed sweet oil on the dead man's forehead, whispered a prayer into his ear. Then the freedmen had rolled the body into a shallow grave—hoping that someone would come to build a proper crypt before the rains came—and hurried away.

A week later, word had arrived at Far Water of the burial.

It would be ten more weeks before the epidemic would finally begin to burn itself out, and what was left of the family could return to the city.

They'd been back in New Orleans over a month now, and though the dying outside the door had slowly ground to a stop, inside the mansion, the echoes still sounded, searing to ash the life Margot and her sister had known.

"I am going out."

Margot started as Catherine Hannigan brushed past her in the dim hallway.

"Mistress, wait," she cried.

Her mistress stopped, only half turning as she pulled on a pair of black riding gloves. "What is it?'

Her voice was sharp, the tone with which she said everything these days . . . when she spoke at all. Margot hesitated. Her mistress looked up, a deep line of displeasure creasing the space between her brows. In the months since the deaths of her husband and daughter, her pale skin had become nearly translucent, her face all hard, sharp angles.

"Was there something?" she snapped.

"It is early yet, Madame. Every morning you are up nearly before the sun." Margot tried to smile. "Let me get you some *café*, perhaps a sweet biscuit, *oui*?"

But her mistress was already moving down the hall toward the front door. "No . . . *merci,* no. I must go. I must make sure that James is properly laid to rest."

She smoothed a hair from her face, fixed the lace collar of her mourning suit. Margot watched, uneasy. In black from head to toe, Catherine Hannigan looked like a ghost.

"But . . . ," began Margot.

The white woman whirled, her wide crinoline skirt whispering against the narrow walls of the hallway. Desperation and sorrow rolled off of her in waves.

"The gentlemen from the shipping yard will be here again today." Margot spoke fast, trying to hold her mistress there. "They will want to speak with you. What shall I tell them?"

In the early morning light, her mistress's face seemed to collapse on itself. Catherine Hannigan's mouth quivered, her eyes blinking rapidly. For a moment it looked as if she might crumple, but she quickly regained her composure, her expression hardening. She fingered the brooch at her throat, the one made from the hair of her dead husband.

"Tell them . . ." She breathed out a short, irritated sigh. "Tell them I have gone to visit my beloved husband."

She turned and disappeared through the front door. Margot followed, her heart pounding in her chest. Girard, assisting the mistress into the barouche, caught her eye. Under the porte cochere, the two slaves gazed at each other, a silent eternity passing between them, until the groom gave a nearly imperceptible shrug and climbed up into the driver's seat. Margot watched him pull out into the street. From somewhere on the other side of Sixth Street, she could hear the milk wagon rattling across the cobblestones.

Fall had come to New Orleans and the air was sweet and cool, but she struggled to catch her breath. She had seen it in Girard's eyes. Fear. Because he knew, just as she did . . . that whatever the spirits had whispered in Grandmere's ear, there were still more bad things coming to this house.

The white men came. And kept coming. The cotton men. The timber men. The sugar men. All wanting to speak to the mistress. All bringing with them thick sheaves of paper: bills of sale, orders of lading, shipping requests, receipts. Catherine Hannigan refused to meet with any of them. Every morning, just as the sun cleared the trees, she left the house, not returning until late in the afternoon, when she would then take to her bed.

She acted as a woman possessed. She had one purpose now: to see her husband moved from the Lafayette Cemetery to the Rousse vault in the St. Louis Cemetery. Nothing could distract her: not her children, not the increasingly insistent businessmen that came daily to her door.

Every morning Girard drove her to see a different city official, a different priest. And every morning she was met with resistance on every front. Though Catherine Hannigan came from a well-respected French Creole family, she had married on the wrong side of Canal Street. Her family had tolerated James Hannigan because of his wealth, his business connections, but the priests of St. Louis were not so impressed. Worse than his birth, it was well known throughout the city that he was a nonbeliever. His gods were the things he could buy and sell, the silver and paper currency that lined his pockets. Let him stay in Lafayette, it was whispered, it is good enough for *les Américaines*.

"You have to speak to her, you have to make her listen. Those men that come grow angrier by the day. They curse. Make threats now."

Margot was in the kitchen house with her sister and grandmother, canning tomatoes and peaches to be put up for the winter. Steam from the boiling pots had plastered her hair against her neck.

Her grandmother made a sound in the back of her throat without turning around. She shook her head as she strained boiled peaches through a cheesecloth.

"She will listen to you," persisted Margot.

"And what should I tell her, *chére*? To stop begging at the feet of those priests? That they will never allow the master's bones to taint their graveyard? That she has two living children that she should be tending to?"

"*Oui*, Grandmere! That, and more."

Grandmere grunted as she squeezed thick juice through the cheesecloth. "No, *chére*. She listens to no one."

"You should at least try," said Margot. "You—"

"*Assez, chére!*" cried Grandmere. "It is a white-folks affair. If the woman wants to drown in widow's weeds and spend her days howling at the church's door, it is not our place—"

"There is no money!"

The old woman froze. From the corner of her eye, Margot saw Veronique jerk, the knife she'd been holding to skin tomatoes hovering in midair.

"There is no money," Margot whispered. She stared down into the swirling water, unable to meet her grandmother's eyes, her tears mixing with the steamy sweat on her face. She could feel them, her sister and her grandmother, watching her, waiting in shocked silence. Taking a deep breath, she turned. Her grandmother stood at the table, still holding the cheesecloth, golden peach juice dripping down her arm onto the floor.

"They come day after day," said Margot. "Those men. Asking for Mistress Catherine. At first polite. Asking that I give my condolences to the mistress."

She stared at her hands.

"Then, when she wouldn't see them, not so polite. They don't believe me that she is not at home. They force me to take the papers—even when I say that I cannot. Some of them don't even go away. They sit for hours, watching the door from their carriages."

The three Hannigan slaves stood in silence breathing in the heavy, sweet aroma of boiling fruit.

"You read them," said Veronique—a statement not a question.

Margot nodded.

"*Mon Dieu,*" murmured Grandmere. She sank into a chair.

Margot nodded. "I had to. Finally. When they kept coming. And the mistress refused to look at them."

"But . . . ," said Grandmere. "Master James . . . the money."

Veronique was watching her, her eyes wide.

"There is no money, Grandmere. Only debt." She sighed. "He owes money to everyone. To cattlemen from Texas, sugar and coffee men from the islands. There is a promissory note for nearly twenty thousand dollars silver to a bank in New York. And another to a shipyard in Cuba."

She stopped, unable to go on.

"But what does it mean?" asked her sister.

Margot turned to look at her sister, so tiny and fragile looking. "It means," she said softly, "that Mistress Catherine is in trouble whether she wants to hear it or not." She looked pointedly at her grandmother.

"It means that she may have to sell everything." She swallowed hard, choking on the next word. "Everyone."

"Margot!" Their grandmother was on her feet again. She glowered at her granddaughter. "Enough. The mistress would never sell us. Never. We have been a part of this family since her father was a child. She would never. . . ."

Margot pressed her lips together and said nothing. Her grandmother knew even better than she that nothing was guaranteed for a slave. It was her grandmother's hope talking.

"And the master promised you girls your freedom at eighteen," Grandmere pressed on. "For you, that is only two months away."

"He also always said he was the richest man he knew," snapped Margot.

The three of them exchanged looks.

"James Hannigan was a rough man, coarsely spoken," said Grandmere finally. "He may have had no god, but he had his word."

Margot sighed and closed her eyes. Dark images whirled through her mind. She thought she might throw up. "I pray the saints that you are right, Grandmere. I pray for all of us."

6

"*Mere de Dieu!*"

The banging felt as if it had been going on all her life. It reverberated through the house, working its way into her dreams. Jerked awake, she leaped from her bed. One ankle caught in the covers, and she crashed to the floor, landing hard on one knee. A few feet away, Veronique murmured in her sleep, oblivious to the pounding—and the cursing.

"*Merde,*" she swore again as she hobbled from her room behind the butler's pantry and down the hall to the front door. It was barely dawn. Who could possibly be pounding at the door at this hour? And more importantly: how in the name of the Virgin could anyone still be sleeping through all the commotion? It sounded as if wild horses had been let loose beneath the portico. A vision of the angry businessmen that had been haunting the mansion flashed through her mind. What if it was one of those white men Master James owed so much money to? What if they had come at this ridiculous hour hoping to surprise the mistress at home?

She hesitated, her hand hovering over the doorknob. The pounding suddenly became so fierce that the walls themselves shuddered, the doorframe threatening to crash into the foyer. Margot snatched open the door.

"How dare—" She stopped midsentence and gaped. It was not a white man at the door but a white woman: a short, very round, very old white woman.

"Well, it is about time," the old woman declared. "I had begun to think that everyone in this house was deaf as wood. I've been out there banging away since Methusalah was a young boy."

She pushed her way into the foyer, followed by a servant, a dark-skinned, gaunt-faced slave in a satin waistcoat.

"Margot? It is Margot, isn't it?" She spoke with a faint French accent. Margot nodded.

"Get your mistress for me, *si vous plaît*. And I am desperate for your grandmother's coffee since I am forced out at this obscene hour."

Margot clutched the bodice of her dressing gown and stared mutely. Ninette Rousse stood in the dim foyer like a bright hummingbird. Her green brocade traveling suit was decades out of date yet looked newly made. The trademark red hair of all the Rousse women had faded to all white but was meticulously curled, two neat spirals bobbing on either side of her round face.

She thrust her bonnet at Margot, who took it wordlessly. Like her suit, it was old-fashioned: broad brimmed, extravagantly decorated with colored ribbon and bright feathers, a design from the twenties. She frowned at Margot's silence.

"The mistress is still sleeping," Margot managed finally.

The old woman flicked an impatient hand, brushing the words away. Despite her wealth, Margot noticed she wore only a simple wedding band and a small cameo at her throat, so unlike the layers of pearls and diamonds Catherine Hannigan encrusted herself in.

"Of course she's still sleeping," said Ninette Rousse with an irritated chuckle. "My granddaughter has never seen the sunrise a day in her life." She cocked her head and peered at the slave girl with narrowed eyes. "Except now I hear she has developed a most distressing new preoccupation and manages to rise much earlier."

Margot glanced uneasily at the stairs leading to Mistress Hannigan's bedchamber. "I will wake the mistress," she said. "Grandmere will be pleased to make you her *café*."

She was talking to the old woman's back. Ninette Rousse was already heading for the parlor, leaning only slightly on her cane. Margot glanced at the servant. His face remained expressionless.

She woke her mistress, who stared at her in bewilderment before rising from her bed, then Margot went to wake Grandmere.

"What does it mean, Grandmere?" asked Veronique as the three of them scrambled about the kitchen.

"I don't know, *chére*," muttered Grandmere, pulling ginger cookies from a tin. She shrugged, sighing. "Madame Ninette follows her own mind. Always has. And now, old as she is, it's most likely she always will."

She took the hot water from Veronique and poured it over the newly ground coffee beans, following it with a sprinkle of cinnamon; a teaspoon of dark molasses.

"She looks harmless as a pigeon, all soft and round, all that white hair." She chuckled grimly. "But more than one white man has found out the hard way that it is a mistake to cross her. She is more alligator than pigeon."

"I don't like her." Margot inspected the silver service for spots while she waited for the coffee to brew. "She follows you everywhere with her eyes, always watching. Like she is waiting for something."

Grandmere sighed and strained the coffee into the carafe. "Guess the old woman has her reasons to be cautious of the world."

Margot had been arranging the cups on the tray. At her grandmother's words, she stopped and faced her, frowning. "And what would the matriach of the great Rousse family have to be so cautious of?"

"It was her husband that had the first Far Water, the one across the sea, in Haiti," said Grandmere. Margot was silent.

"He died there," the old woman added. "Killed by his own slaves, they say."

She glanced anxiously at the door. It would not do for the mistress to know that her slaves even knew the story. Slaves killing whites. The unspoken fear of every slave owner. Such talk would result in the harshest penalty.

Margot snorted. She'd heard the stories—nearly every slave in New

Orleans had. There had even been a slave revolt here in New Orleans years ago. Short lived and ending in tragedy for the slaves. But still . . .

"One white master for all the Negro men, women, and children killed," she said. "How sad."

Her grandmother drew a sharp breath as Veronique gaped. "Margot!" Grandmere's eyes were wide with fear.

Margot pressed her lips together as she picked up the tray. What was it to her that the old woman had lost her man? Ancient history, and nothing to do with her. Besides, she had kept her money. She had kept her son, *non*? And even if she was only a woman, she was free and she was white. Soon she, Margot, would be eighteen, and she would be free. But she would never be white.

"The Yon Nwa once belonged to her."

Margot jerked, whirling to face her grandmother. Hot coffee sloshed from the spout of the carafe, dampening some of the cookies. Veronique stopped pulling bits of straw from the broom by the stove and stared.

"What?" Margot saw a shadow cross the old woman's face.

"The Yon Nwa isn't real, Grandmere," said Veronique. She laughed uneasily.

The Yon Nwa. The Dark One. The Evil One.

She was a character in the stories the old superstitious slaves told the little ones to get them to behave: Go to sleep or Yon Nwa will come for you in your nightmares. Do not tell lies or Yon Nwa will cut out your tongue and use it to sweeten her poisons.

The oldest ones said she had come from across the water, from Haiti before it was Haiti, that she lived deep in the bayous and conversed with the alligators and panthers, that she could stop the tides from coming in, cause a bird to fall from the sky with a single look. They said no priestess had ever been born more powerful.

"*Oui*," said Grandmere. "She is real. Or at least used to be. And old Madame Rousse used to own her."

"Own the Yon Nwa?" Margot felt the hair on the back of her neck prickle.

Her grandmother nodded. They stared at each other in silence.

"Is it true what they say about her?" asked Veronique finally. "That at night she turns into a raven and flies about the world listening to your secrets? That she can turn water into molasses?"

The old woman was shaking her head. "She was a great priestess, a *babaloo*. The spirits ran through her like blood, used her. She could do things, real things. People disappeared around her, just . . . vanished. She could draw metal to her. Make clocks run backward."

Margot laughed but she felt something dark lurking in the shadows just out of sight. "You saw this? Yourself? The whites would never have allowed it. They would have stopped her. Slaves have been killed for less."

Grandmere's eyes burned into her, and Margot felt a surge of fear. She gripped the tray harder to stop the cups from rattling. "She was no longer a slave by then. And the whites were terrified of her. She came and went as she pleased. And when she was gone, no one knew where she went. Few had the stomach to look for her. Most were happy to be shed of her."

She was silent for a long while.

"I saw her once," said Grandmere.

Margot grunted in surprise. The air in the kitchen seemed thick as soup.

"I saw her," Grandmere repeated. She stared off into the distance. "I was a young woman then. Master Julian had just bought me. As a wedding gift for his new wife. We were visiting his mama. Madame Ninette had asked me to go to market with her. We weren't but a few blocks from the house when Madame turns pale as water. She jumps out of that carriage and goes running down a back street quick as a cat. I lit out after her."

Grandmere stopped and hung her head, remembering.

"Did you find her?" asked Veronique.

"*Oui,* I found her." Grandmere sighed. "She was standing behind an old outhouse, hair undone and falling down her back, filth up to her ankles, but it was like she didn't even notice."

She shuddered.

"There was a black woman standing there in front of her, tall, broad as a man through the shoulders. Skin the color of ink. She had these big eyes that burned like fire. Madame and this colored woman, they just stare at each other across the alleyway. They don't speak. They don't move. They just stare. Like there was no one else in the world."

She looked up, her eyes moving between the two girls, who stood still as death, listening.

"I grab hold of Madame. Try to pull her away. Because whatever that black woman was, she wasn't from this world. But Madame Ninette, she doesn't come. Just stands there like she is carved from stone. And that black woman just look and look. And then she look at me and it was like I split in two. If the whole sky had crashed down on my head then, I couldn't have run away."

The old woman was breathless, reliving that long-ago moment. Margot glanced at her sister. Veronique's face had gone pale, her knuckles white from gripping the table's edge.

"The Yon Nwa. I knew it was her. I could taste all the lives inside her. Feel her power. She look at old Madame, points a finger and she says just one word. 'Liar.' Then she throws back her head and growls. That sound a cougar makes when it kills a deer. I thought she would tear us to bits then, me and the Madame. But . . ."

She stopped and shook her head. Margot saw the tremor in her grandmother's hands and was suddenly jolted by the realization that her grandmother was an old woman.

"But what, Grandmere?" Veronique's voice was barely above a whisper. From deep in the house came the sound of a bell: their mistress demanding her coffee.

"Come, *chére,*" said Grandmere. She tapped the tray Margot'd nearly forgotten she was holding. "The mistress will already be out of sorts. Take her the tray lest we find ourselves cleaning out the chicken coop."

But Margot made no move to leave. "What?" she asked. "What happened, Grandmere?"

Her grandmother stared into the open flames of the cook fire, fists clenched at her side.

"I saw . . . I saw an old man, taller even than the Yon Nwa. A man with no eyes. He spoke to the Yon Nwa, said something in her ear that made her smile. But it was a smile to freeze your blood. She held up one hand and I fell into another place. A dark place, where carriages swallowed up men and carried them into the clouds and a Negro lady in blue trousers held the beating heart of a man in her hands."

Fortuna Rousse crossed herself, and Margot saw sweat darkening the fabric under her arms.

"What happened to her? To the Yon Nwa?" asked Veronique in a small voice.

"No one knows. Some say she still roams the bayous waiting for a time when she can kill all the whites, just like was done in Haiti. Some say she died."

The bell rang again, summoning them, the sound sharp and insistent. The three slaves stood listening, unmoving, until it stopped.

Grandmere wiped her hand across her face and looked at her granddaughters. "After that day, the Madame bought the house in Natchez. Came to New Orleans less and less. I heard her say the Yon Nwa was waiting for her, wanting something from her."

"What?" whispered Margot. Her throat was dry. "What did the Yon Nwa want?"

Grandmere picked at the tray, absently removing the damp ginger cookies.

"I don't know, *petit*. She never said. But whatever it was, I don't think old Madame had it to give."

She pushed her granddaughter toward the door and said, almost to herself, "And she did not call her Yon Nwa. She called her Abigail."

Part Two

1791

Haiti

Abigail

Nearly a half mile up, through thick stands of banana and coconut trees, so high that sometimes, especially in the rainy season, it was covered in dense clouds, was her place, her secret place.

The air was clean here, free from the smoke and stench of the coffee camps. But the air was also thinner, and she was forced every so often to stop and catch her breath. High above, in the bright tree canopy, she heard the screech of an island parrot and smiled.

"*Se bon,*" she murmured. "The bird of luck."

She climbed faster, pushing herself. She wanted to have time in her secret place before the sun set. It was Sunday, and the Code Noir—the Black Codes—decreed that slaves must not work on Sundays, but the royal commissioner was far away, in Cap-Français, and the colonies across the seas were mad for their coffee.

"*Lajan avan lwa.*" Abigail spit into the trees. "Money always over the law."

Still, Monsieur Rousse was better than most of the other planters, the ones who worked their slaves to death because it was cheaper to replace one than to rest one. On Eau Lointaine—Far Water—slaves only worked the groves for two hours on Sundays and were given an extra ration of pork and raw cane on that day. Far Water slaves were not whipped, and Thierry Rousse believed it was a sin to sell a child away from its mother before the age of twelve. The master even freed the old ones—the ones wrung dry from all the years of forced labor in the brutal sun of Saint-Domingue's coffee fields—"so that they could spend their last years knowing the grace of French citizenship."

The other planters thought Monsieur Rousse a fool. They predicted that one day his *nègres* would cut his throat while he slept. Rousse merely smiled. "I am a good Catholic," he told them; "God will protect me." He was a good Catholic and he held to the Code Noir as closely as his profits would allow.

Abigail pressed on, her legs aching, her heart fluttering in her chest like the jeweled hummingbirds that flitted in the shadows.

Suddenly, the forest opened up and she was there: at her secret place.

She was standing on a wide ledge of stone, a break in the dense blanket of trees that covered the cliffs surrounding her. High above, the mountain continued up and up, vanishing into the clouds, while below, the forest ran downhill, all the way to the sea. Hibiscus flowed down the mountainside, swaying in the thin air like pink and white silks.

Abigail flung herself to the ground and fanned the sweat from her face with a palm leaf before pulling a small coco *vert* from her skirt pocket. Slicing open the top, she threw back her head and drank, openmouthed, the coconut water warm and sweet.

Far below, rimming the edge of the jungle, she could just make out the red roofs of Cap-Français and, just beyond, the small, pale dots scattered on the surface of the sea that she knew were ships.

The sea.

She hated it. Hated the sight of it, its warm, salty smell like the breath of a great beast. Abigail squinted. The water was so blue that it seemed to swallow all the light of the sky.

When the *blancs,* the whites, had come for her, when they'd snatched her from the banks of the shallow river that ran near her village, she couldn't have understood then, would never have believed, that there could be so much water in the whole of the world, and that on the other side of that huge water was a world so foreign, so far away, that she would never see her family again.

Ama, her second sister, had been collecting reeds on the riverbank with her that day, and they'd both been taken and thrown into the same dark place on a ship to cross the never-ending water. Ama never spoke another word. She sat rocking back and forth in the stinking darkness, silent, arms wrapped around her long legs. On a cool, windless night, when the *blancs* brought them out of the dark place to throw salty water on their skin and make them walk back and forth, yelling at them in their strange language, Ama had jerked away and clamored to the top of a railing. At the last minute she turned and smiled at Abigail. And then she was gone. As if she had never been in the world at all.

A sob escaped from somewhere deep inside, and Abigail began to punch herself in the face, her fists striking her cheeks, her eyes, harder and harder until that memory, and all memories that came before, were beaten back into that dark, unreachable part of her soul. There was no "before." There was only this place of sky and water and trees, this place of endless work, this place in which there were a hundred ways to die a horrible death.

And now Hercule was gone.

Eleven days and more. He had come to her that Sunday, come to see her and their sons. Hercule. Her blessing from the gods. Her piece of dry land in this cursed place. Henri and Claude had tumbled like monkeys between their father's feet, laughing, as he'd tried to show them how to shape wood with heat and water. He was a cooper, the best on the island, and it gave him a freedom few other slaves enjoyed. But his sons were only five and too restless to pay attention, so Hercule had finally given up and tossed coconut shells for them to chase while she fried the plaintains and the bit of fish he'd brought.

She gnashed her teeth. She should have known. When it had come time to leave, he'd held her face a little too long, stared too hard into her eyes.

Hercule's master came racing into Far Water three days later, tumbling from his horse, yelling for the master.

Monsieur Rousse had been having dinner and he came to the door, shirtsleeves undone. Abigail saw it all from the door of the cookhouse.

She gripped a bag of rice so tightly that it ripped, the white grain spilling into the dirt at her feet.

"That boy has run off," bellowed Monsieur Quennelle. "I told you, things are out of hand. We must crack down now, or it will be our ruin."

Monsieur Rousse spoke softly, too softly for her to hear. He leaned into the sweating Quennelle, his dinner napkin still in his hand.

"You're a fool, Rousse! The *nègres* are arming themselves against us, and that Hercule is with them."

Abigail cried out, and the two planters turned just as her knees buckled. Hercule's master was a big man, fat and soft as a maggot. He stormed toward her, yanking her roughly from the ground.

"You are his *épouse,* no? His wife?" He shook her. "Where did he go? What did he tell you?"

In the next instant, her master was there. *"Assez!"*

Quennelle shook her harder and she gritted her teeth against the pain, forcing herself not to yank away, not to slap his doughy face.

"This woman knows something," he cried. "They all know something. We are French men, *non*? Should we let these animals simply turn on us like rabid dogs? Have you forgotten that *fils de chienne* Macandel in 'fifty-eight? The women and children he slaughtered in their beds? Or do you think your kindness, your extra bit of *porc,* will protect you and your pretty white wife?" He spit.

"I said, enough!" Rousse grabbed Quennelle and spun him around. "This girl is my property and, as far as I know, has done nothing to warrant this rough handling."

The fat planter glared at him. Rousse returned the look, then shook his head before turning toward Abigail, who stood trembling, clutching her throbbing arm in one hand, the shredded rice sack in the other.

"Do you know anything about Hercule, Abigail?" he asked. His voice was firm but gentle.

Abigail shook her head. *"Non,* Monsieur."

Rousse nodded and started to turn away.

"But . . ."

He stopped, waiting.

"He would not just run off, Monsieur."

"Ha!" cried Quennelle.

Abigail stiffened. She was a large woman, tall, broad through the shoulders, and muscular from years of hard labor. She glared at Hercule's master, defiant. He would not touch her again, not with Monsieur Rousse standing there.

"He would not just run off, Monsieur. Not without a word." She spoke the words in French, not Creole, speaking slowly to make sure the words were right. "He is husband to me, father to my sons."

"Husband." Quennelle spit again in the damp earth. "As if that means a thing to a *nègre*." He stomped back toward the house.

Abigail dug her nails into the soft meat of her palms to keep from throwing herself on his back and sinking her teeth into the fat, sweaty neck.

Thierry Rousse watched him go in silence. He sighed.

"Abigail . . . ," he began finally.

"I swear on the Virgin that I know nothing," said Abigail. Her voice shook, all defiance gone.

Her master worried the dinner napkin between his fingers for a moment, then patted her lightly on the shoulder. "*Ça ira*. It will be alright."

He sighed again, then turned to follow after his uninvited guest.

But it wasn't going to be alright. Eleven days and now the sun was preparing to set on yet another one. And still no word of Hercule. He had gone to join the rebels. She was sure of it.

There were more of them every day, slaves running into the mountains, deserting the coffee and indigo fields, fleeing the sugar plantations. There were rumors, murmurings in the slave quarters, in the cookhouses, behind the laundry sheds. Slaves exchanging furtive glances as they picked coffee cherries from the trees: the mountains have claimed another, they whispered.

Abigail slid down on the ledge and closed her eyes.

Maroons.

They were called maroons: those slaves who escaped into the wilds of the forests high above the plantations. They crept down from the

mountains like smoke—raiding the plantations, stealing food, weapons, even white *enfants,* to turn them into slaves, it was said, or maybe
to hurl them into the sea as an offering to the orisha, the gods. Abigail
had heard both.

And now Hercule was one of them. Abigail felt that as surely as she
felt the breeze on her skin. Hercule had become a maroon.

She lay there on the ledge and held herself still. Her grandmother
had been an honored priestess of their people and, more times than
Abigail could count, had forced her to lie silent in the grass and listen.
"The world will tell you secrets. But you must be still and ready to hear."

It was a lesson Abigail had had little patience for. But now, as she
lay on her little wedge of rock, she tried. She closed her eyes, stared
at the dark space behind her lids, focusing. From where she lay, the
distant sea was silent, its voice lost in the trees far below, but she could
hear monkeys arguing in the treetops, the wind rustling the palm
branches. Somewhere above her, a coconut fell to the ground, and she
felt the vibration beneath her hands.

She stared at that dark place and felt the air moving around her
skin, felt the roughness of her shift, the grains of dirt beneath her
back, felt the humming of the earth, its energy.

Then she was no longer on a rocky ledge high over Cap-Français.
She was moving, sliding through space, the air around her warm then
cool, as she passed in and out of shadow.

Hercule.

She felt something fold inside herself, and the world bloomed like
a flower, its many petals each a perfect world in itself. In one, she saw
a huge bird made of metal roar through the blue sky over where she
lay; in another, a glass box with people singing inside. The images confused her but she forced herself to lay still, watching but not feeling,
the way her grandmother had taught her.

Suddenly, her breath caught in her throat.

Hercule.

There. Imperfect. As if through dust-streaked glass. But there. Her
Hercule. His skin the blue-black of a coffee bean, his lips full and soft.
His face seemed thinner, bruised. But his eyes . . .

Abigail gasped and for a moment felt herself spiraling away from him, hurtling toward a crack in the universe, toward one of those other worlds, and she struggled to calm herself, to see but not feel.

Hercule's eyes . . .

They were hard, cruel. Where was the laughter that she knew? Where was the kindness? This Hercule was not her Hercule. This Hercule was a stranger.

"*Kiyes ou ye*," she whispered. "My heart. *Kisa ou ap fe?* What are you doing out here?"

Hercule's head shot up and he frowned. He seemed to search the trees, the shadows around him.

"My love," she whispered. Her husband caressed his throat, the last place she had touched her lips before he'd run down the mountain trail, away from her. She reached for him, even as she knew that she would feel nothing beneath her hand. And then the world exploded, throwing her out of that seam between worlds, slamming her back onto her high mountain ledge.

Abigail lurched upward. "Hercule!"

She sat blinking in the lowering sun, confused. A thick column of black smoke rose from the hills above Cap-Français, appearing like a feather on the mountain's cap of green. As she watched, a pinpoint of bright orange formed at its base, growing wider inside the trees with each passing second.

The sun was setting over the city there at the edge of the sea, and at first the orange glow seemed to be just a reflection of the sunset. And then she saw that it was not.

"*Bondye*," Abigail cried. "My God."

Fire. Cap-Français was on fire.

Another explosion rocked the countryside. She felt it in her teeth. Whirling, she began to race back down through the jungle, back toward Far Water. Back to her children.

8

She could no longer see the orange tongue of the flames as she raced down the steep mountainside, but she could smell the smoke. Or maybe it was not the smoke she smelled but the pent-up rage of all those maroons swarming from their hiding places, high in the cloud-wreathed mountains.

"Sweet Virgin, Holy Mother, keep Hercule safe. Keep him safe." She muttered the prayer over and over as she crashed through the trees.

Down and down, her descent barely controlled, her bare feet out in front. Her work-toughened heels digging into the hillside, steering her like a rudder. Something screamed in the trees and Abigail veered sharply, losing her precarious footing. The scream came again, and she added her own panicked voice to it as she tumbled, gracelessly, a dozen yards through the trees.

"Merde!" She lay sprawled on her back, panting for breath. Something crashed in the forest above her and she cried out.

Maroons.

A pair of wild pigs erupted from the trees and brushed past her, close enough for her to smell their stink. They ignored her, disappearing into the gloom, their squeals sounding just like the scream of a wounded child.

"Merde," she swore again.

Groaning, she pushed to her feet and began once more to make her way back toward Far Water. As she moved farther down the mountain, mahogany and rosewood gave way to fruit trees—banana, orange—and thick ferns as tall as a man. The air grew thicker, warmer against her skin. Though the fires in the mountains were now invisible to her, the whole sky was aflame as the sun set in the far-off sea.

As she entered the groves she slowed. It was quiet, the neat rows between the coffee trees empty. Abigail held her breath and listened. From the quarter, she heard the murmur of song, an occasional child's laugh. Tree frogs sang from the shadow of the groves. The *grand kay*—the big house—was visible against the darkening sky, every window aglow with lantern light.

A basket of coffee cherries sat at her feet, and she bent, pushing her hand deep into it. The cherries were still warm from the day. Abigail looked around, then squatted over the basket. Hot urine streamed into the cherries and she grunted, forcing the last bit from her bladder.

"To sweeten the drink of the *blancs*," she muttered.

She moved quickly down the deserted rows. Her sons had probably worn old Edynelle to the bone. The ancient slave woman had been freed in her old age by Monsieur Rousse to spend her final days gumming sugar cane and rocking on a low stool in the shade. She was supposed to watch over the ones too little to go out to the coffee groves and cane fields, but mostly she either ignored the children or screamed curses at them with words no one understood.

The last time Abigail had left the twins with Edynelle, she'd come back to find the boys taunting the old woman after having tied her stool up in the branches of a guava tree.

Maybe the fires had been nothing. Maybe it'd simply been another *blanc* clearing the forest to grow more coffee or rice or whatever it was these ghost men wanted next for their fancy tables across the water. Or maybe it had been one of their warehouses used to store gunpowder. She sniffed at the air. There was only the scent from the frangipani trees that stood at the edge of the big house.

An image of Hercule, his eyes black and dull, flashed through her mind, and for a moment she saw him running through the thick smoke around Cap-Français, head back, teeth bared. Like a *zombi*, one of the soulless dead. She crossed herself.

Non.

That was not her Hercule. He would not have joined the maroons. Left their sons. Left her.

She straightened and moved quickly through the quarter where the cook fires still burned, lighting the doors of the squat mud-and-palm-leaf huts. The boys would have eaten by now. Someone, not likely Edynelle, would have given them something, but if she didn't hurry, she was afraid that she might find it was the old woman herself lashed to the guava tree this time. The thought made her smile.

"Manman!"

Two small figures detached themselves from the shadows and ran to her. Henri and Claude flung their arms around her knees, nearly bringing her to the ground. They were dirty and scratched, their dark hair white with dust.

"Look at you two," she clucked. "Like wild animals."

Claude released her and dropped to his hands and knees, snorting like a pig.

Abigail sucked her teeth. "*Arret!* Stop that, child." But she laughed, hugging Henri tighter to her side.

"We fed the wild things," called one of the women from the door of her hut. Edynelle was nowhere to be seen.

"*Mèsi*," said Abigail. "*Vini*, boys. It is late."

She gathered her sons to her, relishing their warmth, their sweaty boy smell, and bundled them toward their hut.

The sun had not yet cleared the horizon and already the air was thick and wet. Up and down the quarter, the slaves were beginning to stir. Abigail stretched, moaning softly, her body reminding her of her tumble on the mountain the night before.

Her eyes burned. The night had been filled with bad spirits. They'd ridden her back, scratching at her eyes, pulling her hair. When they'd tried to whisper evil words in her ears, she'd shaken them off and refused to hear, but the effort had worn her down. And now the day was set to begin and she'd barely slept.

Abigail splashed water on her face from the jug by the door and sighed. The boys were still sleeping. She poked at the coals of the cook fire and unearthed three ears of corn that had roasted in the cocoon of heat through the night. Stoking up the fire to brew coffee, she poured water into a tin cup before tucking back into the hut.

"*Bonjou, petits,*" she whispered. "It is morning."

She smiled. Her sons were splayed across their straw mattress like spiders, arms and legs tangled.

"Wake now. Wake." She dipped her fingers in the cup and sprinkled water across their dark brown faces, so like their father's. Both boys stirred but neither opened their eyes.

"Up, you lazy creatures." She pretended not to see Claude's grin as she leaned and planted kisses on their eyelids, the tips of their noses. Eyes still closed, they began to giggle, squirming like frogs in her embrace. When Claude could stand it no longer, he leaped from the mattress.

"We are not lazy, Manman," he cried, hopping from foot to foot. "See? We are awake."

Henri, content as usual to let his brother speak for them both, reached up one warm hand to stroke her face. She turned her head and kissed his palm.

"Eat," she said and handed them each an ear of steaming corn. "Then go find Mama Edynelle."

At five, they were old enough to begin working the coffee, but Monsieur Rousse had not yet sent for them and Abigail was content to let them taste their freedom as long as they were able. It would be the only freedom they would ever know.

"Such a dirty thing," she said, wiping Henri's face with a damp rag. "You would follow your brother into . . ."

She stopped and sniffed at the air, trembling. Henri, who had been wiggling under her ministrations, froze. Even Claude stopped his bouncing and watched her warily. Something was coming. The bad spirits had come again and were whispering at her neck.

"Stay," she commanded her sons. She stepped from the hut.

Abigail smelled the coffee brewing on the cook fire, ready for the boys to drink before they were sent to Edynelle, but she made no move to take it from the coals.

A man was crossing the grass from the big house. She squinted, trying to see, but the sun was at his back and his features were lost in the brightness. Behind her, the boys jostled each other in the doorway. She ignored them.

The man stepped from the glare of the sun and her heart thudded in her chest. A white man in the quarter usually meant trouble.

"*Bonjour,*" he said.

It was Monsieur Dreyfus, the master's friend from Gonaïves.

Abigail bobbed her head and dipped slightly, a simulation of a curtsy.

"*Bonjou,* Mét," she said, returning his greeting in Creole.

André Dreyfus was a small man, slight, with hair the color of dry grass. He was a Jew. It was what all the other *blancs* said when they spoke of him: *Il est un juif.*

Abigail didn't know what a Jew was. To her, he seemed not much different than any of the other *blancs*. His clothes were a bit shabbier, his skin less sun-reddened, but perhaps that was because he lived in the city and didn't work the land like the other *blancs*. Abigail thought that perhaps a Jew was a white man that owned no land, but Hercule told her once that it had something to do with the gods they worshipped.

She watched him, wary. The few times he'd spoken to her, he'd aimed the words at her face and not to the air behind her. And he seemed more interested in Monsieur Rousse's whiskey and books than in the slaves of Far Water. But whatever else he was, he was still a *blanc*.

"*Vous êtes* Abigail, *oui?*" The little man's pale face was sweaty and splotched with red.

"*Wi.*"

"The mistress wishes to see you."

Abigail nodded and turned to her boys, who were trying to peek around her skirts at the white man. Dreyfus smiled and wiggled his fingers at them.

"*Bonjour,* young sirs," he said.

The twins stared, openmouthed, and Abigail pinched them both hard on their necks until they bowed.

"*Bonjou,* Mét," they said in unison.

"Go now," said their mother. "Go to Mama Edynelle. And mind yourselves." She turned to follow André Dreyfus back across the lawn to the big house.

"Your boys are lovely," said Dreyfus.

"*Mèsi,*" murmured Abigail. She clenched and unclenched her hands, trying to slow her thoughts. She had been in the big house many times before. She had a way with roots, a feel for healing, and the mistress often sent for her, especially these past few months. But never before had a white man been sent to the quarter to find her. What could this mean? The bad spirits whispered all around her.

The big house of Far Water was not as grand as some. Abigail had been to Monsieur Quennelle's estate twice with Hercule, and his home dwarfed the Rousses'. But her master's house was bright and airy. Low-slung and perched on a hill overlooking a valley, it had a broad porch and tall windows to catch the breezes that found their way down the mountain. The windows had no glass, but rather louvered shutters to keep out bugs and let in air.

When they reached the porch, André Dreyfus climbed the steps, but Abigail hung back. Slaves didn't enter through the front door. The white man turned.

"Abigail?"

When she didn't move, Dreyfus came back down the stairs and touched her shoulder. "Come, the mistress is waiting."

Reluctantly, she followed him into the house, across the cool mahogany floors and into the small parlor near the back of the house.

"Ninette?" said the white man. "I have her here."

Ninette Rousse turned from the window.

"Shall I stay?"

The white woman seemed to think this over, then shook her head. "No, but . . . I may need you later."

Dreyfus nodded then left the room, softly pulling the door closed behind him. For a long moment, her mistress didn't speak. Abigail stared down at her bare feet, instinctively moving away from the large clock that hung over the fireless hearth. She mistrusted clocks. They seemed an unnatural way to track the passage of time. And they did odd things when she was around. The mechanisms inside whirred and broke, the tiny pieces spewing into the air. The little hands ran backward or stopped moving altogether.

She heard her mistress moving around the room but didn't raise her head. Her heart beat hard in her chest. It was not like the mistress to be so quiet.

"Abigail."

Abigail looked up. Ninette Rousse had perched on the edge of the chair nearest the hearth. The slave looked away quickly, biting her lip to hold back a nervous laugh. Short and round by nature, the white woman was now also heavily pregnant, looking like a ripe fruit about to burst.

"*Metréss?*" Abigail exhaled sharply through her nose, blowing the laugh away.

Madame Rousse said nothing and Abigail looked up again. The white woman was pulling nervously at the lace cuff of her sleeve.

"You are well, Madame? The baby is well?" It was a breach for her, a slave, to speak first, but Abigail thought she might begin to scream if the silence wasn't broken.

The corners of her mistress's mouth turned up. "It is fine. We are fine. Thanks to you."

Abigail bobbed her head then looked away again.

The mistress had come to Saint-Domingue from a small village north of Paris to marry her husband not long after Abigail arrived at Far Water. Barely out of her teens, wide-eyed and cheerful, Ninette Rousse had taken an inexplicable liking to the sullen slave girl. Abigail suspected she'd been lonely, the only white woman for miles. And they were close in age. She'd taught Abigail French, brought her into the *grand kay* to work in the kitchen instead of the coffee groves. And it was she who'd introduced her to Hercule. She'd also been the one to discover that Abigail knew the ways of curing sickness. It was after she'd lost her babies—one to fever, another dead before it had even drawn a breath—that she'd come to Abigail and begged for her help.

"Please," the white woman said now. "Sit."

Abigail's head snapped up in surprise. She glanced at the chair nearest her, then at her mistress and shook her head.

"Non, Metrés."

"I need you to sit, Abigail." Madame's voice sliced through the thick air, sharp as a cane knife, and Abigail started. Her mistress had never raised her voice to her, never spoken a word in anger.

"Please." Madame Rousse's voice was soft again, but her face was flushed and she was trembling.

The edges of the room went soft and her mistress seemed to blur. For a moment, Abigail sensed something else in the room with them: something angry and dark.

"Abigail?"

Her mistress gripped the arms of her chair and stared at her. Abigail ducked her head and shuffled to the chair. She gazed at it for a moment. The red swirls of fabric on the cushions were like the inside of a mouth and she felt her stomach turn. Swallowing hard, she balanced her hips stiffly on the chair's edge.

The white woman didn't meet her eyes. She gazed instead at the hearth, frowning as she ran a hand over her pregnant belly.

"Mistress?"

Ninette Rousse raised her eyes and Abigail rocked back. It was here, in this room. The bad thing. The thing that had haunted her dream, the thing she had felt licking at her neck all morning.

"Bondye," she whispered, leaping to her feet.

"Name it." Her voice was harsh, strangled. "Name it."

"What?" Her mistress quivered on the edge of her chair. "What do you mean?"

"There is evil here. Death." Abigail could barely get the words around the knot that had formed in her throat. "Say its name."

The white woman made a noise but no words came out.

Abigail had a horrible thought. "You have sold me away. Me . . . or my children."

"What? Never . . ."

The spark of relief that flared in Abigail's stomach was short-lived. She held her breath and waited.

"They . . . ," began Madame Rousse. She stopped and her blue eyes filled with tears.

Abigail said nothing.

"They have found Hercule."

Abigail staggered backward, sitting hard when her knees found the chair. Eyes closed, she rocked back and forth.

Thank you, God. Thank you, Legba. Thank the saints.

Her body shook with joy. She would go to him. Surely the mistress would let her. She wouldn't have given her this news only to keep them apart. She would . . .

It took her a moment to hear the silence that filled the room. Abigail opened her eyes. Ninette Rousse had risen and was standing in front of her, so close that the fabric of her gown puddled around Abigail's bare feet.

She bent as much as she was able and clasped the slave girl's hands in her own. "Oh, Abigail, I am so sorry."

Tears ran down her round face and Abigail jerked, confused. She tried to pull her hands free but the white woman held on.

Sorry?

"He was with a band of maroons that attacked a garrison near Trou-du-Nord."

Abigail shook her head. What was the mistress telling her? She didn't know that place.

"They had weapons. They burned several rice plantations, killed the owners, their families, even the dogs. Marcel Quennelle has gone to bring Hercule back. To punish him himself."

"*Manti!* It is not true." She wanted to cover her ears, to make the words stop, but her mistress's tiny hands had suddenly become like the mouth of a snapping turtle, trapping her, as the terrible words rained down on her head.

"He is to be made an example," said her mistress, the words barely audible. "I wanted you to know. I thought you should hear it from me."

"I will go to him," whispered Abigail. The world had gone soft and fuzzy again. She was in the parlor, her mistress standing in front of her, her rosewater perfume floating in the air. But she was also in the quarter, the dirt warm under her feet, the coffee scorched now. She needed to take it from the flame. Her head throbbed.

"You will not," snapped her mistress.

Abigail was jolted back as if slapped. Madame Rousse still gripped her hands but she wore an expression Abigail had never seen before.

"You will not," she repeated. "Hercule . . . Hercule has done a terrible thing. I can barely believe it myself. He . . ."

She shook her head and went on, her expression softer. "And it will be the most terrible thing to see. You would not want . . . Quennelle is a hard man, brutal. It will be terrible, Abigail."

Abigail had stopped listening. She wanted the white woman to move. She would go to Hercule and nothing—not this woman who had always been kind to her, not that *bata* Quennelle—would stand in her way.

She stared up at her mistress and a black void opened inside her. Inside that dark place, she could see her hands around Madame's throat, could actually feel the warmth of her mistress's breath against her wrist as she strangled the life from her.

Ninette Rousse fell silent and loosened her grip on the slave girl. Abigail dropped her eyes to her mistress's pregnant belly and leaned forward slightly. It was a boy, this baby, she knew that as surely as if the baby already rocked in her arms. She could see him curled there under his mother's heart. He would have his mother's red hair and fair skin, his father's slim build. She felt the baby's heat, a small furnace in the womb, its heart thrumming quickly.

But she felt cold, as if she had just clawed her way from the grave. The spirits had followed her to this room. They whispered in her ear, waiting for her to acknowledge them. She ground her teeth. If the mistress did not release her, she would call their name. They would speak through her mouth, see through her eyes. And she would let them stroke the fine, golden red hair of the unborn Rousse. She locked eyes with her mistress and Ninette Rousse swallowed hard—Abigail could see her throat working—and stepped away.

The slave girl rose and began to walk toward the door.

I will go to him and they will not stop me. They cannot stop me.

Halfway across the room the floor seemed to buckle and a sickness filled her. She fell to the floor.

"Hercule!"

9

Abigail gripped the straw saddle. It would have been easier on foot, but the mistress had insisted that she ride the donkey. The slave girl stared at her mistress's back. Ahead of her, Ninette Rousse sat awkwardly astride the back of a spotted mare. She was a poor horseman in the best of times, and now, heavily pregnant, slogging downhill through thick vegetation, she rolled side to side in the saddle like a pea in a bottle.

Abigail had come to on the floor of the little parlor, Dreyfus and her mistress leaning over her, her mistress so close she could see the vein pulsing beneath her eye.

"We leave for Quennelle's immediately," was all she said.

Marcel Quennelle's plantation appeared like a wound in the forest.

Spread out on a narrow plain tucked against the mountain, the three riders could see the straight line of the cocoa trees and beyond that, the coffee groves, all eerily empty. Dreyfus halted his horse at the edge of the forest and peered over his shoulder at the two women.

"Ninette, you are sure of this?" he asked. "Thierry . . ."

"André, Thierry is meeting with planters near Saint-Raphaël. Quennelle is *un porc*. He respects no one. Respects nothing except the *écus* that line his pockets. But he fears my husband. Needs his connections—and his goodwill—if he wishes to continue shipping his coffee at a fair price. We will come to no harm here." She laughed, but her round face was gray and there were dark red blotches beneath her eyes. "Besides, André, you seem to think that I am some delicate flower that wilts without the protective cover of her husband."

The corner of Dreyfus's mouth turned upward and he bowed in his saddle. "As you wish, Madame."

They moved cautiously out into the open, riding side by side in silence. They had nearly cleared the cocoa trees before they saw anyone. An old man stood at the base of one of the trees swinging a machete. With one smooth movement, he freed a sun-colored cocoa pod from a branch and slipped it into the sack that was slung across his shoulder. He glanced up at their approach, his dark, wrinkled face blank, then returned to his task, as if they were of no more interest to him than the flock of birds overhead. The white man and woman exchanged a glance and rode on.

Quennelle's house was as large as Abigail remembered, but as they rode closer, it was clear that its prime had long passed. The white-washed stone was faded and peeled. Shingles were missing from the roof. A dark blue shutter hung crookedly from a top window. As they rode into the courtyard, a tall, dark-haired man, barely out of his teens, stepped from the porch and walked slowly to meet them. Abigail inhaled nervously and gripped the saddle, damp from sweat after the long ride. The man was armed, as were the other men she could see lurking at the edges of the yard.

"*Bonjour,*" called Dreyfus.

The dark-haired man stopped a few yards away, feet planted widely, his eyes hidden in the shadow of his hat. He didn't return the greeting.

"We have come to call on Monsieur Quennelle," said Dreyfus.

"Monsieur Quennelle is busy," said the man, his tone insolent. Ninette Rousse made a sound in the back of her throat, and the man raised his head to look at her.

"I am Madame Rousse, mistress of Far Water," Madame Rousse said. Her voice was tight. "We will speak to Monsieur Quennelle."

"He is not receiving guests . . . Madame." The man smirked. "But I shall let him know you called."

Abigail felt her mistress stiffen beside her.

"I do not need a serving boy to relay my messages for me," snapped Madame Rousse. "Especially one who does not know how to speak to those above his station."

The man's face went white. Abigail desperately tried to catch her mistress's eye. She knew men like these *blancs,* men who swam up from the sewers of cities and towns everywhere. They came to this place because even their own people would not have them. They did the dirty work of the plantations: the beatings and tortures, the hunting of the runaways. She had heard that they were even rewarded on some plantations for siring babies with young slave girls. Thierry Rousse called them garbage and would not have them at Far Water.

These *blancs* might dress like men, might even speak the language of men, but they were not men. They were dangerous animals. Her mistress would have been safer poking a wild pig with a stick.

"My station?" snarled the man. His hand tightened on his gun.

Madame Rousse waved her hand dismissively. "Run along, boy. Get your master."

Abigail stared. Perhaps it was the heat, the strain of the ride. Ninette Rousse was not a stupid woman. So she must have gone mad. Why was she deliberately provoking this boy, speaking to him in a tone she never even used with her slaves? She felt the heat of the *blanc*'s outrage even from where she sat.

Dreyfus was off his horse in an instant.

"Sir," he said, speaking as calmly as if he were standing in the Rousse parlor. "Madame Rousse is very tired and is, as you can see, with child. I'm sure if you let Monsieur Quennelle know we are here . . ."

Abigail watched the muscles work in the younger man's face. He looked from Madame Rousse to Dreyfus and back again, his hands locked on the grip of his gun.

"I told you he was busy," the man said, finally.

"And we do so hate to impose," said Dreyfus gently. "But it is imperative."

The man caught her looking and Abigail flinched, quickly dropping her eyes to the donkey's back.

"And what is this *nègre* then?" asked the man.

"She belongs to Madame."

There was a long silence before the man spoke. "*Bien,*" he said at last. "*Attendez ici.*"

He turned sharply and disappeared around the side of the house, the other men following, leaving them alone in the courtyard. Dreyfus whirled on Madame Rousse, his face twisting.

"Have you completely lost your mind, Ninette? Baiting that boy like that? He was ready to knock you from your horse!"

The white woman's eyes flashed fire.

"Those men are nothing. Less than nothing. It is creatures like them—*basse classe*—that are the root of all our problems," she said, her voice hard. "They torture the *nègres,* steal their children, do unthinkable things to their women. No wonder the maroons hate us."

"That may be," snapped Dreyfus. "Or not. But your name . . . and your husband's will give no protection against men like him."

Ninette Rousse trembled in her saddle, her knuckles white where she gripped the reins. Abigail leaned and wrapped a hand around her mistress's wrist. The white woman started but didn't pull away.

"Mistress Ninette," she said softly. "A snake may be beneath your feet but its bite can still take your life."

The young white woman blinked, and then slowly a grin spread across her face. Abigail released her wrist. She didn't love her mistress but she didn't hate her, either. She had been kind to her and her boys. And it would be to no one's advantage if this crazy woman got them all killed.

"I shall remember that, Abigail," said Ninette Rousse. She threw her head back, laughing out loud.

Dreyfus frowned, then faced the *gran kay,* turning his back on them. "*Femmes,*" he muttered.

"*Bonjour, bonjour.*"

Marcel Quennelle came waddling from the shabby estate house, his graying hair limp in the heat, his face as red as a coffee cherry.

"Dominic told me we had guests. What a pleasure." He strode up to Madame and kissed her hand. The mistress caught Abigail's eye as she surreptitiously wiped her hand on her skirt. Abigail bit her lip and pretended not to see.

"And Master Dreyfus," exclaimed Quennelle, pumping the smaller man's hand. "It has been long since we last met."

The fat man made a great show of looking around.

"But where is your husband, Madame?"

"I come in his service," Dreyfus said quickly, before Madame Rousse could answer. "We heard there was . . . some trouble with your slaves."

"No trouble," said Quennelle. Abigail could feel his eyes on her. "No trouble at all. I had a slave that was lost but now he is found."

He laughed and bile rose in Abigail's throat. She twisted the straw saddle in her fist.

"It is this slave we have come to speak to you about," said her mistress.

"Yes?"

Madame Rousse nodded. She reached out one hand and Dreyfus lifted her to the ground. She walked quickly to Quennelle.

"Yes," she said quietly. "It will not take long."

The planter frowned and glanced over his shoulder toward the house. Pulling a kerchief from his waistcoat, he wiped at his flushed face.

"*Pardonnez-moi,* Madame," he said, bowing slightly. "I am a poor host. It comes from long years as a bachelor. Please come in from this heat. We can drink something cool while we visit."

Madame Rousse glanced back at Abigail.

"Your slave can wait in the quarter, if you like," he said. The three whites disappeared into the house.

For a long moment Abigail didn't move. She kept her eyes fixed on the donkey's back. The animals stiff hair appeared almost as red as her mistress's in the afternoon sun.

What did the mistress want with that cur, Quennelle? Ninette Rousse hated him. Maybe she was going to plead for Hercule's life. Maybe she would buy him and bring him to Far Water. It was unlikely that she would try and save a slave accused of raising arms against the *blancs.* Even if that slave was Hercule. But maybe . . .

Abigail moaned and slid from the donkey, leading it toward the quarter. The quarter was as quiet as the cocoa fields and coffee groves had been. Slaves stood in the narrow spaces between their huts, still as ghosts. She recognized a few faces, had met them on the rare trips here to visit Hercule, but when they saw her, they turned away, their eyes wide, terrified.

She made her way to Hercule's workshop. It stood empty, the door ajar. She tied up the donkey and stepped inside. The tools of her husband's trade were arrayed neatly around the sparse shop: there were the staves, the wooden pieces that made up the sides of a barrel, all different lengths, and the winch for shaping them. There were the planes for smoothing the wood, and hoop hammers for pounding the metal rings onto the barrels. She fingered a round chip of wood, the size and smoothness of a coin, then laid her hand against a half-finished butter churn. She could smell him here, his thick, woody scent.

Oh, Hercule, what have you done?

A commotion outside brought her back to herself. Slipping the wooden disk into her pocket she pushed open the door and stepped back outside. All the slaves were heading for an open area beyond the grind house: men, women, children, their heads down, faces grim, were being herded like cattle down a narrow lane toward it. Abigail clenched her teeth and followed, the evil spirits whispering, whispering in her ear.

At the end of the lane the space opened up and the slaves stopped moving, but there was a murmuring, an angry vibration making its way through the crowd, like bees preparing to swarm. Abigail squinted to see what was happening, but tall as she was, all she could see was a sea of angry, dark faces. She pushed closer and a movement caught her eye. It was Dreyfus, looking ill, standing near a storage shed with Quennelle, away from the gathered slaves. He was staring at something. Abigail followed his eyes and screamed.

Through the crowd she could see that the ground rose slightly. Straw had been piled on the top of the mound, and tied to a pole, in the center of all that straw, was her Hercule.

Abigail clawed her way through the slaves and threw herself on him.

"Hercule," she cried.

He barely seemed to register her. His battered face was shiny with swelling, blood matted the side of his head. She put her hand there and gagged. His ear was missing. Someone pulled at her from behind. She turned her head and snarled, spit flying from her lips, before turning back to her husband, no thought in her mind except that he should see her. She gritted her teeth and placed her palm against his head once again. Gently, she turned his face toward hers.

"Hercule," she whispered.

He moaned and opened his one good eye.

"You missed supper last week," she said, her face close to his. He struggled to say something, seemed to try and smile. "Do not think I will forget that, husband."

More hands were on her now, yanking at her, grasping at her arms, her waist. Someone called her name. She wrenched free and wrapped her arms tightly around her husband, who was clearly looking at her now.

"*Mwen renmen ou,* Hercule. I love you. *Mwen telman fache avék ou!*"

"*Mwen regret sa,*" he murmured through torn lips. "I am so sorry, Abigail."

They tore her hand from his face and still she clung to him, her fingers clutching at his clothes. "You will look at me," she cried. "Only me. *Ou konprann?* Do you understand? Only at me."

The white man called Dominic tore her free and threw her to the ground. He kicked her once, twice, but she felt nothing. Her eyes were locked on Hercule's.

"Look at me," she screamed. "Keep looking at me."

Someone lit the straw and she saw Hercule jerk.

"Hercule. At me. Look at me. See only me, my love."

His eyes were locked on hers, even as unseen hands tried to pull her away, even as the smell of cooking flesh began to fill the clearing. As the fire worked its way up his body, Hercule began to scream, an agonized, inhuman sound, and still she fought to stay near.

"Look at me, Hercule. *Ou konprann?* See only me."

Abigail screamed the words again and again, until there was nothing in front of her but the roaring fire that drowned out her voice.

And even then she stood there, shivering despite the hellish heat. "Come."

It was Madame Rousse. But she didn't respond. Abigail stood as if dead, her mind a black empty place, silent except for the roar of the fire. André Dreyfus picked her up, and the slaves of the Quennelle plantation silently stood aside as he carried her to the donkey and back to Far Water.

Gaelle

She was dreaming again, but this was not her dream. The air was thick and fragrant, the trees draped in moss. Everything—the house, the trees, the smells—were foreign to her. She heard the clip-clop of horse hooves on cobblestone, smelled smoke, thick and oily on the air. There was a flash of beautiful cloth, the color of a spring sky.

And then . . .

She was standing on the slope of a mountain. She knew this place. She felt a hitch of pain deep in her gut and inhaled sharply. Her grandmother had grown up in the nearby village and she and Rose had come every summer to these mountains, high over Gonaïves, far away from the dust and soot of the city. They'd spent countless hours running through the ruins of the old coffee and sugar plantations. But now Rose was in college in California and Grann . . . Grann had vanished on that horrible day when the earth had shaken Haiti to dust.

The forest spread out like a green carpet beneath her feet, as far as she could see. On the horizon, outlining the blue of the sky, was a darker band of blue, the Atlantic. Gaelle frowned, confused. There was something wrong about this place, something different.

And then it struck her.

She had never seen the mountain so green, so lush. Grann had spoken of the old days, the time of her grandmother's grandmother, when their land had been a paradise of wild hibiscus and banana groves, when jaguars and monkeys roamed wild. But that was before the mountains had been stripped of the trees to make charcoal, the plains cleared to farm, and the bare hillsides scoured clean by mudslides.

A hint of smoke and something else, something she couldn't quite name, caught her attention. She swallowed hard, then swallowed again, tasting it on her tongue. This was a dream, but not her dream, and she wanted to wake up. There was evil hiding here beneath all this beauty, she could feel it. But she was trapped here, in the Haiti of her ancestors. And she was alone.

She caught the scent of smoke again. And it felt more like a memory, a bad memory, than a dream.

There, off in the distance, a fire was burning, the smell sharp, organic, nearly overwhelming. Her mouth watered as bile rose in the back of her throat. There was something inside the flame, something that looked . . .

"Gaelle!"

She bolted upright. Toya was kneeling beside her, her round face pinched with worry. Mrs. Orr, the DON, and another nurse hovered nearby.

"Guy, what happened? Did you fall? Are you okay?"

She noticed the blood pressure cuff around her arm and tried to stand.

"No," cried Mrs. Orr. "You need to take it slow."

Gaelle glanced behind them. The old woman sat motionless in the chair, her eyes fixed on the television screen.

"I . . . I am fine." Toya held her firmly by the wrist, checking her pulse. "I was dizzy."

"You fainted?" asked Toya, alarmed.

"I . . ." She ripped the cuff from her arm and pushed herself to her feet. "No. I am quite fine." She shot another glance at the old woman.

"Gaelle, I think you should go home for the rest of the day," said Mrs. Orr. The DON was a squat, nervous woman with dyed red hair. She stood gripping her cell phone in one hand, the clipboard she carried everywhere pressed against her chest with the other.

Gaelle shook her head, and for a moment everything swam out of focus. For a brief second she thought she smelled smoke.

"Yes," she agreed reluctantly. "I will go home." She felt an odd sensation in her wrist, an echo of the pain where the old woman had grabbed her.

"Should you see the doctor?"

"No." She said it too quickly and saw everyone's eyes widen. Taking a deep breath, she forced a smile.

"No. I just got dizzy," she said again, feeling a wave of relief when the DON finally nodded.

"I'll walk her out," said Toya.

Stepping into the hall, Gaelle chanced a final look at the old woman, who sat still as stone in her chair. Minutes later, as she dragged her coat from her locker in the lounge, she could feel her friend's eyes boring into her back.

"What is it?" she snapped, turning around.

Toya crossed her arms across her chest. "Don't be gettin' all snippy with me, girl. I ain't the one."

"I am sorry. I just . . ." She sighed.

"You didn't just get dizzy, Guy. You were out cold."

"I got dizzy."

"Okay, fine." Toya held her hands up in surrender. "Let's go with that then."

Gaelle rolled her eyes. As she pulled on her coat, she suddenly remembered the remote in her pocket. "Here, you give this to Mrs. Orr, yes?"

"What the hell, man?" Toya stared at it. "Is this the TV remote? What'd you do to it?"

She flinched, remembering the surge of heat down her arm that had finally made the old woman release her. It had seemed to come from everywhere. And she had not been in control. "I did nothing! I found it in the old woman's bedcovers."

"It looks . . . melted." Toya was still staring at it. "What'd she do? Microwave it? Man, Orr's gonna lose her shit. She has a hissy when she even has to replace paper clips."

Gaelle shook her head, and once again she had the sensation of tilting into another place. "I will see you tomorrow."

"Don't you come back in here if you're still feeling 'dizzy,' you feel me?"

She grinned. "Yes, I do feel you."

Gaelle stood for a long time in the middle of the front room that served as her living room, slush from her shoes melting onto the threadbare rug. She glanced around the sparsely furnished space. She didn't know what she should be doing. Despite all her years in Cleveland, her only real friend here was Toya, and it was barely 6 a.m. in California, too early to call Rose. Sinking to the couch, she stared through the room's one narrow window.

The old woman flashed in her mind, and she held up her hands to examine them once again. Other than the faint tremor, there was nothing unusual about them: long, bony fingers like Grann's, short, ragged nails—she was really trying to stop biting them—skin the color of hickory wood.

Nothing unusual at all.

But there was.

"*Cho tankou soléy la,*" Grann said. Hot as the sun.

She remembered all those doctor visits, Grann scraping money together to take her to see specialists in Port-au-Prince, insisting that there had to be something wrong with her, because she was always so hot, always felt like she was burning with fever. She remembered the needles, the bright lights, the sharp smell of disinfectant. But they'd all said the same thing, all those doctors. That it was just how she was born. That she had a fast metabolism. She wasn't sick. She just ran hot as a furnace, like Toya said. She stared at her hands. It was nothing.

She could keep her coffee from getting cold, warm Toya's fingers. A weird trick of her body's chemistry, a nice perk on a winter day.

Except this morning it hadn't been nice. It had been terrifying.

She had never felt so hot. Had never used it *against* anyone.

She leaned her head against the back of the couch and closed her eyes. In a few hours it would be late enough to call Rose. They would talk about her finals, the cold weather here in Ohio, figure out a way to get her home for the holidays. She would tell her sister about the remote and they would laugh.

The knock on the door startled her. She glanced at her watch. She almost never got visitors. Even the Jehovah Witnesses avoided navigating the broken concrete driveway that led to her front door.

"Yes?"

A young white man stood smiling at the door. Young white men were a rare enough sight in the neighborhood that she stepped back, startled, immediately suspicious.

"Morning," he said.

"May I help you?"

"My name is Beck Gardner."

She said nothing, waiting.

"You haven't responded to any of the letters we've sent you."

She frowned. "Letters?"

"I'm the new owner of this property. This one and the one next door. We've sent several letters informing you that you have ninety days to find a new place to live." He glanced down at the papers he held in his hand. "Well, sixty-four days now."

"What?" She blinked, confused. "What happened to Mr. Howard?"

Marvin Howard was the elderly man who owned the carriage house and the decrepit mansion in front of it.

"Mr. Howard lost this property to the bank almost a year ago."

He held the papers out to her, but she stood unmoving, staring at them. With a sigh, he bent and placed them on the floor behind her. Straightening, he stood there, as if waiting for her to speak, but she was gazing, stunned, at the envelope on the floor.

"You'll need to vacate the premises by the end of February, Ms. Saint Pierre. You understand?"

She didn't answer, and after a moment he turned and walked away.

She stood there for an eternity staring at the envelope before slumping to the floor and picking it up. There had to be some mistake. They could not do this, could they? Take her home away? Where would she go? This was the first place, the only place, she'd lived since they'd been forced to flee Haiti. They could not, they would not take this away from her, too. She sat for a long time in front of the still-open door, oblivious to the cold, oblivious to the fact that the envelope she'd crumpled in her fist had burnt to ash.

Margot

1857

"Mar?" Veronique's bony finger jabbed her between the shoulder blades. "Mar, are you awake?"

Margot arched away, but there was nowhere to go on the tiny mattress, except onto the floor.

"Mar . . ."

"*Allez dormier,*" hissed Margot.

For a long moment the only sound was the chirping of the crickets on the other side of the wooden shack's thin walls. The single window was open for circulation, but the air was a living thing pressing down on them. Margot sensed her sister, lying behind her in the dark, trembling with the effort of keeping silent. With a grunt, she flung herself onto her back, swatting damp hair off her cheek.

"Alright! Spit it out," she hissed. "Before your head explodes."

Veronique pushed herself up on her elbows. Margot could just make out her silhouette in the dark.

"What do you want for your birthday?"

"My birthday?"

The word sent a jolt of rage through Margot. She dug her nails into the rough ticking of the cornhusk mattress. Her birthday. She'd been promised her freedom for her last birthday. Instead, she'd been ripped from her home, her family; sold away like livestock to the sort of people she never would have even spoken to on the streets of New Orleans. What could a birthday ever mean to her again? Veronique leaned close and Margot could feel her sister's breath against her face.

"My birthday is months away," she said, finally.

"*Oui,* but this is something to think about before the day, *non?*"

Margot bit her lip to hold back the retort.

"I know what I will give you."

Margot grunted. "And what is that, *oie?*"

"I am going to get you a ticket on that freedom railroad."

"Ce qui?" Margot bolted upright, hissing in pain as her head struck her sister's. "Are you mad? You have been talking to those *noirs* again, *non?* To those *garçons?* Francis? Ned?"

Veronique said nothing. Margot sucked her teeth and rolled from the cornhusk mattress.

"I have told you not to speak to them. They are field slaves . . . common."

"They are kind." Veronique pushed her face close enough for Margot to read her expression. She was frowning, her eyes that of Grand-mere's, disapproving. Margot looked away, shamed. She rubbed the space between her eyes. Each beat of her heart sent a pulse of pain through her head.

"Yes," she conceded. "They have been kind to us. But they speak of this . . . this railroad, this road that carries slaves to freedom—where they can disappear and never be found. Even if it were not foolishness . . ."

"It is not foolishness . . . !"

Margot placed a hand over her sister's mouth. Veronique's lips were soft and cool beneath her palm, even though her face was twisted in anger.

"Even . . . ," Margot went on, her voice hard, "even if it were not foolishness, it is foolhardy to speak of. Do not think the *blancs* do not listen to the whispers of *leurs esclaves.* If they hear the talk of escape, of running away, then it gets only worse for us."

"How worse?" Veronique's mouth moved against her fingers. Margot jerked her hand away.

"Do not be *stupide*," she snapped. She glared at her sister in the darkness. "You know how it could be worse. These . . . people . . ."

She could never bring herself to speak the name of the white people to whom she now belonged. Could not, even now, think of them as her masters.

"They are not so terrible," Margot went on. "At least here, the woman is too sick to take notice of us, and the man is always in his fields with his tobacco. All we have to do is keep the house."

"And mind those ugly, stupid *enfants*," sniffed Veronique.

Margot laughed bitterly. The master's children truly were four of the dimmest, most unattractive creatures she had ever laid eyes on—with their thin, limp hair and sallow skin, their noses constantly running.

"*Oui*," she agreed. "And mind the ugly, stupid children."

Veronique coughed and said nothing.

"Goose, *oie*," said Margot finally. "We are together, you and I. *Non?*"

Veronique leaped up and threw her arms around her neck, surprising her. She returned the embrace, frowning. When had her sister gotten so thin, so insubstantial? Her light shift felt as if it held only bones. And there was something else. As she held her sister, she felt a vibration beneath her hands, soft as a cat's purr, but unpleasant. It spread up her arms and into her chest, turning the world to shades of muddy blue and gray, souring the spit in her mouth. She could taste the bad moving through Veronique's lungs, filling them with poison.

"*Je t'aime*, Margot." Veronique sank back to the mattress, pulling her sister with her. "Sing to me."

Margot inhaled sharply through her nose, forcing back a howl of despair. She hated them. All of them.

Catherine Hannigan. James Hannigan. Ninette Rousse. Every *blanc* who walked the earth. All those forces in the world she couldn't control, that had torn her away from Grandmere and landed them here.

"*Je t'aime aussi*," she said roughly. "Though I have no idea why. Your head is as hard as a cooking pot and just as empty, and you are sure to get us both in trouble one of these days."

Veronique giggled and tucked her head beneath Margot's chin.

Margot closed her eyes and breathed in her sister's scent: sweat and apples and smoke from the woodstove. She forced herself to ignore the sharper, sickly smell that drifted just underneath. She breathed deeply, waiting until she was sure that the tears wouldn't overwhelm her, and then she began to sing.

> *Dodo l'enfant do.*
> *L'enfant dormira bien vite.*
> *Dodo l'enfant do.*
> *L'enfant dormira bientôt.*

> *Sleepy time the little one sleeps.*
> *The little one will sleep soon.*
> *Sleepy time the little one sleeps.*
> *The little one will sleep soon.*

Carefully, Margot untangled herself from Veronique. The little girl snorted then rolled on her side. In her sleep she coughed, a rough, low-pitched sound. Margot watched her for a moment, then leaned to lay her hand on her sister's back. Almost immediately, the vibration stirred beneath her palm.

"Oh, *bébé*," murmured Margot. Veronique coughed again and Margot stroked her hair, running the fine strands between her fingers, tensing each time a cough wracked the thin body. After a while, Veronique's breathing seemed easier, each cough coming farther and farther apart.

Margot stood and made her way out into the night. A giant hickory tree grew a few yards from the shack door, and she made her way to it, slouching at its base. The night was still warm but a breeze stirred the air, freshening it.

The tree sat on a high rise of land, and by the light of the quarter moon Margot could make out the dark shadows of the rolling hills. Everything was wrong here. The way the land rose and fell in no discernible pattern, the dry, dark earth. Even the moon seemed to hang oddly in the sky. She had the overwhelming sense that somehow her spirit had made its way into someone else's body and become trapped in this terrible life. In her mind's eye, she could clearly see herself, the real Margot, wandering, soulless and lost, through the streets of New Orleans.

A single tear made its way down her cheek. She wanted to go home. She wanted Grandmere. She wanted the color to come back into her sister's gaunt face. She took a deep breath and then she was sobbing, her fists pressed against her mouth to muffle the sound.

It had been the old woman, Madame Rousse, who had come to them. Margot had been in the backyard beating dust from the parlor carpets. Veronique was emptying ash from the fireplace into the rose beds.

Margot felt her before she saw her and turned to find the old woman standing on the stone path that led from the outdoor kitchen. Ninette Rousse had stood silently staring, her lips pressed into a hard line, her eyes bright blue in the morning light. Margot would remember that always, how old Madame's eyes were the color of bluebells.

Veronique had come from the garden then, and the two sisters stood side by side, waiting wordlessly for Madame to speak, forever it seemed, and when she finally had, Margot had not been prepared for the words.

"*Ma petite-fille est une imbécile,*" she said, shaking her head.

Without another word, she turned, and the girls watched her walk away, her gold-tipped walking stick clicking loudly on the flagstones that lead back to the house. Five days later they'd been loaded into a carriage. They were to be sent by boat up the Mississippi to a family friend of the Rousses'. Girard was not driving, and Margot wondered dully if he had been sold as well. Grandmere was nowhere to be seen.

The night before, her shrieks had echoed through the Prytania Street house, begging the mistress, pleading with her to spare her granddaughters, but she had nothing to bargain with.

Finally, in the early hours of the morning, Fortuna Rousse had curled together with her granddaughters by the fire in their room one last time, trying to pour a lifetime of love and hope into them. At dawn, just before Madame Rousse sent for them, she fastened a tiny locket around each of their necks. Inside each one was a curl of her hair, fine, steel gray. She touched her lips to their foreheads, then left their room.

Madame Rousse and Mistress Hannigan had been there to watch them leave. The old woman stood stiffly in the doorway, her eyes hidden in shadow. Mistress Hannigan at least had the decency to shed a tear.

"I'm sorry," she said. "I didn't know. I am so sorry."

She tried to hug Veronique, but the girl shrank away, as if she were one of the poisonous snakes that swam the black water of the bayous near Far Water. Catherine Hannigan stood in the drive then, crying and crying, her face flushed, her red hair a tangled mess down the back of her wrinkled dressing gown.

"Catherine!"

Ninette Rousse stepped from the shadows of the doorway, her eyes hard and flat as stones. She glared at her granddaughter until the younger woman fell silent, her arms limp at her sides, her eyes fixed on the side of the wagon, unable to meet the gaze of the two girls she was selling away.

Madame Rousse stepped to the wagon and grasped Margot's hand. Margot tried to jerk away but the old woman's grip was as strong as a teamster's. She pulled her close.

Eyes the color of bluebells.

"Be brave," she said. "Always be brave." She released Margot's hand, then turned and disappeared into the house.

Slowly, the wagon pulled out of the drive and turned onto the street, heading for the port. Margot gripped her sister's hand and gazed back at the house, hoping for one last glimpse of Grandmere.

"Wait! Wait!"

The wagon jerked to a stop and Margot and Veronique exchanged a look. Running down the street after them was Catherine Hannigan. Her dressing gown billowed around her, exposing her thin nightdress. Margot winced, embarrassed for her, even as she was aware that it should no longer matter to her.

"I have something for you," panted Mistress Hannigan when she caught up to them. She thrust a cloth-wrapped bundle into Margot's lap. Margot glanced up at the driver, an American, who sat scowling up at the sky. She peeled the cloth back. Laying in the center of a sheet of folded muslin was a ham, and next to that lay a small Bible. Veronique made a noise.

Margot looked up. Her former mistress was smiling, her expression hopeful. Margot stared with narrowed eyes at the white woman, until the mistress's smile collapsed and she backed slowly away from the wagon.

"*Bien,*" whispered Catherine Hannigan. "Alright, you can go then."

The wagon began to move once again down the bricked street. Margot stared at the Bible and the ham in her lap until she felt Veronique's hand on her arm. She looked up. Her sister was pointing at the ham and silently laughing, her mouth wide, her shoulders shaking. Margot blinked, and then she began to laugh as well, ignoring the looks of the white driver.

She leaped to her feet, Veronique's arms locked around her waist to hold her steady and keep her from being thrown out onto the street.

"*Maîtresse!*" she yelled. Her voice echoed off the houses in the early morning fog.

Catherine Hannigan looked up and Margot launched the ham at her. Their former mistress screamed and stumbled backward, the ham landing with a wet thud harmlessly, more than a foot in front of her. Veronique handed Margot the Bible. It was small, not much larger than a teacup, but heavy. Margot took careful aim, and just before they turned south onto Washington Avenue, hurled it with all her strength.

Mistress Hannigan was still staring at the ham in the street; they could hear her sobs all the way at the corner, and the Bible struck her like a miniature cannonball, just above her left breast. She cried out and fell—her legs bare and sickly white—in the middle of Prytania.

The two girls cheered and hugged each other, laughing all the way to the port. At some point, though, Margot couldn't remember exactly when, the laughter had turned to tears.

Margot laughed now, though it was bitter in her mouth.

What fools! To throw perfectly good meat into the street.

Now, from the shack behind her, Veronique was coughing again.

The sound pricked at Margot like the point of a knife. She rubbed the chain that held the locket between her fingers.

Don't be sick. Let this just be the thin Kentucky air.

She prayed, though she no longer believed in God. What sort of God would allow her family to be destroyed because James Hannigan had been such a vain and careless man? What sort of God would allow one group of people to have that much power over another?

Please, don't be sick, oie.

Because if Vee was sick, there would be nothing she could do. If they were home, Grandmere would know what to do. She would rub Veronique's chest with turpentine oil or wrap her in a poultice of sage and vinegar. Her grandmother would know how to draw the sickness out of her, how to make her strong again. But in this ugly, gray place of empty spaces, Margot felt alone and helpless. The coughing drifted to her in the darkness, tearing at her heart.

Rest. She just needs to rest. And to get away from those snotty-nosed enfants. It was the strange food. It is that white woman, already half dead. She infected Veronique with something. She would be fine if only she could feel the right kind of sun on her face.

Maybe.

Margot tugged her shawl around her head, trying to shield her face from the biting insects.

Maybe they *should* go on that railroad to freedom.

She stood and walked back to the shack.

12

It was death that decided for Margot.

The master's wife was dying. For the past fortnight she'd managed to drag herself from her bed and into the parlor. Most days she spent sitting in a battered rocker in front of the unlit fireplace. Sometimes she sewed. Other times she brushed the youngest girl's hair or listened as the oldest boy painfully sounded out his letters. Mostly she slept, her chin resting on her skeletal chest, her limp hair hiding her face.

The master seemed to take this small spark of energy as a good sign, the fact that his wife had at least risen from her bed. He smiled often, an expression Margot had rarely seen on his face in the ten months since they'd arrived on his farm. Each day, as Margot stirred oatmeal for the children, the master kissed his wife's pale, sweaty forehead before going out into his tobacco fields. Most mornings, she could hear him whistling long after he'd passed behind the curing barn.

He thought she was getting well. But Margot knew better. Rot drifted around the dozing woman like smoke from a grease fire. The master's woman was like a candle, the wick of her life flaring up and burning brightly just before going out forever.

So it was decided.

They had to leave.

They had to leave before the woman's life flickered out. Margot had no intention of ever again allowing her and her sister's fate to be decided by the dying breath of a *blanc*. On a warm fall night, by the light of a full moon, Margot took her sister's hand and they walked quietly into the night.

There were five of them: a middle-aged woman and teenaged boy, Margot and her sister, and Ned. Margot had never seen either the woman or the boy before, but through the long night, as they walked in silence, staying in the shadows, it became clear that the boy was Ned's brother, and that the woman was their mother, both from another plantation down the road.

The runaways said very little to each other. They walked by night. By day, they made makeshift hiding places beneath fallen trees, in shallow ditches, anywhere they could find, and tried to sleep. Veronique's cough grew stronger, lasted longer. Margot scoured the woods for the herbs she remembered Grandmere using for a cough: marshmallow root, peppermint, but this far from home, everything looked alien and she found nothing she thought might help. As they walked at night, moving farther and farther north, Veronique's breathing became more labored, though she insisted she was fine.

The warm October night they'd run away had been a tease, and the nights quickly turned frigid. By the third day, their meager supply of food had nearly run out. Still, they pressed on. With whispers and hand signals, Ned led the way. He'd told them they were headed for the Ohio River. There would be someone there, he said, a conductor, to guide them across the water into freedom.

On the fourth night, the ground was softer, wetter. In the darkness it was hard to see. Frost-glazed mud sucked at their clothes. Behind her, Veronique struggled for each breath.

"*Allez!*" panted Veronique when Margot stopped to wait. "Go on. I will catch up."

But the next time Margot looked over her shoulder, her sister was no longer there.

"*Mon Dieu!*" She spun and began to retrace her steps.

"Veronique," she cried. "Veronique where are you?"

Behind her, Ned hissed for her to shut up. If they were being followed, her shouts would lead the slavers right to them. Margot didn't care. She had to find her sister.

She thrashed wildly in the marshy forest, falling again and again, tangling herself in half-submerged branches and dangling vines, reckless in her panic. She turned, then turned again, lost.

"Veronique!" she screamed.

"Mar?"

The voice came to her from the shadows. It took many long, disorienting minutes, but finally she found her. Veronique lay crumbled near the roots of an upended tree. Dark water covered her to the waist, her breath coming hard and uneven.

Margot fell to her knees and cradled her sister's head. "What are you doing, goose?"

"All this water," panted Veronique. "I thought I should bathe."

She was shivering, hard. "I am so cold, Margot."

"I know, *bébé*. I know," whispered Margot. From the corner of her eye, she saw Ned and his family crouching in the shadows. She tried to stand but her sister's arm snaked around her waist.

"Don't leave," she whimpered. "Don't leave me, Mar."

Margot tasted bile in her throat. "I am not going anywhere, Vee, except to get something to make a fire." She struggled to keep her tone light. "Since you insist on bathing."

She lifted her sister out of the water to the driest place she could find. It was like moving paper, her sister's weight barely there.

"We gotta go."

Margot cried out. Ned had appeared silently at her side.

"Can't stay here no longer," he said. "Gotta get goin'. Them peoples at the river ain't gonna wait forever."

"Then go," snapped Margot, using her hands to search the cracks and crevices of the fallen trees. "Take your family and go. My sister must rest."

But he made no move to leave. He watched in silence as she collected a fistful of moss and a small bundle of the driest wood she could find.

She rooted in the pocket of her skirt for the flint she'd stolen from the barn on the day they'd fled. On the second try, the fire caught and Margot inhaled deeply, grateful for the small circle of light.

"You will be better after you rest awhile," she said, squatting next to her sister. She bit her lip to keep from crying. Veronique's face was the color of day-old fish. Her eyes had sunk deep into her thin face. Blood had dried at the corner of her mouth.

"*Oui*," she said smiling weakly. "I will be better."

"They gon' see that fire," said Ned, quietly. "They gon' see and they gon' come."

Margot felt something break inside her. "*Allez*," she shrieked. "Just go. Leave us alone. If they come, they come, but my sister must rest."

Ned looked at her sadly.

"Go," screeched Margot.

Ned turned and melted into the shadows with his family. Margot pulled Veronique closer to the fire.

Except for the harsh sound of her breathing, the girl was silent, still. Margot stroked her sister's face, her mind flooded with barely coherent thoughts.

"Vee?"

Veronique's eyes fluttered open. She stared up at Margot blankly and then she smiled. "*Ce qui?*"

"This is the most terrible birthday gift you have ever given me."

"*Désole*," said Veronique. Her laugh quickly dissolved into another fit of coughing. As it wracked her body, Margot could feel her sister's lungs tearing themselves apart. Bloody foam dribbled from Veronique's mouth; her body stiffened as her eyes rolled up in her head.

"No," screamed Margot. "No, no, no. Breathe, *oie*. Do you hear me? Breathe."

She hugged her sister's tiny body against her chest and bent her forward, pounding hard on her back, tasting the thing in her lungs go from blue to black, then break up. A little. Veronique's coughing eased, then stopped. She sagged against Margot, her breathing ragged but regular.

Margot clung to her, rocking, sobbing, and humming softly. Something splashed in the woods and she fell silent, every muscle tense. She glanced at the fire, but there was no point in dousing it now. Surely whoever was out there had already seen it. She heard voices and her heart pounded. What would they do to her when they took her back? Beat her? Sell her away? She glanced at her sister sleeping fitfully in her arms. Maybe it was for the best. Maybe they would take pity on Vee and find some way to nurse her back to health. Or maybe she would grind apple seeds to a powder. She and Veronique would drink it in a tea and be free forever.

Something moved in the shadows and Margot cried out in fear. Ned's mother stepped into the small circle of light and knelt in front of the sisters. She opened the small handkerchief she had tied to her waist with string and pulled out a shriveled sweet potato and the remains of a roasted rat.

"Wish I had more to give but . . ." She shrugged.

Tears welled in Margot's eyes as she gazed at the pitiful offering, everything this woman had.

"I . . ." She couldn't go on.

Ned's mother smiled and touched Veronique's cheek. And then she vanished into the darkness.

"*Merci*," murmured Margot to her disappearing shadow.

"Mar?"

Margot looked down into her sister's eyes.

"I want to go home. I want to go home to Grandmere."

"Me too, *oie*. Me too." She tossed the last of the moss onto the fire and pulled Veronique close, trying to warm her with her body heat. After a time, she dropped into a restless sleep.

It was the silence that woke her. Sometime in the middle of the night Veronique had stopped coughing.

Margot blinked. The sun was coming up over the trees, the sky the color of fresh melon. She tried to sit up and Veronique shifted oddly in her arms.

"Vee?"

There was no answer. The little girl's eyes stared, unseeing, toward the dawn sky.

Margot screamed. She grabbed her sister, heavier in death than she had ever been in life, and began to stagger from the swampy woodland, the only thought in her mind that she had to get to Grandmere. If she could just get home, if she could just get Veronique to their grandmother, then everything would be alright. She would wake up in her bed on Prytania Street, this whole past year a terrible nightmare.

Margot tripped, dropping her sister's body. She tried to get up, tried to pick Veronique up and keep running, but her arms, her legs refused to obey. She lay there in the cold mud, staring into her sister's eyes, and began to howl. She howled until her voice gave out and her mind went dark.

When she opened her eyes again, the sun was at the top of the sky, giving light but little warmth. She was soaked through and ached with cold. For a moment she lay blinking, confused, her lids sliding painfully over the grit in her eyes.

"Vee?" she croaked, her voice hoarse.

And then recognition crashed into her, knocking the breath from her lungs. With a sob, she rolled on her side. Veronique lay next to her, and Margot clutched at her, pulling her close. Her sister's body was as cold and rubbery as a leg of mutton in the smokehouse, but she held on, humming a tuneless lullaby.

"*C'est bien, oie*," she murmured. "Everything is going to be alright."

She drifted, oblivious to the day growing later, not cold, not afraid, humming and humming.

"*Allez!*"

Margot jerked.

"Vee? Veronique?"

She'd heard her sister's voice, felt her warm breath against her neck, and she pushed herself upright with a groan. Veronique still lay on the ground, eyes closed, clothes mud-caked, face gray, waxy.

And yet . . .

Margot scanned the trees. Was this one of Grandmere's spirits? Was her sister's spirit here with her now? Watching her?

"Veronique?" she whispered.

"Allez." The word was soft but clear, carried on the wind, rustling from the dry underbrush. "Go. *Now.*"

The hair stood up on her arms and she bent to touch her sister's face. But Veronique was gone. She was completely alone.

Margot found a hollowed log. It wasn't quite big enough, but it would protect her sister in some small way from the animals and the elements, at least for a while. Gently, she tucked pine boughs around her sister's body. Veronique had always liked the smell of fresh pine. Then, bending, she swapped the lockets Grandmere had given them, hers for Veronique's. They were identical, but she would always know this one had belonged to her sister.

In the end, she simply walked away—no more words, no more tears—because there was nothing else to do.

Abigail

1791

Révolte!

Monsieur Quennelle, the pig, had been right after all.

For months, the rumors had drifted in the slave quarter like ghosts, roiling through the coffee groves, gaining strength by the day, whispered from slave to slave, managing to penetrate even Abigail's fog of grief.

There was a man, they said, a priest, who had spoken to the spirits. And this man had declared war on the *blancs*. He meant to drive them—every man, woman, and child—into the sea.

Every night, they said, plantations burned and the *blancs* were killed in their beds. The warrior maroons carried as their standard, not a flag, but the head of a white baby on a pike.

And, they said, when it was over, this war, when the last *blanc* had been driven from the last cliff, there would not be a single slave left in Saint-Domingue, only free black men and women. And every day the cocoa fields and coffee groves grew emptier as the slaves melted into the mountains to join the fight.

Révolte!

Abigail moaned. She lay curled into a fetal position, hidden among the rigging and other ship's stores that cluttered the aft deck. They'd been at sea . . . three days? Five? Since the night the mountains surrounding Far Water had finally exploded and what was left of her world had gone up in flames. She struggled to focus, but her memories of that night were broken, jumbled.

Monsieur Rousse appearing at her door, no waistcoat, blouse pulled free of his breeches, reeking of stale sweat, ordering her to the main house.

Angry white men with guns, crowding the halls, Monsieur Rousse's study, watching her as she walked by, hatred and fear naked on their pale faces.

Ninette Rousse, her mistress, in the center of the drawing room, wringing her hands, her red hair matted and tangled, her yellow dress bright in the gloom.

Révolte!

They were leaving. Taking the last ship from Port-de-Paix to some-place called Cuba, then on to New Orleans. They were leaving, before the maroons reached Far Water. But "they" did not include Thierry Rousse. He would stay, stand with the other planters and defend his holdings. He had been good to his slaves and they would stand by him. He was sure of this. And "they" did not include her sons, Claude and Henri. There was no space for them on the ship, no accommodations for them in New Orleans, but Abigail was needed, to look after the mistress and baby Julian.

Abigail moaned and pulled her knees tighter to her chest. She had a vague memory of blocking her master's exit from the drawing room, of screaming "No!" into his startled face. She remembered falling, the taste of blood in her mouth. Had he struck her? She couldn't re-member. She was stuck, frozen in the last moments with her boys, her *enfants*. Bending over their sleeping forms, inhaling their musty, little-boy scent, touching her nose to theirs. She clawed at her face. Ama had been the brave one. She should have kissed their beloved faces then slit their throats, so they would never again know fear or sadness. Not have to wait and hope for the freedom promised by the maroons, for they would already have the one, true freedom. But she had been a coward. She let herself believe the master's promise that he would send them to his smaller estate in the South where it was safer, that she would see them again.

The deck pitched and Abigail pulled herself up, back in the present, leaning over the splintered railing to retch. She'd been sick nearly from the moment she'd boarded. They were on a two-hundred-ton French merchant ship, designed for cargo, but the only cargo it now carried were several dozen terrified whites and their handful of slaves. The whites, mostly women and children, huddled in small groups on the decks, the blacks, for the most part, confined to the hold.

All except for Abigail.

On that first morning, after their fevered race down the mountain, a deckhand had tried to force her into the hold with the other slaves. The opening yawned before her like a great black mouth, and her nostrils suddenly filled with the memory of rotting flesh, shit, and blood. As she backed away, she thought she heard Ama laughing at her from the shadows below.

"Nigger," snarled the deckhand as he tried to push her forward. *"Chienne."*

She smelled the stink of rum on his breath as she planted her feet, digging her nails into the wood framing the hold. Something hard struck her between the shoulders, but she was a big woman, and strong, and she would not be moved.

"Get your ass down there, now. *Entendez-vous?*"

Abigail whirled and threw herself at the sailor. He would have to kill her to get her into that hole. Or she would kill him. She no longer cared which. Only the intervention of her mistress had prevented either outcome. Now they left her alone. And she tried to be invisible.

She opened her eyes. She tasted metal and her head hurt, the pain slowly worsening until she was seeing double. But no, not double, not exactly. Abigail ran a hand over her face and squinted. She was seeing a double image, but the images were not precise mirror images of each other. She squinted. There was the deck, a dark-haired boy of seven or eight squatting near the railing, rolling a green marble between his hands, a woman sobbing quietly near the bow, a sailor, his legs deeply bowed, cursing as he threw the contents of a slop bucket into the sea. But the other image . . . the other image was different. There was the deck, but it was empty save for a lone gull standing on the railing. She could hear the crack of the sails as the wind whipped them, feel the salt spray on her skin. The pain in her head was a clanging hammer. She squeezed her eyes tight, and when she reopened them, there was only the deck with the little boy and the sobbing woman.

"Abigail?"

The slave woman started and looked up. A few feet away, her mistress stood watching her. Ninette Rousse was smiling, her eyes wild in her pale face, red hair frizzed by the sea air, her infant son clutched to her bosom.

"You must come out of there, *chére*," she said. "We will be in Cuba in a few hours, then just three more days and we will be safely with my cousin's family in New Orleans."

Abigail ground her teeth. The pain in her head was starting again, and for a moment she saw that other deck, hiding behind this one, empty of everyone, empty of her mistress and her mewling, maggot-colored child.

"Abigail, you come out of there this instant," snapped Ninette Rousse when the slave didn't respond. Her voice was loud, bordering on hysteria.

Abigail saw the other whites watching. Her mistress saw, too. She whimpered and pulled the baby tighter against her chest.

"Please," she whispered. "It's going to be fine. I promise. Please."

Abigail stared at her mistress for a long moment, then turned away, curling back into her fetal position.

Behind her, she heard Ninette Rousse whispering, "*Tout ira bien.* Everything is going to be fine."

They stood side by side in silence at the railing.

New Orleans.

The smells and sounds were overwhelming. Ships of every shape and size crowded the pier, dark coal smoke belching from the smokestacks of some, blackening the sails of the others, turning the rising sun an angry scarlet. Below and behind, teamsters swarmed crates the size of houses, and men of every shape and color pushed their way up and down gangways shouting curses in English and French and a half dozen other languages. And from somewhere, through the murky dawn, came the sound of church bells.

And then there was the water.

Gone was the aquamarine blue of the seas surrounding Saint-Domingue. The little French merchant ship now floated at anchor in water that reeked of kerosene and human waste and was the color of old potato skins. Mixed into the stench of the foul water was the smell of rotting fish, overripe fruit, burning cane.

When finally able to disembark, they were met by the husband of Madame's cousin, a gaunt, narrow-faced man with hair the color of moldy straw. He reminded Abigail a bit of Monsieur Dreyfus, and she wondered if Madame's cousin was *un juif* as well. She had no idea of the rules that governed the worshipping of the *blanc* gods.

The cousin turned and led them through the crowd to a small carriage, where two black men were loading her mistress's trunks onto the platform behind the seats. An image of Hercule flashed in her mind, and she bit her lip to keep from crying out. She stared at the ground as one of the teamsters helped Ninette Rousse and the baby into the carriage.

The slave woman gripped the iron railing to pull herself up beside the luggage, then froze. For a moment she had a rush of fear, the sensation of a sharp blade tip tracing her spine from neck to tailbone. She turned, scanning the crowd. It seemed a solid wall of noise and chaos, but gradually, she began to distinguish details. People pushing and shoving their way between the horses and carts. A wagon filled with pigs rumbling by. A woman standing near a makeshift shed, roasting peanuts.

Abigail felt eyes on her.

There.

A woman, the oldest woman Abigail had ever seen, stood at the mouth of an alley. Short and round, with skin the color of creamed coffee, her bright white hair was tied back with a kerchief. She was staring directly at her, and when she caught her looking, she stepped from the shadows and smiled. Abigail felt the hair on her arms stand up.

"Abigail?" Ninette Rousse had turned in her seat and was watching her with the same wide-eyed confusion she'd had on the ship. "What is it?"

Abigail pressed her lips together and shook her head. She pulled herself up onto the platform at the back of the carriage, balancing her weight against the trunk and valises piled there. She glanced back. The woman had vanished, absorbed back into the bedlam that was the New Orleans street. It was nothing. One old colored woman and these maddening streets. One old woman.

She could feel the mistress's eyes on her.

"Nothing," she said finally. "It is nothing, *Metrés*."

As the carriage lurched into motion, she felt that knife blade down the center of her back, and shivered.

14

The strap of the basket dug deep into her shoulders, and she arched her back to shift its weight. It had been mid-August when they arrived in the city, in the very teeth of summer, but now, two days before Christmas, a glaze of ice coated the dark water that filled the muddy canals passing for streets in New Orleans.

Abigail had never known such brutal cold. The wool cloak she wore stank of another, and every inch of her body itched under its weight, but it kept out most of the chill. It would warm later, but now, just after sunrise, the temperature lingered just above freezing. She blew out a breath and watched it fog in the frigid air, both intrigued and horrified, as it hovered a moment in front of her lips, like some restless winter spirit.

The city reeked of kerosene—she could taste it on her tongue—the smell growing stronger the closer she got to the river. It burned her eyes. The city was preparing for the huge bonfires that were to be lit along the Mississippi as far as the eye could see, to light the way for Saint Nicholas. It was to be an incredible spectacle—or so her mistress had assured her, though she had never seen it, either.

Abigail shifted the basket again and rubbed her stinging eyes. New Orleans was an ugly place: cold and dirty and crowded, the foulness of so much humanity oozing from the very buildings. She was shocked at how much she missed Saint-Domingue. And not just her boys. She missed the warm air sweetened by hibiscus, the translucent blue of the sky. She missed the wild green of the mountainside and the singsong rhythm of the quarter.

She hunched her shoulders and forced her way through the throng. She was on her way to the market. Eva, the cook, had already slaughtered the goose for the Revillion supper—the celebration after Christmas Eve mass—and had sent Abigail for last-minute supplies: sugar and wine for the eggnog, oysters to smoke for the dressing.

Despite the cold, Abigail was glad to be out of the house and away from Eva. The cook rarely spoke to her except to spit orders or to sneer at Abigail's fractured French.

The house where they stayed was a modest town home owned by Madame's cousin. The cousin's husband, the man who'd met them the day they arrived, was a tobacco agent. Aside from Eva, there was only one other young slave girl who looked after the children and the housekeeping, and a groom who tended the horses and did handiwork. With the arrival of Madame, the little house was filled to overflowing, and they'd had to cobble a space for Abigail just off the fruit cellar, where the sickening sweet smell of rotting apples seeped into her pores night after night.

Abigail picked up her pace. The town home was some distance from the market at the edge of the river, and if she didn't hurry, it would be so crowded that it would take forever to make her few purchases.

The market was on the far side of Plaza de Armas and was already swarming with people despite the early hour: holiday shoppers, soldiers in bright uniforms whom Madame had told Abigail were from another *blanc* country called Spain, workmen engaged in the building of the great St. Louis Church. She had just stepped into Decatur Street when she felt that familiar sense of unease.

"Out of the way!" cried a teamster.

She jumped back, barely avoiding being run down by the wagon. She studied the crowd. Everyone was busily going about their tasks. No one seemed to notice her and yet . . . someone was watching her. She could feel it. She rooted around in her pocket until her fingers brushed against the small wooden disk she'd taken from Hercule's shop, all she had left of him. She squeezed it and shivered. A wet wind was blowing off the Mississippi. The smells of the river mixed with the ordinary market smells and the kerosene of the bonfires, making her head ache.

She crossed the street and entered the market. Ignoring the steadily growing sense of being followed, she moved quickly, purchasing each item on Eva's list before turning back toward home.

"Merde," Abigail swore, nearly dropping her basket.

There!

Standing in the center of Plaza de Armas. The old mulatto woman and her companion.

On that first day, there'd been only the old woman, but nearly every day since, there'd been the two of them. The woman and the man. The man was much younger, tall and broad of shoulder, his skin as dark as ebony. And they were there. Always there. At the market, at the far end of the street when she emptied the ash pails, at dusk, in the shadows just beyond the carriage house as she lit the lamps for the evening.

At first, she'd thought she only imagined that they followed her. Perhaps they lived nearby, ran errands in the same way that she did, but nothing explained how they were always on the same streets, in the same shops, how they always seemed to be there at the end of the alley when she stepped out to empty the slop basin every morning.

And they watched her.

Abigail felt their attention on her, even when they seemed to be haggling for tobacco for the man's pipe or peering into a barrel of freshly caught crabs.

They never came near, but they were always there.

She hurried across the street. She had tried to approach them before. But somehow they always managed to vanish down some side street, disappear into the crowd before she could reach them. But today she would know. Today they would tell her who they were, what they wanted from her. They watched her come, the man's face impassive as he raised his pipe to his lips, the woman wearing a faint smile.

This time Abigail was close enough to see that the woman had no teeth. A small group of Spanish soldiers cut in front of her, and she stopped to let them pass, swearing again under her breath. She was already late, and Eva would be unbearable for the rest of the day, cutting her with sharp words and dirty looks, but she had to speak to the old woman. She felt the need deep inside.

She fought the urge to push through the soldiers, but finally they were past.

And . . . they were gone.

Abigail dashed to where the man and woman had stood just moments before, turning wildly, scanning the crowd. It was impossible for them to have disappeared that quickly across the broad open space of the square. But everywhere she looked, there were only workmen and harried shoppers to be seen.

She let out a cry of frustration, ignoring the looks of passersby. She waited for them to reappear, scouring the crowd as she paced from one edge of the square then back again. But they were gone, and despite the warming sun, the sharp river wind had worked its way deep inside her cloak. With one last look around the square, Abigail turned and headed back to the house.

It was barely a week into March and already the city seemed to have completely forgotten the gray, wet winter. A sheen of sweat coated Abigail's face as she knelt at the edge of the vegetable cellar digging for the last of the previous fall's potatoes. A bolt of sky-blue satin suddenly appeared under her nose.

"You will need to deliver this to the dressmaker's on your way to the market." Abigail glanced up. Eva stood in the doorway, the fabric thrust out in front of her. Abigail frowned and thrust her trowel deep into the damp soil.

"*M'entendez-vous*, girl?"

Abigail gritted her teeth, ignoring the cook. She found two large, slightly shriveled potatoes and placed them in her apron pocket. Eva shook the satin and the bright cloth unfurled, dangling dangerously close to the dirt floor.

"Do you hear me, *nègre?*" snapped Eva.

The cook stumbled backward as Abigail shot to her feet.

"*Ou bliye tét ou,*" snarled Abigail. "You think yourself my mistress now?"

"Speak proper French," commanded Eva, recovering herself. "You are no longer on that devil island. You are in civilization now."

Abigail hissed and stepped toward her. Eva blinked and thrust the bolt of fabric up between them. The cook was perhaps not quite thirty, a year or two older than Abigail was. And though her clothes were fine—the hand-me-downs of her mistress—her hands were rough and swollen from long hours of kneading and chopping in the kitchen and the strong soap in the laundry.

"*Ou twompe,*" said Abigail in Creole before switching to French, rolling the words around in her mouth. "Pretty clothes and fancy words do not make you a master . . . or protect you from them, either."

Eva flinched, hot patches of color blooming on her ginger-colored cheeks. "And yet it is you who sleep in the fruit cellar like a stray cat."

Abigail laughed bitterly. "Fruit cellar. Feather bed. Are you any less a piece of property than me? *Twompe,*" she said again. "Fool."

Eva made a noise in her throat and drew back her hand as if to strike. Abigail locked eyes with her as rage bloomed in her chest. For a second her vision blurred. She saw Eva standing before her, eyes wide with terror, and she saw beyond her, through the courtyard, to the bridal wreath in full bloom along the front of the house, the tulips pushing up from the earth, still damp from the previous day's rain. She staggered as pain ricocheted from behind her eyes and down her spine. Blinking, she fought a wave of nausea, and then there was only Eva, standing there, staring at the trowel Abigail gripped in her hand.

"*Toi . . . ,*" she snapped finally, breathing hard, as Abigail dropped the trowel. "You will go to the dressmaker. They are waiting for this fabric and I am too busy."

She thrust the blue cloth against Abigail's chest, forcing her to take it, then smoothed back her hair. Her face fixed itself back into its mask of disdain. "And do not soil it," she said, before turning and crossing the courtyard back to the house.

The morning was warm and growing warmer. Abigail's feet were soon soaked, as water from the mud-clogged streets seeped through the thin leather of her slippers. She hated wearing shoes. They were uncomfortable and protected her feet against nothing. But Madame Rousse insisted.

The air rang with sound as she pushed her way through the market: dirty-faced children hawking newspapers, the clang of a blacksmith's iron, the lowing of cows in their pens. And the voices—French, Spanish, Creole, English—more languages than she had names for, as if the whole world had tipped over and people from every corner had spilled onto this spit of land that curved along the Mississippi.

Abigail forced her way through the mob, heading for the docks. Sidestepping a dray heavily loaded with cotton, she hurried along the streets, downriver toward the slips where ships loaded and unloaded night and day. When she passed a high brick wall topped with shards of glass, she ducked her head and pretended not to see. It was but one of the dozens of stockades in the commercial district where slaves were kept until auction.

The pier was chaos. Men and animals and wagons and ships stretched in every direction. It took her eye a moment to sort out individuals as they descended the gangplanks of the closest ships, house-sized bundles of cotton and massive wooden crates creaking dangerously over their heads on ropes.

Seven months.

It had been seven months since their escape from Saint-Domingue. Every Sunday, Madame sent Abigail to the docks. Every Sunday, no matter the season, no matter the weather, she was there to meet the ships as they arrived from every corner of the world. But there was only one part of the world that interested her mistress. That interested her.

Seven months and there'd been not a single word, not a single letter from Far Water. The news they did hear of Saint-Domingue was bleak. More and more whites were fleeing the island, arriving in the city pale and wild-eyed, whispering of a freed slave, one who spoke the language of the *blancs,* who led the maroons against their masters.

Yet every Sunday, Ninette Rousse sent Abigail to the docks, to wait for word of the fate of Far Water and of her husband. Abigail didn't know why Sundays. A ship from the island could just as easily arrive on a Tuesday . . . or a Friday. And if there was word, wouldn't someone come to them, appear at the town house with a message? Or would not Monsieur Rousse himself appear at the gate, her babies in tow, Claude wiggling like a minnow. Abigail shook her head and tucked herself into the shadows next to a crate of turtles packed on ice and straw. From where she stood, she could easily watch the arrivals. So many ships. So many desperate men, women, and children. And not a one from Far Water.

Since New Year's, Madame had barely left her room. In the mornings, when Abigail brought her coffee and biscuits, she barely acknowledged her. Her round cheeks had become deep hollows beneath her eyes, and her once-bright hair hung limply around her face. The only light Abigail ever saw in her mistress's eyes was when she was with her son.

Abigail herself could barely tolerate being in the same house as the child. As the days and weeks and months grew with no word from Far Water, her nights were filled with longing for her children, and her days, increasingly, with visions of ways to kill the boy. She could mix something into his food. He was just learning to walk. It would be simple to leave the nursery door open so that he might tumble down the steep stairs.

As day after day passed with only silence from Saint-Domingue, her hatred for little Julian grew darker, deeper, his rosy cheeks and baby laughter a constant rebuke. Were her children any less precious than this one white boy? Wouldn't he simply grow up one day to tear another black family apart? Just as Monsieur Quennelle had done. In the same way as his own father. The mistress seemed to sense this in her and rarely left the slave woman alone with her son.

A black man passed close by, a three-foot-long alligator tucked beneath one arm. He touched a finger to his cap.

"Mornin'," he said in English.

Abigail nodded, eyeing the twitching reptile suspiciously. *"Bonjou."*

The man disappeared into the crowd, and Abigail turned her attention back to the disembarking passengers. Across the narrow wooden walkway, a thin, beautifully dressed quadroon served coffee to customers in white china cups. Suddenly, Abigail felt the hair rise on her arms. Lurching from her resting place, she jerked her head back and forth, scanning the crowded booths, the shadows beyond the stacked crates and heavily piled wagons. She saw no sign of the old woman and her companion, but they were there, somewhere in the crowd, watching her. She could feel them.

Something caught her eye.

Passengers were descending from the ship closest to her. It was a fine vessel, small but well fit out, its sails furled neatly against the masts. A man was slowly making his way down the gangplank. His face was hidden beneath his hat, but there was something familiar about him.

Abigail forced her way down the pier, heart quickening. *I know him,* she thought, I know this *blanc.* She reached the end of the gangplank and planted herself in front of him.

"Pardonnez-moi," said the man, head still down, as he stepped around her.

Abigail froze and she watched as the man began to walk up the pier. In a moment, he would disappear into the crowd. Two black freedmen passed between them, the thick bundles of tobacco slung across their shoulders momentarily blocking him from view. Her paralysis broken, she ran after him, the satin filled satchel for the dressmaker bouncing against her thigh.

"Mét," she called. "Monsieur."

But the man didn't turn. He was moving quickly, his hat pulled low, barely seeming to register the crowd around him. At the street he stopped, waiting for a break in the heavy traffic.

"Monsieur," she called again. "Monsieur Dreyfus."

The man raised his head and when he turned, Abigail let out a cry.

It was André Dreyfus, the friend of her master. But it was an André Dreyfus terribly changed. The Jew was nearly skeletal, his blue eyes blank. A horrible scar deformed the left side of his face. An eye patch covered one eye.

"*Je suis* Abigail," she said, speaking French. "Abigail, Monsieur. You know me, yes?"

The white man blinked, then raised his face to stare silently into the sky. He seemed to be having problems standing upright. She grabbed his sleeve to steady him, and he brought his eyes down to meet hers.

"Abigail?"

"*Wi, Mét.*"

André Dreyfus nodded and made as if to cross the street, to walk away. Abigail grabbed hold of his sleeve once again.

"Monsieur Dreyfus, please," she cried. "What has happened to Far Water? What has happened to my sons?"

Far Water.

At the name, Dreyfus's face cleared, and for the first time he seemed to truly see her.

"Abigail?"

"*Wi.*"

"Abigail." His eyes began to fade again and she shook him hard.

"Monsieur Dreyfus, what of Far Water?" she pleaded. "Monsieur Rousse. *Mes enfants.* You remember? Claude? Henri? You called them lovely? You remember, *wi?*"

Her voice was shrill as she clutched the front of his stained waistcoat in her fist. People had begun to stare.

Dreyfus's mouth worked but no sound came out. "Far Water," he said at last, his voice barely above a whisper. "Far Water is no more."

Her heart seemed to stop in her chest and she forced herself to say the next words. Because she had to know, had waited all these long months to know. "*Petit mwen yo,*" she murmured. "*Mes fils?* What of my babies?"

He looked at her for a long moment, his one good eye bright with tears. "I am sorry," he said at last. "I am so very sorry."

There was a roaring in her ears. The satchel slipped from her fingers, pale blue fabric spilling out into the mud. Dreyfus stroked his eye patch and stared at the cloth, his expression confused.

"*Mes enfants,*" she shrieked. "My babies. He promised. He promised to look after them. He said they would be safe. You are liars! You are all liars."

She would have thrown herself at him them, would have torn at his ruined face, but suddenly the strange black man was there, the old woman's companion. He grabbed her from behind, holding her as easily as if she were a child as she flailed and howled her rage, her grief.

Sailors, teamsters, merchants stared, but no one approached.

"I am so sorry," murmured André Dreyfus again. He turned and shuffled across the street, vanishing into the crowd that was heading upriver toward the market.

The big man held her until she was spent. When he released her, she stood silent in the mud, staring numbly at the wide swatch of blue satin splayed in the road, her mind empty of everything except a quivering, bright hot pain.

Someone took her hand. She looked up and into the face of the old woman with the long braid who smiled kindly. She smelled sweet: of sugar and cinnamon.

"Come," she said softly. Her voice was deep and she spoke French with an odd lilting accent.

"I am called Simona," said the old woman in her singsong French. "And this is Josiah."

Abigail glanced at the man. Up close he was even taller. His thick black hair was pulled back with a leather tie, and he wore a bracelet of red and white beads around one dark wrist. She looked at his face and inhaled sharply. Both of his eyes were covered with a thick white film, and though he stared at a point just beyond her shoulder, it felt as if he were peering deep into her being.

"Come," Simona said again.

Abigail shook her head. She had to get back to the town house. Madame would be waiting for her.

"No," said the old woman, as if reading her mind. "There is nothing there for you now. That part of your life is forever gone. You come with us now."

She wrapped a warm hand around Abigail's wrist and began to lead her across the street. Abigail allowed herself to be pulled away from the market, toward the back of the town, where the streets petered out into thick forests and dark bayou.

"Where?" she asked finally. She felt as if she were dream-walking. "Where are we going?"

Simona stopped and turned to face her, touching her face. Abigail felt a shiver of warmth. "We are taking you to the place you have been traveling toward forever. So that you can learn."

"Learn?"

"What you are. What you can do." Simona grinned toothlessly at the bewildered expression on her face. "Ah, *chére.* You have no idea."

Abigail had a sense that she had seen all this, heard it all before. The road where they walked seemed to split apart, then melt back into itself, but not quite, the edges blurred, askew.

"When all is done you will have nothing else to fear from this world, but the world will have much to fear from you."

Behind them, Abigail heard Josiah laugh.

Gaelle

"Girl, what in the world is the matter with you?"

Gaelle looked down. The carafe she'd been filling for coffee had overflowed, and water was pooling on the floor around her feet like a small lake.

"*Méd,*" she swore, grabbing a handful of paper towels.

"What is going on with you, Guy? I thought we agreed you'd stay home until your 'dizziness' passed." Toya's tone was light, but the worry in her voice was clear.

"That is not it." Gaelle stopped sopping up the water and rooted through her purse until she found the letter. She thrust it at her friend.

The letter Beck Gardner had left was little more than charred scraps of paper—she tried to put that out of her mind—so she'd spent the morning and most of the afternoon ransacking her apartment for any evidence of the other letters the new owner said he'd sent. Finally, just before dark, she'd found them, mixed in a pile of papers meant for recycling. She sat on the kitchen floor, her back against the stove, reading them over and over until long after midnight, when she'd fallen into a fitful sleep. Hours later, she woke, curled on the floor, feeling achy and punch-drunk. She managed to dress and get to work on time only out of long habit.

"Shit," said Toya behind her.

"Yes, shit."

"Man." Toya sighed. "Why's it always got to be so hard for folks like us? We scratch and save and work and go without, and the world just still comes along and kicks us right in the teeth."

She stared down at the paper in her hands, her lips pressed in a hard line.

Gaelle stood, blinking back tears.

"Sweetie, you're okay." Toya tossed her head and forced a bright smile. "It's gonna be alright. You know you got a place at my house anytime. And Rose, too. I'll just throw those boys out in the garage. House'll smell better anyway."

Gaelle threw her arms around her and squeezed hard.

"Oh, lord! Get off now," cried Toya, pushing her away with a laugh. "You're making me sweat with your hot self."

"It is going to be okay, sweetie," she said again. "I promise. We ain't got much, but we survive. It's what we do, right?"

She gave Gaelle's hand a quick squeeze. The two aides put on their badges.

"Oh, and don't forget those Joint Commission certification folks start comin' in today. Boss lady is runnin' around here losin' her damn mind."

Gaelle groaned. The entire facility had been on edge for weeks. How could she have forgotten that the state inspectors would be on site for the next few days?

Toya grinned. "Yeah, this ain't turnin' out to be your week, is it?"

In the hall, Gaelle grabbed her arm. "*Mèsi,* Toya. You are a good friend."

"Yeah, yeah, whatever. Just be on the lookout for Orr. She is seriously on the war path."

A half-dozen inspectors were swarming the facility, the receptionist had called off sick, and the phones had been ringing nonstop. The director of nursing flitted in and out of rooms and around every corner of Stillwater like a rabid squirrel, barking orders, peeking into storage closets, snatching stray pieces of paper from every desktop. At one point, Gaelle passed Toya in the hall. The DON was rooting through Toya's med cart muttering under her breath. Her friend pantomimed shooting herself in the head as Gaelle hurried away, lips pressed together, to keep from laughing.

She actually liked the DON, despite her constantly harried demeanor. Melody Orr truly tried to do the best by all of the residents. It had actually been her who'd fought to get the mysterious old woman with no name the benefits she needed so that she was allowed to stay in their nursing home.

Near the beginning of the shift, the director of nursing had grabbed her by the arm. "Gaelle, please! Could you man the front desk and answer the phones? We're just so short-staffed. I'm sure I can get someone to cover your residents."

Though she would never admit it, even to herself, Gaelle was relieved. She'd felt a stirring of unease all morning at the thought of entering the old woman's room. All day she fielded calls from relatives asking about their families, hospital social workers inquiring about bed availability, insurance companies seeking additional information. Stillwater Care Facility was in muted chaos, and she was grateful for the distraction.

As the hours wore on, the foggy disbelief that had enveloped her since the day before gradually gave way to a simmering anger. It sat like a hot film on her skin. She would not lose her home again. She would fight. Somehow, she would fight. She had survived the earthquake, the loss of her family. This was nothing.

Survive.

Like Toya said, it's what they did.

It wasn't until a woman named Angie came to replace her that she realized the day had passed. Toya and nearly all of the early shift had already left for the day, and Stillwater was finally settling down. After signing the messages over to Angie, she headed to the lounge for her coat. She would not tell Rose about the letter, she decided, not yet. Not until she figured out what she was going to do.

The hallways were quiet as she headed for the door. The inspectors were gone for the day and the residents were either sleeping or on the other side of the building in the activity room, waiting for dinner.

As she passed the old woman's room, she slowed. Despite her unease, it felt odd not to have spent time with her. She was about to turn away when she heard an unfamiliar voice coming from inside.

Gaelle frowned. The old woman had never had a single visitor, and except for the staff, no one should have been in there. Warily, she stepped to the door. In the dim light from the hall, she could see a male figure sitting on the edge of the bed. He was bent over the old woman, speaking to her in a low voice.

"Winter, can you hear me? Bad times comin' and we got to be ready."

"Excuse me." Gaelle flicked on the light. "May I help you?"

The man turned slowly to look at her, seemingly unfazed by her appearance at the door. Gently, he laid the old woman's hand on the bed and stood.

"Good evening."

"May I help you?" she asked again.

The man smiled. He was late-middle-aged, slightly stooped but still powerfully built. His dark hair was streaked with gray and pulled back from his face with a leather tie. Gaelle took in his expensive jacket, the pipe jutting from one pocket. Despite the dim lighting, he wore darkly tinted glasses.

"My name is Josiah." He held out a large, work-worn hand, and she took an instinctive step back. There was something unsettling about him. He seemed to radiate a chill that had nothing to do with the December weather.

"I'm looking for the director of nursing," he said, dropping his hand.

"She is not in here."

"No," he said with a chuckle. His voice was thick with the South. "She is certainly not."

"Who are you?"

"I'm with Joint Commission." He flashed a card.

Gaelle's eyes narrowed. Everything about him felt like a lie. She studied him a long moment, then stepped out into the hall. He followed, brushing past her, and once again she felt that unpleasant chill. She glanced into the room, but the old woman seemed no different than usual. The television blared an announcement about a bombing in the Middle East.

"At the very end of this hall, then take a left," she said finally.

He gave a small bow and turned to walk away.

"Excuse me."

He turned back toward her.

"A minute ago. Did you call her Winter?"

"I did."

"Why?"

He grinned. "Because that is her name."

"What? How can you know that?"

But he walked away as if he hadn't heard.

Part Three

1852

Remembrance

Winter

Winter woke with a start, heart tripping wildly in her chest. The night had been filled with vaguely remembered nightmares: snarling dogs, screaming children, fire. It clung to her still, mixing with the sweat on her skin, chilling her. She kicked free of her blankets and sat up, feeling jittery and out of sorts.

Crawling from her bedding, she splashed cold water from the basin on her face, in her armpits, pausing for a moment to stare at the reflection that rippled on the water's surface. Broad face, the color of a pine cone, hair tangled wildly about her head. She tugged at it, trying to separate the matted strands, but it was useless. With a sigh, she pushed one finger into the bowl of soda powder and quickly scrubbed her teeth, then pulled the cloak from the peg near the door. Wrapping it around her shoulders, she stepped into the cold fall morning.

It was barely an hour past dawn and Remembrance was already buzzing with activity. From the highlands far up in the hills that ringed the settlement, the mournful lowing of cows drifted down to her through the trees, punctuated by the high-pitched ringing of Thomas's hammer as he worked the metal in his smithy.

Remembrance.

To Winter, it was simply the place she'd grown up, the only home she'd ever known. But to everyone else who lived here, down to the last man, woman, and child, it was a place of sanctuary. A place where people like her—colored people—could live in peace and safety.

Remembrance.

A place within a place.

Spoken of with a pride mixed with disbelief. A place that should not exist, yet did. A place created by some sort of poorly understood magic. Created by Mother Abigail. Priestess. Practitioner of vodun.

Instinctively, Winter turned to look up the wide, worn trail that led to the highlands. Mother Abigail's cabin lay nearly at the summit of one of the highest hills, just below the wide, flat clearing where the men worked a few acres of crops and their small herd of sheep and cattle grazed. The priestess's cabin was no different than all the others in Remembrance, a simple structure of rough wood planks and river stone.

Something's coming—something big. Something terrible.

The thought came out of nowhere, like a slap in the face, and Winter inhaled sharply as a shiver snaked up her spine. The nightmares seemed to have followed her into the daylight. Clutching her cloak, she sniffed at the air. There was an uncomfortable sensation in the center of her gut, as if the settlement was just the smallest bit off-balance.

With a soft grunt, Winter stepped onto the path, following it as it sloped gently downhill, away from Mother Abigail's cabin. The air was clean, crisp, the trees glowing scarlet and gold in the muted sunlight. The damp earth felt wonderfully cold beneath her bare feet. She waded into a mound of leaves, inhaling the scent of forest and earth just as Will, the blacksmith's younger son, passed her, heading toward the highlands. The boy grinned, shaking his head at the sight of her standing shin-deep in wet leaves. By the time she reached the trailhead and entered the clearing for the Central Fire, the feeling of foreboding was fading.

A handful of women still hovered near the fire circle. They nodded but didn't speak as they quickly rearranged the firewood near the canning shed before disappearing, laughing, down a narrow path through the woods. It was washday, and most of the women of Remembrance would spend it down at the creek washing the bed linens and clothes.

It was peculiar to be alone at the Central Fire, the massive fire circle that marked the very core of Remembrance. It was where the settlers gathered for meals and fellowship, for announcements and celebrations, but the effort it took to keep Remembrance running smoothly, the urgency of chores to be done, especially now, in preparation against the coming winter, had scattered the settlers to their tasks. Everyone had their job to do in Remembrance. Everyone except her.

Despite the fact that she had been in Remembrance longer than anyone aside from Mother Abigail, despite the fact that Remembrance was her only home, somehow she drifted just outside the beating heart of the settlement, circling round and round but never quite absorbed into its soul.

The ex-slaves, the men and women who had managed to find their way to the safety of Remembrance, were polite, but distant. Because she belonged to Mother Abigail? Because she was not one of them?

She had not been born here, in this place that should not even exist. She had been born out there, in the world, like them. Mother Abigail told her the story every day on the anniversary of her finding.

Her mother, her real mother—a woman whose name she would never know—had placed her in a basket and covered her with a woolen shawl, and then she had run. Run from one of those bad places Winter only knew as names in other people's stories. Her nameless mother had looked not much older than Winter was now. Had she run from Kentucky? From Alabama? Perhaps one of those island plantations that grew rice off the coast of South Carolina. All Mother Abigail could tell her was that her mother had run, made it all the way to Remembrance, made it almost to freedom.

Except . . .

Except a freak late-spring storm had roared in off the lake. Birds froze solid to tree limbs. The sky filled with snow thunder.

Mother Abigail had found them there, on the other side of the Edge, that thin boundary separating Remembrance from the outside world. Her mother was wrapped around the basket, giving her baby the last, the only thing, she had to offer—her body's dying warmth.

"Named you Winter," said Mother Abigail every time she told the story. "And you been mine ever since."

Winter glanced up at the lightening sky. She was one of them. Even if she couldn't remember the horror, the fear. The Outside had taken something from her, too.

Winter's stomach rumbled and she moved inside the ring of logs surrounding the massive Central Fire. There, at the fire's edge, she found a skillet of fried apples and potatoes, still warm. She fixed herself a plate and plopped down on the log nearest the fire.

Something's coming.

She jerked and shoved the thought away, leaning closer to the fire. The sharp October wind cooled her back, while the fire toasted her face. At a sharp noise, her head shot up, but it was only Belle, gathering ash into a pail on the far side of the fire circle. The woman glanced at Winter, her face expressionless, before picking up the battered pail and heading back down the path that led to the wash hut at the creek's edge, leaving her alone once again.

Winter gulped down the rest of her breakfast and stood. The heat from the fire had become almost uncomfortable. She took a step back and stared into the flames. Unease settled around her again. After washing her plate, she turned and wandered aimlessly toward one of the paths leading away from the circle. Briefly, she considered joining the other women at the creek but quickly dismissed that idea. Whenever she was around, they were tense, laughing awkwardly, shooting her looks from the sides of their eyes.

And their scrutiny made her clumsy, inattentive. The clothes she was washing drifted downstream. The biscuits she was baking would refuse to rise. Once, while stirring lye for soap, she'd even managed to catch the hem of her shift on fire. No. She didn't want to be around them any more than they wanted her around.

She found herself at the clearing, a flat open space filled with knee-high grass, turning from green to yellow in the deepening fall. Sinking down, she lay on her back and stared up at the sky. Clouds moved overhead and the sun disappeared behind them for a moment, taking the illusion of heat with them. Winter shivered. This was considered the boundary to Remembrance, and almost no one came out this far. But she knew this was an illusion, knew that you could walk for days and days and never leave Remembrance, never see a soul who had not been allowed in, never be Outside. Only when Mother Abigail willed it, only when she dropped the Edge, would they become one with the rest of the world.

Winter had asked Mother Abigail to explain it to her once, how it was possible, and the old priestess had laid a faded handkerchief on her lap.

"See," she said, smoothing it flat, "this is the world for everybody else."

Then carefully, she had folded it, pleating it so that it had folded on itself like an accordion.

"But this how the world really is." She ran a wrinkled finger inside one of the pleats. "I just bent space a tiny bit and made us this place here. Inside a' one a' these folds."

"World there. And another world. And another yet." She stroked the parallel folds. "Us? We here. And folks only see what they expectin' to see. So they don't really see."

"But how, Mother Abigail?" she'd asked. "How do you fold up space like that?"

The old woman frowned and then she laughed. "How does that ol' man Willie wiggle his ears? Just something I can do."

But there was more to it than that. Even as a little girl Winter had known that. She lay in the grass, watching the clouds slowly move across the sky. The cold seeped through her cloak and then her cotton shift, but still she lay there. A flock of geese cut across the sky, their discordant honking drifting down to her.

Mother Abigail would surely be looking for her, but for now she felt calm and at peace.

The grass rustled in the wind. And something else. She felt it. A slight crackling on her skin: sharp, unpleasant. She sat up. A dozen yards away, the clearing disappeared in a line of thick trees. A tall mulberry, its branches already bare after the first frost, marked the beginning of the forest. She was alone, and yet . . .

Something had changed, she could feel it. The skin on the back of her neck, between her shoulder blades, felt hot, as if she were standing directly in front of the Central Fire once again. The ground beneath her feet seemed to sag, as if some great weight were settling there beside her. There was no one in the clearing with her that she could see, but all her senses sounded an alarm. Something was wrong. She didn't know what, but she knew she needed to leave. She needed to get back to the settlement. She stood just as the mulberry began to shake violently. A man burst from the forest into the clearing, and Winter cried out, stumbling backward. He fell once, then fell again. Rising to one knee, he stared at her, his eyes wild, terrified.

"Help me!" he croaked.

She stood, frozen, horrified, and then Mother Abigail was there. And Josiah, her constant companion, as always, never far behind. They went to the man, the priestess wrapping one strong arm around his waist lest he fall again. Together, Josiah and Mother Abigail half dragged, half carried the man back across the grass to where Winter still stood, too shocked to move.

The man looked to be in his early twenties, five or six years older than she was. He had skin the color of a hickory nut, and curly black hair that hung past his shoulders. His bottom lip was swollen and there was blood caked near his left temple.

Winter understood immediately that he was a runaway. But how was that possible? No one just appeared in Remembrance. Mother Abigail had to lower the Edge, to flatten out the folds that separated the spaces between worlds. She was about to ask, when she felt the clearing shift again, felt the painful crackling down her back. Her hair stood on end, sparking with energy, and she knew without touching it that it would be hot to the touch.

"Hey there, Zeus."

They all spun toward the voice. From the corner of her eye she saw Mother Abigail stagger and nearly drop the runaway, who moaned softly. She gawked as a white man emerged from the trees. Though she had never seen one before, either a white man or a slave tracker, she knew him instantly for what he was. And in spite of her fear, she was curious.

The man wasn't, in fact, white at all, but a sort of grayish pink. His black hair looked greasy and hung limply in his eyes. The tip of his thin nose was red and pockmarked. Except for the gun that he carried loosely in his arms, there was nothing scary about him, and yet, she sensed the runaway's terror. And Mother Abigail's tension.

"How you holdin' up there, Zeus?" asked the white man. His tone was calm, friendly.

"Kinda poorly, Master Clay," said the runaway through his swollen lips.

"Zeus, you got to come on with me now, you hear?" The rifle rested in the crook of the slaver's arm, the barrel pointed toward the ground. "You got the Gilliams all in a lather, boy. And frankly, I think you rather hurt their feelin's runnin' off like that. Come on back with me now. I hear tell they hardly ever beat their niggers. You might even get away with just a good, stern talking to."

He smiled, but his eyes were hard beneath the lank hair.

Mother Abigail shifted the weight of the slave against Josiah and took a step toward the slaver.

"Get yourself away from here, you white Satan," she snapped. "You'll not be takin' anyone from here. Not for no beatin', not for no talkin' to. This man has his freedom on him now. He belongs only to his own self. You can take *that* back to the Gilliams."

The white man stiffened and his mouth dropped open as he glanced at the other three Negroes in the clearing. He shifted his gun, and Winter could see the muscles working in his jaw. He turned his attention back to Mother Abigail, his pale eyes narrowed, flashing rage.

"Look, Auntie . . . ," he began.

"I ain't your auntie," snarled the old woman. "My name is Mother Abigail. You'll need to be rememberin' that."

Clay shook his head and brought the barrel of the gun up slightly. "Ma'am—" He stopped short.

The air around them had begun to warm, and from the corner of her eye Winter could see the far end of the clearing warp slightly, lose its shape. She looked from Mother Abigail to the white man and back again. The slaver could feel the shifting around them, too. She could see it in his eyes. He didn't know what it was yet, but if he didn't leave soon, he would. And it would be bad for him.

"Ma'am," Clay began again, "ain't got no truck with y'all. I just come for Zeus. He ain't got no right to steal hisself, and I been paid to bring him back."

He glanced at Winter and she saw him hesitate. She saw something else as well, the dawning of fear, the look of a man beginning to realize that he doesn't know quite what he's walked into.

It was hot in the clearing now and Winter was sweating under her wool cloak. A searing wind had begun to blow across the yellowed grass, bending the blades. The runaway had recovered himself a bit and looked around in confusion. The slaver cleared his throat, a soft sound that Winter seemed to hear more in her brain than in her ears.

"Zeus, you come along peaceful," he said, his voice just the tiniest bit higher than before. "You know the law says I can drag your friends along, too, if they cause a ruckus, but they really ain't none a' my business."

Zeus took a hesitant step forward, but Josiah seized hold of his tattered shirt, holding him back. The slaver grunted his displeasure, and the thin veneer of civility evaporated.

"Enough of this now," he snapped, and moved to reach for Zeus, but Mother Abigail stepped in front of him, blocking his way.

"Heed me," said the priestess. "You can leave this place a whole man or broken, but you will leave."

Winter bit her lip. *Go. Just go,* she silently pleaded. *Go now, before it's too late.* This slaver man was no real threat to them. He had to feel that. Maybe Mother Abigail would just let him go.

But she wouldn't. Not now. Rage had hold of her. Winter felt it, they could all feel it, pulsing off the priestess in waves as Mother Abigail's fury, her hatred of this slave catcher, twisted and warped, transforming from emotion into pure energy. If the slaver didn't run, run now, then the Gilliams and Zeus would be the last thing on his mind.

The heat in the clearing had become nearly unbearable. Sweat rolled between Winter's shoulder blades, pasting her cloak against her back. The air stung her throat, her nose. The slaver's eyes swung between Mother Abigail and Josiah, then back again, sweat beading on his lip. He took a step back and Winter saw him raise his gun.

Beside her, Zeus was trembling, and Winter grabbed his hand before he could bolt. She could sense his heart racing and held on tight.

When Mother Abigail's powers were unleashed like this, it was best to stand very still. It was better to be nowhere near her, but there was no hope for that now. All they could do was hold still and hold on. Overhead came a crash, like thunder. The sky had turned flat and gray as a dinner plate. Hot, superheated air whipped the gentle wind into a swirling gale. It lashed the high grass, and a cloud of Ohio dirt rose up and engulfed the slaver in a tornado of rich black soil, scouring his skin. He cried out, dropping his gun as he fell back. For a moment he seemed to disappear and the world spun around them. Winter gritted her teeth, fought for balance.

The slaver was there, farther into the trees, then gone. For a split second she saw him again, standing in a bright clearing, the winds calm, the sun shining. His mouth was open in a silent scream and he seemed not to see them from where he stood, trapped in the folds of time and space. Lost.

Mother Abigail raised her hands.

"No, Abigail!" cried Josiah. He lunged for the priestess and there was another clap of thunder. The ground pitched, throwing them all to the ground.

And then . . . silence.

Mother Abigail whirled toward Josiah, eyes blazing.

"You let him make you lose the thread like that, Abigail?" he asked, calmly returning her gaze. "You one of one. He just one of many."

The old woman was breathing hard. Winter got slowly to her knees. It was cooling off again. The wind a normal wind now. She tasted grit in her mouth. She glanced at the slaver. He sat, legs akimbo, in the dirt. His face was bloodied and scraped, his dark hair gray now, coated with dirt. He stared at them, unseeing.

"One less," said Mother Abigail, her voice hard, staring with disgust at the white man at her feet. "Don't need to kill him. Just need to lose him. Remembrance not the only world I know how to make."

She laughed grimly, and the sound made the hairs stand up on the back of Winter's neck. Josiah pulled his pipe from his shirt pocket.

"You lose him, another one just take his place," he said, tapping tobacco into his palm.

Mother Abigail said nothing for a long moment, then she grunted and bent over the prostrate slaver. Winter tensed.

But the old priestess peered into Clay's blank face. "*Ou se kaka, blanc,*" she whispered. "Remember this place and never come here again. Remember my name."

The slaver flinched and tried to scrabble away. Mother Abigail straightened.

"Get the boy," said Mother Abigail, pointing at Zeus, who still lay trembling on the ground.

She raised her arms, seemed to falter for a moment, then suddenly the air was fresh and cool. The slaver was gone, as if he had never existed. Once again, Winter felt the familiar hum against her skin. The Edge had been restored and Remembrance was once again safe, separate.

Without a word, Mother Abigail turned to follow the trail that would lead them to the center of the settlement, as Josiah helped Zeus to his feet. Winter, her heart still beating wildly, turned to follow. At the trailhead, she turned to look back at the clearing. From somewhere deep in her head, she thought she heard the slaver scream.

17

Mother Abigail

The sharp splinter of wood bit into her palm.

Pain.

Pain was good.

Pain was real. Because that was the problem, wasn't it? Telling real from memory, slipping from memory to the imagined. Staying tethered to the now. It was happening more and more often, this slipping. So many mornings waking and reaching for her babies, her boys. Calling out for Hercule in the night. But if they had survived the uprising at all, her boys were no longer babies. They were grown, old men: fathers, grandfathers. And Hercule . . .

She moaned and gripped the small lump of wood tighter, relishing the sting of it. Once, it had been perfectly round, smooth, a remnant taken in last-minute desperation from her husband's woodshop. But after more than sixty years it had splintered and worn away to nearly nothing. But it was real, a reminder of a time when she had been someone else.

It was cold in the cabin, and Mother Abigail lay shivering, drifting in and out of time, in that gray place between awake and sleep. A day passed, then another, the old priestess vaguely aware of the settlement's rhythm outside her door. She had a broken memory of Louisa, Remembrance's healer, forcing hot corn mush between her lips, the steam washing over her forehead, but mostly she'd been left alone, shaking on her low cot, the wooden disk clenched in her hand like a talisman.

Slavers.

A white slaver here in Remembrance.

Impossible.

She controlled the Edge, that unseen boundary separating Remembrance from the Outside. *She* was the one that saw the seams that existed in the spaces between all things, the only one who could slip between them, fold them up, move them, so they became bigger or smaller . . . or disappeared completely. She was the one who'd created this sanctuary, this impenetrable sanctuary, for her people.

But he'd been there.

Real.

As real as the roof of her cabin, as this sliver of wood she held in her hand. Somehow, the Edge had lost its shape, collapsed on itself, at least for a moment. A moment long enough for the slave Zeus and that abomination hunting him to enter.

Abigail had been at the smokehouse, her face raised to catch a bit of morning sun, when she'd felt it: a quickening behind her heart, a sense of the world tearing into halves. She was standing in Remembrance, the wood of the smokehouse rough against her back, the smell of hickory smoke thick on the fall air. And then she was standing in an empty field, the wind whispering through the grass, geese flying in formation overhead.

Then . . . pain.

Her head pounded and there was a ringing, like a hammer against metal. She'd staggered, bile rising in her throat. She knew this feeling, had lived inside it, nearly died from it, wanted to die from it, in those black days and months after Simona and Josiah pulled her from the streets of New Orleans.

But that had been more than a half century before. Before she'd learned what it was. What she was. Now she knew to skate along the fissures rather than fight through them, knew the way of drawing the energy that was in all things—the rocks, the water, a beating heart—into herself and transform it how and when she wanted. And what she created responded to her will and her will only. Until three days ago. When the Edge had fallen of its own accord like a broken window. And now fear ran through her veins, cramping her gut.

"*Tout bagay anfòm.*" The old priestess ground her teeth. "Everything is fine." She rolled to her side, moaning as she curled into herself. She was so very tired. The slaver's pale, pockmarked face flashed against her closed eyes. His smell was still sharp in her nose, his sour sweat mixed with fear. She'd wanted to shred him, wanted to tear him apart. Would have scattered bits of him through all the worlds she could find if Josiah hadn't been there, if he hadn't called her back to herself. She knew he hadn't stopped her because he feared for the slaver's safety. He'd have gladly destroyed the *blanc* himself. No, Josiah had stopped her because she'd lost control. She ground her teeth.

"Abigail."

She started. She'd not heard him come in. But that had been his way from the first. Josiah, lurking in the shadows, but always there. In the beginning, she'd assumed it was Simona who led the way through the darkness. Only many years later did she come to understand the truth of it.

"Abigail."

She rolled to her back but would not look at him, silently willing him to leave. His stare was a hot coal against her face, and she could hear the unasked questions. He wanted to know about the slaver. He wanted to know how the Edge could have been penetrated. But mostly he wanted to know about the change in her. But there were no answers she was ready to give.

The silence grew between them, a weight pressing her deep into her straw mattress.

"*Merde,*" she swore. She sat up. Josiah was there in the corner, staring silently at her, as she knew he would be.

"What?" she snapped.

He calmly lit his pipe. "What is it?" he asked, finally. He raised the pipe, the beads of his bracelet clicking in the silence.

She swore again, then struggled to stand. When he reached to help, she swatted his hand away. "*Mwen byen.* I'm fine!"

Leaning heavily on her walking stick, she limped to the door, knees and back aching. She was so tired.

After days in bed, the air felt sharp against her skin. She smelled snow on the wind. She had a sudden flash of bright blue satin unfurling into the dirt, bridal wreath blooms crowding the empty space in front of her stoop, and she staggered in the threshold, confused. She felt Josiah's hand press against her back. She grunted a protest but did not push him away.

The sun was still hours from rising, and for that she was grateful. She was too unsettled yet to face her people. She and Josiah drifted through the moonlit settlement like two restless souls, and the thought made her laugh to herself, that they should move along the same plane as the *loa,* the spirits. They walked in silence past the smoldering Central Fire and the smokehouse, past the path leading up to the smithy, through the cemetery, until they found themselves moving downhill, back toward the clearing.

The clearing.

The most powerful place in Remembrance.

All those years before, she'd walked away from Simona's shack in the depths of the bayou. She didn't know where she was going, only that she needed to go. She walked for months, crossing half-frozen streams, sleeping in open fields, until she arrived here, at this clearing, the grass as tall as her shoulders, ribbons of energy crisscrossing in the Ohio air. She'd known immediately that she was home, and she'd known what that home would look like.

"Tell me," said Josiah.

The aroma of cherry tobacco hovered around them as she stared across the clearing at the tree line, which was just a darker shadow against all the other shadows, remembering those first warm nights in this unfamiliar place.

"Bad times coming, old man," she said finally, not answering the question she knew he was really asking.

Josiah made a noise that landed somewhere between irritation and amusement. She shot him a look. His still-thick hair, pulled back from his face with a leather tie, had only a few strands of gray, and his coal-black face was as unlined as the first day she'd seen him over sixty years before. In all that time, she'd glimpsed a hint of his true age only once. When he'd come to pull her from the bayou. She shook her head, not wanting to remember that time of despair.

"Bad times," he echoed. "It always be bad times for black folks."

"Not funny."

"No," he agreed. "But true all the same."

He pulled on his pipe, and she knew he was still waiting for her to tell him about the slaver. She pressed her lips together and gazed into the darkness.

Josiah sighed. "What your white lady say?"

She sucked her teeth. He was talking about Quaker Mary. Once a month, more if circumstances warranted, Mother Abigail met the white woman on the Outside of the Edge. They met to trade Louisa's liniments and honey and the flawless horseshoes and whimsical fancies from Thomas's smithy the *blancs* seemed unable to get enough of in nearby Ashtabula. The priestess traded for the things that couldn't be grown or made in Remembrance: salt and sugar, buttons and iron ore. But most importantly, she traded for news of what was happening Outside.

"Quaker," said Mother Abigail.

Josiah grunted. "Quaker a white lady, ain't she?"

"Quaker's different kinda white. Some kinda different god."

A faint echo sounded in her head, and a face swam up from deep in her memory. Pale blue eyes, a scar puckering the left side of his face. *Le juif.* The Jew. André Dreyfus, as he'd looked the day he'd stepped from the ship in New Orleans. The day she lost everything she'd had before and started on the road to becoming someone, something else. Her mouth went dry and she swallowed hard. Why was that time haunting her today?

"She Quaker," she said again.

She had never heard of Quakers before arriving in this valley. A *blanc* was a *blanc*. Creatures not to be trusted, creatures who might smile with white teeth, then bite your neck with them. But these quiet, strange-dressing *blancs* had proven different. Over time, she developed a wary trust of them, a working relationship, especially with the one called Mary, enough so that if a runaway decided to move on from Remembrance, to continue farther north, the priestess entrusted their safe passage to her.

"Last time we meet, she show me a paper. Say it say the *blancs* allowed to take runaways back to they masters now. Even if they make it this far."

She felt Josiah tense.

"She say them trackers go where they please. Even into that big town. Ashtabula. Be snatchin' free mens off the street less they prove they free. She say that paper say it okay to do now."

Beside her, Josiah had gone rigid as stone, his pipe clenched in his fist.

"So still harder times comin' then," he said. His voice was low and hard. "They not gon' stop. Ever."

The old priestess shrugged and gazed at the sky. Daylight was coming.

"But that ain't the whole of it, though?" he asked.

"I'm gettin' old, Josiah. Old and . . ." She hesitated.

She was on the verge of telling him how some days she woke, confused, and reached for Hercule, wondering why there was no sound of workers heading for the coffee fields. How sometimes she saw the spires of St. Louis Church looming from the Ohio mist and smelled the coal-fouled Mississippi River. She was right at the brink of telling him that in the past weeks, the past months, those things seemed more real to her than Remembrance, that the bright rivers of energy that she rode, that she needed to keep them all safe, seemed faded and dull.

They had been together so long. He'd been at her side as she lay naked in Simona's cabin without food or water for days, fires burning in the corner under the low roof until her sweat turned the ground she lay on to mud. Until the ghosts of her husband, her sons, her sister whirled around her in flashes of oranges and yellow, speaking a language she didn't understand.

She was right on the edge.

But in the end, she turned to him, the person she'd known longer than anyone else in life, and said, "It will be day soon and the people are scared."

He watched her, eyes narrowed as she brushed past.

"Come," she said.

18

Winter

She moved through the settlement, head down, eyes fixed on the ground under her feet. The whispers, the stares washed against her back like a soft wind. It had been three days since Zeus appeared in Remembrance, the slaver right behind. Three days since anyone, aside from Josiah and Louisa, had seen Mother Abigail.

A group of women were working near the root cellar, and as she passed, they fell silent. She hunched her shoulders and walked faster, feeling their eyes burning into the back of her head.

Remembrance was on low simmer, but with each day that passed with no sign of the priestess, it moved closer and closer to boiling over. Rumors crackled through the settlement like lightning, each one more horrifying, more unbelievable than the last. The wells were poisoned, though no one seemed ill. Slavers were sneaking into the settlement in the dead of night and stealing children, though none were missing. Mother Abigail had abandoned them, disappearing into the night, heading across the lake to the north and into Canada.

Near the path that led to her cabin, she passed an elderly man. She met his eye and smiled, but the look he returned was so filled with hostility that she faltered, stumbling on the uneven ground. She glanced around, but there were no friendly faces to be seen. She hurried up the path, not looking up or slowing until she reached her cabin and was safely inside. Closing her eyes, she let out a shaky breath.

That first night she'd climbed the trail toward Mother Abigail's cabin to find Josiah standing guard in front of the door, a silent black mass, and felt the familiar tingle of revulsion. She'd never liked Mother Abigail's companion, never understood what he was to her, why he was always just there, hovering at Mother Abigail's shoulder. Was he a relative? A friend? Lately, Winter's dislike of the man had begun to morph into something more. Something closer to hate. She hated the odd, opaque eyes that seemed to follow her everywhere. Hated the way he slipped through Remembrance, silent, stealthy, like smoke. And she hated the way that just being near him set her teeth on edge. A current surrounded him that caused her hair to stand on end, repelling her.

He had never said a harsh word to her that she could remember, yet she sensed he detested her in equal measure. That morning, when he smiled at her there at the threshold, the spit soured in her mouth.

"Can I see Mother Abigail?"

"She restin'."

She waited for him to say more, to tell her to come back later, that Mother Abigail was fine, but he'd said none of those things. He stood, silent, unmoving, that smile fixed on his face. For a moment, she stood her ground. He would not run her off without seeing Mother Abigail. She wasn't afraid of him.

Except, she was.

Inexplicably and definitively afraid. Without another word, she turned and ran all the way back to her cabin. And now, two more full days and nights had passed with no sign of the priestess.

Pulling her cloak tight, Winter leaned against the door and tugged hard at her hair. The walls seemed to close in around her, pressing the air from the space.

She whirled and flung open the door, startling a boy who was walking by leading a goat on a tether. He blinked, then hurried past. She glared at his retreating back, then charged up the trail toward Mother Abigail's. At the top of the trail her resolve wavered and she veered off into the brush, heading for the small penned area where the priestess kept her coop.

A flock of chickens rushed forward as she eased into the pen, but immediately lost interest when it became clear that she had nothing to feed them. She slumped, shivering onto a metal pail near the gate.

What would happen if Mother Abigail did disappear? The thought had never occurred to her in any real way. Mother Abigail was like the earth or the sky: ancient and somehow never-ending.

Remembrance existed inside a wrinkle in space created and maintained by Mother Abigail. If the priestess were to leave or, unimaginably, die, would that space simply cease to exist? Would the Edge smooth out like a freshly ironed shirt, exposing them, merging them with the Outside? And what about her? As much as she'd never really felt a part of Remembrance, it was the only place she knew. Outside was a universe that lived only in her imagination, fed by the horrific stories of those who'd escaped and the scars they bore on their minds and their bodies. And yet, in spite of that, there was the tiniest longing, the faintest flicker of curiosity about "out there." She shot a glance at the back of the cabin on the other side of the pen.

A chicken pecked its way close. Small and gray with streaks of amber, an Easter Egger, it was Mother Abigail's favorite for the pale blue and green eggs it laid. She stared hard at it. Bands of pale gray lay atop bands of darker gray, strands of golden red running through. She focused on the way the soft feathers curved along the chicken's round body before splitting like a fan at the tips. She concentrated until she could see the place where the feathers entered the gray pink chicken flesh.

Winter couldn't do what Mother Abigail could do—pull space apart, fold it up on itself. But she could do this.

She could see the pieces that made up a thing. And if she focused hard enough, then that thing—a table, a tree, this chicken—became just particles spinning in space in the shape of a table, a tree, a chicken. And if she focused really, really hard, she could change the way the particles spun, speeding some up, slowing others down, drawing them to her or pushing them away, as if she were some giant magnet. She couldn't explain how she did this any more than she could explain why her heart beat, but she could. The way Mother Abigail could bend space or Willie could wiggle his ears.

Sometimes, when the adults were away working, she entertained the smaller children by making miniature tornadoes of dirt. Or she would make the Central Fire leap and dance, pushing it to form shapes in the air: a fish, a flower, sometimes a face. But faces were hard and the effort left her feeling dizzy and hot. Whenever the adults caught her at this, they yanked their children away, giving her the evil eye. They never said anything. Of course not. She was Mother Abigail's pet, after all.

Winter ground her teeth, an ember of resentment glowing in the pit of her stomach. It was true that when she was little, this thing she could do had sometimes gotten away from her. Water flashed to steam, scalding a boy. A load of horseshoes being readied for Outside slightly melted and ruined. But nothing like that had happened in a very long time. But still, many in Remembrance looked at her as if she were a stray cat that had wandered in to warm itself at their fire. It wasn't fair. She belonged in Remembrance more than any of them.

The only one that truly seemed to enjoy her company was David Henry. He had come to Remembrance three summers before, when she was fifteen. He was old. He didn't know his exact years, but she guessed him at thirty or so. David Henry didn't talk much, he just smiled and appeared in the exact place the settlers seemed to need him the most, setting traps and fishing lines, digging out the root cellar, repairing the shelters.

He was also the best tracker in Remembrance. Since the spring thaw, he'd been teaching her. She liked being out in the woods with him, liked listening to the tales he spun about the woodpeckers and the red foxes. He said she was a natural. She didn't tell him it was because she sometimes could see the trail a deer or a rabbit left behind, little particles drifting in the brush, like sparks. Not always, but sometimes. She thought about going to find him, to see if he was going out today, but the thought of walking back through the settlement again clenched her stomach into a fist.

The Easter Egger pecked closer to her feet, searching the dirt for bugs. She stared at it, the soft gray feathers, the tiny round body. She could see all that made up the little chicken, minute particles spinning round and round each other, the bits that made up the feathers; the eyes, spinning faster than the body. The chicken wasn't really a solid thing. There were spaces there, like tightly packed, whirling grains of sand. Spinning, spinning. The shape of a chicken. And deeper, beneath the warm flesh, spinning faster still, blood. Moving fast and hot. But even here, there were spaces. The blood not one thing, but a million things. Traveling together. Faster and faster . . . the shape of blood . . .

"Winter?"

She cried out as the world jerked, dropped from under her. Spots flashed before her eyes and she fell, vomiting in the cold dirt. She felt hot and sick, confused. It took her a long moment to remember where she was. Taking deep breaths, she felt the cool beneath her hands, smelled vomit, smelled . . . blood?

Mother Abigail's.

She was in Mother Abigail's chicken pen. She pushed herself to sitting, head pounding, her skin on fire despite the morning chill. She clawed clumsily at her cloak, trying to rip it off.

"Winter?"

She raised her head. Mother Abigail stood over her, Josiah a few feet beyond. The priestess reached down and pulled her to her feet, gripping her hand so that the cloak stayed on.

"What happen here?" she asked. "What you do?"

Winter frowned, then looked to where Mother Abigail pointed. Blood was spattered across the pen, her feet, the hem of her shift. Feathers covered the ground like gray and red snow.

"I . . ." She staggered as the world seemed to shift beneath her feet, then vomited again. The two old companions watched in silence.

"I don't know. I don't . . ." She shook her head, felt a wave of dizziness. She had been focused on the Easter Egger. Had been there, inside it.

"I don't know," she said again. Her skin burned. She swallowed again and again, fighting against the nausea.

Mother Abigail and Josiah exchanged a pointed look, and a flicker of fear pierced her cloud of confusion. She couldn't stop looking at the ground around her. There was so much blood, so much . . .

She'd been concentrating on the Easter Egger, on its feathers and the spaces inside it. Concentrating on the blood . . .

"Winter!" Mother Abigail's voice was sharp.

Winter jerked and looked up at the priestess.

"Leave it, *petite*. Leave it, now!

"A fortnight," she went on. "The freedom train brings passengers to our door."

Winter tugged at her hair and tried to concentrate on what the priestess was saying. A rescue? There'd been no rescue since Zeus. And that had not gone well. And how was it possible that Mother Abigail could even know such a thing without ever having left her cabin?

"How many?" she asked finally. The smell of blood was nearly over-whelming.

The old priestess gazed into the woods beyond the chicken pen. "Freedom quilt hung in the tree on the other side of the Edge. Five pins in the center of the star."

Five. Five runaways escaping on the Underground Railroad.

She knew that Outside, people hung quilts to signal that runners were being passed from station to station, places where people would help them escape slavery.

Winter followed Mother Abigail's gaze. There was no quilt, just a stand of birch trees and a cloudless blue sky. She looked back at the priestess.

"They will come," repeated Mother Abigail, still gazing off into the distance. "And when they do, you will be there to help guide them in."

Winter inhaled sharply. She had never been to a crossing. No one had, except Mother Abigail and Josiah. Fear wrestled with excitement inside her, and she opened her mouth to ask Mother Abigail the million questions that were suddenly swirling in her head, but the priestess turned and walked away.

19

Margot

Margot barely registered him when he appeared from the shadows. She'd been walking for hours, head down, mind blissfully empty. She thought—if the vague consciousness that propelled her forward could truly be called thought—that it might have been two days since she'd left her sister. She couldn't remember when she'd last eaten, when she'd last slept. It no longer mattered.

If the man had not stepped directly in front of her, had not grabbed her by the wrist, she would have most likely walked straight into the river. It wasn't until he spoke to her that she finally looked up. And there it was, the Ohio River, the last rays of sunlight spreading across its flat, silver surface like melted butter. Dark bluffs rose jaggedly against the golden red sky on the other side. She turned to look at the man who'd stopped her, touched his face, then collapsed, spent.

When she woke, she was on horseback, shivering, damp, wrapped in a moth-eaten blanket. It smelled like horse, but it was warm, and for the first time in days she was not alone.

He told her his name was Benjamin, but after that said very little except to offer her food or water. As they rode, she wondered vaguely about Ned, about his mother and brother, but there was a part of her that didn't want to know. It was better to imagine that they had crossed this way and were making their way toward Canada, were there this very moment sitting safe and warm in front of a roaring fire.

They traveled through the night and all the next day, stopping only to rest and eat, and to water the horse. Aside from her name, Benjamin asked no other questions, and for this she was grateful.

Near dusk of the second day, they stopped at the edge of a clearing and crouched, half hidden among the branches of a massive mulberry.

"Once you with Mother Abigail's people you be safe." The man's eyes glittered in the waning light. He pulled a quilt from the tangle of mulberry branches and ran a finger over the five pins that glistened in the star at the center. He gave her a sad look before squatting beside her, the quilt folded on the ground at his feet.

"This place you goin' . . . it different," he said softly. "Mother Abigail's sort of a holy woman. Coloreds that go with her, they don't never get found. They just . . ."

He made a going-away motion with his hand, wincing in pain as he did so. Margot looked away. She'd felt his sickness during the long ride. Her arms, wrapped around his waist for hours, had thrummed in agony as his heart stumbled over itself in his chest. Outwardly, he looked healthy, but she doubted he would live another full year. Once more she thought of Grandmere, who would know some potion that might strengthen him. She pushed the thought away.

"Some folks 'round these parts call this place an abomination." He chuckled. "They say it a affront against God. Don't seem to stop 'em tradin' for Mother Abigail's liniments and healin' herbs, though it sho' do keep 'em from hangin' round longer than necessary."

Margot frowned, not understanding. How could anyone guarantee that no one in this Remembrance would ever be found? And why would people think such a place was an abomination?

"You've been there?"

"What? To Remembrance? Oh, no, ma'am!" Benjamin laughed out loud. "Remembrance ain't exactly a comin'-and-goin' kinda place."

He patted her arm, and once again she felt his heart, big and weak, struggling in his chest.

"Trust me," he said. "It gon' be alright."

She made a disbelieving noise, then fell silent as he moved away from her to watch the clearing. She thought of the stories Veronique had whispered to her in the dark of the shack, of the railroad that took slaves away to freedom. She ran a hand over her face and blinked back tears.

Benjamin tensed. Someone was coming. In the pale moonlight she could make out a figure, small, moving fast across the clearing.

"Stay," he hissed.

He stood but clung to the shadow of the bush, one hand on his rifle. Somewhere, off in the darkness, his horse nickered. Margot pulled the thin blanket more tightly around her shoulders. The figure stopped a few yards away, the tiny lantern they held moving in a slow arc, searching.

"Hello?" The voice of a young girl.

"Who the hell is you?" snapped Benjamin, stepping from the cover of the mulberry. He pointed the gun directly at the girl's chest and she stumbled back with a cry, the lantern swinging wildly.

"Mother Abigail! Mother Abigail sent me!"

For a long beat, he seemed to think this over, then slowly lowered the rifle.

"Never sent no one before," he said, his distrust palpable in the dark clearing.

"No," agreed the girl. "But I know you're Benjamin. I don't know why, but she wanted me to bring the passengers in tonight."

At the mention of his name, the conductor visibly relaxed. He turned and motioned for Margot to come out.

The girl frowned. "Mother Abigail said there'd be five."

Benjamin looked away, his expression pained.

"Light load," was all he said.

Margot had a flash of realization that the five had included Ned's family and Veronique. She pressed her lips together, then looked at the girl standing in front of them for the first time. She was tiny, about the same age as Veronique, wild-haired and barefoot despite the cold ground. When she saw Margot looking, she smiled.

"I'm Winter."

"*Bonsoir.* Margot."

The girl raised her eyebrows and grinned.

"Here," she said. She held a packet out toward Benjamin. "Mother Abigail says give this to you. It's from Louisa's garden. She says it'll help make you stronger."

The man accepted the packet with a slight bow. "Nice meetin' you, Winter, but I best be gettin' on. No need to draw extra attention. Give Mother Abigail my regards."

He smiled at Margot. "Welcome to freedom."

He turned to go and Margot grabbed for the young conductor's hand. "*Attente.* Wait."

He stopped, and she could feel a pulsing rising up her arm and settling between her breasts, could see swirls of dark gray fluid filling her lungs. She could see what was broken inside him, but knowing was not fixing and she was not a healer. He was watching her, eyes narrowed. She swallowed hard.

"*Merci,*" she murmured, then dropped his hand.

He frowned, then with a final nod to the two girls, melted away into the night. Margot followed him with her eyes as long as she could.

"We need to be going, too."

Margot started; she had nearly forgotten the girl. In the dim light, she squinted. Even standing still, the girl quivered with a nervous energy. She reminded Margot of the terrier the farmer in Kentucky kept by the smokehouse to chase away rats.

"Come on," said Winter.

She turned to walk back across the clearing, toward the blackness of more forest. Margot watched her go. The night wavered around her and she lifted her face up to the sky. She no longer felt the trembling in her legs. She no longer felt her legs.

Freedom was in front of her—or so the Underground Railroad conductor had said—somewhere beyond that clearing the strange girl was crossing. Her sister was behind her, her body swallowed up in some nameless forest on the other side of the river. And she . . . she was caught in between, unable to take another step.

"I made it, Vee," she whispered to the night sky. "I am free."

"Christmas!"

Margot looked down. Winter was several feet away, waving her arms, cloak flying about her head like a flag.

"Girl!" she cried. "Margot! What are you doing?"

Margot took one step then stopped once more.

"*Je suis si désolé!* I am so sorry," she murmured. "Just go. Please!"

The sky stretched overhead like velvet and, faraway, in the high branches of the trees, she thought she heard Veronique laugh. The tiny girl came back to where Margot stood, muttering angrily. Stopping a few feet away, she flapped her arms at Margot again.

"What is it? We can't just stand here. We have to go."

Margot stared at her.

"I don't understand? Are you sick? Is something hurting you?" cried Winter. "It's only just a little ways now. Hardly anything at all. Come on. Here, you can lean on me. I'll help you."

"No!" Margot jerked away, eyes wild.

Now it was Winter's turn to stare.

"I just . . . please. Leave me alone. *Aller-en.*" Margot gave a harsh bark of laughter that ended in a sob. Freedom? What would she do with freedom? Without Grandmere? Without Veronique? In this cold, strange place that even the man who'd delivered her here had never seen. She was so tired and so empty.

"Come on," Winter said, finally, her tone gentle. "It'll be alright. I promise. You can move just this tiny ways more, can't you?"

Margot had a sense of how dangerous it was for them to be standing out in the open like this, knew what this girl was risking. She wanted her to leave, to let the girl know that it didn't matter anymore—that she was fine. She opened her mouth to tell her this but the words died on her lips.

Winter had dropped into a crouch in the high grass, as she peered narrow-eyed into the woods at the far end of the clearing. Instinctively, Margot crouched, too. The grass was autumn dry but still high, and from where she squatted, she could just make out the top of Winter's head.

"*Quoi?* What is it?"

She strained to hear something, to see something, but there was only the ordinary night sounds . . . and the sour smell of the other girl's panic.

Something . . . on the wind, just at the edge of hearing. There was the rustling of the trees and the wind across the grass, the sound of her blood pounding in her ears. There was . . .

There it was again! Barking! Weaving in and out of the wind, whispering through the grass . . . the barking of dogs. Her throat locked around a scream.

"Come!" Winter's voice came to her across the short distance, brittle with fear. "Come, now!"

Margot's head snapped around. The other girl's hand extended to her through the grass, and Margot made her way toward it, keeping as low as possible; her resolution of just moments ago—to give up on this night—forgotten.

The younger girl jerked her head toward the woods, and the two leaped to their feet, dashing for the cover of the trees on the opposite side of the clearing. The dogs were closer now, their barking high-pitched, wild. They'd caught the scent and were crazed with the chase.

"*Saint Dieu!* What are you doing? Why do we stand here?"

The tiny girl had whirled and stood facing the dogs that had crested a short rise at the end of the clearing. She stood there, watching them come.

The dogs raced down the low hill and Margot screamed and bolted for the trees. Winter still hadn't moved. From the corner of her eye, Margot saw her standing, motionless, staring as the dogs came. And then she saw her falter.

"*Course!*" she screamed, though there was no hope now that the girl could ever outrun the dogs. "Run!"

The dogs were nearly on them now, their wild barking drowning out every other sound in the clearing. Margot saw a tree several yards away, a small V-shaped opening low on its side. If she could just make it there, if she could push her way inside . . .

And then someone else was there with them, a tall, broad woman, her pale cloak glowing white in the moonlight. The woman stepped out into the clearing and turned toward the rushing animals. Barely acknowledging Margot, who'd stumbled and fallen to her knees, the cloaked woman pointed at Winter.

"Go," she cried, her accent foreign to this part of the world but somehow familiar to Margot. "Get the *tifi* moving!"

Winter whirled and scrambled to Margot's side, the dogs only a dozen yards behind her now. "Get up," she screamed. "Get up now!"

She grabbed Margot's arm and yanked her to her feet, dragging her toward the shadows of the woods. It sounded as if the hounds were right on top of them, but with Winter pushing frantically at her back, Margot couldn't see.

As they stumbled along the dim path, the night sky began to glow an eerie green. The air crackled and hissed, and sparks of light flashed above their heads. The hair on Margot's neck stood up. There was a crack, like a gunshot, a terrifying yelping. And then silence. The only sound was the wind rustling through the grass, and their panicked breathing..

"Be a good night for Josiah's cider." The foreign voice spoke, very near her.

Margot cried out. The big woman stood just a few paces away, leaning lightly on a walking stick, calmly studying her. There was no sign of the dogs.

"I'm Mother Abigail," said the big woman. "What name you go by?"

Margot ran a trembling hand through her hair and stared. Mother Abigail took a step toward her and Margot flinched. The priestess stopped.

"You safe here, *petite*," she said. Her voice was low, gentling, the voice one used with frightened children or the ill. "You safe now."

She turned to Winter, who was lurking wide-eyed at the side of the trail. "Come then, this girl looks like death walkin'. Let's get her into the settlement."

"I'm sorry, Mother Abigail," said Winter. "I'm so sorry."

Mother Abigail turned back to look at the girl. She was the oldest woman Margot had ever seen. Her dark skin was smooth but wrapped tightly around the bones of her skull. Snow-white eyebrows sat above deep-set, burning eyes that moved constantly, seeming to take in everything. The old woman stared at Winter, an expression on her face Margot couldn't read.

"It's late, child," was all she said before turning to walk up the path.

"The dogs," Margot croaked, her voice hoarse. "What happened to the dogs?"

Mother Abigail turned once again and gave an enigmatic smile. "They lost the trail. No need to think of them again."

"Lost . . . lost the trail? But . . . ," she said. *"C'est impossible."* They had been right there, close enough to touch. She closed her eyes. It was hard to focus. Her thoughts were coming so slowly. "Where there are dogs, the slavers will be right behind."

She looked over her shoulder.

Mother Abigail laughed, and Margot saw that her teeth were brilliantly white and widely spaced.

"Child," said Mother Abigail. "No slavers gon' ever find their way here. This here all Mother Abigail's. You got off the railroad in the safest place there is."

Winter stepped to her side and began to guide her up the trail, gently this time. Margot trudged behind the old woman, listening for danger. But the dogs were gone. There were no enraged white voices.

Safe? Nowhere in the world was safe.

"And where is this place, please?"

The old woman turned and looked at her. "Remembrance, *petite.* This is Remembrance."

20

Mother Abigail

It was after midnight.

The new girl had barely managed to stagger into Remembrance. Though her eyes were barely open, they'd managed to get a bowl of warm turtle soup into her. From their place around the fire and from the doors of their small cottages, the other settlers had watched, curious yet maintaining a respectful distance, giving her space as was the custom. There would be time for questions at the welcoming.

Mother Abigail had watched as Winter led the girl—Margot—away from the Central Fire and down the trail behind the bakehouse, taking her to one of the empty shelters hidden along a winding path, far back in the trees.

Low to the ground and enclosed on three sides, the half-dozen triangular log shelters were packed with dry straw and heavy quilts, warm and watertight. They were kept ever ready, the straw changed, the quilts aired regularly, the chinking in the logs patched as needed. Despite the signal on the quilt, only one shelter would be occupied tonight, not five. She gripped her walking stick, anger igniting in her gut. At least the *blancs* had been denied this one.

A shelter just like these had been the first structure in Remembrance, back when the spirits still spoke to Mother Abigail regularly, whispering in her ear that after her journey of a thousand miles, this was the place to create her world.

When . . . if . . . the girl decided to stay, she would be moved to one of the whitewashed cottages near the Central Fire.

The excitement of the new arrival had kept people up much later than usual, that and the lingering anxiety that still permeated the settlement, but finally, slowly, everyone had drifted away to their cottages and Remembrance was quiet.

The priestess skirted the Central Fire, now a pile of smoldering embers, and limped toward the baking shed, her knees aching in the damp air. For a long moment, she gazed into the darkness where the shelters were. From where she stood, she couldn't see them, but she knew the structures were there. Part of Remembrance yet separate, they were a place where runaways' hearts could settle and heal while they adjusted to the fact that the air they now breathed belonged to them.

She turned and headed back toward her cabin. A deep silence covered Remembrance, but Mother Abigail was restless.

Five. There should have been five. But there had only been the one, and that one so unraveled that it was a wonder she'd made it.

And then there were the dogs.

Mother Abigail ground her teeth, unconsciously quickening her pace.

Quaker Mary's paper had been right. The new law was making the slavers bold. Making it worth their while to travel this far north. Twice now, in less than a week, they'd come this close to threatening Remembrance. The first time . . .

Mother Abigail shook her head. No. She wouldn't think on that. That had been a momentary lapse. The first she'd ever had since coming full into her power back in New Orleans all those years before.

Nothing.

It was nothing.

One lapse in nearly sixty years.

And they had saved Zeus, no? And the girl. She inhaled sharply. No. It was of no consequence.

The old woman pursed her lips and grunted. Sleep would not visit her this night. Slowly, she climbed the path that would take her to the highlands, passing her own cottage on the way, the path gradually narrowing as she neared the top. Remembrance sat in the space between a bank of rolling hills carved out millennia before by moving ice. Even without the Edge, the hilly topography, the thick stands of birch, pine, buckeye, and maple provided some bit of protection.

Merde!

Mother Abigail swore as her knees and shoulders and back and ankles screeched in protest of the climb. She was old. She wasn't sure how old. Did it matter once so many long years had passed?

She sat, leaning against the large boulder that marked the crest of the highlands, to catch her breath. She pulled a rag from her sleeve to wipe her brow, feeling her heart beating in her ears.

Remembrance was her sanctuary. They'd taken everything else from her: her husband, her children, even her name. Quaker Mary's paper was nothing to her. They would never take this. She spat into the dirt. Let them come. Let them try. She felt a sharp pain in her head, a rush of dizziness, and closed her eyes, waiting for it to pass.

Where had the time gone? Could it have been so very long ago since she'd worked the coffee fields of Far Water? It felt like just yesterday that she'd hidden in the muddy bayous of Louisiana, learning the Art, the way to listening to the *loa*—the spirits. How many days had she lain—naked, with only a sheet between her and the rough wooden floor, no food, no water—as Simona prayed and poured hot holy oil over her breasts, her stomach? Until time was simply a river that carried her along. Space a thing to jump between.

And Josiah had been at her side ever since he and Simona had led her away from those New Orleans docks that dreary March morning. Simona was High Babalawa: the highest of priestesses. The blacks of New Orleans revered her, the whites feared her, and all left her alone.

"What art is it you practice?" Abigail had asked in those first few weeks. "Is it vodun?"

Simona had laughed, her eyes disappearing in the deep wrinkles of her face. "Do not think so small," she said. "I use whatever 'art' I need.

I call on the wind god of the red man and the spirits of our ancestors. I even talk to the god of the *blancs* when I need him. Learn, my child."

And Abigail had learned. She learned everything Simona could teach her, until one day the student was far more powerful than the teacher. She'd left to live on her own, deep in the bayou, wandering the streets of New Orleans at her pleasure, more feared than Simona had ever been. And always Josiah was there, standing in the shadows, watching, waiting.

At first the pain of pushing space, folding it around itself had been agony. Abigail thought she might die, hoped she might die. Simona instructed her to pray, to ask the *loa* for help, but even then she was losing her faith. The *loa* were fickle creatures and God a capricious entity. How else to explain the fact that she was given such great powers, yet she and so many others were still left to the mercy of the *blancs*? If there truly was a God, would he not have given her the power to strike down these *blancs*? Would she not still be fishing on a riverbank an ocean away with her sister? No, she could not pray. She and the *loa* would develop a business arrangement, not unlike the one she would later have with Quaker Mary. She would use the gift they'd given her, but otherwise largely ignore them. They were not her allies.

She started as something moved in the shadows.

"Who is there?"

She waited, but the only answer was the far-off squeaking of bats feeding on the apples rotting up in the orchard. Squinting, she tried to see, but her eyes were as old as the rest of her and showed her nothing but shadows beating against shadows.

"Damn!" she swore again. "Crazy old woman."

But she wasn't crazy. She knew that. Something was happening. Something bad both Outside and in Remembrance.

"Tired," she muttered. "Tired."

Things were changing. She felt it. She needed to protect Remembrance, to keep it safe, but time was a river and she could feel herself getting close to its end. She moaned. For the first time in a long time, she didn't know what to do.

Winter.

The girl's face flashed in her mind and the old priestess's face softened. She'd found the child curled up like a bug under her mother in the snow, eyes wide open, calm as you please, as if waiting for her. Even then, she'd felt it. That current of power coursing through that little body, generating its own heat. But while it had grown as Winter grew, it remained disordered, sloppy, despite her efforts. She thought of her Easter Egger spewed across her chicken pen and frowned. Josiah said she coddled the girl. Was he right? All she knew was that Winter was not ready to protect Remembrance.

"Manman!"

The priestess shot up with a cry, pain corkscrewing through her head.

"Claude?" she cried.

A small crowd of gens de couleur *crossed the narrow street in front of her, the ribbons of their bonnets shimmering in the moonlight, their silk skirts whispering on the brick pavement. The free women of color, beautiful as they moved together, laughing, down the street. A street vendor called out from the alleyway. Her son. Where was her son?*

The pain in her head worsened, as if a hot poker were being pushed into her brain, leaving a trail of fire. *She was standing on the pier, waiting for the fish Eva would prepare for dinner. . . .*

No.

She was in Remembrance.

Remembrance?

Was that right?

She gripped her walking stick and hit her forehead with her fist, breathing hard.

"Abigail?"

She jerked, felt something break apart inside her head, and suddenly she knew herself again.

Josiah.

The old man had materialized from the shadows like a phantom.

She stared at him, dazed, sweat rolling between her breasts despite the cold. Trembling, she clenched her walking stick to the point of pain. He stood at her side, watching her, not touching but close enough for her to feel the warmth radiating off his body.

"*Ou pé m'*, Josiah." Her voice was raw. "You scared me."

He said nothing.

She grunted in irritation, inhaling his scent, apples and smoke and damp wool, until her heart began to slow, the pain in her head fading to a low thrum. It had always been this way, for nearly sixty years, him appearing at her side in times of trouble. And there was trouble coming.

"What you think of the new girl?" he asked finally.

She shrugged. "That she new."

The old man grunted. "She by herself."

"*Wi.*"

The two old friends stood in silence, offering up a quiet prayer for those whose road to freedom had led elsewhere, not needing or wanting to dwell on the possible fate of her companions.

"She look starved and halfway to crazy, don't she?" asked Josiah, breaking the silence.

Mother Abigail smiled bitterly. "Like they all do at first."

Side by side they looked out over a darkened Remembrance.

"What you doin' up here, Abigail?" Josiah asked, after a long moment.

"Just ponderin' on things," she said, not looking at him.

"Hmm," was all he said.

She turned. "You got somethin' to say?"

"Why you send that girl out there tonight?" he asked, his eyes like two raw oysters in the faint light.

"It was time. She gon' have to do it. Sooner rather than later. Need to learn. It will be her time one day. I gettin' old. I gettin' tired."

"She won't never be able to control the Edge, Abigail. Not sooner. Not later."

The priestess bristled. "She powerful."

"She feral!" Josiah took a deep breath. "She got powers, I grant you that. But she undisciplined. Unfocused. And she got no real idea what Remembrance means. What she gotta do."

"Winter loves Remembrance."

"Abigail, she love it the way you love somethin' that always been there. Don't even think about it. Just takes it for granted. She ain't seen that other world outside, not with her own two eyes. Ain't been branded by it. So she don't know the things you got to be ready to do to defend what you hold dear. What it cost." The old man held his face to the night sky and sighed. "You ever tell her the truth? 'Bout why you left New Orleans? The whole truth? How you end up here."

Her head snapped up. "I tell her the truth. I never lie to her."

When he said nothing, she turned her back on him and began to work her way back down the hill. She would not talk of that time. Would not speak of that one gruesome week, when the maroons had revolted on the sugar plantations outside New Orleans and the whites, drunk on fear and revenge, had ravaged the city. Chopping off the hands and feet of slaves and free people of color alike, lighting them afire. Lining their heads on pikes at the city gates, a warning. On that cold January day in 1811, she'd turned her back on New Orleans, on the *loa*, and started walking.

"You want me to tell you everything's gon' be alright, Abigail?" He was behind her again, following her. "You want me to lie to you the way you lied to me when that slaver walk through the Edge the other night?"

She whirled on him, nearly losing her balance. "Lied . . . ?"

"Everything is fine," he said, mocking her.

She growled a warning.

"After you left, after they took Simona, who was it found you in that bayou waitin' to die?" He was speaking low, his voice hard. "Layin' up, measurin' all the wounds the world done put on you? Even after all Simona and I taught you. After all you became. You give up. Layin' up there waitin' on death. But then I found you again. You don't never have to answer to me, but don't never play me for no fool."

She laughed, the sound harsh and loud in the darkness. "You didn't do that for me. You do that for you. My power is your power. You needed me like you needed Simona."

She laughed again.

"I know the creature you are. Feed off me. Feed off Simona. Until we used up and die."

He stepped close, hissing. "I used you? And what was you when we found you, eh? A slave standin' in the mud, screamin' about her dead babies."

"You think you made me?" Choking on her outrage, the priestess could barely get the words out. "That what you think? Don't mistake yourself, Josiah. This power is mine."

"Not made you. Taught you. And the only thing you knew about power before that was makin' massa's dinner."

She snarled and raised her hand. Unflinching, he grabbed it, and she felt the energy she'd released break apart and flow around him. In that same instant, she felt herself fall, though he still held her, falling into a pit where pain and darkness lived. She felt the heat of him, heard the rumble of thunder in the distance. She tried to pull free but could not. She stumbled, felt herself getting lost and then . . .

She was free. Tiny lights flickered before her eyes. Swearing, she slumped to the ground. He folded himself up beside her and pulled a pipe from his pocket. He lit it, the tremor in his hands barely noticeable. Long ago, they'd discovered that though neither was strong enough to destroy the other, they could inflict a great deal of pain on each other. They sat in uneasy silence for a long time and then she laid her hand on his thigh. Without comment, Josiah covered it with his own. A truce.

"Tell me what you see." He sounded slightly breathless. "Or not. But don't lie to me, Abigail."

She gripped his hand and told him: how the then was sometimes becoming muddled with the now. How sometimes she lost herself.

But she didn't tell him everything. Could not even admit it to herself. That sometimes, she even lost Remembrance.

"Then change truly done come," he said when she was done. He squeezed her hand.

"And so?" she asked.

"So we do what we always done, old girl. We wait and see and then we fight back. Just like we always done."

21

Winter

She moved along the deer track, pushing her way through the tangle of vines that threaded through the trees, skirting the much easier trails that wound through the settlement. As she climbed over moldering tree trunks, her bare feet sank deep in the thick moss and damp earth. Overhead, branches of maple and birch intertwined, casting shadows everywhere.

In a few minutes, she'd pushed her way into a small opening in the woods. She stopped to catch her breath. She was at the north end of the cemetery, surrounded on three sides by sugar maples. Last season's sap buckets still hung from the trunks.

Goodwill of the ancestors make the syrup sweeter.

Winter smiled. When she was little, that was what Mother Abigail said to her every sugaring season when they came to collect the sap.

She picked her way through the small graveyard. She liked it here, liked the sense of peace. In summer, honeysuckle and wild rose grew uninhibited around the gravesites, perfuming the air. She stooped and ran a palm lightly over a wooden grave marker, the engraving already worn away. She felt a strong urge to lie down next to the now-unmarked grave, but she was on an errand for Mother Abigail, so with a sigh, she straightened and moved on.

Several hundred yards on, at the other end of the cemetery, nearly invisible in the trees, were the half-dozen temporary shelters that housed the new arrivals. Far enough away from the center of the settlement that the newly freed didn't feel overwhelmed, yet close enough that they understood they'd not been abandoned; the structures were small, but sturdy. Winter had taken less than a dozen steps toward the one where the newest runaway lay, when she heard the sound of a struggle coming from inside. Dashing toward it, she bent to look. The girl, Margot, though still asleep, was thrashing wildly, calling for someone, crying out in another language. One arm slammed into the side wall and, alarmed, Winter grabbed for the girl's hands to prevent her injuring herself.

Margot's eyes snapped open. She blinked in confusion.

Then. "Veronique?"

"No." Winter frowned. "Winter. It's alright. You're alright. You're safe now."

The other girl stopped struggling and confusion was slowly replaced by something else. Disbelief? Anger? She laughed, a harsh, hysterical sound that bounced off the walls of the small shelter. Winter let her go and backed through the opening. Margot followed seconds later and stood, wobbling slightly.

"I know you," she said. "You were there last night."

"Not last night," Winter corrected her. "Three nights ago. You've been asleep for three days."

"Three days?" Margot's head snapped around. "Impossible!"

Winter shrugged, watching as the other girl took in her surroundings.

"If you're feeling up to it, we can take a walk down by the creek," she said. "Get you some fresh clothes. You could wash." She looked pointedly at the girl's torn and dirt-caked garments.

Margot glanced down and, even beneath the grime, her embarrassment was obvious. With a nod, she brushed a tangle of hair from her face and took a few steps. She staggered, nearly fell, and Winter leaped to steady her, inhaling sharply when Margot jerked away. The two girls stared at each other a long moment before Margot looked down, lips pressed into a thin line.

Winter sighed. "Come."

As they walked, she was sharply aware of Margot stumbling clumsily along behind her. Every few yards or so, she paused to glance over her shoulder and study the girl in her charge.

Margot was tall, a café-au-lait Negress—cream-colored with just a drop of coffee. Her eyes were green . . . or brown, Winter couldn't decide, her long curly hair a matted mess. Her face was long, too angular to be pretty, her mouth a bit too wide. Nonetheless, she was striking, a bad thing for a slave trying to disappear. Margot tripped over a tree root, but Winter bit her lip and pretended not to notice.

There were a million questions roiling in her head, but Winter remained uncharacteristically silent. Everything about this girl set her teeth on edge: the flashes of anger, the burst of wild laughter back at the shelter.

Runaways had appeared in Remembrance since Winter could remember, more men than women, almost always young. When they arrived, they were nearly always at the end of their endurance, so beat down by exhaustion or the whip or fear that they could barely speak their names. And they'd all, almost to a man, woman, and child, lost someone, been forced to leave someone behind. What they all had in common was an overwhelming gratitude for their freedom. Even those who believed that Mother Abigail must be some kind of witch. The other emotions—despair for those left behind, the thirst for vengeance, the fear for what the future held—those came later. Sometimes days. Sometimes weeks. But this girl was different. Her darkness rode right at the surface. And if she was grateful, she was hiding it well.

The memory of Margot standing still as death in the moonlight, refusing to move despite the dogs, flashed through Winter's mind. She shot another glance at the girl who was still picking her way along the trail.

At the creek's edge, a heavy pot sat in a shallow pit, surrounded by smoldering coals.

"You can wash yourself up there," said Winter. "Washday was yesterday, so there's clean clothes on that dry line over there. Should be something there that fits you." She eyed the tall girl doubtfully.

Margot stared at the steaming pot but made no move toward it, and

Winter felt a flicker of pity for the girl. "Wash. Don't wash. But Mother Abigail wants to see you, and I got to tell you, you're a little ripe." She grinned, trying to elicit a smile. When there was no response, Winter touched her wrist.

"*Ne me touche pas,*" Margot hissed, whirling on her, teeth bared.

"Christ on a horse!" Winter cried, stumbling backward. Shock quickly gave way to anger. "Are you touched in the head?"

Margot stared at her, unblinking, for a long moment, then bowed her head. "I beg your pardon," she said. She was trembling badly. "I am feeling a bit . . . unsettled."

"A bit unsettled?" Winter eyed her uneasily. She looked around. They were alone. She took a deep breath. "Well . . . why'n't you just go on ahead and wash up."

She went to sit on a rocky mound a few feet away. She turned her back to give the other girl privacy but watched her from the corner of her eye, wary. She dug a bare toe in the ground and fidgeted. Since the rescue, the priestess had been like a ghost. Winter hadn't caught even a glimpse of her. She hadn't even come herself to tell Winter to get the new girl settled in. Instead she'd sent the message by Belle, a young mother of twin girls, who'd come to Remembrance more than five years before.

Once again, the image of the dogs flashed in her mind. She shivered. There'd been a moment standing in that clearing, a very brief moment when the Easter Egger had sparked in her head and she'd had the bizarre thought that she could do to the dogs what she'd done to Mother Abigail's chicken. And then the thought was gone. There hadn't been any spaces between things, only the braying of the dogs and the roaring of blood in her ears.

And then Mother Abigail had been there. Had been there all along. She had done the thing only she knew how to do. Bent space, folding the Edge up around them, making the dogs . . . vanish.

Winter gave a grunt of resentment. Why had she even sent her out on her own to get the girl in the first place? Had she known about the dogs? Was this another one of her tests? Everything seemed to be a test with her lately. And she seemed to be failing them all.

She shot a cross look over her shoulder. Margot was bent over the pot of water, splashing her face, pulling her fingers through her hair, trying to work out the tangles.

Winter tugged nervously at a tangle of her own hair, twisting a strand round and round her finger. Would Mother Abigail even acknowledge her when she showed up with Margot? Would she be angry? The priestess hadn't seemed angry about her chicken. She hadn't even seemed angry about the rescue. More . . . disappointed. Winter cringed. She wasn't sure what it was she had done to disappoint Mother Abigail this time. How could she have known about the dogs? What could she have done differently? She couldn't do what the priestess could do. How many hours had she been forced to stand in the woods, in the cold and the heat, Mother Abigail's exhortation to "focus" ringing in her ears?

"*Merci*. Thank you."

Winter started. Lost in thought, she hadn't heard the other girl walk up behind her. She turned. Margot had washed and put on the new clothes. The gray shift and heavy blue overskirt were far too short, but they were clean. Margot's old ragged clothes lay in a pile at the creek's edge. The runaway glanced at them, then away.

"Thank you," said Margot again, and for the first time she gave a true smile.

Winter squinted at the newly scrubbed girl and tugged self-consciously at her own matted hair. "Well, don't you look fresh as a peach," she said, nodding her approval.

Margot replied with a tight smile. Winter turned and began the trek back toward the Central Fire.

"You were speaking . . . French?" Winter asked, after they'd been walking awhile.

"Pardon?"

"French?" Winter turned to study Margot. "When you woke up. You were calling for someone and speaking French. It was French, wasn't it?"

The other girl's face darkened and Winter tensed, preparing for another outburst.

But Margot simply nodded and said, "*Oui*. French. Do you speak it?"

"Me? No!" snorted Winter. "But Mother Abigail does. Some. Mostly bad words, I think."

Margot's lips twitched upward. "Your Mother Abigail speaks French?"

Winter nodded. "And Creole. Which is kind of like French I guess, but different."

"Where did she learn French?"

Winter shrugged. "No one in Remembrance has to talk about the before time . . . unless they want to. Including her," she said. "But before Remembrance, she lived in a place called New Orleans. . . ."

Margot made a strangled sound in her throat and Winter stopped to look at her.

"What?" she asked.

The other girl shook her head.

"Mother Abigail says lots of folks speak French there," she went on, watching the girl through narrowed eyes, wary. When Margot said nothing to this, either, Winter sighed and resumed walking back toward the settlement.

"Mother Abigail left New Orleans after a bad fever there." The girl's silence was beginning to spook her. "I mean I think that's why she left. Because people were always dying of fevers there. She told me stories about how people would just sit down in the streets and die, blood leaking from their eyes and ears. Said there were graves filled with the dead and people piled one on top of the other like firewood. She said the fools, that's what she called them, the fools would fire off cannons night and day, trying to scare off the sickness. But mostly it just scared the sick to death."

She glanced back at Margot. The other girl was bent forward, as if walking against a headwind, head down, fists clenched, the muscles working in her jaw.

"When the rains came, all those bodies popped right back out of the ground and floated down the streets," Winter went on. "Can you even imagine that? It's no wonder she left."

"*Oui*," murmured Margot. "I can imagine that."

Winter cut her eyes at the girl. "Are you . . . are you alright?"

"*Oui.*"

Winter waited for the girl to say more, but the silence stretched out between them.

"Mother Abigail was living outside the city when the worst fever any-one ever saw came. She left. To come here with Josiah," said Winter.

"Josiah?"

"He's . . ." She hesitated.

The thought of Josiah started an uneasy fluttering in Winter's chest. If Mother Abigail had secrets that filled the skies, then the old man was a mystery as big as the world. No matter that his eyes looked like snot, Winter knew that he still saw. She was certain of it. And lately, she felt those opaque, wet eyes following her wherever she went. Judging. Disapproving.

"He's . . . Mother Abigail's friend," she said, finally. "Since the fever time, back then. Since forever."

"And what happened to *les chiens*? The dogs?"

The question caught Winter off guard. She eyed the girl. How to explain Remembrance to someone already so skittish, so ready to bolt?

"Maybe they remembered a prior engagement," she said smiling. A joke. Margot stared at her blankly.

She sighed. Usually, it was left to Mother Abigail to explain Remembrance to the new arrivals, but nothing about this was usual, and Margot had been her rescue . . . mostly. Slowly, and as simply as she could, she tried to explain the mystery of Remembrance to her. When she was done, Margot stared at her, disbelief and disgust twisting her features.

"So you believe that your Mother Abigail has created a . . . a world, where no white people may enter?"

"Yes. We're standing in it."

"And you believe that with a wave of her hand, the old woman sent a pack of dogs to . . . where? A prior engagement?" Margot gave a bitter, hard-edged laugh. "Then you are either a liar or a fool. Or you must think I am."

Winter bristled but didn't respond. There was no point in defend-ing Remembrance. The girl would see soon enough. She turned on her heel and resumed walking, not looking back to see if Margot fol-lowed. She walked without stopping until she reached the top of the hill that marked the edge of the main settlement.

"This Mother Abigail must be truly powerful to have survived such a fever and the swamps," said Margot coming up behind her. Winter said nothing.

"I am sorry," Margot went on. "I am sure this . . . Remembrance . . . must seem a magical place to you. But a world between worlds? Invisible to the outside? A *conte de fée, oui*? A fairy story?"

Winter sucked her teeth and moved off down the hill.

"I know those fevers. Have seen them. They destroy everything in their path. Even if you do not die from the inside out, you still die. I was born in New Orleans."

Winter turned, surprised. A single tear ran down the older girl's face.

"They take everything," she hissed. "They take it and destroy it."

"They?" asked Winter.

Margot made a noise in the back of her throat, a swallowed sob, and without another word began to walk down the hill. Winter watched her go, glad she hadn't told the girl all of it. Glad she hadn't told her that whenever Mother Abigail told that story, whenever she described the sight of the dead, rats feeding on rotting flesh as they rode the corpses through the streets like life rafts in the smoky sunlight, the priestess would throw back her head and laugh and laugh until tears ran down her face.

22

Mother Abigail

From her perch on the low stool in front of her cabin, she watched the two girls approach. The new girl was fair of skin, closer to white than Negro, with curly, honey-colored hair pulled back from her face, her sharp features oddly put together. From where she sat, the priestess could see the tightness in her jaw, the tension in her movements.

There was a painful thrumming in Abigail's head. It was almost always there now. She closed her eyes, and fatigue fell over her like a blanket, threatening to suffocate her. Not for the first time, she questioned the wisdom of having confided in Josiah, even the bit that she had. She felt him watching her all the time now, measuring her steps, her words, waiting for a show of weakness, even now, when he was elsewhere in the settlement. *Bondye*, she was tired.

She pushed a hand into the pocket of her overskirt and felt for Hercule's disk, rubbing it between her fingers. It was worn almost to nothing. Like her.

Opening her eyes again, she studied her girl. Barely reaching Margot's shoulders, Winter was short and wiry. As usual, her headdress had come loose and hung carelessly about her shoulders, leaving her dark hair a wild tangle in the breeze. The girl was a muss-and-fuss bundle of messy energy. Mother Abigail shook her head. She remembered Josiah's description of her as feral, and in spite of herself, she smiled. He wasn't wrong.

Winter bounced up the trail in front of Margot, kicking at stones, leaping to slap at a low-hanging branch. The old woman watched as they met a heavily pregnant woman making her way down from the highlands. Winter ran to her and threw her arms around her, nearly knocking the woman off her feet.

The old woman shook her head. The girl was all emotion, her moods, like her energy, tumbling and twisting: light, dark, light. Many years before, long before Remembrance, Mother Abigail had saved the daughter of a spice merchant, and after, along with her silver payment, the grateful father had gifted her with a kaleidoscope. She'd kept it in her shack, deep in the bayou, fascinated by the changing colors, the lights. Winter reminded her of that old long-lost kaleidoscope: bright and random, changing with the whisper of the wind.

And then she was standing there, shifting anxiously from foot to foot. "Mother Abigail."

The old woman nodded and struggled to stand, wincing as pain shot through her knees. "Child."

"I brought Margot." Winter visibly relaxed at Mother Abigail's greeting. "She's from New Orleans," she added, twisting a lock of hair 'round her finger, bouncing on her toes.

The priestess's eyes widened and she felt a shift around her. Suddenly she smelled the stink of coal smoke from the ships docked in the Mississippi, saw the sun reflecting off the broken glass that topped the wall of the slave stockade. She blinked, and there was Winter, looking at her strangely. Margot stood indifferently nearby, her gaze fixed on the chickens clucking in the dooryard. Mother Abigail fixed her face into a mask of mild interest.

"Yes?" she said.

Margot did not acknowledge this; instead, she turned toward the sounds coming through the trees from the Central Fire. From Mother Abigail's cottage, tucked deep into the hillside, it was difficult to see what was happening down by the main clearing, but every now and then they caught a glimpse of a short, round mulatto running back and forth through the trees.

"That's the Reverend," said Winter. "He teaches anyone who's interested to read." The round man bounded through the trees and partway up the hill. Seeing the three women, he stopped, gave a quick wave, then charged back toward the Central Fire. "Can't really say for sure what it is he's doing right this minute, though."

Margot might have been carved from stone. Only her eyes moved in her pale face. The priestess studied her.

"Mother Abigail?"

The priestess sighed.

Winter hesitated and Mother Abigail fought the urge to roll her eyes. "What you want, Winter?"

"I . . ." Winter rocked from foot to foot, her eyes on the ground. "Are you . . ."

Mother Abigail sighed again. "*Petite,* go find Josiah," she said. "Send him to me. Then I need you to go up to Louisa. Time for the next exchange time, and Quaker Mary askin' for some special things. Outside *blancs* go through Louisa's honey and liniments like they breathin' air. All the good to us, though, yes?"

The girl hesitated and Mother Abigail touched her gently on the cheek. "When it quiet, we talk. Go. It Margot's time now. We need us to get acquainted."

Before Winter could turn away the old priestess stopped her.

"Girl, why you always look like a stray? Tell me this." She brushed Winter's hair behind her ears and retied her headdress.

"Mother Abigail!" protested Winter, pulling away.

"*Il est fait!* It's done!" The priestess released her, waving a hand dismissively. "Go on, wild thing."

Winter rewarded her with a quick smile, then was gone.

Once they were alone, Mother Abigail turned her attention back to the runaway, who stood quietly, listening to the buzz of activity around Remembrance.

"You didn't run here from New Orleans," said Mother Abigail. "*D'ou sont vous?*"

The French words felt slippery, putrid in her mouth. Since abandoning Louisiana she'd rarely spoken the language. Except to swear. And that felt right. To curse in the language of the *chein* who'd stolen so much from her. It was only with great effort that she kept from spitting in the dirt as the words left her mouth.

For a long moment, it seemed Margot might not answer. She stood motionless, erect, facing the path leading down to the Central Fire. When finally she turned toward the priestess, Mother Abigail suppressed a gasp. The girl stared at her, her amber-colored eyes cold, hard.

"*Nous sommes venus d'Kentucky,*" said Margot quietly.

"From many days away. Just the other side of the Ohio River," she added in English.

"*Nous?*" asked Mother Abigail. Margot had said "we," but she'd been alone when the conductor found her stumbling, starved and half mad, through the woods.

The girl didn't respond. Mother Abigail lowered herself back to the stool, swearing as something popped painfully in her back. Margot raised an eyebrow but remained silent.

"Come," said Mother Abigail, indicating an upturned log. "You come sit by me. We exchange stories. Yes?"

Margot made no move to sit. Mother Abigail pretended not to notice.

"You know your years, child?"

"I am twenty," answered Margot. "I was born on New Year's Day, in the year 1839."

Mother Abigail nodded. A house slave then—the fair skin and straight back, the parlor French, suggested as much—but the accuracy of the birth date confirmed it. Birthdays for field hands were as useful as frog's teeth.

"Good to know where your story begins," she said mildly.

Margot stared at her.

"So young. Brave to risk escape," said the priestess, narrowing her eyes. "What made you run to freedom?"

She did not know this Kentucky, but from what she'd heard, there were not many fancy French families there. How had this house slave gone from a town house in New Orleans to Kentucky? Debt? A mistress's jealousy?

Margot opened her mouth as if to answer, then closed it again. She shrugged. Mother Abigail waited, but the girl seemed to have nothing more to say.

"This place called Remembrance," began Mother Abigail when Margot remained silent. "I created it. Not important how. Important is that you safe here long as you choose to stay."

Still Margot said nothing. She might have been a stick of firewood.

"There be no whites here," the priestess continued. "Don't need 'em. Don't want 'em."

A shadow passed across Margot's face and was quickly gone.

"The Edge . . ."

"*Oui*," interrupted Margot, speaking at last. "Your girl explained all about this Remembrance. This magic that allows no one in or out without your permission."

She made no effort to hide her disdain.

Mother Abigail raised an eyebrow and leaned forward. "Not magic," she said evenly. "Art."

She focused on a space just beyond the girl's feet, a tiny seam. She let her mind reach for it, give it the faintest caress. She saw Margot's expression change from contempt to confusion, saw the flicker of fear as she sensed something change around her. The priestess held it for a minute, the wrinkle in space, then let go. She sat back, expressionless.

Margot clenched and unclenched her hands. "Am I a prisoner here, then?" she asked.

"What?" Mother Abigail gave a bark of laughter. "Of course not. Remembrance is a sanctuary. But it's good to know the nature of a thing, yes?" she went on. Margot pressed her lips together.

Feeling a flicker of irritation, Mother Abigail inhaled sharply through her nose. Something about this girl, this Margot, both repelled her and intrigued her in equal parts. It was unfair, she knew this. The girl should have no more effect on her than the wind against a mountain. After all, what horrors must the child have endured, what force of will must it have taken to survive alone in the wilderness while making her way to Remembrance? But nevertheless, there it was.

"Some stay with us," she said as calmly as she could manage. "They find work that keeps us strong. Working the land or metal. Tending to the little ones, building things. Cooking. Sewing. Others rest a while, then move on. What you good with, *petite*?"

Margot gazed off into the distance, beyond the priestess's shoulder. "I can play the piano and I can embroider. I can read and write in English, Latin, and French. I—"

She stopped abruptly as Mother Abigail began to laugh. "Well, not much call for fine stitchery or piano playin' in Remembrance, as you can see. But the Reverend down there, he could use the help learnin' the babies to read and write. And English'll be fine and plenty for the time bein'."

Margot looked into the middle space, her eyes focused on something unseen by the priestess, the muscles of her jaw working.

"Winter is my daughter," said Mother Abigail. "She'll help you get your bearings. Roam as far and wide as you like. Other than the animals in the hills, there are no dangers to you here."

At this, Margot blinked. "No danger?"

"None."

The two stared at each other, the old priestess and the young runaway. Mother Abigail had the sense that she was being challenged, though Margot stood quietly before her.

The priestess leaned forward once again, saw the girl flinch. "How you come to be in Kentucky, girl?"

It was the second time in just a few minutes she had asked the girl her story—against the rules she herself had set for Remembrance, that no one need share their story until they were ready—but there was something about this one, something that made it seem a matter of some urgency.

Margot stood there in her dooryard in her too-short dress, staring down the hill where the sound of children playing drifted up to them, her face revealing nothing. She turned toward Mother Abigail.

"We were sold to pay a debt, my sister and I. Our mistress's *grand-mère* came to the house after Master Hannigan's death. Madame Rousse . . ."

The effect on the old woman was electric. She shot to her feet with a cry, the pain of her arthritic knees forgotten. Margot stared at her in alarm.

"What?" gasped the priestess. "What name you say?"

"I . . ."

Mother Abigail gripped the girl's arm. "What name you say?"

Margot tried to pull away but the old woman was surprisingly strong.

"*Je ne sais pas!* I do not know! Master Hannigan? Madame Rousse?"

Mother Abigail released her so suddenly that Margot staggered backward, nearly falling. "What is the given name of Madame Rousse?"

The girl was shaking her head, her pale skin even more pale. Mother Abigail knew she was scaring her, knew she was pushing too hard, but she couldn't stop. Something had ripped open inside her.

"Her given name," she hissed.

"Ninette. *Son nom est* Ninette Rousse."

The priestess went cold. She stepped toward the girl again. She wanted . . . she had no idea what she wanted, but this girl had seen her, had talked to her, had been sold away by the very *blanc* that had caused her to lose her boys all those years ago. She needed . . .

"Abigail!" Josiah's voice broke the spell.

"Josiah." Mother Abigail froze where she was, her eyes still locked on Margot. The young girl stood motionless, dazed confusion mixed with fear on her face.

"I am Josiah," he said. He held one hand slightly forward, as if testing the air currents, and moved to stand between the two women. "I am the old man of Remembrance to Abigail's old woman. Welcome."

He held out his other hand and, after a moment's hesitation, Margot took it.

"I am Margot," she said, before pulling her hand free and clenching it tightly against her chest.

The air around them crackled with tension.

"You can wait for Winter by the Central Fire," the old woman finally managed to say, struggling to control the shaking that had suddenly taken hold of her. She pointed toward a path that led downhill through the trees. "She's gone up in the hills to hunt up Louisa. Our healer."

She noted the interest that flashed across the girl's face.

"When they come down, have Louisa give you something to build your strength," she went on. The pain in her head was building once again. She ignored it. "You weaker than you think. The next few days are for learning and resting."

The girl nodded and, without meeting her eyes, moved off in the direction Mother Abigail had indicated. Josiah propped himself onto the porch beside the priestess. Mother Abigail felt his eyes boring into her.

"Tell me, Abigail," he said after a full minute had passed.

She took a deep breath, trying to expel the weight that lay against her heart. "She belonged to the family that took my babies from me."

Josiah grunted in surprise.

"It cannot be coincidence," she murmured. "It cannot. That this girl from New Orleans should end up here now. That she belonged to the same family that once claimed me."

"No," he said quietly. "Not coincidence. The gods don't work like that."

She hissed. "The gods."

He chuckled mirthlessly.

"Well, what it mean, then?" she snapped.

He shrugged and she shook her head. She had closed off that part of her heart. She would not, she could not feel that pain again. She began to punch herself in the face.

"No, Abigail." Josiah grabbed at her flailing hands. "Don't do this. You stop this now.

"Look at me." He seized her hands and held on. "Look at me."

She looked.

His mucoid eyes locked onto hers and she couldn't look away. As he gripped her hands, she tasted the potatoes he'd had for breakfast, the sweet tobacco from his pipe. This is what he could do: take over a body and make it his, command blood, lungs. She felt his fire, his heat. Felt his power mix with hers. He was inside her now; she felt him there. Even if she had wanted to, she was powerless to stop him. And as his hands curled around hers, she felt a lightness, a lifting of the terrible weight. He held on until the pain went away. No, not away. It was still there, reverberating in the deepest shadows. But it was bearable for the moment. He released her and she sagged against him, a vague soreness in her chest.

"What does it mean, Josiah?" she whispered again.

He snorted. She sat up and gave him a sharp look. "Old woman, I gave up a long time ago to figure out the secret messages the spirits be sendin'. An' you an' them barely on speakin' terms."

She gave him a weak smile. "You're an old fool."

They sat side by side in silence.

He blew out a plume of sweet-smelling pipe smoke and began to hum as the voices of the children singing their alphabet wafted up through the trees.

Gaelle

She was exhausted. She'd slept poorly again. Weird dreams about the old woman and the strange man, about her grandmother and foul-smelling fires, had rolled around in her head all through the night, and she'd wakened feeling foggy and irritable.

As she headed out the door, she glanced at the calendar stuck on the refrigerator. Rose would be home soon, and though she hadn't yet figured out what she was going to do about the letter ordering her to vacate, she was excited. Having her sister back with her, even for a little while, would make things feel normal again.

She sighed and carefully pulled out of the narrow drive that led from the carriage house to the street. It was snowing heavily, and the old car desperately needed snow tires, making the drive precarious. Nearly half the homes on this stretch of her block were abandoned, and at this hour the few that were occupied were still dark. At the corner was a bank that had been converted to a church long before she and Rose had moved into the neighborhood. In the dark, hard-blowing snow, the giant cross that hung near a second-floor window seemed to float in midair, its bright red lights glowing like some sort of omen.

She had just passed the church, easing up on the gas to let the car coast around the corner, when she caught a glimpse of a familiar figure from the corner of her eye. Hitting the brakes harder than she intended, she felt the back end of the car skid. It fishtailed wildly and jumped the curb, narrowly missing a fire hydrant before sliding to a stop. Gaelle gripped the steering wheel, heart pounding in her ears, then swearing; she yanked off her seat belt and threw open the car door. Standing in the dark street, she squinted in the blowing snow toward the church, slush soaking the hem of her scrubs.

He'd been standing there. Right there on the corner. That peculiar old man from Stillwater, the red light from the church's cross casting a sickly glow on his dark face. She felt a shiver of fear and crossed herself. She stood a bit longer, the wind swirling the snow around her face and down the collar of her thin coat, but there was no sign of him. Swearing, she got back in her car and continued on to work.

When Gaelle rushed into her office, Melody Orr was on the phone. The DON held up a finger, indicating to give her just one minute, then went back to typing on her keyboard, seeming to do a dozen things at once.

"Gaelle, good morning," she said, after hanging up. "Are you alright? Are you feeling dizzy again?"

"Did a man come in to see you last night?"

The DON frowned, raking a hand through her stop sign–colored hair. "A man?"

She laughed, the worry lines fixed between her eyes. "There were dozens of men in here yesterday. It's review time, remember?" she added, as if Gaelle might not have noticed.

Gaelle shook her head. "Older. Dark hair with streaks of white. He was wearing sunglasses?"

"No." Mrs. Orr stood and began pushing papers into a pile. She tucked her clipboard under one arm and began scrolling through her phone as she came around the desk.

"Near the end of the day shift?"

The DON, who'd been nearly out of the door, turned and peered at her. "No. Gaelle, what is it?"

Gaelle told her how she'd found the man hunched over the mysterious old woman, how he said that he worked for Joint Commision. She didn't mention that she thought she'd seen him standing in the snow near her home just a short time before.

"He was in her room?" The DON looked alarmed. "And he had a card?"

She nodded.

Mrs. Orr swore and raked at her hair again. "He didn't hurt her?"

"No. I do not think so." She fought the urge to pat the DON's hair back into place.

"Damn it," swore the DON again. "That sounds really suspicious. Why would he be in a resident's room, especially alone? I'll need to talk to security. And the staff. Thank you, Gaelle."

She hurried out into the hallway.

"He said her name was Winter."

"What?" The DON whirled back to face her, eyes narrowed. "Why?"

For the entire time the old woman had been there, they'd called her Jane, for Jane Doe. Or, more often than not, simply, the old woman.

"Why would he say that?"

Gaelle said nothing.

"For the love of . . . ," muttered Mrs. Orr. "If you see him again just stay away and call security, you understand?"

She nodded, but the DON was already halfway down the hall.

Gaelle moved around the old woman's room. Winter's room, she reminded herself, if the old man was to be believed. She freshened the linen, changed her gown, moving quickly, efficiently, without the usual banter. She was on alert, her muscles tensed for any sudden movement. But the old woman sat still, her eyes fixed as always on the unremittingly bleak news scrolling across the television screen.

Gaelle took the pitcher from the table to fill with ice. At the door she hesitated. Turning back toward the room, she stared at Winter for a long time, the woman seemingly oblivious to her presence. She glanced over her shoulder into the hallway. They were alone.

"What is your name?"

No response.

"Winter? Is that your name?"

The old woman slowly turned her head and locked eyes with her, and she inhaled sharply. The look sent a wave of dread through the center of her gut, and she was glad of the bed between them.

She swallowed hard. "And that old man? Who is that old man?"

The woman's mouth widened in a toothless smile.

"Josiah," hissed the old woman. She threw back her head and shook with soundless laughter.

24

Winter

For the second time that day, she found herself trudging down the path toward the creek. However, just before reaching the gravelly bank, she veered sharply left, taking another, barely perceptible trail. Mother Abigail had told her to find Louisa, and if the healer wasn't tending to the sick in the center of the settlement, then there was only one other place she was likely to be—up in her gardens, tending her hives.

But Winter was in no hurry. Aside from Josiah, Louisa was the person in Remembrance she disliked the most.

Louisa had a sort of magic. Much as it pained her, even she had to admit that. Plants whispered to Louisa, told her their secrets. From them, she extracted the salves and liniments, the tonics and elixirs that healed Remembrance's wounds, eased their babies into the world, and fought the sicknesses that threatened the settlement in every season of the year.

And then there were her bees and their honey. Of all the things they traded with the Outside, Louisa's honey was their most valued currency: bright, golden yellow, the color of sunflowers, her honey was said to cure everything from burns to rheumatism. When the hives came in, the people on the other side of the Edge—black and white alike— traded them all the salt and nails, buttons and needles, iron ore and cotton goods, canning jars and sealing wax they could ever need. Louisa worked magic with her plants and her bees. That was true.

But what was also true was that in spite of her gifts with medicine, Louisa was mean as a snake. She had no great love for anyone in the settlement, as much an outsider as Winter, though she seemed to prefer it that way. But her greatest antipathy seemed mysteriously reserved for Winter.

Winter kicked at the fallen leaves lining the path. She bent to pick one up, holding it so that the sunlight shone through. Most of it had already been eaten away by worms and the damp, but what was left flowed from the leaf's spines like lace. She ran a finger tenderly over the graceful pattern, seeing where the light leaked between the spaces. A flash of sunlight through the trees caught her attention, reminding her of her errand, and, sighing, she picked up her pace. She couldn't drag this out much longer.

Winter trudged uphill, ducking the tree branches that aimed for her face, muttering to herself along the way.

"Can't stay on flat ground with everybody else. Course not. Like her precious bees wouldn't be just as happy on lower ground. They're bees—what do they care? Even the highlands. Why couldn't they be in the highlands? At least there's a real trail up there! Christ on a horse!"

Near the summit, Winter stopped to catch her breath.

Still spitting curses, she pushed on until she staggered, finally, out into a broad open space: Louisa's garden. The healer's garden was perched at the top of a bluff overlooking a river—the same river that fed their washing creek. Tucked among a cove of twisted buckeye trees were the hives. Up here, despite the lateness of the season, many of the flowers still struggled to bloom. Insects and birds flitted among spiky coneflowers near gone to seed. Three-foot-high goldenrod hummed with bees.

Behind her, Remembrance was invisible through the treetops; in front, the sheer stone-studded hill rolled out in a carpet of greens and reds and golds—all the way to the distant river—silver in the afternoon light.

High and inaccessible, except for the steep and rocky trail she'd just climbed, it was the perfect place for the reclusive healer and her gardens.

"What you doin' up here?"

Winter whirled. "Christmas!"

The herbalist had come up silently behind her and stood a few feet away, clutching an herb-laden basket. She stood glaring at Winter. The herbalist was older than Winter by a few years. She was thin to the point of gauntness, most likely the result of the ghastly injury that deformed the left side of her face and made it difficult for her to eat much except soft foods.

"Mother Abigail wanted me to come find you," said Winter evenly.

"You found me then."

Winter rolled her eyes as Louisa turned away and headed toward a small shack half hidden in the vegetation, the place she lived and worked, far from everything except her beloved flowers and bees. Winter followed, keeping a wide distance between them. Louisa was not above hurling things at people when she was in a snit, which was most of the time, as far as Winter could tell.

"Well, I got the impression she wanted to see you. She wants to know if you have everything ready for the exchange."

The herbalist spun around and Winter tensed, prepared to duck.

"She wants to know if I'm ready? I ever *not* been?"

Winter inhaled sharply, trying to hold her temper in check.

"Louisa." Winter made her voice like spring sap, slow and sickening sweet. "She's not doubting that you're ready. She says the outsiders have some special requests, that's all."

"Special requests. Special requests," muttered Louisa, hitching her herb basket tighter against her side. "Do I look like a mercantile? Do I?" She bent to examine a rosehip.

"Ask me, shouldn't be havin' nothin' t'all to do with them devils. Remembrance makes its own way. That's what I say," she mumbled.

Winter threw her arms up, exasperated, keeping a wary eye on Louisa's basket.

"Sweet baby Jesus, girl," she snapped. "I'm just bringin' the message. The rest? That's something between you and Mother Abigail."

"Got the message," replied Louisa flatly.

"Fine!" Winter turned to leave, the herbalist's hatefulness churning in her stomach. How could anyone be so full of poison?

"You know," she said, turning back. "If you treated people halfway as good as you treat your stupid flowers, maybe you wouldn't be by yourself all the time. Maybe you'd even have friends."

"Ain't nothin' wrong with bein' alone, 'specially if the choice is sufferin' a fool," Louisa spit. "As for friends? You be marching around Remembrance like you the queen of the ball, grinnin' so wide it's a wonder your face don't split plain in two."

She smiled then and the effect was unnerving.

"And somehow," Louisa went on, her eyes glittering, "I don't see no crowds of folks fallin' all over theyselves tryin' to be *your* friend."

Winter reared back, Louisa's words like a slap in the face. She blinked back tears.

"You know," she said, taking a step toward Louisa, who stood smiling dangerously at her, "you might be the nastiest person I ever met. Remembrance did just fine before we dragged your half-dead carcass in here. You'd think you'd be the tiniest bit appreciative. But no! You think 'cause you can take sickness out of folks, that gives you the right to just flash your hind parts in everybody's face. You think you're so special! What I just don't understand is how you manage to heal folks when you don't even like them!"

"Well, you're not special!" Winter snarled, the words nearly choking her. "You're just evil!"

Louisa laughed, a harsh, broken sound. "Naw," she said. "I ain't nothin' special. Not like Mother Abigail's precious Winter. The girl who's gone look after all us po', pitiful slave folks after Mother Abigail gone."

She shifted the basket. "What I just don't understand is, how you s'posed to take care of us folks when can't nobody even let you near the cook fire 'cause you most likely to set your fool self on fire?"

"*Femèl chein,*" snapped Winter. "Bitch!"

They stood inches from each other, breathing hard. Winter trembled with rage, fighting the urge to launch herself at Louisa, to slap her damaged face.

When Louisa had first arrived in Remembrance, her face broken, barely able to speak, barely alive, Winter had pitied her. But no more!

Louisa, who was inches taller, stood unmoving in front of Winter, the undamaged side of her dark face fixed in an expression of loathing, her eyes challenging.

Winter felt the other girl's hatred crash against her, washing over her in waves. She wanted to push the other girl aside, to slap that hateful expression off her face. How dare she speak to her like that? This deformed nobody that they had dragged across the Edge. She would have been dead if it hadn't been for them. And this was the gratitude she showed?

Winter narrowed her eyes. She stretched her fingers wide and felt heat flow from her hands up into her arms, her neck. That scar on Louisa's face. She could see inside the puckered skin, the spaces in between. The bits there, spinning slow, sluggish, not quite dead but not living tissue either. It was ugly. She was ugly. And she hated her. Her fingers were warm, a painful crackling at their tips.

"You don't know me! I *am* special!" she hissed.

Louisa blurred in front of her. Beneath that scar, where her jawbone should have been holding her face together, were jagged pieces of bone, pieces missing like an old puzzle. And they were spinning, spinning. Her tongue, that hateful tongue, spitting venom.

Louisa's expression changed, the bitter smile slipping into something like bewilderment. There was no sound in the garden now. The bees were silent, the wind still. Winter's skin felt singed with a fire she couldn't see. She smelled fire in her nose, heard nothing but the roaring in her ears.

She hated her. Louisa didn't know. She did have friends. How dare she? She was special and she would show her.

She tasted blood in her mouth, coppery like a penny. Louisa's terror.

And then the healer screamed, a low-pitched, guttural sound, and suddenly Mother Abigail's chickens flashed in Winter's head. The blood splattered across the pen. She had an image of Louisa torn apart like the little gray Easter Egger. Horrified, she spun away, wrapping her arms around herself.

"No," she cried.

Pain spiraled through the top of her head, an agonizing pain that left her breathless, staggered her. And in that very instant, Louisa was flung backward, as if slapped by a giant hand, the basket and its contents flying in an arc high over her head.

"No," moaned Winter again through gritted teeth.

She felt sick and bent, hands on knees, breathing hard, waiting for the heat, the feeling of everything spinning around her, to bleed off. Waiting to feel like herself. Louisa lay sprawled on the ground a few feet away.

"Louisa!" she whispered, hoarse.

Louisa jerked. Her eyes blazed in her damaged face. "You . . . you are a foul, unnatural thing . . . a . . . an abomination! You will never be Mother Abigail!" The girl scrambled to her feet and disappeared into the trees without another word.

Winter stared after her, her body still pulsating, hot.

Unnatural?

She threw back her head and screamed.

Louisa had called her unnatural. The word echoed in her head.

Was there anything natural in Remembrance?

She had wanted Louisa gone and the power had come, unbidden, rising up and catching fire inside her, as if it had a mind of its own. The desire, the need to see inside the spaces, to move them, nearly uncontrollable.

She could still feel that instant, that fraction of a moment when she'd had a sense of Louisa coming apart, of being ripped to pieces and shredded like Mother Abigail's chicken. Bile rose in her throat at the image, and she swallowed hard, forcing it down.

"I wouldn't have hurt her. Not really," she whispered. She took a shaky breath. "I just wanted her to shut up. I wouldn't have hurt her."

She closed her eyes. She would leave this place, run so far even Mother Abigail wouldn't find her. She wondered if Canada was like Ohio. She would live in a city. She had never seen a city. She tried to imagine a place where colored people were free to walk the streets with whites, where they could go to the market together. To real schools.

She would get a dress shop, with big windows made of actual glass to let in the sun. Ribbons and lace of every color would line the walls like a rainbow, and white women and colored women would come in together to have her make their fancy dresses. People would clamor for her beautiful things, the way they did for Louisa's honey. And she would be normal. Like everybody else.

There was rustling in the trees below her.

"Louisa?" She straightened.

Was she coming back up?

"Go on, now," she called. "Just leave it be, alright? Just go on and see what Mother Abigail wants."

She sighed; shame and fatigue crept up her spine. Even so, she would never apologize to Louisa. Never. Not after the vile things she'd said.

The rustling grew louder, seeming to be coming from the grove of buckeyes, downhill from the hives. Winter frowned. The only real way up to the summit was the path Louisa had just taken. Beyond the buckeyes and the hives was a rocky, murderously steep incline, nearly impossible to climb. Besides that, it was unlikely anyone would dare be around Louisa's bees without her permission. Winter moved warily toward the grove.

"Hello," she called softly. "Y'all better get on out of there. Louisa'll skin you alive if you mess with her bees."

There was no answer. She was about to call out again when she heard voices. Male voices. The accents strange and fluid. The hair on the back of her neck stood on end, and she froze where she stood. She'd heard voices that sounded like these just the week before. They were the voices of white men, the same kind of voices as that slave tracker.

There was more thrashing on the downhill side of the buckeye grove, and still she couldn't move. The voices faded in and out, sometimes seeming to come from just inside the shadow of the trees, then dropping to the faintest of whispers. Words came to her. Something about spineless preachers . . . about a horse. There was laughter followed by long silence.

For a moment, Winter thought she had imagined it. It was her nerves, her guilt over what had just happened with Louisa. It wasn't possible. Slavers in Remembrance? Again?

A shot rang out from beyond the trees. The paralysis that had locked her in place shattered, and with a cry, she whirled and raced down the path toward the settlement, oblivious to the sharp stones grinding into her bare feet or the branches tearing at her face.

There were white men in Remembrance!

25

Margot

She turned her back on Mother Abigail and Josiah and walked down the path toward the Central Fire, back straight, each step deliberate. The old woman had terrified her, they both had, but she would never let them see. She rounded a curve, out of sight of the cabin, and doubled over, gasping for breath.

What was this place? Who were these people? That man with his ghost eyes? That old woman?

Babalawa.

The word popped into her mind. A high priestess of vodun. The stories Grandmere told of a priestess that would come from across the ocean and free all the slaves. Who had the power to drive men mad and make them disappear where they stood.

At the thought of Grandmere, she sank to the ground with a sob. It had been a mistake. They should have stayed on that miserable farm in Kentucky. Maybe then Veronique would still be alive. Maybe the farmer would have kept them both together, even after his wife died. He would have needed even more help with his repellent litter of dim children, *oui*?

She covered her face with her hands, weeping softly.

"You alright?"

Margot looked up, startled. Two identical, dimpled, brown-sugar faces stared down at her. She swiped at her face and tried to smile.

"Yes," she said. "I am well, thank you."

The little girls exchanged a look.

"You're pretty. Where you come from?"

"New Orleans," she answered without thinking. It was at least the second time that day she'd been asked the question.

The girls seemed to be thinking this over.

"Is that far away?" asked one finally.

Margot nodded, matching her serious expression to theirs. "Yes," she said. "Very far."

The girls nodded solemnly.

"You are twins," said Margot. She felt foolish as soon as the words were out. Of course they were twins. They were like peas in a pod, impossible to tell apart. The sisters exchanged another look and rolled their eyes.

"Of course," said the twin that hadn't yet spoken.

"What's your name?" asked her sister.

"Margot. What is yours?"

"I'm Esther and this is Hannah. We're six."

Nervously, Margot brushed a strand of hair off her forehead. Children made her uneasy. She felt big and awkward around them, unsure of how to talk to them. Back home—in Louisiana, she corrected herself—she had treated the Hannigan children like smaller, occasionally cantankerous adults. She began to edge her way around the twins.

"You talk funny," said Hannah.

Margot stopped and looked down at the two small girls. "Do I?"

Two brown heads nodded in unison.

Margot smiled. "Where I . . . where I come from, everyone speaks like I do. Shall I teach you a little French?"

Hannah grinned.

"How old are you?" Esther interrupted.

"Esther!" admonished her sister. "That's rude."

Esther crossed her arms across her thin chest. "I don't understand why it *ain't* rude to ask where somebody from, but *is* rude to ask how old they are."

"You not supposed to ask grown-ups, that's all," muttered Hannah, sounding unsure.

"She ain't no grown-up," declared Esther peering intently up into Margot's face. "She just . . . bigger."

Margot laughed, startling herself. It was something Veronique might have said. The tightness uncoiled in her chest, and she inhaled deeply for the first time all day.

"I am twenty," she answered.

"Wanna see my doll?" asked Esther. She thrust something into Margot's hands. It was about the size of her hand and as thick around, carved into the general shape of a torso with a head—no arms, no legs—nothing like the fine porcelain dolls with their painted faces and silken hair that Catherine Hannigan had had shipped to her from Paris.

"Winter made her clothes," said Hannah proudly.

Margot had been about to hand the doll back, but at that, she pulled it close and examined it more thoroughly. The material was common, not silk or taffeta, but it had been pieced together cleverly and adorned with bright ribbon. The tiny stitches were expertly done, she noted with surprise, something she would not have expected from the excitable Winter. She nodded her approval and handed the doll back.

"*Elle est très belle*," said Margot. "She is very beautiful."

"No she ain't," said Esther sadly. "She just a big ol' hunk a' wood. But Momma say one day, she gonna get us a real live baby doll. With real hair. And a face."

Margot laughed again at the girl's honesty. She hoped that it was true.

"We can show you everything," said Esther. "Come on."

She opened her mouth to protest. She just wanted to get as far away from Mother Abigail and Josiah as she could. She wanted to find her shelter, curl up in a ball and hide. Until she could figure a way out. But the girls had already grabbed her hands, one on each side, and were dragging her down the trail. As they pulled her along, they pointed out all the important places in Remembrance.

"That's the baking house. They make bread there."

"Up that way is where they keep the cows."

"Everybody lives up there," said Esther. "Well, not you yet."

Margot followed her gaze and saw tiny cottages climbing neatly up the hillside like stair steps.

"And we learn out letters right by that tree. I can write my name."

Halfway down the trail, they ran across an old man screaming obscenities at a goat who brayed at him from the safety of the trees.

"That's Sir Galahad," said Hannah, giggling. "He's crazy for his goats. David Henry says he likes 'em better than people."

"David Henry?" asked Margot.

"He's nice," answered Hannah.

"Hannah loves him," said her sister.

"I do not," screamed Hannah.

"She wants to marry him when she grows up."

Hannah looked stricken, then grabbed for her sister, who went racing off down the trail screaming with delight, leaving Margot alone once again. She stood a long moment in the sudden quiet, pain throbbing dully in her chest, missing her own sister desperately. She blinked back the tears that were threatening to fall again and kept walking.

She came out into a wide open area, a circle of stones surrounding a massive firepit, sanded logs grouped together and clearly meant for sitting. The Central Fire. Winter had mentioned it and Margot vaguely remembered it from that first night. They'd given her something to drink here, soup she thought.

People milled about: stacking wood, peeling vegetables, raking debris from around the circle, coming and going from the many trails that fed into the open area by the Central Fire. They acknowledged her with a smile, a nod, but no one approached her. She leaned to peer into a pot that was steaming over one of the smaller fires. A giant hog's head floated in a broth. Bile rose in her throat and she backed away, pulling her cloak more tightly around her shoulders. The sun was bright but gave little warmth. She shivered. The old witch was right. She was weak. The muscles in her legs trembled and she ached with fatigue.

The old woman had wanted her to wait for Winter. To wait for the healer, but all Margot wanted to do was sleep. To dream of her grandmother, her sister. Of a place that made sense. She turned in a slow circle. All of the little trails looked the same.

She had just decided on one, hoping it would lead her back to the little shelter or perhaps to the healer she was to meet; just taken a few steps into the shadows, when a woman came bursting through the brush. She saw Margot standing in the middle of the trail and skittered to a stop, clutching a reed basket tightly to her chest.

The woman was frail looking, young, perhaps mid-twenties. But it was her face that seized Margot's attention. The right side was smooth, the color of milk chocolate, her eyes almond shaped. But the left side . . . the left side was a ruined horror, collapsed, the deep purple-hued scars running like melted wax from her hairline to the corner of her lips, twisting her features, distorting her mouth.

Mon Dieu!

Her own face burned in sympathy.

"Well?" snapped the girl.

Margot blinked and looked away in embarrassment, then, glancing at the basket of herbs, forced herself to meet the girl's eyes. "I was looking for the healer. Louisa?"

"What for?"

Margot flinched at the woman's sharp tone. "Mother . . . Abigail said she would have something . . ." She stopped. The girl was glaring at her, openly hostile.

Margot was both startled and amused by the girl's aggressive unfriendliness. She was like a badger that she and Veronique had once cornered near the Kentucky woman's henhouse. Biting her lip to hold back a smile, she asked, "You are she? You are Louisa?"

"Yes," said the girl after a long, narrow-eyed pause. "I'm Louisa."

"Mother Abigail sent me to you," Margot began again. "She said you would give me something for . . . strength."

Louisa sucked her teeth. "Course she did. Special requests. Something for strength," she grumbled. "Think I was back on the plantation, folks makin' demands. Well, come on then. Can't make it standin' here, can I?"

Margot stepped aside to allow the herbalist to pass. "My name is Margot," she said to Louisa's back. The other girl did not respond. This healer was a curiosity to her but she held her tongue. She doubted that the cantankerous girl would answer any questions anyway. As they stepped back into the clearing, Louisa flicked a hand toward the Central Fire.

"Go. Wait over there. It'll take a bit to mix up something. Not like I got nothin' else to do. Might as well be warm while you wait."

There was a sudden commotion behind them. Margot turned in time to see Winter careening from the trees, her face wild, her headdress undone. They locked eyes and then she was on her, pulling at her, her eyes crazed.

"Mother Abigail? Where is she?"

"I don't . . ." Margot shook her off. "What is it?"

She took a deep breath, but it was too late. Winter's fear had already begun to infect her. From the corner of her eye she saw the other settlers edging closer.

"What is it?" she asked again.

Winter shook her head, as if whatever it was was too terrible to put into words. She spun away and dashed toward the cottages. Margot looked uneasily toward the woods that she'd just exited but saw nothing.

She found herself following Winter as the girl wove frantically among the cottages searching for Mother Abigail.

The old priestess was coming down the slope from the highlands, laughing softly at something Josiah was saying into her ear. Her face froze as her frenzied charge skidded to a stop in front of her. A young couple walking nearby turned to stare.

"Child, what . . . ?" Mother Abigail began.

For a moment, Winter said nothing. She stood gulping mouthfuls of air, one hand clutching the priestess's cloak, the other pulling nervously at her hair. Finally, turning her back against the staring couple, she spoke.

"Pattyrollers!" she gasped, her voice strangled. "In Louisa's garden."

Pattyrollers?

Margot frowned. For a moment, she couldn't place the word, and then she remembered. It was what some of the slaves called the slave hunters. Her blood turned to ice. The shocked expression of the others around them told her that they'd heard it too.

Around her, the world had gone silent. Time slowed, oozing around her like cooling molasses, images coming to her in fragments: Louisa's basket falling to the ground, Mother Abigail's frowning confusion. And the old man, Josiah, his face as bland as milk, smiling gently, as if he hadn't understood the words Winter said. That night at the mulberry, the sickly farrier had said she would be safe here in this place. Winter had said it as well, and the old woman. They all said it.

A lie! It was all a lie! Nowhere was safe! All this, everything has been for nothing!

Sound slowly seeped back into Remembrance as time caught up with itself.

"What you sayin', girl?" hissed Mother Abigail, grabbing one of Winter's flailing hands. "No white mens in Remembrance! *Silans kounye a!* Hush now! That is impossible!"

The priestess's touch seemed to gather the girl. "I heard them," she cried. "White voices. Up in the gardens. Just now." Her voice shook.

"Liar!" snarled Louisa. "Ain't nobody up there. I just came from up that way. How any white men gon' get in Remembrance in the first place? And if they did, how they gon' get way up there without makin' a big ol' ruckus. Don't nobody come in my gardens."

The priestess sliced an impatient hand through the air, silencing her, then pulled Winter into a space between the cottages, out of earshot, Josiah close behind. This time, Margot did not follow.

"Lies," Louisa said aloud. "All of it."

She shot Winter a withering look, then bent to pick up her fallen herbs. Margot smelled the terror lurking just beneath the girl's anger. She stood there, uncertain of what to do. Go back to her shelter? Wait by the Central Fire? She wanted to run: as far and as fast as she could. It didn't matter where. All this, and Veronique had died for nothing. She rubbed a thumb over the bridge of her nose.

Margot looked around. A young couple stood with their heads

together, vigorously whispering. The man's hands waved about in agitation. People were milling about the fire, looking up to where Mother Abigail had disappeared among the cabins. A restless murmur filled the area.

Louisa had disappeared and there was no sign of Winter, Mother Abigail, or Josiah. She ground her teeth. There was a phrase her grandmother had said many times when things sometimes seemed to go from bad to worse. Margot whispered it now under her breath.

"*De la pot dans le feu*. From the pan into the fire."

26

Mother Abigail

She'd sent them all away so she could think—except that she'd been standing in the exact same spot at the trailhead for an eternity without a single useful thought. Winter's words had struck her in the face like the flat side of an ax. The girl had said the same words over and over, though the priestess had needed only to hear them the once: white men in Remembrance. The only reason Mother Abigail remained silent was because so many conflicting emotions—rage, fear, disbelief—had seized up her tongue.

She'd sent them away, Winter and Josiah, everyone. She needed to be alone. It felt as if those terrible words had rubbed the very skin off her body, exposing the nerves underneath.

The girl had wanted to charge back up the hill to the gardens, to confront the white demons that dared invade Remembrance. And do what? the priestess wondered. Demand that they leave? Snatch them down from their horses and hold them hostage?

It is what they would have done if they'd found the slavers, but she'd sent two men back up to Louisa's gardens and they'd found . . . nothing. But the priestess had no doubts about what Winter had heard. It was slipping away from her; each day it grew harder and harder for her to find the seams running through space. Even that moment with Margot in the dooryard, something that should have required no more effort, no more thought than flicking a mosquito, had left her feeling drained.

She closed her eyes. The barrier between them and Outside was still there, but it was weakening, *she* was weakening. She felt it like an ache in her gut.

The Edge.

Her creation.

Those years of studying the Art had opened a place in her brain where her boundless rage, her hate, could be turned into the power to manipulate space. She had made this place. A sanctuary. This one thing they could never take from her. But now . . .

The slavers were not in Remembrance. Not now. Not yet. But they were coming. She could feel it, and even so, she could not rouse herself to action. She stood shivering at the head of the trail leading up into the gardens and moaned. Time was a slim thread running before her, and it was running out.

She needed to . . .

She shook her head, trying to clear it. She didn't know what she needed to do.

A branch snapped in the shadows.

"Who's there?" she cried, wincing at how old, how frightened she sounded.

"Who's there?" she called again, forcing the quiver from her voice.

"Just me, Mother Abigail."

A young man stepped from the cover of the trees and she relaxed.

"What you be doin' out here, David Henry?" she asked.

"Josiah asked me to bring you something to eat." He held a cloth-covered bowl out to her and looked up at the gray sky. "Look like snow comin'."

The priestess glanced up without comment. Her hands shook as she took the bowl and lifted the cloth. The sweet smell of corn chowder wafted up, and her stomach growled in appreciation. She thanked him and eased herself to the cold ground to eat. When he didn't turn to leave, she rested the bowl in her lap and examined him.

David Henry was what Josiah called "an invisible Negro": average height, average weight, skin just a nondescript average brown. He was one of the few who'd chosen not to share his before story, though the thick scars crisscrossing his back told them most of what they needed to know.

Remembrance had come to depend on his quiet, cheerful strength. She had come to depend on it. And when he had his "spells," disappearing into the woods for days, only to return near mute and wild-eyed, Remembrance gathered around him, holding him, until his demons went back to sleep.

He stood now, watching her quietly, his skin glowing reddish in the late-afternoon light. He was holding a rifle. He had been one of the two men that had gone in search of the slavers near the hives.

"What you got, David Henry?"

He smiled but said nothing, his eyes never leaving hers.

"So you think Remembrance be needin' protection with a gun now?" she asked.

He ran a hand lightly along the gun's barrel. "There's protection and then there's caution." He smiled and cocked his head. "And a man can't never have too much a' either."

She nodded and studied him a moment. "What you hear, David Henry?"

He shrugged and stared up the darkening path toward the gardens. "Just things on the wind."

Still watching him, she slurped her chowder, savoring the crisp cracklin' between her teeth.

The young man turned and gazed off into the distance, his back straight. "Mother Abigail, Remembrance be my home. It be the place I born as a true man."

He stopped and took a deep breath. She nodded again and waited for him to go on.

"If I gon' have to die," he said, "then it's gon' be here in Remembrance. For Remembrance . . . dyin' as a man should die, protectin' his own."

"So that what you be hearin' then? Dyin' talk, David Henry?"

He looked at her and she saw a dangerous, simmering anger behind his smile. "Whenever you got white mens lurkin' in the shadows hopin' to catch nigras, 'specially nigras with no intention of cooperatin'," he said, "somebody's bound to die."

Mother Abigail felt a chill. Were the *loa* speaking a warning through this man? For just a moment, the world tilted on itself, blurring her vision.

"Don't understand much a this mumble jumble about Remembrance, how it come to be and such. How it works," he went on. "Don't much matter, anyhow. Remembrance's real. That's all I got to know. It's real and it's mine. And if the white folks ain't here now, it just be a matter a' time. Always is."

His brown hand caressed the gun.

"It ain't like I don't believe in you, Mother Abigail. Nothin' like that." He chuckled, a pleasant, rumbling sound. "It's just like I say. There's protection and then there's caution."

"Well . . . ," she said. The world righted itself again. "That . . . sounds most sensible, David Henry."

He peered at her intently, his face deadly serious again. "What you gonna do, Mother Abigail?"

The old woman grinned at him. The shaking in her hands had slowed a bit. "Well, *jenn gason,* right now, I'm fixin' to eat me the rest of this fine chowder."

The sun was barely peeking over the trees when she arrived at the clearing the next morning. Josiah was already there, slumped against the hollow tree, smoking his pipe. Winter squatted several yards away, her face closed. The priestess frowned, looking from one to the other, sensing the hum of anger in the air. Josiah blew fragrant smoke into the morning air. He nodded as she stepped clear of the trees. "Abigail," he said mildly. Winter just stared.

She stopped a few feet from them and gazed across the yellowed grass. The air sparkled in the predawn crystalline fog, turning ordinary trees and shrubs into magical creatures. David Henry was right. An early snow was on the wind.

The priestess peered at Winter. "Most days have to near 'bout set

you afire to get you out of bed. But today you be out in the freezin'
cold and the day barely broken," she said dryly.

Winter shot a look at Josiah. "Couldn't sleep."

"Mmmm," replied Mother Abigail, one eyebrow raised.

She cut her eyes at Josiah. "And you couldn't sleep either, old man?"

He chuckled and blew another plume of smoke into the frigid air.
"Abigail, you know I ain't slept in nigh on sixty years. Too much happenin' in the world."

"*Wi*, always."

"Mother Abigail? What about the slavers, the pattyrollers I heard?"

The priestess turned to Winter. Absently licking her thumb, she
smoothed a stray lock of Winter's hair. The girl half-heartedly batted
her hand away.

"Mother Abigail?"

The old priestess sighed and pulled her hands inside her cloak to
hide them. The shakes had come back. And the pains in her head.
Thoughts came to her like fireflies, flickering for a moment, then disappearing. She heard the sound of carriage wheels on the cobblestone
street and dug her nails into her palms.

She tried to smile, to reassure the girl. "They not here, *petite*."

"I wasn't lying. I heard them!"

The priestess held up a hand. "I know child. You heard them. But
they not here."

Winter frowned. "I don't . . ."

Mother Abigail felt Josiah watching her. Her head swam and she
ground her teeth. Winter sat uncommonly still, waiting.

"The Edge," she pressed on. "It . . . weak. That why you heard them.
But they still Outside."

"What?" Winter leaped to her feet. "What do you mean 'weak'?
What does that mean?"

Mother Abigail closed her eyes, opened them again. "Things change
always, child," she said, forcing her voice to stay calm. "The Edge . . .
been around a long time. It just wearin' down a bit. Like me."

Winter stared at her, eyes wide in shock. "Can they . . . ?" She took a
deep breath. "Can they get in here?"

Josiah, still slumped at the base of the hollow tree, puffed quietly on his pipe. Though he said nothing, she sensed something in him, a heightened vigilance . . . and something darker.

"No!" Mother Abigail swallowed, the word sticking in her throat.

"You can fix it?"

The priestess looked away, fighting that peculiar sense of falling, of drifting off the world's edge.

An image of David Henry with his gun popped into her head and she pushed it away. Of course she would fix it. She had made it, hadn't she?

"*Wi, petite.* I can fix it."

"Abigail." Josiah got to his feet with an ease that defied his years.

She waited.

"Let's walk, old woman," he said. "You wait here, girl."

He hooked an arm through Mother Abigail's, and she let him lead her into the clearing.

"Makin' promises you not sure you can keep, Abigail?" he said when they were out of earshot of Winter. "Lyin' to the girl."

She whirled on him. "That the second time you call me a liar, Josiah!"

She turned her back to him. There was a fluttering in her gut, faint but there, an echo of the day Zeus had appeared in Remembrance with his slaver.

"Abigail!"

She started and realized that Josiah had been talking to her the whole time. She frowned. "What?" she asked irritably. "What you tryin' to say to me?"

He was standing in front of her. Those strange, dull eyes that should not have been able to see and yet missed nothing locked onto hers, and she felt the familiar rumble in her soul as she sensed the quiet force within him. She knew their relationship confused the others. He was not just her friend. It was more complicated than that. They fed off each other, back and forth, trading strength and knowledge. By now, after all these years, in some way they were nearly one creature. She was weakening and he knew it. Her weakness weakened him.

"What?" she asked again, impatient.

He hesitated. He was afraid, too. She saw that now and dread washed over her.

"How long we been here, Abigail? How long Remembrance been?"

The priestess glanced over her shoulder. Winter was standing near the hollow tree, her thin arms wrapped around herself, watching them.

"Near to a lifetime," she answered. The world spun and she closed her eyes, trying to concentrate, the uneasiness in her gut stronger.

"We got led to this place, Abigail. We got led here 'cause you was special. You was touched by the gods, chose 'cause you got a gift. You made this place. Saved lives needed savin'. Kept us safe . . . but . . ."

"But what?" She could barely get the words past her throat.

He sighed. "But maybe Remembrance done reached its natural life. Maybe you not meant to fix it. Maybe this ain't no longer the way."

"No!" cried Mother Abigail. She glared at him. "No," she said, chopping at the air with her hand.

"Abigail, you . . ." He stopped, then tried again. "They's signs everywhere. Listen to the spirits. They talkin' to you through that. What they tryin' to say?"

"The spirits got nothin' to say to me. Nothin'. I need nothin' from them," she snapped. "I did this."

The old man was silent.

"You sayin' you don't believe Remembrance still our purpose?" she asked. "What to do then, old man? Let Remembrance die? Walk away? We got near two hundred souls that give everything to find their freedom here. Everything! And what we tell them then? Where they got to go? Where *we* go? Out in the world? Out there?"

Josiah shook his head. "I am sayin' we might have to think on somethin' else . . . some other way. Be ready if . . . if you not strong enough to make the Edge right again. Everybody . . . everything serves a purpose. But it not always the same one forever. And we need to be ready."

The world lurched—hard. And her mouth filled with hot saliva. She swallowed, then swallowed again.

"Nothin' else to think on, Josiah!" Her voice was raw. "*Anyen!* Nothing on the other side for us but blood and sorrow! Won't never live in that world again! Never! I'll fix the Edge. I made it! I fix it!"

"That is pride speakin', old woman, not good sense! Back away! Just for a bit! Talk to the spirits. Maybe you meant to do somethin' else. Think on some what-ifs. Pray. . . ."

"The Edge is my concern," snapped Mother Abigail, interrupting him. "Those two hundred souls back there? They belong to me."

Josiah stiffened.

"Your concern?" His tone was incredulous. "Belong? You they master now, Abigail?"

She stood silently raging, breathing hard until finally he stepped aside, giving an exaggerated bow. "Then go. Go and fix *your* Edge. We be quiet as can be, boss."

Mother Abigail gave him a fierce look. She felt Winter's worried gaze on her back. Her palm itched to slap Josiah's face, to replace her growing panic with action, any action.

"It is mine to fix, old man," she hissed through gritted teeth.

"Pride can rot a body's insides," he said tightly. "Pride can get a body killed."

She turned her back and stomped into the clearing.

Ase! Moun sot! Fool!

She was trembling. Josiah's words had spooked her. But it was impossible! Remembrance would never end. It was all she had. All she was.

The Edge was everywhere, surrounding them like the skin of a soap bubble. It had been here, on this very spot, that she had driven herself to the limits of her mind, forcing herself to near collapse as she bent space to her purpose. This place had spoken to her. Spoken to them both. Soft and green, the hills rolling out as far as the eye could see. So different from New Orleans, so quiet. And then they met the Quakers. Watched them hide people who looked like her and Josiah from other *blancs*, and she knew that if there was any place on earth for her, that it was here. With Josiah at her side.

Even all these years later, she remembered how it felt to be so strong, so full of energy, as if she were a star fallen to earth, and her hands, her eyes, her mind were nothing but pure white light and power.

Remembrance was her revenge. Each soul she helped escape was one more she stole from the *blancs*.

Josiah's words echoed in her ears: "Pride can get a body killed."

Mother Abigail moaned.

I am Remembrance! Remembrance is me! Not pride! Truth!

She moved slowly along the tree line, straining to hear. The discomfort in her belly had not changed, and she allowed herself to hope, just for a moment, that everything would be alright. The brittle grass crunched under her feet as she peered into the shadows. She shot a quick look behind her. Winter and the old man were watching her—being quiet. She clenched her jaw.

Horses!

Her head snapped up. She heard horses!

Something contracted inside her, a spasm so severe that her bladder gave way, hot urine pouring down her legs.

It was gone!

The Edge had collapsed.

She spun about wildly. There were only the three of them in the clearing, but the sound of hoofbeats was nearly deafening—more than one rider, moving fast. Pain shot through the back of her head and she faltered. From the corner of one eye she saw Winter step away from the hollow tree, into the clearing.

The priestess staggered.

Go! Go back, now! But the warning was only in her mind. Her voice no longer obeyed her!

The trees shifted before her eyes and she saw blue sky, a mountain covered in green flowing down to an even bluer ocean. She tasted blood, felt something give way inside her head.

Then they were there!

The horsemen!

Five white men on horseback roared from the trees, crashing through the giant mulberry, shouting, churning up the muddy ground. The lead rider saw her, pulled up hard, nearly toppling his horse. She heard cursing, the screaming of the horses, but the pain in her head—such pain—made every thought lunacy. She smelled colors, tasted sounds!

I am Babalawa! You cannot enter here.

Suddenly Winter was at her side, pulling at her, saying something to her. The priestess tried to answer, but her words were nonsense, even to her own ears. She was on her knees. So hard to think. So hard to see. There were men on horses everywhere, and colored men with guns.

David Henry? Josiah? No, that couldn't be right. No one needed guns in Remembrance. She was all the protection they needed.

"Mother Abigail, get up! Get up now!"

The pretty little girl pulling at her looked familiar. And so afraid! She smiled and reached for the girl's face. Alright. It was going to be alright, *petit*.

"Mother Abigail!"

That's not my name, the priestess wanted to tell her. I have another name from long ago, from when I was younger even than you.

Kianga! That my name. It means "sunshine."

"Winter?" said Mother Abigail. "What . . . ?"

"They're here!" screamed the girl. "They're inside Remembrance. You have to fix it! You have to fix the Edge! You have to close it!"

The Edge was gone! And Remembrance was open to the world. She remembered now. She had to close it again, had to hide Remembrance from the Outside. She struggled to get to her feet, but even with Winter's help, couldn't manage.

She heard gunfire and screams and she realized hazily that David Henry was not the only black man in the clearing with a gun.

Josiah! Where was Josiah?

She closed her mind against the noise, tried to focus, tried to see the spaces between worlds. Beneath her, the earth quivered and she felt the familiar slide.

Relief.

And then . . . it was gone, replaced again by that fierce agony in her head. She bit back a scream.

"Winter," she gasped. She could feel the girl gripping her hand, but the world had gone black. "Help me, child."

The girl moved behind her, wrapping her skinny arms around the priestess's waist, and with the last of her strength, Mother Abigail focused once more. Her head, her eyes, were on fire. She gasped as her power met Winter's. The Edge bowed out, rippling around them, through them, then sealed itself off.

Remembrance was safe.

The old woman collapsed in blackness onto the cold ground. She never heard Josiah's curses or Winter's screams. Never felt the thin arms ripped away.

27

Winter

When Josiah appeared at the door to her cottage, hours before sunrise, Winter had asked no questions, simply followed him into the dark woods. She'd have gone mad anyway if she'd stayed in that cabin alone with her thoughts a second longer. She didn't know where they were going or why, but anything was better than staring up into the darkness, waiting for something to happen, someone to do something.

With only a tiny lantern for light, they made their way to the edge of the small clearing marked on one side by the hollowed-out oak tree and on the other by the massive mulberry bush, the same clearing where, days before, dogs had come racing out of the moonlight to tear her and Margot to pieces.

At the hollow tree, Josiah dropped to the ground and pulled a pipe from his jacket pocket. He tapped out the ash, refilled, then lit it. He gave a grunt of pleasure as he inhaled. Winter waited for him to speak, waited for him to explain why they'd slipped away from the settlement before dawn and come here, but he silently smoked his pipe and gazed sightlessly across the clearing, almost as if he'd forgotten she was there. She looked around. Everything—the drying grass, the tree limbs—was covered in a glaze of frost and twinkled in the half-light. A translucent fog hovered just above the ground, throwing odd shadows everywhere. She'd come to this place countless times in her eighteen years—it was here that Mother Abigail had found her as an infant, just past the mulberry—but on this early morning, the place felt foreign, frightening.

Something rustled in the brush and she inhaled sharply, but it was only a possum and its mate. She swallowed, forcing down her nerves.

"Josiah?" she whispered. "What are we doing out here?"

"Waiting," came the reply.

"What," she asked as calmly as she could manage, ". . . are we waiting for?"

"For Abigail."

Winter frowned. They were alone. "Well . . . where is she?"

"She'll be 'round directly."

"Why didn't we all just come out here together?"

"Cause we ain't together."

The hair stood up on the back of her neck. She shook her head, confused. What did that mean? Why couldn't he just speak plainly for once?

"What about the pattyrollers, Josiah?" she said through clenched teeth. "You think they'll come this way? Is that why we're here?"

He puffed on his pipe, not answering. With a grunt of irritation, she made to stand. His hand shot out and locked around her wrist, and she cried out as he pulled her back down, hard, beside him. She could smell the cherry tobacco from his pipe.

"Just sit a while, child. Quiet your mind."

Winter lurched forward so that her face was only inches from the old man's. His flat, gray-white eyes seemed to absorb the little light there was.

"What are we doing here, Josiah?" she hissed again. "Something's wrong, isn't it? That's why we're here? Because something's wrong? Where is Mother Abigail?"

The old man stared at her, unblinking, and her breath caught in her throat. She felt his anger coming at her and she flinched, trying to back away. She couldn't move.

"She lost her faith," he said. "But me and Simona, we showed her. What she was. What she could do. That she was strong."

He closed his eyes. "They took our women and Abigail got strong. They took our children and she got stronger. They took our manhood. . . ."

He opened his eyes and Winter saw an expression she'd never seen before. A chill snaked down her spine.

"And when she got strong enough," he went on, "not even as strong as she would get, but strong enough, we took our revenge." He laughed and the sound made her stomach clench. She tasted bile.

"They came to us to cure their sickness, but we made it so they couldn't make no more babies," he went on. "Made their businesses fail, their houses catch afire. The whites? They never knew. Called 'em Acts of God."

He laughed again. "But only if Abigail was a god."

Winter tried once again to pull away, but he tightened his grip and she felt her bones grind against each other.

"But then the others, those out on the plantations, fought back, too. And the whites chopped them into little pieces, burned 'em up like they was hogs in the street. It broke her. She lost her faith. She didn't want nothin' else in this world. Except a place. This place. Remembrance. And then you. And you weren't never worthy."

Winter gasped. The old man leaned into her, his hatred unmistakable.

It suddenly felt as if he were reaching inside her, gripping her heart in his fist. She could see it, feel it, though Josiah had barely moved a muscle. It didn't hurt, not quite, but there was a feeling in her chest, heavy, unpleasant, and the sound of her heart was loud in her ears. He squeezed and it beat slower and slower still. She reared back as far as she could.

"You don't have a smidge of her power. She wanted this for you. And I . . ." He grunted and waved his arm, indicating all of Remembrance.

"But you lazy. Got no understanding a' nothin'. Of what this is. What you got. She gave you love but love ain't shit!"

He smiled. And then he released her.

Winter scuttled away, gasping for breath, shivering as she gulped in the icy air.

Across the clearing, the priestess was barely visible. The fog had lifted a bit but a brittle haze still shrouded everything. "Stay here," Josiah had commanded, and then he and Mother Abigail had walked away across the grass together.

They had argued. Winter couldn't hear their words but she saw Josiah stiffen, felt the world quiver with his anger, even from a distance. She saw him bow, a gesture she didn't understand, then saw Mother Abigail stalk off into the shadows past the massive mulberry. She was there still, stomping along the boundary to the forest on the other side of the clearing. Josiah stood in the clearing, halfway between Winter and the priestess. Tears rolled unheeded down Winter's face. In one terrible night, her world had turned inside out.

Unworthy!

Josiah had spit the word in her face. Had looked at her with such hatred. And the Edge? Mother Abigail said something was wrong with the Edge. Winter thought she might vomit.

She watched as Mother Abigail strode back and forth, hands out, as if feeling currents in the air. She was talking to herself . . . or to the spirits. Winter could see her lips moving but she was too far away to make out any words.

How could the priestess have ever thought she, Winter, could control the Edge? That she could protect Remembrance?

She yanked nervously at a lock of hair, vainly trying to untangle it. Finally, giving up, she wrapped her arms tightly across her chest. She was cold and she was scared.

Suddenly, the priestess stopped. Standing rigid, her head whipped wildly about as if tracking something only she could see.

Mother Abigail suddenly whirled toward her. Their eyes met and Winter leaped to her feet, stepping into the clearing toward her.

What was it? What was happening?

As if in slow motion, she saw Josiah's pipe fall from his hand, saw Mother Abigail crumple soundlessly to the ground.

A loud *FOOMP* filled the clearing, the sound of gas igniting, and Winter froze as the clearing filled with men on horseback. White men on horseback.

The screams, from men and horses, were deafening. A horseman with pale skin and dark hair wheeled sharply in front of her. Icy mud from the horse's hooves peppered her face, breaking the spell that locked her in place, and she dashed toward the center of the clearing.

For a moment, she lost sight of both Mother Abigail and Josiah but ran in the direction of the old mulberry, ducking away from grasping hands, dodging flying hooves. Something struck her hard in the back, nearly throwing her off-balance, but she kept going, not even turning to see.

There, at the base of the mulberry, was the old priestess. She was half kneeling, as if she'd tried but failed to get to her feet. Winter slid into her, nearly toppling her.

"Mother Abigail! Get up! Get up now!"

The old woman looked at her and smiled vaguely. She was speaking, but the words were garbled, gibberish. Then the priestess turned her face up to the sky and laughed.

"Mother Abigail," screamed Winter. "You have to get up. They're here! They're inside Remembrance! Get up! The Edge! You have to fix the Edge!"

"Winter?"

The girl wrapped her arms around Mother Abigail and tried to pull her up, but the priestess was dead weight.

Oh, Jesus! Oh, sweet Jesus!

A gun blast exploded near her ear and she screamed, tightening her grip on Mother Abigail. Through her tears, she thought she saw David Henry and Thomas, the blacksmith, charging from the trees, followed by a handful of settlers, all heading straight for the horsemen.

"Winter?"

Winter looked down. Mother Abigail's eyes had cleared.

"You have to help me, *ti m*."

"What?" she cried. "What do you want me to do?"

And then she knew. All the days of standing in the woods, Mother Abigail exhorting her to "focus." It had been training, preparation, for this, for Remembrance.

She locked her arms tightly around the priestess and closed her eyes. She tried to block out everything, everything except getting back inside Remembrance and closing the Edge behind them. She felt heat flow from Mother Abigail's hands into hers. Sounds—the shrieking animals, the cursing men—faded away and the ground heaved slightly beneath them.

The chaos faded and she was falling, not into silence, but into the spaces between sounds. The Edge. It was back. For a brief moment, she felt it all around them, like a low hum against her skin. Then Mother Abigail went limp in her arms and it was gone again.

Winter was seized from behind and yanked hard upward. Her feet dangled awkwardly off the ground. From the corner of her eye she saw the hand of the man who had grabbed her, dark hair covering dirty white knuckles, knuckles the color of maggots. She tried to scream, but her cloak, gripped in her captor's fist, twisted tighter and tighter around her neck, choking off her breath.

"Winter!"

David Henry appeared as if out of thin air. Wild-eyed, bleeding from a cut on his forehead, he swung the butt of his rifle at the man holding her. For just a second the slaver's grip loosened and she tore free, dropping to the ground. Scrambling to her feet, she spun to find David Henry facing off with the tall, barrel-shaped white man whose head and face were covered in the same greasy black hair as his hands.

"David Henry?"

David Henry didn't answer. His eyes never left the slaver who was now circling him, his face contorted in rage. Around them, a dozen black men were fighting the slavers with guns, with clubs, with their bare hands. Josiah, older by decades than every other man in the clearing, stood before one slaver and his horse. He threw out one hand and the horse collapsed, trapping its rider beneath. Somewhere, someone was screaming.

"Run, Winter! Run and warn folks!" cried David Henry.

Her head swung violently around, trying to take in what was happening, trying to make sense of it. She needed David Henry to come with her. She needed someone to help her get Mother Abigail back to the settlement. She hesitated, torn.

Was that her? Was she screaming?

Her mouth snapped shut and she spun toward the path leading up to the settlement.

This time she saw the man. Thin and malnourished, the slaver materialized from behind the hollow tree, where a million years ago she'd sat shivering next to Josiah. She tried to sidestep him, but he was too fast. He grabbed her arm, pulling her against him. His shirt was damp with sweat, and she could smell the stink of him, the hint of something rotten. She thought of the fat man fighting David Henry, and a hysterical laugh escaped her lips, startling the white man. He pulled his face back to look at her, and with a snarl she launched herself at him, clawing his eyes, scratching his face and neck, biting wherever skin was exposed.

Cursing, he struggled to hold on to her. He grabbed a fistful of hair and threw her down, knocking the wind from her lungs. She sprawled on the ground gasping.

For a moment, she felt the earth pulsing beneath her, trying to speak to her. And she tried to listen, struggled to bring her terror under control so she could hear it clearly, but she was lost in the cacophony of screams and curses and gunfire saturating the air around her.

The thin slaver raised his fist, and she saw hate and hunger in his ice-blue eyes. Her last thought before the fist crashed into her face and her whole world went black was of Mother Abigail's Easter Egger.

28

Margot

She knew she was dreaming again, in that odd broken way that people have of knowing that what they're seeing and hearing and smelling is not real, not quite. But even knowing it was a dream, Margot smiled.

She was in the washhouse. Grandmere was standing over the metal washtub, steam from the water making her dark face glow in the morning sunlight. The aroma of powdered sugar and chicory for the breakfast coffee drifted from the kitchen, competing with the smells of lavender and strong lye soap rising from the laundry. Margot heard a noise behind her and turned to find Veronique standing in the door, her eyes still slitted from sleep, creases from the sheets imprinted on her cheek.

Margot reached for her sister, but Veronique didn't move, simply squinted blearily at her through sleepy eyes.

"Help," said Veronique, her voice flat.

Margot's dream-self frowned. "*Que?* You need help?" she asked her sister in French.

Veronique shook her head slowly from side to side. "Help," she said again in the same lifeless voice.

"I don't understand, *chérie*," cried Margot.

From outside the washhouse came the sound of running, shouting— chaos.

Margot turned back toward her grandmother. The old woman stood calmly stirring clothes with a paddle. Veronique stared at her, unblinking. Margot stepped toward her sister but, in that peculiar way of dreams, found that no matter how she tried, she could not get closer.

"Veronique!

"Help," was all the little girl said again. And then she smiled.

The shouting outside the wash shed grew louder. Margot thought she heard someone crying. Veronique turned to the sound and began to move toward it.

No! Not yet!

Over her shoulder, Veronique smiled at her again, her familiar, one-dimpled smile, and then she was gone.

The sound of gunfire propelled Margot up. Crawling out of the tiny log shelter, she stood swaying in the cold, confused for a moment. She heard another shot and jerked. That part hadn't been a dream. Grabbing her cloak, she dashed up the short trail toward the center of the settlement.

Remembrance was pandemonium.

Some people ran around willy-nilly, others stood murmuring in small panicked groups. She was shocked by the number of people, and it struck her then that she had no real idea how big Remembrance actually was. Searching for a familiar face amid the chaos, her eyes fell on two identical little heads peeking up from behind a woodpile. She threw her cloak around her shoulders and hurried toward them. At her approach, the twins looked up, their eyes wide with terror. They clung, trembling, to each other.

"What is it?" she asked, dropping down beside them. "What is happening?"

"We don't know," said Esther. "We heard screaming. It woke us up."

"We can't find Momma," whispered her sister. Tears had traced gray tracks down her round cheeks.

Margot looked out from behind the woodpile. More people were milling around the Central Fire, quieter now, panic slowly giving way to confusion. She could smell the crowd's bewilderment.

She turned her attention back to the frightened girls. "Where do you live?"

Esther pointed to a neat cabin at the foot of the hill leading up into the highlands. Red curtains flapped from an open window.

"Go there," commanded Margot. "Close the door. Your *maman* will come and find you soon, *oui?*"

She stood. She needed to find out what was happening.

Winter.

If she could find Winter, surely *she* could tell her what had happened. But before she could move away, Hannah grabbed hold of her skirt, whimpering. Margot leaned over and softly touched her head.

"It will be fine, *chérie,*" she said, though she wasn't sure of that at all. "But your mama will be looking for you. You must go where she can find you easily."

Gently, she pried the girl's hand from her skirt and pointed her toward the cabin. "Hide," she said. "Stay as quiet as you can. Do not come out until someone . . . someone you know comes for you. You understand this, yes?"

She looked at Esther as she said this. Nodding, Esther grabbed her sister's hand and began to pull her toward their cabin. Though her lips were trembling, her eyes were dry. Margot smiled, admiring the little girl's spirit.

Stepping from the dubious cover of the woodpile, she scanned the scene before her. An eerie half-silence had fallen over Remembrance. A group of women stood huddled on the far side of the Central Fire. One woman cradled another who appeared to have fainted.

Margot's throat tightened. There was blood in the air. She could taste the sharp, metallic bite of it on her tongue. Swiveling her head slowly, she searched for it, sniffing at the cold air. There! She caught the scent and moved warily toward it, even as her every fiber screamed *NO!*

There were four of them, crouched in the shadow of a tree halfway up the trail that led from the mulberry clearing. The blood smell was overwhelming. She clenched her teeth as her mouth filled with hot saliva. One of the men whirled, his gun leveled at her heart, and she staggered back, hands out. She thought she recognized him, a medium-brown-skinned man, a half head shorter than she was. He was bleeding from a head wound, but she sensed his injuries were not serious.

"David Henry?" The name came to her in the very moment that she spoke it. The man little Hannah wanted to marry when she grew up. She almost smiled.

"What has happened?" she asked.

David Henry lowered the gun slightly but his face was rigid with tension. "Pattyrollers," he said, spitting out the word. "Pattyrollers got into Remembrance somehow. Took Winter!"

There was a roaring in her ears and Margot moaned. "Safe" the farrier had said that night he'd brought her here. "You be safe with Mother Abigail."

Suddenly, she became aware of another smell, worse than blood, more malignant. David Henry followed her eyes, his face stone.

"Thomas," he said.

She crouched beside the mortally wounded blacksmith. His companions tensed but made no move to stop her. Thomas lay on his back, his blue shirt and overalls turned black with blood, his intestines spilled out onto the damp leaves like new sausages. His eyes were open but he stared unseeing at the pieces of gray sky peeking through the treetops.

"He got gut-shot tryin' to protect Mother Abigail," said David Henry behind her. His voice was flat, emotionless. "First one out. Tried to take that pattyroller down with his bare hands. Woulda torn that cracker to pieces if he hadn'a gotten blasted."

Her head felt heavy on her neck, as if it might shatter with too quick a movement. David Henry's words registered in her mind finally, and she turned to look at him.

"Protect Mother Abigail?"

The most desperate of slavers would not take an ancient slave woman like the priestess back south. She would not be worth the food wasted to keep her alive that long, even she knew that. David Henry was silent.

"Somethin' happened to her out there by the mulberry," said the man nearest her. He drew each breath in as if it was fire, and she knew without even touching him that several of his ribs were broken.

"They took her?" asked Margot.

The man shook his head, winced. "No. They didn't touch her. Least-ways, not that I saw. Was a slaver near abouts, but she just . . . fell out. Then Thomas . . ." His shoulders sagged and he looked away.

"And Winter was with her?"

David Henry made a strangled noise in the back of his throat. "They snatched her up. I saw that myself." He leaned over Thomas and gently brushed his eyes closed. "Couldn't stop it."

Balling her fists beneath her cloak, Margot fought the urge to touch him. "Where is Mother Abigail now?"

"In her cabin," said the third man, speaking for the first time.

"Sent someone to fetch Louisa so she can heal her," said David Henry. "If she can."

The men fell silent then. Margot felt rooted to the spot, her legs made of wood. She breathed through pursed lips, sipping at the air, trying to take in as little of the scent of blood and death that swirled around as possible. Her eyes burned and she rubbed a thumb between her aching brows.

"What," she asked finally, her voice a fragile thing in the morning shadows, "what will happen now?"

David Henry stiffened and she saw his grip on the gun tighten. Though he couldn't see the settlement through the trees, he seemed to sense the growing panic gripping Remembrance. The surviving men exchanged guarded looks, there in the shadow of the trees.

Margot watched the muscles work beneath the skin of David Henry's jaw. "What happens now?" he said. He turned to look at her, and in the morning light his eyes were wild. "We protect what's ours."

Gaelle

"I don't see any difference." Toya stood staring down at the old woman.

Gaelle had run from the room and found her friend, dragging her back to Winter's room.

"She spoke."

Toya crossed her arms over her chest. "Yeah, she's a brilliant conversationalist."

Gaelle punched her lightly in the arm.

"Hey, I'm just sayin'."

They stood side by side in silence, but the old woman barely seemed to register their presence. She gazed past them at the images flickering across the television screen.

Gaelle suddenly had an idea. She walked to the television and, reaching up, turned it off.

"Shit!" cried Toya.

Gaelle turned to find Winter glaring at her. But unlike the times before, there were no animal wails of protest. Toya waved a hand in front of the old woman's face and Winter shifted her attention to her.

The aide grunted and took a quick step back. "Okay, that is not disturbing at all."

"It gives the heebie-jeebies, yes?"

"Oh, hell yeah."

Gaelle leaned down so that her face was level with Winter's, yet out of reach. "You can speak," she said. "Why will you not speak?"

The old woman merely blinked.

"Come on, our break's almost over," said Toya, touching her arm.

"But she *can* speak."

"You know, I'm not sure I even want to hear whatever it is she has to say."

Gaelle turned and looked at her friend, surprised to see Toya frowning, her eyes narrowed as she studied the old woman.

"I don't know, Guy. There's somethin' not right about this lady. Everything about this just feels wrong. You gonna tell me you don't feel that?"

She nodded. She did feel it.

"Whatever she's got locked up in that head a' hers, probably best kept where it is."

Gaelle gave the woman another look, then straightened. "Okay."

She turned the television back on and immediately saw the tension melt from the old woman's face as she turned her attention back to the screen.

Back in the staff lounge, she told Toya about the strange old man.

"Hmm," said her friend, grinning. "Older man with a ponytail and sunglasses. Sounds sexy. A little borderline creepy, but sexy."

Gaelle rolled her eyes.

"Are you sure it was him you saw this morning near your house?" Toya was suddenly serious. "I mean, it was dark, and in this weather, can't hardly see my hand in front of my face."

"I am sure. I could see him clearly in the light from the church cross. It was him."

"Did you tell Orr?"

Gaelle shook her head.

"Guy, you need to be careful. I don't know what's going on, but if this dude doesn't work for Joint Commission then we're talkin' some crazy stalker mess."

"Yes."

"Hey," said Toya, brightening. "I got something for you."

She rooted around in her pocket and pulled out a card. "My cousin's boyfriend works down at the courthouse. He gave me this card. Said this lawyer handles real estate stuff. Merry Christmas, girlfriend."

Gaelle pressed the card to her heart with a smile.

"You know sometimes the world just keeps beatin' you down," said Toya.

"But we survive, *wi*?" She held a hand up for a high five.

Toya hesitated, then took a deep breath, slapping her palm. "Yeah, girl. We survive."

She saw the bright yellow envelope taped to her door as soon as she drove up. Even before she'd ripped it open, before she read the lines threatening legal action if she did not vacate the premises the week after Valentine's Day, she felt a surge of rage. Beck Gardner's toothy grin flashed in her mind.

Beck—what a stupid name.

Why couldn't he just leave her alone? This rundown garage in this rundown neighborhood meant so much to him that he would see her homeless?

She snatched at her scrub top, trying to get it off. She was hot. So hot. And she wanted all these clothes off so she could breathe. She kicked her shoes off and hurled them across the room, one by one, feeling the heat inside her build with rage.

Grabbing the jar of cooking utensils, she flung it against the wall with a howl of fury. Why couldn't they just all leave her alone? It took her a moment to register her phone ringing. She yanked it from her pocket and saw the number.

"*Bonjou, sè*. Why are you out of breath?" The sound of her sister's voice brought her back to herself, and she sank to the concrete floor, feeling the coolness against her back.

"Rose, *bonjou*! I was . . . I just ran in from outside. It is snowing and cold." She laughed. "You will hate it, but I cannot wait for you to come home."

There was long silence and she was immediately on guard.

"Rose?"

"Gaelle . . ."

She sat up. "When are you coming home, *ti sè*?"

"Gaelle, the money won't come through until after the new year. I can't afford it."

Where moments before she'd been so hot she'd felt she might combust, now suddenly she felt as cold as ice. "But it is Christmas."

"I know. I am so sorry. Please do not be angry."

"I can take out a loan. There are places that do that. I could send you the money."

"No," cried Rose. "You already said you need work done on your car and new tires. And those places are *kriminèl*. They steal your money. I will be home for spring break. I promise."

Gaelle held the phone in silence. She felt hollowed out, empty.

"Gaelle? Are you angry with me?"

"No." What she felt had no name. "I will call you tomorrow."

"Mwen renmen ou."

"I love you, too."

She held the phone for a long time, then, dropping it, she reached for the warning letter. There on the cold floor she held it in her hand, feeling nothing as it burst into flame and burned away, the embers floating in the cool air like stars.

Part Four

Outside

Winter

There was murmuring all around her, the sound ebbing and flowing, and she felt herself slipping, sinking deep into the spaces around her, becoming one with everything. She imagined that she could slip inside a tree, hover there, her particles blending with its particles until there was no difference, creating a new being, a Winter tree.

She stretched her neck, and pain corkscrewed through the bottom half of her face. She opened her eyes. At first she could see no difference. Everything around her was bathed in an oily darkness, but as her eyes slowly adjusted, she saw that she was lying in a huge building, a barn. High above her head, a half-dozen hooks, a band saw, and other farming tools dangled from the ceiling.

Why? Where?

She turned her head, and the ground seemed to wobble beneath her back. Her mouth felt swollen, tight. Muddy light seeped through the cracks in the walls of the barn, forming a pale crisscross pattern over the piles of broken furniture and discarded tools that littered the floor. She tried to sit up and another lightning bolt of pain shot through her jaw and teeth. Moaning, she crumbled back to the cold floor.

"You're awake."

Her head snapped around and a violent wave of nausea washed over her. She jerked her head to the side and vomited again and again into the moldering straw heaped next to her, until she lay gasping for breath.

"You okay?"

Cautiously, she raised her head to peer into the shadows toward the voice, her teeth clenched against another wave of nausea. A man, a boy really, stepped from the gloom by the door, into a finger of light.

Winter tried to scramble away, her palms and knees scraping against the barn floor. One ankle was suddenly gripped hard and she went sprawling spread-eagle onto her stomach. Screaming, she rolled onto her back kicking fiercely at what held her.

A thick band of rusting metal was clamped around her ankle, connected by a thick chain to a loop in the floor.

She was chained to the floor.

She stared, incredulous, the scream dying in her throat. She blinked, unable to make sense of what she was seeing.

"Are you okay there?" the boy asked again, approaching slowly.

There was a horse stall a few feet behind her, and Winter dragged herself painfully toward it. She pushed her back against it, ignoring the metal band slicing through the skin at her ankle, a low gurgle of panic rising in her throat.

"Whoa, whoa there," cried the boy. "Settle down there, now."

Winter opened her mouth to scream again, to tell him to stay away, but no sound came out.

"It's alright," said the boy, squatting down a few feet away. "I ain't gonna hurt you. I just brought you somethin' to drink."

Winter stared. He was thin, almost skeletal, his face made up of sharp angles and lines. His hair was the color of winter wheat and hung limply against his face. His pale eyes were rimmed with dark circles. He smiled at her.

"I ain't going to hurt you," he said again.

He leaned toward her to get a closer look, then recoiled in shock as she lunged at him, clawing at his face.

"Hey!" he cried.

Winter slid down against the stall wall and wrapped her arms around her chest, tears running unheeded down her face. The boy watched in silence for nearly a minute, then, shaking his head, turned and walked away.

Winter stared at the barn door, straining to hear, afraid the boy would come back. When he didn't, she looked down at the chain. She pulled on it, gently at first and then harder, and harder still, until her ankle had swollen tightly inside the rusting band and blood streaked the top of her foot.

"No," she screamed. "No."

She collapsed to the floor and buried her head in her arms.

"No," she sobbed.

When she opened her eyes the next time, the barn was brighter. She raised her head and looked around. Now she saw that there were in fact three horse stalls, but it was clear there'd been no horses in them for a long time. Still lying on her side, she gingerly ran a hand over her face. Her lip was swollen and two of her bottom teeth were loose. There was a goose egg on her forehead. But nothing was broken and none of her injuries seemed permanent.

Something moved behind her and she shot upright, her lips pulled back in a snarl. It was the white boy again.

"Frank said to bring you somethin' to eat," said the boy. He set a pot of something steaming near her, then backpedaled so that he stood just beyond the reach of the chain. When Winter remained motionless, watching him warily, he gestured toward the pot.

"Go on," he said. "It's oatmeal. Got real butter in it and everything. Frank says it'll perk you up some."

Her stomach growled and she tried to remember the last time she'd eaten. She wondered what day it was, how long she'd been here. Wherever "here" was. The boy nodded encouragement as Winter slowly rose to her feet and shuffled toward the steaming pot. Bending, she picked it up, cradling the hot cereal gingerly with her fingertips. She stared at the lumpy gray goo. There was indeed butter, sitting like a yellow sun in the center of all that gray. A lump formed in her throat and her stomach hitched.

"Go on, now. Eat it," urged the boy. "Paddy made it, so it likely ain't all that good, I gotta admit. Best to gulp it down while . . ."

The rest of his sentence was swallowed up by an agonized scream as his face vanished beneath a layer of scalding oatmeal.

"Damnation!" he screamed, staggering blindly into one wall, bringing a washtub down on himself. "Damnation and hell!"

His screams brought a man to the door. Framed there, the sunlight lit him from behind so that all Winter could make out of him was that he was big. She added her voice to the white boy's.

"Let me loose!" she shrieked. "Let me loose! Let me loose right now! Let me loose!"

The big man strode into the barn. She recognized him instantly— the man who'd first grabbed her in the clearing, the one David Henry had bashed with his gun. He wore the purplish bruise from that blow on his left cheek. The slaver caught the howling boy by the scruff of his neck. "What in hell . . . ?"

He shook the boy like a wayward puppy until the boy's screams settled into pained whimpers. Winter yanked wildly at the chain on her ankle, twisting this way and that, ignoring the throbbing in her face and in her knees.

"Let me loose!" she screamed. "They're coming to get me! They're coming to get me and then you'll be sorry!"

The big slaver strode toward her, the boy still grasped by the neck. "Shut it!" he roared. He pushed her hard, sending her sprawling onto the filthy barn floor. Her swollen ankle flared red hot.

"And you," he yelled, giving the boy another shake. "We got no food to waste. You just lost your supper, boy! Feedin' you puts no coin in my pocket. Feedin' her does!"

He thrust the boy through the barn door, then followed after, yanking the doors shut, leaving Winter once again in half darkness.

Curling on her side, Winter squeezed her eyes tight, her breath coming in strangled bursts. Something crawled up her leg and she whimpered.

In a minute Belle will call me to breakfast. I'll have baked apples and then Mother Abigail will come and fuss at me about practicing my skill. I'm in Re-

membrance and it's almost breakfast time. Any minute . . . any minute now, Belle will call me to breakfast.

Outside the barn there was a crash, followed by cursing. Winter flinched and pressed her fists against her ears.

I'm not here! I'm in Remembrance!

She murmured this over and over until everything else—the curses of the slavers, the rustling of the mice in the straw, the throbbing of her face—receded into the background, drifting there like a half-remembered nightmare.

31

Margot

The settlement was bathed in scarlet light as the sun began to sink behind the hills. Though there was snow in the air and it was bitterly cold, all of Remembrance was out. Every man, woman, and child lined the path leading to the cemetery, silent as ghosts, even the babes in arms.

Four men carried the rough pine coffin, two at the head, two at the feet. They had come to bury Thomas, the blacksmith. A night and one full day had passed since the attack on the settlement, and initial disbelief had settled into a numb outrage. And now night was falling again and Remembrance was pulled taut, waiting, waiting for the trigger that would send all that emotion—rage, fear, revenge—bursting out into the open.

Margot watched from the shadow of the tree, near the top of the trail. These were not her people. This was not her grief. Not quite. She had her own sorrows.

David Henry passed, following the coffin, his jaw set in a hard, straight line. He caught her eye and something flickered across his face, a moment of recognition. She nodded and then he was past her, moving slowly down the trail. In her old life, she would never have noticed a man like him. So . . . ordinary.

But not ordinary, no.

After the attack, she'd watched as he moved through the settlement: dragging people from their cabins where they hid like sheep, pushing them to the job of living, with a joke, a calm word, and, if necessary, a threat. But beneath the smiles, Margot sensed steel. His eyes never stopped moving, scanning the trees, the trails, his finger never off the trigger of his rifle.

From her place in the shadows, she stared after him and felt a stirring behind her breastbone. She tried to imagine David Henry as a slave, tried to imagine him cowering beneath the blows of a whip. She could not.

At the entrance to the cemetery, the men laid the coffin gently on the ground, and a frail-looking woman, her headdress undone, her hair streaked with gray, threw herself across it, sobbing silently. The men who had been at the coffin's feet, boys really, wrapped their arms around each other and then the woman, shielding her within the cocoon of their bodies. They held each other like that until the woman straightened. Holding herself rigid, chin out, she laid a horseshoe on the coffin and then folded with her sons into the ranks of her neighbors.

And then he appeared, as if shot from the ground.

Josiah. Mother Abigail's friend.

There was a collective gasp as the old man strode to the coffin and slammed his palms against the top, once, twice, three times, then jerked upright, as if poleaxed. From somewhere deep within his throat came a sound like a growl. An elderly man not far from Margot began to hum, the sound a refrain to Josiah's growl. Then a young boy a few yards in front of her took up the sound, and the woman next to him, who appeared to be his mother. And the man to her left. Until the whole cemetery reverberated, pulsing with a dark, primitive, primeval noise that echoed in Margot's head, cutting off her breath.

"*Mere de Dieu!*" she whispered. "Mother of God!"

She stumbled backward, tripping over a tree root. And then Josiah seemed to be staring at her, through her, his mucoid eyes holding her in place. The sound in the cemetery grew and Margot struggled to breathe. The air around her throbbed. It was cold, but she felt sweat forming beneath her cloak. The boy in front of her raised his arms.

"Yes," he moaned. "Yes, Jesus, yes."

On and on it went, until Margot's heart beat to the rhythm of the chanting in the cemetery. Everything, the faded wooden grave markers, the trees, even the dirt on the trail where she stood, seemed to glow. Looking up, she thought she saw shapes twisting in the treetops.

He is calling to them! The old sorcier *is calling the spirits. And they answer,* mon Dieu, *they are answering him!*

A memory came to her: her grandmother on her knees in the back gardens, alone after a night of wandering the dark streets of New Orleans, whispering, her face a ghostly mask in the light of a candle. Margot had been what? Eight? Nine?

"Who are you talking to, Grandmere?"

"The spirits, chére. *They are everywhere, always. And if you are quiet, they will speak to you."*

"What do they say?"

Her grandmother smiled and blew out the candle, leaving them only the light of the moon. "They tell you the things you must know, chére. *They guide you toward what you are meant for."*

The cemetery pulsed: light, dark, light. She saw the flash of faces in the darkness, caught for a broken piece of time in the flickering lamplight. And those faces were calling to her, speaking in the voices of all the settlers. Around her. Inside her. Trying to tell her . . .

Grandmere?

And then, as suddenly as it started, it was over. Once again the cemetery was filled with a thick silence, broken only by muffled sobbing. Josiah seemed to shrink at the side of the coffin, his years suddenly writ large on him.

"This a day of homegoing, for Brother Thomas," he said. "The spirits will guide his way to heaven. He truly free now."

Sir Galahad, the goat man, stood over the coffin and shattered a small mirror, scattering the pieces around the grave. "This is so the spirits can see their reflection in Thomas. They will see themselves in him and him in themselves. We sad, but they be pleased that he joins with them . . . with all the ancestors," he said.

Josiah placed an egg in the grave, his hands trembling slightly. "For his new life just beginnin'."

Margot clenched her fists tightly against her chest. For a moment her vision blurred and there was a roaring in her ears. She felt something brush against her arm and jerked, but there was nothing there. Something flickered deep in the trees again, a movement just over her shoulder. But whatever it was, whoever it was, stayed just outside her line of sight. Shivering, she turned and hurried back to her little shelter.

By the time she crawled out again, it was completely dark and she was light-headed with hunger. The smell of things cooking drew her toward the Central Fire. She remembered the floating hog's head from a few days before and winced.

She glanced up at the stars that twinkled like crystals against the black velvet sky. She was on edge, disoriented. She'd never planned on staying in Remembrance. This stop in Ohio was simply to have been a way station on the journey to Canada, the land of the Northern Star, a place Veronique had spoken of as if it existed in one of their fairy tales. Somehow, someday, in that place far beyond the reaches of the slave catchers, they would earn money and then they would go back to Louisiana and buy the freedom of their grandmother. Veronique had believed that, and though Margot had teased her sister mercilessly about holding to childish wishes, she had wanted to believe, too.

After things had gone so horribly wrong, after Veronique . . . all she'd wanted was a safe place to hide from the trackers, to catch her breath, to recover from the long trek north. And she'd ended up here. In this Remembrance. This *asile*. This madhouse. Where an old woman convinced people that they were invisible to the whites. She laughed bitterly. She'd been here less than a week and that had already been proven a lie.

No, she had never planned on staying here, but now she didn't know what to do. There was snow on the wind now, promising a mean, early winter. This would be only her third winter season outside of Orleans

Parish, the last one spent on a rocky hillside farm in Kentucky. She'd seen snow before: icy crystals that coated the cobblestones of St. Ann Street like sugar glaze, powdery coatings that covered the ugly rocks and dirt in Kentucky. But she had never experienced the true winter she'd heard some of the white visitors to the Prytania Street mansion— those who came from the East and Middle West—speak of, the kind that buried the world, caught and killed the unsuspecting.

That was what she smelled on the wind now, what the conductor had hinted at before turning her over to Winter by the mulberry. No, she had no experience with that kind of winter, and if she left Remembrance now, she would surely perish. But if she stayed? With the slavers lurking in the shadows, waiting, mightn't that be the greater risk?

Margot inhaled sharply, fighting tears. "A fine mess, *non*?" she muttered.

"Hello."

The voice startled Margot from her dark daydream. She'd been so absorbed in her thoughts that she'd nearly tripped over the woman hunched at the edge of the Central Fire.

"Pardon me," said Margot. "Hello."

The woman smiled up at her. Everything about her was round. Her face, her large eyes, her hugely pregnant belly. She looked like a little doughball.

"Would you mind helpin' me up?" said the woman. "I sat down to shell peas and pure forgot I can't hardly get to my feet by myself no more. I just roll around like one a' these peas myself."

Margot extended both hands and helped rock the woman upright.

"You are having twins!" She'd felt the two heartbeats as soon as her fingers closed around the woman's hands. Strong. Healthy. One boy. One girl.

The woman narrowed her eyes, then broke into a broad smile. "Well, that's a relief to know. I was sure I was 'bout to birth a calf. 'Sides, ain't no surprise there, I reckon. Everybody who makes a baby inside Remembrance makes two."

Margot frowned.

"Girl, don't think about it too hard," said the woman, laughing. "Or your head's liable to bust open like a overripe tomato. It's just one of those Remembrance things. You get used to it." She patted her belly.

"I'm Petal," she said. "So much excitement, we never got introduced formal."

"*Enchanté,*" said Margot. "I am Margot."

"'Course you are. I probably know all your business by now better than you do your own self. Even if some of the busybodies had to make up a bucketful." Petal laughed. "New folks comin' in is big news around here."

Her face darkened. "Though not as big as recent doin's, I expect."

Petal squinted at the basket of peas at her feet. She smiled when Margot bent and reached it up to her.

"Where has everyone gone?" asked Margot.

Another shadow crossed Petal's face. "Folks scared. Hidin' mostly. Plannin' on what to do next. Winter's gone. Mother Abigail's took sick. Thomas . . ." She shuddered in the flickering firelight.

"And can't no one seem to find Louisa now, either," she went on softly.

Margot rocked back. "What does this mean?"

Petal turned her round, pretty face toward Margot, her expression answering for her.

"What happens now?" asked Margot, an echo of the question she'd asked David Henry earlier.

Petal smiled but her eyes were hard. "This my home. I ain't runnin'. Me. My babies. This our home, and I'm not about to let some yellow-bellied driver man scare me off . . . or carry me off."

If she had not been so uneasy, Margot would have laughed. The pregnant woman looked barely able to walk, let alone able to take on a team of slave drivers. "What about . . . the Edge? Was it not supposed to stop this from happening? Keep out people like the slave catchers?"

Petal shifted the basket and stared into the fire. "I don't know," she answered at last. "It was good here. For a long time. Everything Mother Abigail promised. More. This . . ."

She shrugged and locked eyes with Margot. "Don't matter. Let 'em come!"

She turned and glared in the direction of the cluster of cabins that rose up the hillside, seemingly deserted except for the thin plumes of smoke that drifted from their chimneys.

"Cowards!" she cried, nearly toppling herself over. Peas flew from her basket and scattered in the dirt, disappearing in the near darkness. She touched Margot's wrist. "Folks got call to be scared, I grant you that, but this our home! We got lazy. Forgot who we are. What we can do. With Mother Abigail protectin' us all the time. We took our freedom, ought to be willin' to fight to keep it."

Margot shook her head. "Fighting is not for everyone."

Petal gave her a long look. "I s'pose. But sometimes you don't get to choose."

She turned and began a slow waddle toward the cabins halfway up the hill. "Cowards," she muttered, waving off Margot's assistance.

Alone by the fire, Margot nervously rubbed at the pain in her forehead.

Winter, Thomas, Mother Abigail, Louisa. She stood for a long moment, paralyzed by indecision. Shouldn't she be doing something? Who should she ask? Her stomach growled and she was grateful for the sudden diversion of hunger.

A cast-iron skillet lay in the cooling ashes of the Central Fire. Lifting the lid, she saw to her relief that it contained not an animal's head, but the remnants of potatoes and fried apples, the remains of Thomas's quick, sad funeral repast. It was nearly cold but she ate it with relish, and the act of eating calmed her a bit. She washed the food down with scalding coffee and surveyed the area around her.

The Central Fire lay in a shallow bowl, narrow trails leading out from it like spokes on a wheel. One, she knew, led to the washing creek; another was the way back toward the cemetery, and ultimately to the mulberry clearing where she'd first stumbled into Remembrance. In the firelight it was impossible to see the trail that led up to the highlands, but she could track its course by the gentle meandering of the cottages up the hill.

It was a good place to make a home in freedom, she admitted. Fertile land to farm, good, clean water nearby, protected on three sides by rolling hills.

Veronique would have loved it here.

"Help."

She jerked, sloshing coffee on her hem. She looked around wildly, even as she realized that no one was there. The word whispered in her ear so clearly. Veronique's voice, Veronique's breath against her skin.

She is dead! It was a dream!

But even as she thought this, the fine hairs on her neck stood on end, the skin along her shoulders prickled.

"Stop it! *Arrête!*" she whispered, unsure who she was talking to.

Margot shuddered and gulped more coffee, scalding her throat. She closed her eyes and crossed herself, and still the feeling of being watched, of not being alone, would not leave her. The sound of the funeral chant echoed in her head.

She stared into the cup, absently swirling the grounds left in the bottom. She felt dizzy with uncertainty.

I don't know what to do.

Suddenly, against all reason, she was seized by the need to see the old priestess. She made her way slowly across the clearing toward Mother Abigail's cabin, picking her way with only the fingernail moon to light her path. Once again, shadows seemed to flit in and among the trees just outside her line of vision, and she had the overwhelming sense that, if she could just turn her head fast enough, she might catch sight of her sister crouched among a tangle of wild rose.

"*Merde! Imbecile!*" she muttered. "You are losing your mind!"

A man stood guard at Mother Abigail's door, a suet lamp guttering at his feet, a rifle in the crook of his arm. She advanced slowly, arms out.

"Hello," she called softly. "It is I, Margot."

As she moved into the small circle of light, she saw that the "man" was in fact a boy of ten or twelve. And that the rifle he was holding was nearly as tall as he was. His thin frame trembled, though it was impossible to tell if it was from the cold or fear.

He stepped forward at her approach, bony legs planted, and regarded her silently. The barrel of the gun was pointed toward the ground, but Margot felt the tension in him, the readiness to pull the trigger if it became necessary to defend his priestess.

"Hello," she said again.

The boy nodded, but said nothing.

"I . . . I would like to see Mother Abigail, please."

The boy shook his head. "Can't," he said, his voice surprisingly deep. "No one goes in."

Margot cocked her head and smiled, trying to put him at ease. "How is she, then?"

The tiny Adam's apple bobbed in his throat as the boy swallowed nervously. He cut his eyes at the closed cabin door. "Don't know. We waitin' for Miss Louisa to come take a look at her."

Margot flinched at the mention of the herbalist, and it was her turn to swallow nervously. Keeping her voice as even as possible, she said, "I could check on her, tend to her until . . . I might be able to help. I know a bit about . . . healing."

The boy's narrow spine stiffened, and she could see he was about to refuse her for the second time, when the cabin door swung open, startling them both. Josiah stood in the opening and fixed his peculiar eyes on the boy.

"Jesse, you go on now. I need to talk with Margot a bit," he said.

As the boy's mouth twisted in protest, the old man went on. "The other mens all gone, so I needs you to walk Remembrance. Make sure the womens is safe."

"Yessir," replied Jesse. He turned to go.

"Boy, take your lamp, 'fore you kill yourself."

Jesse tucked the rifle under his arm and grabbed the lamp. With a last suspicious look at Margot, he began to move up into the hills that surrounded Remembrance.

They listened as he crashed through the brush, and after a moment Josiah chuckled. "That boy better than any guard dog. Make so much noise he scare off anything tryin' to sneak up in here."

He turned toward Margot and she bit her lip. His big frame sagged against the doorframe, his opaque eyes glowing a sickly yellow. He seemed, if anything, even more reduced than he had at the gravesite, his skin fitting poorly over his bones. Margot swallowed, tasting the fried apples and scalded coffee in the back of her throat.

"I been waitin' for you," he said, his voice a low rumble.

She blinked.

He stretched a hand in her direction but she drew her hands into her cloak. He smiled and dropped his hand.

"I'm lettin' heat out," he said, when she didn't move.

She inhaled and stepped into the cabin. It was small and dim, and the smell nearly overwhelmed her: candle wax and woodsmoke and apples and old flesh. She shook her head to clear it, waiting for her eyes to adjust. There was some light, but the shutters were closed against the cold, and the tiny woodstove filled every corner with smoke.

Two wooden stools and a sort of rough chifforobe were the only pieces of furniture. Mother Abigail's cloak hung on a wooden knob, a large covered basket on the floor underneath. Opposite the door, against the wall, the old woman lay on a raised pallet. Only the barest movement of her chest showed that she still lived.

Margot's heart stuttered as she stared at the priestess. Despite the coolness of the cabin, she felt hot and light-headed.

"I was waitin' for you," repeated Josiah from a gloomy corner, as if reading her mind.

"I do not understand you," said Margot. She shifted to look at him. She felt damp sweat forming under her arms. "Waiting for me to what purpose?"

The old man shuffled toward the pallet. Turning toward her, he said, "I can't answer that, girl, but from the moment you entered Remembrance, I knew you was supposed to be here. In this time. In this place."

Margot felt behind her, ran a hand over the rough wall of the cabin. It was all real. She wasn't dreaming.

"You are . . . ?" she asked. "You are Babalawo?"

Again, an image of Grandmere flashed in her mind.

"A priest? Me?" Josiah threw his head back and laughed, his teeth unaccountably bright in the dimness, and for a moment he looked like the strong, vital man of just days before.

"No, girl!" he said, still chuckling. "I ain't nothin' like that! I got a little bit of . . . intuition and I got . . . a good sense about things, about folks. But nah! I ain't nobody special."

He was lying. She could see it as clearly as if the words were written in the air between them. Not a priest, *non*! But something else. Something of shadow, of spirit. Unconsciously, she took a step away from him.

"Louisa's gone," he said, seeming not to notice. "Didn't nobody see, but the slavers took her, sure 'nough." All traces of laughter had disappeared from Josiah's face. Margot held her breath.

He was standing over her now, his eyes running thick, gummy tears. She shuddered, tried to back away, but the closed door was against her back and there was nowhere to go. Heat seemed to pour off Josiah in waves, burning her face, singeing her hair.

"What you come lookin' for here?" he asked. Tobacco-sweet breath blew across her face. She shook her head. He was too close. She wanted to bring her hands up, to defend herself, but was terrified of touching him. But it didn't matter, because he touched her.

"What you want here?" he whispered and laid his hands on her shoulders.

The room suddenly pulsed and spun out in front of her in a haze of purple and red. There was something wrong with this man. She felt the darkness, the danger lurking inside him. Not good. Not evil. Just there. The way the copperhead snakes that lived in the bayous of Louisiana were neither good nor evil, but deadly all the same, as was their nature.

She felt him inside of her; her arms and legs, her breath, her will no longer her own!

"*Mary sainte, mère de Dieu,*" she prayed. "Holy Mother, protect us."

She tried to push him out, out of her mind, out of her body, but she was powerless. She tasted milk and honey and whiskey. He was not a single man but many, old and young. Like a cracked mirror, she could feel him reflected in each piece, each reflection just a bit different. She cried out, confused. She'd never felt anything like this before.

The world spun. She tasted vomit in her mouth and she forced it down. Locking her knees, she felt for the door behind her, but her hands were his hands, knuckles swollen and painful, the skin dark and loose, and they would not obey her. His man smell, his old man smell was in her nose, and she felt her skin sag even as his manhood seemed to rise between her legs. And there was nothing she could do.

And then she was on her knees at Mother Abigail's side, her limbs and muscles hers and only hers.

"*Sorcière!*" she hissed, crossing herself. "Witch!"

But the old man barely looked at her, his face tired and blank. Beside her, Mother Abigail moaned softly. Margot studied her, keeping her body turned so she could still keep Josiah in view.

The old woman's eyes were open, though they saw nothing. The left side of her face drooped like warm butter, a thin line of drool escaping her lips. Even without touching her, Margot knew at once what was wrong. A blood vessel had broken in the priestess's head. She felt a faint echo of it in her own.

She felt hysterical laughter rising in her chest. She didn't know what the old man expected her to do, but this woman was beyond her help. All anyone could do now was wait.

32

Winter

"What's your name?"

Winter moaned. Her eyelids felt swollen, stuck together.

"My name's Dixon. Dixon McHugh. Everybody just calls me Dix."

She forced her eyes open and blinked slowly at him. Her mouth was dry. It hurt to swallow. The white boy squatted in the shadows, watching.

"You ain't had no call to throw that food in my face like that," he said. "You best not try that with Frank and them; they liable to beat you near to death."

She turned her back on him, the chain on her leg rattling against the floor.

"Frank says that's how it's done when you catch slaves. That's the big fella that busted in here yesterday. He says you have to do it, chain 'em, else a slave's liable to run off."

She turned her head and fixed him with a look, willing him to die, her nails digging into the soft meat of her palms. He flinched and looked away.

"You shouldn'a run off from your master, then we wouldn't have to chain you," he said, sounding uncertain. "Frank says it's how it's done."

"I didn't run off from anywhere. I'm not a slave," hissed Winter, breaking her silence. "I was never a slave! You . . . you came into my home and kidnapped me!"

Dixon McHugh blinked rapidly. "Kidnap? I didn't . . ."

"I am not a slave," she repeated. It was hard for her to speak. Rage bunched the words up in her throat. "Everyone in Remem—!"

She stopped. She would never speak Remembrance's name to this slaver.

"Everyone in my village is free," she finished.

It was none of his business that nearly everyone in Remembrance once had been slaves. The boy was shaking his head. He looked, if it was possible, even paler than before. Winter watched him through narrowed eyes.

"What happened to your face?" she asked.

From where she sat, she could see a dark bruise running the length of the boy's jaw and down into his soiled shirt collar. It hadn't been there the day before. She was certain of that.

Dix stiffened and Winter inhaled sharply.

"I brought you supper," he said, ignoring her question. "Frank says make sure you eat it. He says you won't be worth nothin' starved to death. Frank's got a sour temper, case you ain't noticed."

"Dixon. Dix. You have to let me loose." Winter took a deep breath. "I don't belong to anybody but myself. I have to go home. Please let me go home."

Her voice broke. "I am not a slave. I have never been a slave. You know this isn't right. Deep down you know that, don't you?"

The boy stared at the ground, not meeting her eyes. His thin shoulders drooped, and for a tiny moment, Winter had a glimmer of hope that he might actually let her go, would see this for the horrible mistake that it was. Then he sighed and looked up at her. His eyes glittered in the grimy light but his mouth was hard.

"I can't do that, miss. Frank took me in. I got no one else." He shook his head slowly from side to side. "'Sides, Frank said we're only catchin' slaves. Only slaves. Not free nigras. So I'm doin' right. Returnin' property. That's all I'm doin', followin' the law. You tryn'a say everybody free where we got you. Well, you know that ain't true, much as you might wish it, cause Frank got papers. He got proof who you all's belong to or we wouldn'a been there."

"He's lying. Did you see the papers? There's no such proof."

Dixon hunched his shoulders as he put a sack on the barn floor where, with some effort, she might reach it. He watched her for a moment, the Adam's apple bobbing nervously in his thin throat. "They took me in when I was in the most desperate way. And . . . and I need that money . . . bad. I ain't particular about no slave-holdin' but the law's the law. That's all. It's the law. Sorry, miss," he mumbled and then he was gone.

"Sorry?" She leaped to her feet again, ignoring the pain in her swollen ankle. "Come back here, you no-account bootlicking cracker!" she screamed. "Let me loose from here, goddammit! Let me loose! Or you will be sorry, sorrier than you know!"

Winter thrashed and kicked, jerking at the chain that held her. She screamed curses and cried, kicking at the nearest horse stall until it splintered. No one came.

Finally, spent, she collapsed to the barn floor, sobbing softly, twisting a lock of hair round and round her finger. She lay curled in a ball motionless as the hours passed, numbed by the cold and her fear. When it had almost become too dark to see, the barn door opened again. This time she didn't look up. What difference did it make what the boy brought her to eat? She wouldn't eat. Couldn't eat it.

"That was quite a little ruckus you kicked up in here this afternoon, gal."

Winter cringed. Not the boy, Dixon, then.

"I'm-a let you have today as a freebie," Frank went on. "But you tryin' my patience. You gonna be fat and sassy by the time we get back to Kentucky if I have to strap you down and stuff food down your gullet myself. You worth way too much silver to die on us. Especially after us losin' one of our best trackers catchin' you."

The memory of Josiah holding up his hand, of the horse flipping over, trapping the slaver beneath, flashed through her mind. She smiled bitterly.

"What you grinnin' at, nigger?" screamed Frank. He rushed at her and she cried out, cowering against the stall wall.

"Frank!"

A white man she'd not seen before stood in the doorway, calmly smoking a pipe. "Leave the girl be," he said.

Frank stopped in midflight and whirled on the man. "Colm . . ."

"Leave her be, Frank! You keep beatin' on her and she won't be worth a half cent at market, well-fed or no."

The man stepped into the barn. "You'll have to excuse my brother. He has no manners. Always a disappointment to our mother."

From the corner of her eye, Winter saw that Colm was a more re-fined version of the bigger man. Dark like his brother, he was mus-cular where his brother was fat, his features handsome to Frank's coarseness. He smiled at her, and his perfect white teeth glowed in the gloom. He glanced at the uneaten supper.

"You don't like Paddy's cookin'?" he asked.

Winter didn't answer. She kept her head bowed but watched him stealthily beneath her lashes. Frank paced a few yards away, growling like a wounded bear, and Winter knew that except for his brother, she would have been beaten half senseless by now.

"No?" Colm went on, as if she'd answered. "Can't say as I blame you. Poor Paddy. Sweet lad, but he thinks food's never really done 'til it looks like charcoal!"

He laughed and Winter stared at him. His tone was friendly, and he stood one foot atop the other, arms crossed, watching her, as relaxed as if they were around the Central Fire. She gaped at him, bewildered by his tone.

"So what's your name, girl?" he asked.

"I . . . ," she said. But the words would not come. Her throat was raw from screaming.

He leaned over her. "Come on, lass," he said. "Give us a name. Or we can give you one. How about Mable? Our mother had a cow named Mable once. Remember, Frank? Stupid thing. Always wandering off."

Behind him, Frank snorted. Colm was still smiling, but now she could see that the brothers had the same eyes, black and full of hate. She blinked back tears. She would not let them see her cry.

"Come, girl," said Colm. "Don't tell me we went through all that ef-fort and you're the simple one."

He reached to grab her arm and she instinctively jerked away. The slaver grunted in surprise and drew back his hand to strike her.

"I'm not afraid of you," cried Winter, tensing for the blow.

Colm's mouth dropped open in surprise. He lowered his arm and turned to his brother, who stood smoldering behind him. "Sweet Mary! We got us a fiery one here, Frank."

He grabbed for her again and held her so she couldn't move. "Don't think all that fire will do you any good where you're going, my girl, but I like it."

"When they come for me, you will be the saddest man on earth," she said. Her voice was trembling but she forced herself to not look away. "They will do things to you . . . I will do things to you. You won't even know your own name, let alone the name of your mother's cow."

For just a moment she saw something flicker in the slaver's eyes, something that looked like fear. He stared into her eyes and tightened his grip on her arm until she cried out in pain. Tears slid down her face.

"Ah, now, none a' that," soothed Colm, stroking her tangled hair, any fear she thought she'd seen, gone. "Maybe she's lonely, Frank."

"Well, can't have that, can we?" said Frank. He stepped from the barn and returned seconds later with a large bundle of rags. He threw it in a corner and Winter heard the rattling of chains, but all she could see was Colm's smiling face and those poisonous black eyes.

Releasing her, he stood. "I won't have all that screamin' again," he said. "It spooks the horses and works on my digestion. If it happens again, then you and my brother Frank here will need to have a conversation. Understood?"

Frank grinned, his lips pulling back from his teeth. Winter nodded and Colm slapped his thigh, delighted.

"Well, now, Mable," he cried, beaming. "I think we're all going to be great friends, then."

He clapped an arm around his brother's shoulders and the two slavers disappeared into the night. Winter covered her face with her hands and sobbed quietly, terrified that one of the brothers might hear and return.

A low moan came from the corner where Frank had tossed the bundle of rags. Winter cried out and clapped her hand to her mouth. But the night outside the barn was quiet. She stared at the bundle, an oddly shaped thing covered in a dirty horse blanket.

She crept slowly toward the bundle, breathing hard through her mouth.

"I'm not scared," she murmured again and again. "I'm not scared."

She could just barely reach the bundle, and with trembling fingers she grabbed a corner of the blanket and pulled.

And then she screamed, the slave-catching brothers forgotten.

The woman's face was barely recognizable, her features swollen and bloody. But Winter did recognize her. She fell backward, then curled up and retched, bringing up dark, stinking bile. When she was done, she wiped her mouth with the stained straw and crawled back to the corner. She could just reach the face of the badly beaten woman with her fingertips.

"Louisa," she whimpered.

33

Winter

Winter jerked upright. Everything hurt—her face, her arms, even her teeth. She'd slept fitfully through the night, propped against the splintered horse stall, watching over Louisa, waiting for some sign of life.

In the cold barn, everything was shrouded in a damp haze. Light leaked through the wallboards, landing in scattered patches on the moldy hay, the broken furniture, lending them a peculiar radiance.

She heard a low moan and pushed herself to her knees.

"Louisa?"

A few feet away, the older girl's eyes fluttered open. In the morning light her face looked like a spoiled plum, purplish and soft. On the already damaged side of her face, the scars had been nearly erased by the swelling. Her blouse was ripped, the pale gray wool stained dark with blood. She stared unseeing into the middle space just beyond Winter's shoulder.

"Louisa," Winter called again softly. She crawled as close as the chains would allow, keeping her voice low. It was quiet outside the barn, and if the slavers were sleeping, she wanted them to stay that way.

For a long moment, Louisa gazed past her, her eyes blank, insensible. Winter tugged at a tangle of hair and willed Louisa to answer. Ever so slowly, a tiny light appeared in the girl's eyes and she seemed, finally, to focus.

"Where . . . ?" she croaked. She licked her lips, wincing as her tongue touched the blood dried there.

"Slavers came. They came into Remembrance." Winter leaned forward. "They took us, Louisa. I don't know where we are."

Louisa's eyes widened. She gazed at Winter for a full minute, then turned her face away and began to make a deep hacking sound, her shoulders shaking.

"It's okay, Louisa," whispered Winter. It sounded ridiculous, even to her own ears.

Louisa's head rolled side to side, the sound growing louder. Winter rocked back on her heels, astonished. Louisa was laughing! Her whole body quaked with the sound; tears rolled from her eyes and still she laughed.

Winter glanced fearfully at the door. Louisa had clearly lost her mind. "Shush, Louisa. Shush! You have to shush now."

What did slavers do to crazy slaves?

"What's the matter with you?" Winter hissed. "They're going to take us south. To sell us!"

Louisa locked eyes with Winter. "Yes," she said simply. She was no longer laughing but she sounded as if she might start up again at any second.

"Well . . ." Winter felt faint. Maybe *she* was the one that had gone crazy. "Well, what do we do?" she asked, her voice shrill.

Louisa's face went blank again, taking on the same unfocused expression as before. She looked at Winter, her eyes empty, then turned her head away once more. A single tear ran down her ruined face before disappearing into her blood-soaked blouse.

Whimpering, Winter scooted away from her and slumped back against the horse stall. The shivering began as a tiny movement that started in her chest and grew until she was shaking the stall behind her. She was as good as alone. No one was coming for her. No one was going to save her. She would never see Remembrance again.

No!

She shook her head. They would come. Someone would come for them. And if they didn't . . . if no one came . . . then, she would save herself.

Except.

She tried to think of how. But her mind was as cold and featureless as new snow. She squeezed her eyes shut and sank into the damp straw.

When the barn door opened, she kept them tightly closed and waited for the boy, Dix, to put down the breakfast of lumpy oatmeal and leave.

"Best to eat somethin', lass. We'll be headin' out as soon as we pick up supplies, and it's a long trip we've got ahead of us."

Winter moaned. Once again, the voice belonged not to the scrawny boy, but to Colm, the dark-haired slaver from the night before, the one with the bright smile and the dangerous eyes. She tried to burrow herself deeper into the straw.

He cleared his throat and she opened her eyes. He was smiling. A sliver of sunlight lit his curly hair so that it formed a gleaming crown around his head. He leaned easily against a barn support, arms crossed, his expression pleasant. The skin on her arms prickled.

He turned to look at the silent Louisa. "Your friend appears to be doing poorly."

"She's hurt," said Winter flatly.

"Yes," said the slaver, still looking at Louisa. His face darkened. "My brother. Dropped on his head as a wee babe once too often, I'm afraid. Doesn't seem to know how to protect his investments. Stupid!"

He looked back at Winter. "Can you patch her up?" he asked. "Otherwise it'll just be a damnable waste." This last he said mostly to himself.

Winter's mouth twitched. They'd beaten Remembrance's healer nearly to death, and now they wanted her to patch her up? Half-crazed laughter bubbled up from her throat, and she pressed her lips together, holding it back.

She shrugged, afraid of what might come out if she opened her mouth to speak. In the blink of an eye the slaver was in front of her, squatting so that he was at eye level. She inhaled sharply and managed not to flinch, meeting his eyes, eyes the color of brackish river water. He smiled.

"You're a lovely lass," he said. "Do you have a special talent?"

She thought of the Easter Egger and gave a bark of hysterical laughter.

The slaver's eyes narrowed dangerously and he squeezed her arm until she cried out. Her pain seemed to please him.

"Ah, no matter. You look like a bright lass."

He looked her up and down, appraising her. "Too soft for a field hand, but might could make a decent lady's maid. We'll do quite fine by you. Even if that other one"—he jerked his head in Louisa's direction—"turns out to be a total loss."

He traced a rough finger slowly down her cheek, her neck. She set her teeth and willed herself not to spit in his pale, pink face.

"And," he went on, "there's always a use for a fair bonny lass in the master's chamber."

He thrust a hand into her blouse and roughly grabbed one of her breasts. She cried out and tried to jerk away, but he laughed and squeezed harder, until it felt as if her nipple was on fire. Leaning against her, he pinned her against the stall, and the stink of him, her revulsion of him, made her go still.

"Ah, yes. A bonny lass. We'll do quite well by you."

He released her and stood.

"I'll send the boy with something to clean her up with. See if there's anything about to tend her wounds. Best you pray she can walk by the time we get back from provisioning . . . or else . . ." He smiled. Without finishing his sentence, he strode from the barn.

Alone again with the insensible Louisa, the trembling started once more. Winter wrapped her arms tightly around herself to keep from shaking apart.

Dix brought warm water, as the slaver had promised, and some almost-clean rags. She tended Louisa's wounds as best she could. To her inexperienced eye, nothing seemed broken, yet Louisa had not woken again. She had the sense that Louisa could wake up if she wanted to but that she was choosing to stay where she was, wandering about in her dreamworld. She didn't blame her. She would have done the same, if her dreams had not been so filled with monsters and dark places.

It was not lost on Winter that she of all people should be the one tending to Remembrance's healer.

"Come on," said Dix.

Winter looked over her shoulder and saw him unhooking her chain from the floor hook. She squinted at him, not understanding.

"Come on," he said again. He rattled the free end of the chain.

"Where?" She felt herself standing on the sharp edge of panic. What was this? Was he taking her away now?

"Colm says I'm to get you some air. Walk you about to keep your muscles strong." She frowned, unmoving, and he rattled the chain again.

She grabbed the end still attached to her ankle. "Don't," she snarled, outrage momentarily supplanting fear. "Don't do that. Do you hear me? I am not an animal!"

She yanked the chain hard, throwing the boy off-balance. Dix slipped on the damp hay, nearly going to his knees before catching himself. She would have charged him then, saw herself closing the small distance between them and gouging out his eyes. But the gun tucked in his waistband made her hesitate. The muscles in her legs quivered, demanding they be allowed to rise up, to jump, to run.

Wait! There will be a better time. She heard the voice in her head and ground her teeth, forcing herself to hold still, burning with frustration. She stared into his eyes and bared her teeth. They would pay for this.

Under her glare, the white boy lost the small bit of color he had. And she had a flash of clarity. He was the weak link. He wouldn't hurt her if he didn't have to. And . . . he seemed . . . scared.

She inhaled, smelling his fear, warm and sour, like old sweat, high up in her nose. The smell of it, the taste of it, warmed her. Her body began to fill with a vague heat and she closed her eyes, trying to concentrate, but her focus slipped away, like the sun slipping behind a cloud. Grunting in frustration, she opened her eyes, and the heat went out of her, a candle extinguished.

Dixon McHugh stared at her, openmouthed. She locked eyes with him, and he took a quick step backward, pulling the gun from his waistband, pointing it at her. The gun shook ever so slightly in his hand.

"Come on," he croaked.

Her eyes burned and she rubbed them. She couldn't . . . Maybe it didn't work here. Maybe it didn't work outside of Remembrance. She needed . . .

She couldn't complete the thought. Everything was all mixed up in her head. Suddenly, all she wanted in the world was to hear Mother Abigail's voice fussing at her to pay attention, to focus on concentrating her power. She needed to hear the old woman's voice.

Winter twisted a lock of her hair and suppressed a sob. Dix made as if to tug on the chain again, seemed to think better of it, then stepped aside to let her pass.

The light outside was nearly as gray as that inside the barn. Dark clouds hung so low overhead that she felt she could bury her hands in their undersides. Everything smelled wet. There was a storm coming, one of those miserable late-fall storms unable to decide between snow or rain and so usually delivered both. She shivered.

Nothing looked familiar. They were standing on top of a steep ridge that looked out over an ocean of more roiling gray clouds. Here and there, gray-green hilltops poked through like fish scales. From somewhere beyond all the clouds and partly hidden forest came the smell of water, dark, fast-running water.

The slavers had set up camp at an abandoned farmstead. There was the barn, a ruined clapboard house, and a half-dozen other collapsing outbuildings, some nearly invisible beneath the creeping vines that were slowly pulling them down.

The three other slavers sat crouched around a fire: Colm—Winter whimpered softly at the sight of him—his brutish brother Frank, and a third man. She recognized him as the gaunt, hawk-faced man that had grabbed her in Remembrance, the one who had punched her in the face. She figured that he must be Paddy, the cook.

Frank sat drinking from a bottle and scowling at the fire. Paddy and Colm were sharing a bottle. They ignored her as she passed. In the firelight, she saw that the cook's face bore the marks of her nails, and she smiled grimly. No matter what happened now, Remembrance had left its mark on these men.

They walked through the remains of the kitchen garden at the side of the old farmhouse, Dix trailing behind, holding on to the chain like a leash. When they reached a damp potato hill, Winter turned on the boy.

"You don't have to hold on to me like that," she snapped. "I'm trussed up like a chicken. Where am I going to go?"

The boy fingered the chain and looked back toward the other slavers nervously. Winter yanked her foot.

"I don't even know where I am. And besides, you have that gun."

She crossed her arms, clutching at her sleeves, and waited. He reminded her of a squirrel, content to hiss and chatter from afar but ready to scamper up a tree at the slightest threat. With a final look over his shoulder he dropped the chain.

"Promise you won't go hightailin' it outa here," he said.

She sneered. "You must be the worst slave catcher there ever was! I won't make any such promise." She smiled bitterly. "You'll just have to trust me."

Red blotches appeared on his pale cheeks. "You hush now!" he snapped. "You just hush!"

He looked from the chain to her face and back to the chain again but made no move to pick it up, and Winter felt wild laughter threatening to break loose once more. She coughed to cover it up, then turned and began to walk through the garden again. Slowly.

This boy's so stupid, he's liable to shoot me on accident, she thought sourly.

They walked around the outside of the house. It was a large house, and tattered lace curtains fluttered through a pair of broken windows on the top floor. On the narrow front porch, a rocking chair sat next to a low table, a glass in the center. Except for the fact that the contents of the glass were thick and green, someone might have just stepped away moments before.

"This looks like good farmland," said Dix behind her. "Someone took a lot of care here. Pity it's goin' to ruin."

Winter said nothing. There was a pump rusting in the front yard. She primed the handle and clear, cold water gushed from the spout. Gratefully, she washed her face and arms, ran damp fingers through her hair, trying not to see the blood mixed in with the dirt as it sluiced into the ground at her feet. It was not a proper bath, but it helped.

She turned to find Dix studying the ground. When the water stopped he looked up, and the misery in his eyes caught her by surprise. He saw her watching him and gave her a weak smile, just the corners of his mouth twitching upward.

"Where are we?" she asked.

The boy shrugged. "About a half day north of Cuyahoga Falls."

This meant not one thing to her. She had never been more than a few feet past the boundary of the Edge, and never for more than a few minutes. She knew the name of the town nearest them that they traded with, Ashtabula, but had never been there. It was just a name to her, the way New Orleans, Kentucky, Virginia, and all the other places the runaways came from were just names to her. She was out in the world. She may as well have been on the moon.

"Long ways from home," muttered Dix, half to himself.

Winter peered at him. "What?"

He sighed. They were walking again. The damp from her washup was quickly seeping into her bones. "Colm and Frank don't hardly ever come this far north to track runaways. If they wasn't tryin' to settle a score they'd a' stayed closer to home to hunt. Like usual."

He glanced at her as he said this last, his cheeks flushing pink. Winter ignored this. It was suddenly important that she keep him talking.

"Where's home?"

"West Virginia."

She hesitated, unsure of how hard to push him, but he was walking beside her easily, studying the farm and the rolling hills: just two friends out for a morning stroll.

"What did you mean . . . 'settle a score'? With who?"

Dix slowed. "Colm and Frank had a brother. Came up here this way a while back, trackin' a slave. A special slave. Had a way with horses. Could break any animal livin'. Worth a powerful lot of money. When their brother finally made his way back home, he didn't have no slave and . . ."

He stopped and licked his bruised lips.

". . . and what?" she prodded.

The boy swallowed hard and looked fully at her for the first time. "And he wasn't right in his head.

"Kept talkin' about this place here in Ohio country. Said it was a damned place. Said a big nigra woman lived there, a nigra woman what had the power to make coloreds just disappear up in thin air. Said she was a witch, that she got inside his head. Cursed him."

She gazed steadily at him even as her heart started to race. She saw that he had eyes the color of a winter sky.

It couldn't be. The slaver who'd followed Zeus into Remembrance. She remembered the screams as they'd turned their backs to climb back into Remembrance. Clay. That was his name. She licked her lips.

"He wasn't right never again after that," Dix went on. "That's what Frank and Colm said. Said it was their family duty to find that witch and all her nigras and teach them a lesson. They didn't believe none a' that mess he was talkin', but they headed back up this way lickety-split. Said it was their family duty to find that place and make the nigras pay. Plus, they still had papers on that runaway."

His pale gray eyes looked into hers. "Are you one of them? Are you a witch?" he asked.

The laughter was out of Winter's mouth before she could stop it. "What pure foolishness! There's no such thing as witches!"

His cheeks turned a deep red. The bruise on his cheek darkened into an ugly shade of purple-black. He frowned.

"What are you then?" he demanded. "You're somethin'! My Gram told me about folks that had the sight. And I can see it in you. I was there, remember? I heard them voices comin' out the trees. Wasn't nobody there and then there was!"

The boy licked his dry lips "The whole place just filled up with y'all folks. That bewitchin' woman? I saw her, too. I surely did. And they was an old man, with funny lookin' eyes. He killed Zeke and his horse. . . . Didn't lay a finger on 'em. Just looked at 'em. Just held up his hands and that horse reared up like he was snake bit. I saw it all. There's somethin' unholy about that place, about you!"

Winter fixed him with an acid stare and Dix flinched.

Suddenly, Winter found herself yanked off her feet and into the air. Frank held her by her collar, dangling her three feet off the ground as if she was no more than a feather he'd plucked up.

"Boy, I'm startin' to sour on you for sure," he roared at Dix. "This nigger ain't no plaything. I told you to go walkin', not talkin'! This here is money! Nothin' but silver money walkin' on two feet. But talkin' to you is like barkin' at a knothole, ain't it?"

He threw Winter to the ground and snarled at her. "Constitutional's over, lass. Back to the barn with you."

She scrambled to her feet, struggling to stay out of his reach, but he had turned his attention back toward Dix.

"Me and Colm're gonna have to ride to the next town over for supplies. Won't make it a week without," he snarled. "Those damnable Yankees in Ashtabula wouldn't even give us the time of day." He spat at Dix's feet. "Hate this place. Can't wait to get back to West Virginny, where white folks are civilized. Can you watch this girl while we're gone? Can you at least do that?"

Dix nodded and Frank strode off with a growl, kicking at Winter as he passed. She rolled, just managing to avoid his boot. Mutely, Dix picked up the free end of chain and jerked it. This time Winter said nothing. She silently let herself be led back toward the barn.

Without a word, Dix fixed her chains back to the hook in the floor. As he turned to leave, she grabbed his arm. The boy jerked as if struck but he didn't leave. He stood, staring at the top of his boots.

"Dix?"

He raised his head and she was startled anew by the paleness of his eyes.

"Why're you doing this? You're different from them. You're no slave man."

So many expressions flew across his face that she barely had time to register them before his eyes went dead. "Shut it!" he said.

He turned and left, pulling the barn door closed behind him.

34

Mother Abigail

That terrible pain, that blinding agony in her head was suddenly gone. Mother Abigail opened her eyes and sat up.

Quiet. It was so quiet.

She was standing in the clearing but something about it was different. She frowned. Where was everyone?

She was dreaming. No. Not dreaming. A vision. A message from the *loa*. So they were speaking to her again?

The sun was rising over the ridge, bathing the clearing in a fiery orange light. And then she saw what it was that was different. The clearing was much wider and the trees were different. And the air, the air was different, too.

Mother Abigail closed her eyes and inhaled. She could smell . . .

. . . the river, sunbaked grass!

"Bone Girl!"

Her eyes snapped open and she whirled. Walking toward her, the sun at his back, was a man. She squinted. There was something familiar about that walk, that voice. And no one had called her Bone Girl since . . .

. . . since they'd stolen her body away! Since the ghost men, the white ones, brought her from the place they call Africa.

When he stepped out of the sun's glare she saw him clearly and clutched at her chest, trying to steady the erratic beating of her heart. She knew him. It had been more years than she could count—she'd been young, so very young—since she'd seen him last, herding their father's goats into a pen, but she knew him still.

"Ajani!" she cried.

The man smiled. He was tall, as was all her family, and broad of shoulder. The last time she'd seen him, he'd been a boy, but it was him. She knew his spirit.

She made to go to him, to fling her arms around his neck and never let him go. What had happened to their mother and father after the ghost men had come and dragged her away? What had happened to the rest of their village?

Her brother held up a hand, warning her back.

"Am I dead then?" she asked.

He shook his head. "No, not dead. Not yet." He grinned, his teeth white in his dark face. "And also not so bony anymore, Kianga."

Mother Abigail laughed out loud at her true name, the name her parents had given her. "No, not so bony. Not in a long time."

They smiled at each other, a wide swath of sunlit grass separating them.

"It is not yet your time, sister," said Ajani, his smile fading. "You have to go back. Your work is not done."

The priestess started. For a moment she had forgotten Remembrance. She was with her much-loved brother and she felt no pain—in her body or in her spirit. She shook her head.

"No! I cannot," she cried. "I am tired! Old! Why can't I go with you?"

Ajani laughed. "Girl, you were always the lazy one. Hiding in the reeds like a grasscutter to avoid pounding the cassava with the other girls."

She knew he was trying to make her smile, comparing her to the giant rats that lived in the marshes of their childhood, trying to take the sting out of his message, but all she felt was despair. "Never! I was never that! I have given, Ajani. So much . . . too much already. More than you know. You can't leave me again. I am old and worn out. What more could the spirits expect of me? Can they be so cruel?"

He took a step toward her. She wanted to reach for him but knew somehow that her hands would never find his. "I'll never leave you, Bone Girl. None of us will."

She saw then that there were others with them, watching. In the glare of the rising sun she couldn't make out faces, but she felt them. Her mother, her father. And there, standing between them, Hercule, young and strong and as beautiful *as the day they'd met in Far Water. He was smiling at her, they all were. She was moaning but all she heard was the sound of her own heart breaking.*

"Finish what you started, Kianga. We are here with you. And when it is done we will come for you."

"No, I will not," she cried. "I am a useless old woman."

Her brother laughed. She could no longer see his features. They all seemed to be fading in the light.

"No!" *She gave an anguished scream.* "Take me with you! Ajani! Hercule!"

Her head filled with such pain she could hardly bear it. She covered her face in despair and fell to her knees gasping for breath. When she finally pulled her hands away, she saw that she was not on the warm, bright riverbank of her childhood village, but in the smoky cabin in Remembrance. She let loose a scream that was equal parts grief and rage.

"Abigail?"

Josiah hovered at the foot of her bed. The new girl, Margot, sat slumped near the door, her eyes wide, bewildered. Mother Abigail tried to speak but her tongue felt heavy and thick. The scream had said it all, in any case. She had no words left. She shook her head and turned her face away.

You should have let me come with you, Ajani. You left me here! What more do you want from me? What more? You should have let me come.

She felt wet on her face and slowly raised one hand to her cheek. She stared at her damp fingertips. It had been so long that, for a moment, she had no name for what it was. And then it came to her. They were her tears.

She let old Josiah pull her up because, truth be told, she couldn't have done it on her own. She was emptied and hollowed out as a gourd. Her thoughts kept drifting away from her. Memories, old and new tangled up in each other, confusing her.

Winter screaming her name. Men, boys from Remembrance with guns.

She'd seen her brother, a boy when she'd last laid eyes on him and now a man, most likely long dead. She'd heard the voices of her mother and father. Simona. Her sister. And Hercule . . . Hercule had been there, too. At the thought of her long dead love, Mother Abigail clutched her chest, as if that might keep her heart from breaking all over again. The world had shattered into bits and she had lost her way.

Her head had been hurting, the worst headache she'd ever had in her life. And she'd fainted. Hadn't she? She couldn't quite remember. The worst pain was gone, but there lingered the slightest ache, like a ghost hovering at the place where her head met her spine.

"Careful, Abigail." Josiah held her fast under one elbow, supporting her until she found her feet.

"Well, quit pullin' at me, old man," she snapped irritably. "I haven't forgotten how to stand at least."

Josiah snorted but did not release her elbow. The priestess sucked in a sharp breath as the room swayed beneath her feet. Wordlessly, Josiah tightened his grip, pushing her walking stick into her other hand. Mother Abigail noted the new strands of gray streaking his hair, the thickening of his knuckles, and felt a surge of fear. She grimaced and gave him a quick pat on the shoulder.

"Best to put on your cloak," he said. "The weather's turned."

"*Dieu,* Josiah! You are my wet nurse now?"

The old man chuckled. "Fuss all you want to, Abigail. Don't change the fact that you weak as a kitten and it's colder than a snowman's teat."

Without further protest, she reached for her warmest cloak. The stiffness in her fingers made the simple act of putting the cloak over her shoulders and fastening it difficult. By the time she stepped gingerly out into the dooryard, she was trembling and out of breath. The cold air felt sharp against her face, wonderful after the stuffiness of her cabin.

Remembrance.

She inhaled deeply, then gasped, shocked, filled suddenly with a true and terrifying certainty. Remembrance—her Remembrance had come undone!

She remembered now. She'd been in the clearing. There'd been shouting and horses. White men on horses!

The Edge had collapsed and slavers had come bursting into Remembrance!

Pressing her lips together, she gripped the walking stick until her knuckles ached.

"What has happened here, old man?" she whispered. A hush gripped the settlement, a flat, unnatural quiet. Remembrance was many things, but it had never been quiet. Beside her, Josiah had gone stiff and silent.

"Josiah?" She clutched her walking stick, bracing for the terrible words she knew must be coming, afraid she might start howling in despair.

"Abigail . . ." He seemed unable to go on. She moved her hand until it was gripping his. He was trembling but it felt more like fury than fear. "You've been laid up for a couple of days. We thought . . ."

She stared at him, her heart stuttering painfully in her chest, stealing her breath away.

"Tell me," she rasped. "Tell it all." The words burnt her throat.

"Winter is gone. Taken. Louisa." His voice was dead, and for a moment she held on to the hope that she had never woken up, that every word from his mouth was happening only in some terrible dream. But the wind on her face was real. The screeching of the jays in the trees was real. And Josiah's worn hand in hers was warm, and real enough. For the first time in many, many years she wished that she had died. Once again, she felt a spasm of grief, that the ancestors had abandoned her, left her here to . . . what?

"Abigail . . . Thomas is dead."

"Enough! Enough!" she cried. "*Il es fait!* Enough!"

She jerked her hand from his and stumbled backward.

". . . and the Edge has given way. Remembrance is in the world."

The weight of his words forced her to her knees. She knelt there, eyes closed, dull with sorrow. She would never rise again. It was impossible. What was the use? Winter was gone. Her people unprotected. And this place that she had made—Remembrance—had broken apart, and her spirit had broken with it.

"Abigail, get up." Josiah spoke directly into her ear. "Get up, old woman! The peoples is scared. You gots to go to them. Give them back their faith. Give them their courage."

If her breath had not been like a lump of coal in her chest, if she could have inhaled to do it, she would have laughed then.

Faith? Courage?

"Remembrance is gone," she murmured.

Josiah grabbed her arm and yanked her upright. Pain shot through her shoulder, forcing her to turn and face him. "Shame on you, Abigail! Shame and shame! All these peoples still here!" Anger blew off him like fire. "I'm still here! You still here! What about the herds and the smokehouse and the gardens? What about the smithy and all those babies in they little cabins? They gone?"

She was silent. She willed his voice to stop. He shook her hard.

"Wake up, woman," he snapped.

"The Edge . . . ," she began.

"Remembrance ain't the Edge. Never was." He dropped his voice and said, "We comin' to the end of our time, Abigail. We mayn't have much left in us, but we got to make sure the peoples ready for whatever comin' next."

"And how shall this happen, Josiah? Just answer me that. I'm to know what comin' next? And what about Louisa? What about . . ." She could barely say the words. "What about *ti fi yo*? What about Winter?"

Josiah released her and she slumped back to the porch. He stood and turned his face toward the quiet settlement, his head cocked. He seemed to be listening to something. With the last of her strength, she pulled herself to standing.

"Josiah?"

A gust of wind blew across the dooryard and she felt icy wetness on her cheek. Shivering, she pulled her cloak tighter.

"What is it, old man?" she asked, watching him closely.

Josiah stepped from the porch without answering. Closing his eyes, he held his arms away from his body, palms down, his dark fingers moving slowly, as if strumming invisible strings.

"Josiah?"

He shot a hand out to shush her. The old woman ground her teeth, trembling with impatience. It seemed as if an eternity passed before he turned back to face her.

"Bad things out in the world, Abigail," said Josiah.

Mother Abigail gave a short bark of laughter. "That right? The spirits tell you that?"

He turned to her and cocked his head. "You mockin' me, Abigail?"

Another harsh burst of laughter. Mother Abigail could feel hysteria bubbling up in her chest and struggled to restrain it. "*Wi*, old man," she said. "*Wi*, I am mocking you. You speak foolishness, what you expect, then? It's bad in the world. Psssh, you can't do better than that? Then I might as well go up pasture and talk to the sheep."

The old man grinned.

"You need to stand it now," said Josiah, his face serious again. "Remembrance wasn't never the war. It was just a long, pretty well done battle."

Mother Abigail moaned.

"The girl's alive but she scared . . . confused," he said.

The old woman inhaled sharply, nearly collapsing again in her relief. "But she lives?"

The old man nodded.

"And Louisa?"

Josiah sighed and shrugged. "You know I got no way of knowing that. She walks a different road than we."

"But if they're together . . . if Winter's with her . . . ?"

"Abigail!"

She struggled to stand and there was a trembling in her arm she couldn't control. "Take me to the clearing."

"What? Why?"

"I need to go there. Josiah, I need to see."

He was silent for a long moment. "Alright. But you must speak to the people first. Let them see you."

She moaned. "What good will that do? I have nothing for them."

He said nothing, merely held out an arm. With a sigh, she took it, and slowly they began to make their way down the trail to the Central Fire, stopping every few yards for the priestess to catch her breath.

"The Edge, it was a good trick," he said.

"No trick," she snapped, interrupting.

He smiled grimly. "No. No trick," he agreed. "You Babalawa. But the Edge ain't all you ever was. Ain't all Remembrance was."

"Babalawa," she whispered.

He nodded. "Remembrance done lasted, what, forty-some-odd years? More? But don't nothin' last forever." His face crumpled, his expression pure sorrow. "Not even this."

They walked together arm and arm, in silence, each lost in their own thoughts

"These your folks," Josiah said finally. "Ain't nothin' over 'til it's over. Got pieces to pick up, so best be gettin' on with it."

"You soft in the head, Josiah," she growled.

He grimaced. "Soft head make a hard behind. Useful in bad times, I 'spect."

"But what about my girl? What about Louisa? We need to go after them."

He fixed her with his opaque eyes for a long moment. He stood straighter, the gray strands in his hair fewer now. She felt power so much greater than her own, so much older.

"She one of us," he said, his voice low. "Can't go after her, but if she strong enough, she will find her way back. If not . . ."

He let the thought hang in the air between them.

The priestess bowed her head, trembling slightly. She had lost so much, and after all this time, she had thought she'd had nothing left to lose.

Moun sot! Fool!

In her mind's eye, she saw her heart, a hard, black, shriveled thing, nothing left to break because there was no longer anything inside. Her mouth stretched wide, a caricature of a smile. Perhaps she was dead after all.

35

Margot

Margot walked unsteadily from the priestess's porch. From the moment her fingers had touched the old woman's face, things had gone badly awry. She was not a healer. Not like Louisa, like Grandmere. She was a *miroir*, a mirror. She could find but not fix. And sometimes in those reflections, as she felt the vibrations of another's pain and sickness in her own body, she also glimpsed their memories. Fragments, bits and pieces, the things that resonated the most strongly for the other person.

She'd felt the sickness in Mother Abigail to be sure, the broken blood vessel in her head, the pool of blood that was squeezing the old woman's brain inside her skull. She'd felt that eerie slide into the other woman's mind, into Mother Abigail's memories.

But almost immediately she'd felt everything snatched from her control. There hadn't just been fragments. There'd been an infinite space, black and hot, and she'd felt a surge of overwhelming despair. She'd tasted death before and this was much, much worse. When she'd tried to pull away, to sever the bond, it was as if somehow the old woman had reached out and into her mind and was clinging to her with everything she had. She had been trapped, a fly stuck in pitch.

Now she was in Mother Abigail's front yard with no memory of leaving the cabin.

Margot staggered, fell to her knees. Her hands were shaking badly. A memory tickled the edge of her consciousness. Something about Julian Rousse and his mother. About Natchez. She moaned and dug her fingers into the damp earth.

Ajani!

The name came into her mind. She was sure it was a name, and the thought of it touched some deep, sad place in her.

Images flashed in front of her. Tall mountains of emerald green rising from impossibly blue water. A handsome man, the color of milk chocolate, a ring of fire at his feet. Two round-faced boys, chasing each other around an old woman who sat smoking a homemade pipe and ignoring them.

Pain.

So much pain.

She had no idea how much time passed before she tried to stand.

She managed to get to her feet, felt her knees buckle. She would have pitched onto her face if strong hands hadn't caught her from behind.

"Steady there, girl! You okay?" David Henry wrapped a firm arm around her waist. "Sweet Jesus, you cold as death. Let's get you to a fire."

He guided her down the short hill to the Central Fire and settled her on one of the sitting logs.

"You hold up right here and don't move. I'm-a get you somethin' hot to drink," he said kindly. "You look like you could stand some fortifyin'."

He was gone and back before Margot could open her mouth to protest. He placed a cup in her hand, then propped himself on the opposite end of the log. Margot inhaled the steam from the cup. She took a sip and sighed. The sweetness worked its way into her head, clearing her thoughts.

David Henry chuckled. "Apple tea. Good, ain't it?" he said. "One of Remembrance's specialties."

"Remembrance appears to have quite a few more than one," she said dryly.

"Mm-hm," he said. "That's surely so." He flashed her a quick smile. He had a nice smile.

"This tea is wonderful," she said after a moment. "It is what you . . . fortify with as well?"

David Henry nodded. "It's good enough for me. I might have me a shot at New Year's but I ain't much of a drinkin' man. Need to keep the little wits I got about me."

She studied him over the rim of her cup. He had a wide face, smooth, the color of a molasses cookie. He wore his hair short, much shorter than the other men in the settlement. He had a tiny dimple in his chin. She decided that she liked the look of him: clean and compact, strong looking.

"You have been in Remembrance long?" she asked.

"Nearly three years," he said. As he spoke, his eyes darted around the settlement, studying the shadows, the trees, the trails that ringed Remembrance. His rifle rested lightly in the crook of his arm.

"When I first got here, I thought folks were havin' a laugh at my expense," he said smiling. "All this talk about some Edge and different worlds and all such."

He shrugged and shifted his gun. "Even after I saw it for myself I thought it was the craziest thing I ever heard of."

"And now?" she asked.

"It's still the craziest thing I ever heard of." He laughed. "But what the heck, beggin' your pardon. I can live with crazy long as I'm a free man, can't I?"

"I suppose." Margot dropped her head in her hands and leaned closer to the fire. A headache was starting to build behind her eyes. She thought about returning to her lean-to but she didn't want to leave the fire just yet, didn't want to leave David Henry's company.

"I like the way you talk," said David Henry.

Margot raised her head and laughed, surprising herself. "You do not think I talk funny?"

He frowned.

"*Les enfants,* the little girls," she said quickly. "Esther and Hannah, *oui*? They say I speak funny."

He smiled. "Ah. Them. Different as day and night. Hannah the little quiet one."

"Yes," said Margot. "She has declared you her beau."

David Henry blinked, then roared with laughter. "So I guess we best be careful, lest we make Little Miss jealous. And that Esther. She liable to say most anything. Ain't scared a' nothin' in this world."

A cloud passed over his face. "Least she wasn't before," he added quietly.

"*Oui.*"

They sat in comfortable silence. The heat from the fire and the fragrant tea lulled her, and Margot found herself sliding toward that in-between place, between awake and asleep. It was eerily quiet. Except for the two of them, no one was around.

"You look tired. I'll walk you to your place."

His voice roused her and she turned her head to find him gazing at her, studying her. She found she didn't mind.

"Your men are guarding Remembrance?" she asked after a moment.

David Henry raised an eyebrow. "They not my men but . . . yes. They watchin' out. Best they can. They not fightin' men but they will fight if need be."

"Most likely they will not come back here, you know. Those slavers," she said. Her headache had found its footing, and the pounding behind her eyes was making her nauseous. She needed to lie down.

He made a noise in the back of his throat, skeptical.

"You made them pay too dearly," she said. "They will move back south. For more . . . pliable prey."

"They paid not dearly enough. And in the meantime they took what don't belong to 'em." His voice was quiet, measured, belying the ferocity of the words.

Margot examined his face closely. His every movement was deliberate, nothing wasted. Once again, she found herself drawn to him, felt that fluttering behind her breastbone she'd first noticed at the cemetery. "And you will go after them, yes?"

"There ain't agreement. Most feel we need to stay put and be at the ready should the pattyrollers come back." He pulled a sliver of wood from his shirt pocket and stuck it between his teeth. "Just in case."

"But you will go after them?" she pressed. "Winter and Louisa?"

He chewed on his sliver and shrugged. "Might'n not be no call for me to stick around here waitin'." He grinned. "Some folks around Remembrance think there ain't no danger of the 'rollers comin' back."

Margot laughed softly. It felt good to laugh. "And do you believe this?"

He gazed at her evenly, one eyebrow raised. "Could be. Never know."

She yawned. "Oh, *pardonnez-moi*."

"Come on, now," said David Henry quietly. "It's late and you 'bout wore to nothin'."

He helped her to her feet and she staggered as a wave of dizziness overtook her. He tightened his grip and gently led her toward the trail that curved behind the bakehouse.

"You saw her?" he asked as they walked.

Margot nodded. He was talking about Mother Abigail.

"And she is . . . ?"

"She is alive." The relief on his face pained her.

"She is very old," she said gently.

"She old," he said hotly, "but she the heart of this place."

Margot shook her head. "Let us hope not," she murmured. She pretended not to see the sharp look he gave her. Once again, she stumbled, and for a moment, Remembrance seemed to pitch beneath her feet.

"I am quite fine," she said in answer to his question, but she gripped his arm firmly as he led her toward her lean-to.

At the entrance to the shelter she held fast to him and met his eyes. He was shorter than she was by half a head. "I fear the Edge has fallen. And your Mother Abigail is too weak to defend Remembrance."

He tucked a heated brick he'd brought back from the Central Fire just behind the lean-to's covering and turned to face her. "You think it matters a whit to me whether I be in the world or out? Remembrance in here." He patted his chest with the palm of his hand. "Mother Abigail done for us; now the time done come for us to do for her . . . and us. We'll defend ourselves. Ain't no point of freedom if you not ready to fight for it, is there?"

He indicated the unseen men hidden in the trees surrounding the settlement. She nodded at hearing the echo of Petal's words.

She placed her hand over his heart. He started but did not pull away. Closing her eyes, she felt his life thrum against her palm, sure and steady. He was a solid man and strong. She forced her own heart to his rhythm, felt his surprise as he sensed the change in himself. And still she held to him.

Unlike the old priestess who clung to her life through force of will, David Henry was vital, and his energy filled her up, soothed the ache she felt from somewhere deep inside.

This was the future of Remembrance, she thought.

He touched her wrist and she jerked, startled. When she opened her eyes, she found him staring at her, an expression of bemused bewilderment written on his face.

"You are going after Winter and Louisa, *oui*?" she asked for the second time that night.

He glanced at his own hand holding her wrist. Almost as if by accident, he rubbed his thumb over the soft skin there, then released her. He took a step back. "I swore, once I got my freedom, that as long as I drew breath, wouldn't nobody take what belonged to me ever again. Remembrance belongs to me, and those girls belong to Remembrance."

Margot nodded. "Yes," she said quietly.

David Henry touched his brow in a half salute, then turned away as she bent to the lean-to.

"Miss Margot?"

She straightened to find David Henry returned, standing just behind her. He pressed something into her hand.

"In case the talk be wrong . . . about the pattyrollers comin' back."

He grinned, then turned and strode between the lean-tos before seeming to vanish into the woods. Opening her hand, she gazed down at what he had given her. In her palm lay a small knife, its wooden shaft intricately carved, the blade very sharp, and very deadly.

36

Winter

A crack of thunder jolted her awake. She had no idea how long she'd slept but her neck felt broken in two. Winter pulled herself upright, hissing in pain. She squinted toward where Louisa lay. In the dimness, she could only just make out a motionless lump.

Dragging herself to her feet, she limped back and forth, trying to force circulation back into her screaming muscles. She tugged the remnants of her cloak around her shoulders, surprised that she still had it. She was cold, and her skin itched from the bites of whatever was living in the damp straw.

"Louisa," she whispered. There was no answer. "Louisa?"

A terrible thought came to her. What if Louisa had died while she slept? Then she really would be all alone. Panicked tears pricked her eyes.

Before she could work up the courage to move closer to the silent figure, the barn door creaked open and in walked Dix, carrying a tray. He placed it on the floor, careful to stay just beyond her reach, then without a word, turned to leave.

"Wait!" She saw him start and forced herself to speak calmly. "It's freezing in here. Without extra blankets . . . or something to build a fire, we're not going to last long enough to get to . . . wherever it is you're taking us."

The boy stood in front of the half-open door, his back to her. In the dancing shadows of his lantern, she could see that he, too, was suffering from the cold. His breath formed a cloud above his head, and beneath his wet, threadbare overcoat, he was shivering. He turned slowly and faced her.

"I brung supper," he said.

Winter glanced at the tray.

"Ain't much," he went on. "Some boiled 'taters and biscuits. Got a bit a' mushroom catsup for taste and some hot coffee. Nothin' fancy but it's edible." He tried to smile. "Just barely."

Winter nodded and pulled the tray toward her. Steam from the potatoes warmed her face. Her stomach growled and her resolve to never eat again disappeared.

"Should be enough for her, too," said Dix, indicating Louisa. He stepped closer and frowned. "She seems to be doin' poorly."

Winter rolled her eyes and bit back a retort. Anger burned like an ember in her gut, but she tamped it down. She was caught, and there was no point in getting the boy stirred up again the way she had earlier. It would do her no good. She needed to stay calm, to think. And she needed to stay clear of the two slaver brothers.

"The cold's not helping much," she said evenly.

"No, don't suppose so," replied Dix. "Colm and Frank's already riled. Things going the way they been. Don't 'spect her dyin'll improve their disposition none. I'll see about gettin' something to help warm y'all a bit in here. She gonna be needin' anything else to put her right?"

Winter shrugged. How should she know? Louisa was the healer. Shooting him a look, her eyes widened when she saw that there was more new bruising starting to form around his neck, just above the collar. He saw her staring and looked away. Still, he lingered.

"You not gonna eat your supper?"

Winter looked down. There were two wooden bowls, each containing three small potatoes not much bigger than her thumb, covered in a lumpy brown sauce. The two flat hardtack biscuits were like iron. It was a meager meal for one, let alone two, but it was warm and would patch, if not fill, the hole in her belly. She picked up one of the biscuits and pushed it into the catsup. While she waited for it to soften, she self-consciously ate a potato and drank the weak coffee.

The warm food steadied her, and the muscles in her arms and legs began to unknot. A gust of wind shook the barn violently, and both Dix and Winter froze, listening as the storm outside built in intensity.

"Bad storm," muttered Dix. "They not gonna make it back tonight, for sure.

"You got people left . . . back there?" Dix asked suddenly.

Winter slowly chewed her bit of potato and studied him through narrowed eyes. He had cleared a place on the floor to set his lantern down and now squatted a few feet away, watching her intently, the lamplight flickering across his face. He had taken everything else away from her and now he wanted this too? Her memories?

When she didn't answer right away, Dix cocked his head and shuffled his feet in the straw. She noted his restlessness and her heart stumbled in her chest. He had no right to her life, but the thought of being left again, cold and in the dark with only the insensible and maybe dead Louisa, was worse.

"I never had a daddy," she said softly. "And my momma died when I was newly born. Froze to death in the snow."

He didn't need to know she was running from slavers.

"Mother Abigail, that old woman that you saw . . . took me in, raised me like her own. Everybody had a hand in, really. The women taught me to cook and sew. Well, they tried. And the men taught me to trap and fish a little bit."

"You don't miss your momma?" Dix asked.

She stared at him, narrow-eyed. Since when did a slaver give two figs about a Negro's family ties?

Winter shrugged. "Never knew her. Would've liked to," she said finally. "Mother Abigail always said she was brave and strong. Gave her last piece of life saving mine, but . . . you can't really miss something you never had."

Dix was quiet for a long time. He seemed entranced by the flame of the lamp. Winter drank the coffee. It had no taste to speak of, but it was tongue-searing hot and if it didn't quite warm her through, at least it thawed her some.

"My daddy went out West to mine for gold," said Dix finally. He stared into the lamplight, speaking softly, as if to himself. "Was gonna send for us when he struck it rich. Didn't never hear from him again. 'Spect he's long dead or . . . maybe he got hisself a new family and just plumb forgot about us. Momma held out hope to the last that he'd come ridin' down that hollow, flush with his gold money, and pack us off to a new, big-city life." He chuckled bitterly. "Then last spring my momma and sister got took by the fever. Last thing on my sister's lips was her callin' for my daddy."

"Sorry," said Winter. In spite of herself, she felt a flicker of pity for this boy, this boy who had helped steal her away from her home and who planned on pocketing silver coins by selling her.

She kept her eyes on the plate of food, but she could feel him looking at her. He was struggling with something. She didn't know what, but she felt it stirring in the air between them. She wanted to jump to her feet and scream at him to let her go, but she forced herself to keep her head down and concentrate on pushing the impossible hardtack round and round in the dark sauce.

Steady, girl, she told herself. Don't spook him. A memory flashed through her mind: David Henry taking her fishing by the river to escape the summer heat. The first time she'd caught a fish, she'd been so excited that she'd snatched her pole back and lost her catch. "Steady, steady," David Henry had said. "Sometimes when you tryin' to catch a thing it's best to let it have its head. If you don't seem a threat, you can sometimes get the wildest beast to eat outa your hand."

Dix sat silently, watching her as she forced down the hardtack. The catsup had made it only slightly softer.

"It ain't true, is it?" he asked.

She looked up, frowning. In the lantern light, his gray face glowed yellow, his eyes glittered.

"About . . . the old woman?" he said. "Her powers? That she can work roots and such? Make folks disappear?"

Holding his gaze, she hesitated only a second. "Yes."

Dixon McHugh lurched to his feet, his pale eyes blinking rapidly. He looked so terrified that Winter had to bite back a laugh.

"What's that you say now?" he asked, swallowing so hard she could hear it from where she sat. "You said y'all weren't no witches!"

She put her plate aside and stood slowly. "Like I said before. There are no such thing as witches."

He stared at her and she stared back. Was it better or worse for him to be afraid of her? She wasn't sure. What if she scared him so badly he ended up shooting her . . . or worse? She twisted a strand of hair nervously around her finger.

Steady. Steady now.

"You scared of me, Dix?" She spoke softly, her voice gentling, the way she'd been taught to speak to an injured animal. She moved toward him, reached to touch the wound around his neck, stopping when he jerked away from her hand.

"Why're you scared of me?" She held herself as still as she could bear. "I can't hurt you."

But she could. She could get inside his spaces. See the pieces that made him a slaver-shaped boy. Turn him inside out.

She could.

If she wasn't so cold. If she could just think clearly. If she could just remember.

She could hurt him. And those other ones, too.

If she could just remember those things—anything—Mother Abigail had taught her. If she could just remember. Then she could go home and there'd be nothing they could do to stop her.

He was pacing back and forth in front of the half-open door, his thin arms beating the air. "I saw it. I saw it with my own eyes. I saw that old nigger and Zeke. I saw you people appear out of nowhere. If you not witches—then what?"

"People," she said. "We're just people."

This stopped him. He peered at her and shook his head, his eyes flitting between her and the door.

"We're regular folks. Just like you," she insisted. *No,* she thought, *not like you.* "Some of us just have a special talent for things. It's no different than being good at trapping or . . . cooking." She glanced at the plate, the brown sauce congealing in the center. "Some folks just have the knack for it."

It was the kind of thing Mother Abigail told the new runaways, the especially skittish ones that needed to hear something they could grab hold to.

He was watching her, his forehead creased, concentrating on her words. "Magic ain't like bakin' taters."

It was her turn to shake her head. Her eyes burned. She was tired, so tired. "Never called it magic. Said it was a talent. If it was true magic I wouldn't be chained up here in this barn, would I?" she asked bitterly.

"Y'all killed Zeke!"

"What would you do if people came riding into your home with guns and whips?" she cried, her voice shrill, unable to hold her temper any longer. "What would you have done if someone had tried to steal away your momma . . . or your sister?"

Dix flushed and looked away, unable to meet her eyes. "I . . ."

"You would have done whatever you had to do, wouldn't you?

"Why're you scared of me?" she demanded again. "Those slavers . . . they're the ones hurting you, beating on you, leaving their marks all over you. You're no better than me! You're just a slave yourself!"

The boy jerked and ran a shaky hand through his limp hair. "That ain't true! You don't know nothin'! I ain't nothin' like you. I'm a white man just like them."

"Not like them," Winter murmured.

She watched the emotions play across his face as he waged some private war. Her shoulders sagged. She was tired and sore and cold and suddenly she just wanted him to leave. As if reading her thoughts, the boy moved toward the door.

"My grammy used to tell of folks touched by the devil," he said, still lingering.

"Oh. Well. Then it must be true." She rubbed a finger across her bruised lips. "Just 'cause something's different, just because folks are too thickheaded and lazy to understand something, doesn't make it evil."

She wanted to curl back into the straw and close her eyes, biting things or not. Wanted him to leave her alone.

"Might could be that your people touched by God, then," he said quietly. She could see him working this out in his head, trying to decide. "I heard a' saints, holy people that could work miracles."

Winter gave him a tired smile. "Well, we ain't saints, either."

Dix pushed the barn door open and wind sliced through the opening, bringing sheets of icy rain with it. As he stood facing her, his pale silver-blond hair whipped around his face.

"I ain't scared of you, you know. And I ain't scared of them, neither." And then he slipped out into the howling darkness.

She gazed at the closed door. *Oh, yes you are.*

"Why you messin' 'round with that white boy?"

Winter gasped. She whirled to find Louisa staring at her from the shadows.

"You're awake!" She rushed to the girl's side and fell to her knees.

"He ain't your friend, you know," said Louisa. She was battered and bruised; her dark face was so shiny swollen it looked as if it might burst open, but her voice was the same, irritable and full of malice. If she could have, Winter would have hugged her.

"How do you feel?"

"Ready for the ball. Stupid." Louisa glared at her. "How I look?" Winter gave a snort of laughter, too relieved to take offense. She poured a tin of coffee and put it to Louisa's lips. "Here, drink."

The older girl frowned but drank it, and after some coaxing, she managed to eat one of the remaining potatoes. But the effort seemed to spend her and her head drooped back onto the soiled blanket. Winter sipped the last of the coffee and stared at her, studying the girl's injuries. She wished she could remember anything at all about healing, but that was Louisa's talent.

And she worried.

What if Colm and Frank did make it back? What if the storm broke and they really did have to leave in the morning? Louisa was in no shape to travel, wouldn't be for days, as far as she could tell. Would they just leave her here? Or would they do something far worse? Winter pushed the thoughts from her mind.

"You think if you keep starin' long enough, you gon' make me beautiful?" snapped Louisa, her eyes still closed.

Winter's lips twitched. "Even I know it would take more than that."

The herbalist grunted and opened her eyes. "You got no idea," she said. There was a long pause. "I ain't goin' back. I sold my soul to get my freedom that first time, and I ain't never goin' back."

Winter turned the tin cup over and over in her hands and listened as the storm threw itself against the walls.

She looked up. Louisa had managed to lift herself up on one elbow. She had the same wild look in her eyes as before, but this time there was no hysterical laughter. "You don't know, girl. You been coddled by Mother Abigail your whole life. Treated special. But you won't be treated special out there. Girl like you . . ." She spat. "Girl like you . . . they'll have you bedded down with the master in no time. And when he gets tired of you, they'll mate you like a hog to some old field hand so's they can get them a big ol' passel of brand-new pretty yellow picka-ninnies!"

Winter sat motionless, Louisa's words washing over her like lye. This was worse than the crazy laughter of before, far worse. She opened her mouth to speak, then closed it again. Louisa's eyes glittered.

"You think they're comin' for you?" snarled Louisa. "Hunh? That what you think? Ain't nobody comin'! Not for you. Not for me."

"You hate me so much?" asked Winter. Her voice trembled

"Hate you?" Louisa laughed. "Hell, yeah, I hate you! I hate the sight of you! I hate the smell of you! I hate the feel of your name in my mouth!"

"I have never ever done a single thing to you, Louisa!" her voice cracked. "Never!"

For a long moment, Louisa was silent, her hard, angry eyes fixed on Winter. And then she said softly, as if all her anger had been used up, "She only ever saw you. No matter what the rest of us did, Mother Abigail only had eyes for you. She treated you like you was some little glass angel. All the time makin' no bones about who would lead Remembrance when the time came. Everybody knew you was supposed to be touched by the gift."

She moaned and fell back onto the blanket. "But I didn't never see no gift. All I ever saw was a high-yellow gal flittin' from one thing to the next like a butterfly." She moaned again. "Butterflies pretty, right enough. They got their place, but they don't do the work of keepin' a place alive, do they? And I just want to know one thing. If you supposed to be special enough to head up Remembrance, how come you still chained up in this nasty horse stall bein' ate up by fleas? Where's your powers now? I ask you that. Where they at?"

Then she closed her eyes and turned her back. Her shoulders shook. Winter thought she heard muffled sobbing. But that couldn't be, could it? Louisa's heart was a stone. There was no room for tears.

Winter sat paralyzed, Louisa's ugly words bouncing around inside her head.

They'll mate you like a hog to some field hand!

I hate the sight of you! . . . I hate the feel of your name in my mouth!

Ain't nobody comin'! Ain't nobody comin'! Ain't nobody comin'!

Winter curled herself into a tight ball and tried to make herself as small as possible. As the darkness deepened, all she heard around her was the barn groaning against the storm's icy assault and the rustling of unseen creatures in the shadows.

It wasn't her fault. She'd never wanted any of it. To be special. To have the ability she had. And certainly not to lead Remembrance.

If you so special, why you still chained up? Louisa had asked her. "Where's your powers now?"

I don't know. I don't know!

She lay shivering on the floor. It was so cold! It was so hard to concentrate! Winter closed her eyes and inhaled through her nose. She tried to see herself back in Remembrance, tried to hear Mother Abigail's voice yelling at her to see more than what was just propped on the tip of her nose. In the freezing barn, she smiled slightly.

The icy rain beat a steady rhythm. It worked its way into her mind, gradually interrupting the words of Louisa's rant, and she let herself be hypnotized by the sound. There was a small metal pail a few feet away, filled with rusting nails. She could see them. See how the rust braided itself into the iron. See how slowly the individual particles moved around each other. And there was water inside the metal, waiting to change it. She could see all the spaces. The pieces that made up the pieces. Spinning. Spinning. And as she watched, they spun faster. Then faster still. The rust unbraided itself as the metal softened and glowed, warming.

Spinning.

Faster.

The nails inside the pail, losing their nail shape, their particles dancing wildly around each other. The pail itself softening, warping.

She fell asleep to the sound of the rain and the vision of all those spinning, dancing particles.

When Dix came in a short time later, bringing blankets and warmed bricks to tuck into the straw, she didn't hear him, didn't hear him call to her in confusion at the small fire that burned in the metal pail by the door. And she didn't know that he stood staring at her in stunned silence, in a barn that now was toasty warm, despite the freezing rain outside.

37

Winter

The storm was getting worse. The barn shook as if giant fists were pounding its sides, and beneath the howling of the wind was the sound of hail being flung against the roof. The tiny bit of light that managed to leak through the planking was such a uniform gray that it could have been either early evening or early morning.

Winter was oblivious to the chaos outside.

She studied the chain around her ankle. It was heavy, a bit over five feet long and attached to a metal loop sunk deep into the barn's dirt floor. She stood and tried tugging at the loop, throwing the weight of her body against it, hoping to dislodge it, but it was sunk too deep. Winded, she dropped cross-legged to the floor and wiped her dripping nose on her sleeve.

She shot a glance at Louisa, who still lay turned away from her, curled in a ball. Whether asleep or simply ignoring her, Winter couldn't tell. Taking a deep breath to clear her mind, she forced herself to concentrate.

More than one way to drive a mule, my girl.

She smiled a little, hearing Mother Abigail's voice in her head, and it calmed her. She held the chain in one hand and slowly began to draw it, link by link across her palm, focusing all her attention on it. She stared at the cold metal, willing herself to ignore everything else, willing herself to see only the links in her hand. There was no storm, no pattyrollers coming to take her away. There was only this chain, holding her in this terrible place.

Nothing was what it seemed. There were spaces between things and spaces between those. One just had to see them. And she knew how to do that. How to peer into the gaps.

She stared at the chain in her hand. It seemed a solid thing but she knew it was not, and as she concentrated she saw that it was made of pieces tinier than a grain of sand. And those pieces were shaped like cubes, millions and millions of cubes. And inside those cubes was an even smaller piece suspended like trousers on a clothesline. She felt herself fall into the space, into the cubes, watched them spin slowly around each other, around her. She raised her hand and touched the outermost particle, watched it move faster, then faster still, spinning, spinning. The other millions and millions of cubes following along.

And as they spun, the chain that she still gripped in her hand grew warm, then hot, nearly unbearably so, but still she held on, falling, falling, into the spaces between the spaces. Feeling the particles that made the iron and the iron that made the chain tumble around and around each other.

"What you doin' over there?"

Something burst in Winter's head, making a sound so loud she was sure it could be heard over the storm. She blinked. The world swam before her eyes, and for a moment, a long moment, she wasn't sure where she was. Then, there was the cold ground beneath her, the raging storm . . . and Dix.

The boy hovered just inside the door. He was carrying a lantern and two food tins and looked near drowned.

"What're you doin'?" he asked again.

Winter blinked. "Nothing." Her voice was hoarse. "I'm not doing anything." Her hand throbbed.

"Well," he said, eyeing her suspiciously. He placed the tins near her. She made no move toward them. "Frank and Colm still not back."

She said nothing to this.

"Never seen nothin' like this storm," he went on. "Never in my life.

It's like the skies just opened up and everything in the heavens just fallin' out."

Still, she said nothing. Her silence seemed to make him uncomfortable. He dug a toe in the straw and fidgeted. "Brought you some beans and biscuits. Ain't got a whole lot left, leastways not 'til Frank and Colm make it back."

Winter stared at the ground. Not for the first time, she wished for a fast river current to carry the slaver brothers away, or a bolt of lightning to strike them both dead. What would happen, she wondered, if they never came back? Would the silent Paddy order Dix to tie her and Louisa to the back of a horse and complete the march south? Or would he think that too much bother and leave them chained in the barn until they starved to death?

Dix shuffled his feet and cleared his throat, but when it became clear that Winter wasn't going to speak to him, he turned to go. At the barn door, he stopped.

"You might get sold to some nice folks," he said. His voice was so low she barely heard it over the hail and wind.

Her head snapped up and she locked eyes with him. Even in the dim light, she saw him flush. She stared until he hung his head and looked away, before disappearing back out into the weather.

A searing pain shot through her hand and Winter sucked her teeth. Hissing in pain, she opened her fist to drop the chain she'd been gripping, crying out in shocked surprise. The chain was gone, or rather the part she'd been holding in her hand was gone. A length of chain was still attached to the metal loop in the floor, and around her ankle the ring still dangled a foot of links, but the part she'd been holding, the little section she'd been focusing on so intently when Dix interrupted was . . . gone. Instead, mean-looking welts pulsed across her palm, like a row of figure eights. Breathing fast, she squatted and pressed her hand against the dirt floor, sighing as it cooled the burning in her palm.

Sweet Jesus on a horse!

The pain in her hand was so bad that it took her a moment—two short breaths—for the realization to hit her, and when it did, she leaped to her feet, the blisters in her hand momentarily forgotten. Barely daring to breathe, staring at the iron band clamped around her ankle, she took a few tentative steps toward the wall behind the horse stall. One foot, then two, and still she moved freely. Heart pounding, she yanked at the chain around her ankle. The newly freed end was as smooth as window glass, as if it had always been meant to be just a tiny spit of free chain and nothing else.

Winter whooped and slapped her good hand over her mouth.

"Louisa!" Winter squatted by the injured girl and shook her. "Louisa, wake up!"

Louisa opened her eyes. Some of the swelling had started to go down on her face and she was beginning to look more like herself. Winter couldn't decide if this was a good thing or not. The herbalist glared silently at Winter.

"Look!" Winter held the length of free chain up for Louisa to see.

Louisa looked and Winter watched with grim satisfaction as the herbalist's expression changed from irritation to astonishment.

"What . . . ?" gasped Louisa, struggling to sit up. "What is that? They let you loose?"

Winter shook her head as she helped the other girl to sitting. "*I* let me loose. I did it."

Louisa looked between the chain's smooth end and Winter's grinning face, her expression unreadable. "Well," she said finally, "what you waitin' for then? You better get on up outa here 'fore those white boys come back."

"I have to get you loose! Yours aren't even hooked to anything. It'll be easier!"

"Get me loose?" Louisa tugged at the chains binding her ankles. "For what? I ain't goin' nowhere! Look at me, I'm a mess. Can't hardly sit up on my own. How I'm goin' to get away from here?"

Winter's smile faded away. "But . . . but you said you weren't ever going back. You said you'd rather die."

"Then I guess I'm-a die," said Louisa. She lay back with a moan and turned her back.

With no thought in her mind except that it was just stinking bad luck that first she should get captured by the pattyrollers and then that she should be captured with this horrible, horrible girl, Winter straddled the herbalist and grabbed her blouse, yanking her roughly upright.

"I am sick of you, Louisa," she hissed. "You hear me? Sick to death of you and your mean-hearted, foul-tongued ways! You want to feel sorry for yourself? Fine! But you're coming with me out of here! If I could find my way back to Remembrance without you, Lord knows I'd leave you. But I can't. So you can just shut up all that foolishness and help me figure out a way to get you up on your feet and moving. You hear me?"

Louisa gaped openmouthed, and for a moment Winter thought she might strike out. It wouldn't be the first time. And then the girl began to laugh. Not the crazed laughter of before, but a deep-throated, full-hearted belly laugh. Startled, Winter released her and climbed off.

"What is so funny?" she asked as Louisa held her sides and cackled on the barn floor.

Louisa took a wheezy breath. "Well," she said. "It looks like the butterfly has a sting."

Winter crossed her arms. "It would serve you then not to forget that."

Louisa rolled her eyes. "I guess the first thing I need to do is fill my belly. Then you can show me how to get outa these blasted chains."

"You're breaking my neck," gasped Winter.

"Then slow down!"

Winter clutched Louisa around the waist, trying to match her gait to the older girl's. Removing Louisa's leg chains had proven to be much easier than getting her up on her feet and walking. The two girls stumbled clumsily around the barn, keeping an ear out for their captors. Winter did her best to help Louisa but only managed to keep throwing the older girl off-balance.

"Alright! Enough! This ain't workin' at all," exclaimed Louisa. She collapsed, sweaty and pale in an exhausted heap.

"Then what?" snapped Winter. "What are we supposed to do?"

"I don't know, but this ain't it. Won't even make it out the barn at this rate."

Before Winter could reply, they heard voices outside the barn. As they came closer, she scrambled to a spot near the horse stalls and motioned a warning to Louisa.

Colm stepped into the barn and silently studied the two girls. "Well, now," he said, looking at Louisa. "Bless my eyes. If you haven't perked up quite fine."

Colm squatted in front of Louisa and poked at her face with his finger, turning her head this way and that. The girl said nothing, but Winter saw her wince with pain at his touch.

Colm stood with a grunt. "Still got the face of a donkey's arse, but we won't be sellin' her for her beauty, will we?"

He smiled at Winter. "We got you for that."

He began to pace, and each time his steps brought him close to her, Winter cringed against the splintered wood of the stall. He stopped and stood with his back to her, staring out of the half-open door at the driving rain.

"Christ Almighty," he swore under his breath. "Never seen weather like this in the whole of my existence. The roads are like pudding. Couldn't get nothin'. No supplies, nothing! I swear on my old Nana's eyes, it feels like we're never to get shed of this devil-be-fucked place."

He whirled and was on Winter before she could take a breath. Grabbing her hair, he yanked her head back hard so that she was forced to look into his eyes. He seemed paler than he had the last time she'd seen him, and there were dark, purplish shadows under his eyes.

Don't let him see the chain. He mustn't see it! Don't let him see the chain.

"You're a sweet little cherry, aren't you, lass?" he hissed. "Do you know what you cost me, gal? Do you? Are you worth it? My man Zeke, my brother? Are you worth my brother?"

He stared into her face, breathing hard, his breath hot and strangely sweet. Her hands were wrapped around his, trying to brace herself against the pain of him yanking her hair. His hands were cold as stone and tangled tightly in her curls. She hung there, helpless, gazing into his eyes, too terrified to speak, until he flung her back down.

Backing away, he took a bottle from his overcoat pocket and drank from it, never taking his eyes off her. His hands shook so badly that he spilled liquor onto his chin, down his shirt.

Run! Run now! The thought a roar in her head.

But she couldn't run. She was afraid of even moving, afraid he'd see then that she was no longer chained.

"My brother," he said. "Did you know my brother? No, of course not. Why would a lass like you know my brother?"

She stared, unblinking, down at her lap. She was afraid that if he looked in her eyes he would know that she *had* seen his brother all those weeks before; had seen him appear like an apparition inside Remembrance, chasing the runaway, Zeus. Had seen Mother Abigail whisper in his ear as he lay sprawled on the ground. Had heard his screams echoing behind them as they carried Zeus across the clearing toward the settlement.

Colm took another drink. This time, he got most of it in his mouth. He smiled and gave Winter a small salute.

"My brother Reavus. The youngest. The finest of the Clay brothers. Full of grit and lightning, he was. Came up to this cursed country a month or so back slave chasin'. Came back to home crazy as a loon."

He plopped down in the dirt next to her. She gripped her skirt, holding herself still as his eyes bored into her.

"Talkin' about ghosts and witches and such"—he took another drink—"you ever hear of such nonsense?"

Winter tried to shake her head but all she could do was blink.

"I said, you ever hear such nonsense?" Colm screamed. He was on his knees, leaning over her. Winter cowered, shaking her head wildly. She brought a hand up to defend against his blows but the slaver didn't strike her. He slumped down once again and sipped from his bottle.

"Me neither," he said, calm again. "I told him and I told him that it was foolishness. And a sin against the church as well, but he would not be moved. Kept saying about how some old woman, a giant mammy, and a nigger with no eyes had cursed him."

He swirled the bottle round and round, staring at the patterns the liquid made inside. She flinched as a gust of wind slammed the barn.

From somewhere high above them came the sound of wood splintering.

"Want to know what happened to my brother? Want to know what happened to Reavus Clay?" he asked suddenly.

No, she thought, she didn't.

She nodded.

"Well," said Colm. He leaned forward and whispered conspiratorially. "When he got back, he went out in the woods and cut a tree for Susie. Susie was his daughter. Tiny little thing. He got Susie a tree. Said it was for Christmas even though it wasn't nowhere near Christmas. That girl surely does love Christmastime."

He drank the last from his bottle then tossed it into the shadows. Winter flinched again at the sound of glass breaking.

"Well, ol' Reave, my fine baby brother, the best of the Clays, put that tree up right in the middle of their cabin. Bloody near took up every inch of the place. Oh, he made them a Christmas, didn't he? He put all manner of fancies under that tree. Toilet water for his wife, a swath of calico cloth, a silver mirror for Susie. Stuffed that place like a rich man's fool. Then he went outside and threw himself down the well."

Winter swallowed hard. She remembered the lanky, dark-haired man that had come to the Edge hunting the slaves, remembered his slow drawl as he'd tried to negotiate with Mother Abigail, how he'd called her Auntie. She tried to ease away, but Colm Clay wrapped his arms around her shoulders and pulled her tight against his side.

"And so we had to come and see, you know," he whispered wetly against her ear. "Me and Frank. Had to come and find the niggers who could do such a thing to our Reave."

Twisting around, he put his lips against hers. She felt the sour/sweet burn of his whiskey. When he tried to push his tongue between her lips, she clenched her teeth, bile rising in her throat.

She stared into his eyes and felt the heat, not in her hand this time, but everywhere. There was no thought in her mind except that he release her. She saw the pink splotching his cheeks, the fine black hairs between his brows. She saw the pores of his face, the specks of dirt settled there. He was just millions of bits shaped like a man, and there were spaces between those bits, and she could touch them and move them. And he was no different than the chain. She could . . .

The slaver jerked away, toppling backward. He lay on his back, breathing hard, then rolled onto his stomach and got to his hands and knees. He looked at her. She looked back.

She could smell him, the weakness of him. His skin, his bones, the things that made him seem like a real, solid thing. Well, that was all an illusion, wasn't it? It would be so easy to take it all apart. Like the chain. Like the chicken.

"Shite," he exclaimed staggering to his feet. "I'm well and truly squiffy."

He squinted at her, seemed to struggle to hold himself upright. He seemed unaware that a thin stream of blood was leaking from his right eye.

"No magic. No witches. You're just a regular nigger gal, right?" His speech was thickly slurred.

Eyes narrowed, Winter smiled through clenched teeth. "Yes, just a regular . . . nigger girl."

Colm stared at her and she held his gaze, rage churning inside her. For a moment she saw something flash in his eyes. Confusion? Fear? The slaver blinked, his eyes narrow, glazed over, then he nodded and walked unsteadily out into the storm.

He's just a thing. Made up of tiny pieces. And he would never touch her again.

"Winter!"

She spun toward Louisa.

Things. They were all just things. Made up of smaller things she could take apart.

"Winter!"

She felt a sudden release, as if a knot had been undone from round her chest. Louisa was gaping at her, her eyes wide. Winter stepped toward her, and Louisa sucked in a breath, drew her knees up under her chin. The two girls stared at each other.

"This storm won't last long," said Louisa at last into the silence, her voice low.

"No?" Winter felt sick to her stomach. She lowered herself to the floor.

"A day, maybe two."

She nodded and roughly wiped her mouth. She could still taste the slaver on her tongue.

"You gon' have to go with or without me," said Louisa. "And it gon' have to be soon."

Louisa was sitting up, her back to the wall. She flinched under Winter's gaze.

Winter noticed, but it hardly mattered. "Yes," was all she said.

38

Margot

She wasn't sure the scratching was real. She'd slept so poorly the past few nights that she was having a hard time telling awake from sleep. During the daytime she wandered through the tense settlement, her eyes burning with fatigue, her head feeling as if it were stuffed with horsehair. She'd just decided that the noise was a dream echo when she heard her name.

"Margot?" The voice not quite a whisper. "Margot? You awake in there?"

She rolled on her side with a groan and pushed back the blanket that covered the opening to her lean-to, and found herself looking into Petal's worried face.

"*Qu'est-ce que c'est?*" she asked, her voice hoarse with exhaustion. "What is it? Are you ill? Is it the babies?"

Petal shook her head. "You best start with coffee." She thrust a dented metal cup through the gap toward Margot. "My Nanny used to always say, wasn't no bad news in the world that couldn't wait 'til after your first cup."

Bad news?

Margot's stomach dropped at the words but she managed a weak smile.

"That sounds like something my *grand-mère* would say."

She pulled herself from the shelter and happily accepted the steaming coffee. Petal's smile flashed on, then off, never quite reaching her eyes. She chewed her lip as she shot nervous looks over her shoulder. Margot sighed, savoring the coffee as it traced a warm path down her insides. Petal was right. Any bad news could wait until she'd finished her coffee.

When, too soon, there was nothing left in the cup but wet grounds, she took a deep breath and turned toward Petal. The girl was kneeling a few feet from the lean-to, turned partly away from Margot. Her body was as tense as a bowstring, her thin arms wrapped protectively around her hugely pregnant belly.

"Petal?"

"It's all a mess," said Petal, struggling to her feet. She motioned for Margot to follow her. "Everybody fussin' and fightin'. It's all just one big cock-a-doodle-doo mess."

At the Central Fire, Margot saw that Petal was right.

Remembrance was unraveling. Uphill, she could see that several cabins, their doors hanging open, had clearly been abandoned. A handful of men stood facing each other on the other side of the fire, their voices raised, gesturing wildly. From where she stood, Margot could not make out the words, but it felt bad.

"What is it? What is happening?"

Petal turned. There were tears in her eyes. "It's comin' undone. Remembrance is comin' apart. Some folks talkin' 'bout leavin'. Goin' on to Canada. Sayin' Mother Abigail can't protect us no more."

Margot pressed her lips together and watched the scene unfolding before her.

"Some of the mens, they sayin' it be death for sure. It's comin' on winter. They say everybody need to stay and protect what's ours."

Margot nodded. It was the thought of winter coming that had made her hesitate about moving on herself. She glanced up at the empty cabins. "Looks like some have already made the choice."

Petal nodded. "A few left for Ashtabula. Said they's more folks there. They be safer there. Maybe."

The two women watched as the argument between the men grew more heated.

"Sweet Lord," murmured Petal. "Wish David Henry was here. Folks always listen to him. He could settle this down, but ain't nobody seen him in days. He wouldn't leave here. He just wouldn't! Somethin' bad musta happened."

Margot said quietly, "He did not just run off."

Petal turned to look at her. "Where is he?"

"He left. Two nights ago. He went to find Winter and Louisa."

Petal stared at her openmouthed. "Oh, Lord," she moaned. "Oh, Lord. By hisself? He think he gon' get somebody back from slaver men? What kinda fool thing is that to do? He gon' just get hisself killed."

"He seems able to take care of himself."

Priez les saints, *please make that so,* she thought.

Petal opened her mouth to say something, then changed her mind. From somewhere in Remembrance, a baby began to cry.

"Where is Mother Abigail?" asked Margot.

Petal blinked, then looked away, chewing hard on her lip.

"Petal?" Margot reached to touch her, then decided against it, her hand hovering just above the pregnant woman's shoulder.

"Ain't nobody seen her since yesterday. Or Josiah, neither. That was the final straw," said Petal. "Folks sayin' that since Winter got stole away, she done gone off in the head."

"Mère Vierge!"

"Well, I'm not goin' nowhere. This my home now. For always," she declared.

Margot's mouth twitched. "So you have said."

"And you? You not leavin', are you Margot? Remembrance could be your forever place."

She hesitated. "I do not know," she said, answering honestly. "It does not seem a place I belong."

Petal stared at her, her eyes glittering. "What place you belong at more?"

Margot opened her mouth, closed it. Where did she belong? Back in New Orleans? Without her grandmother, without her sister, that wasn't home. It was just another city on a map. The thought of walking through Jackson Square without Veronique at her side made her quiver with pain.

"I do not know," she said again.

"You were brave enough to get all the way here. You just have to be brave enough to make your new life."

Be brave. Always be brave.

Old Madame Rousse's parting words echoed in Margot's head. She swallowed hard.

"It was not my bravery." She fingered the locket at her neck and blinked back tears.

Petal saw and squeezed her hand.

"You *were* brave," she said firmly. "You belong here."

She took a deep breath and then she was waddling toward the commotion around the Central Fire. She stopped and frowned at Margot.

"Well, shake a leg, girl," she fussed. "We gotta go see what's happenin'. No matter what them silly mens decides, it gon' make a world a' work for the women."

Margot allowed herself to be dragged toward the milling crowd.

A very short, very fat man, his face shiny with sweat, his skin the color of coal, was standing near the path that led up to the highlands. He held a small ax and pointed it at a cluster of people as he spoke.

"We need to get on up the road to freedom. We need to get to a place where the slavers ain't got no more say over our bodies, over our children," he shouted.

There was a murmuring in the crowd.

"All that talk about the white folks never comin' into Remembrance, well, we saw, didn't we? Just talk. White mens go anywhere they wants. Get anybody they wants. Even got Mother Abigail's gal, didn't they? And where the old woman at now? I says we get ourselves up to the real Promised Land. That's what I says!"

"You ought to be 'shamed a' yourself, Willie!" cried a woman from far back in the crowd. People stepped aside as she pushed her way to the front.

"Ain't you 'shamed?" she cried. "You been here since before me, and

I been here nigh on seven years. In all that time, ain't been no slavers or no other white face been seen up in here. You gon' tell me that don't mean nothing to you? You had a time of peace, now at the first trouble you gon' run off? You run off every time white folks give you trouble, Willie, you gonna be runnin' 'til you die."

"It ain't safe here no more, Belle," cried Willie, shaking the ax at her.

"It ain't safe nowhere," she cried. "And it ain't never gonna be safe if we don't show our grit and stand."

"I ain't gon' just set and wait for them pattyrollers to come back for me. I gots children to protect." Willie's voice trembled.

"I got children . . . ," Belle waved a hand toward where her six-year-old twins stood, Hannah gripping Esther's hand. She took a step toward Willie and stopped. "Where you gonna run when it not be safe in Canada no more?"

The crowd rumbled uneasily around them.

"And it's nigh on winter," someone in the crowd called. "You can't make it to no Canada 'fore the snows come."

"Well, then we make it far as we can," said Willie. "We make it to the next town. Least there's people there. Other coloreds. Safer than bein' out here in the open all herded together like sheep."

"Who you callin' sheep, you fat fool?" cried a middle-aged man with a deep scar across his forehead. "I ain't no sheep. My boy ain't no sheep."

"One of them slavers got killed," yelled Willie. "You think they gon' stand for a white man gettin' killed? Not even northern white folks gonna stand for that."

The crowd shifted uneasily. The men shouted at each other, calling each other cowards and fools, and in the end, Willie and just over a dozen people decided to strike out for Canada, including the couple Margot had seen arguing with each other the day Winter had come charging down from the gardens with her warning.

Margot watched as the other settlers loaded the emigrants with what food, heavy clothes, and small tools they could spare. They were silent now, the arguing done. Sir Galahad, his protesting goat tugging against the rope around its neck, handed one of the women a skin full of milk.

"Good for the babies," he said, nodding at the infant suckling at her breast. "Better than a cow. And this bitch won't be needin' it."

He ducked away from the woman's embrace, pretending to kick at the sullen goat.

Petal rushed in and smothered everyone with hugs and kisses.

"You responsible for these folks now," she said to Willie. She wagged a finger under his nose. "You better deliver them all apiece to that Promised Land up yonder. And don't think I won't know." She tapped her temple. "I got ways."

The fat man wrapped his arms as best he could around the pregnant girl, and the two stood rocking there like two round stones, one brown, one black. Willie released Petal and then wordlessly led his tiny group up the path that would take them to the highlands, past the grazing pastures, and north.

"Well . . . ," said Petal, pressing her thumbs against her eyes. When she pulled her hands away she was smiling but her voice quivered as she said, "It's washday and dirty laundry don't wait on nobody's tears." She turned and waddled as fast as she could toward the river.

The rest of that day, Margot wandered the settlement, restless, lending a hand where she could. She climbed to the highlands and helped an old woman skim buttermilk into small barrels, carried pails of lard to the fire, and helped Belle roll sheets of beeswax for the candles she was making for the exchange. She wondered if there was still going to be an exchange.

The settlers that remained still spoke of the exchange. Of the coming winter. Of churning butter. As if acting like nothing had happened meant nothing had changed, all the while watching the trails, the trees that surrounded Remembrance with anxious eyes.

Remembrance reminded her of an old clock, always, always working. When the slavers came, when Mother Abigail fell ill, it slipped a gear, stuttered a little in its movement, but then seemed to take hold of itself and start up again. As if it had no choice. And it was no different for her. She kept moving because she had no choice. There was still bread to be made, wood to be chopped.

And she thought of her family. Veronique and Grandmere would have loved this place. Especially Grandmere, who hated idle hands.

Blinking back tears, she forced herself to concentrate on the texture of the cool wax beneath her hands, inhaling the faint scent of honey that surrounded her. She didn't want to think, not about the old priestess or the fate of the settlers who were now making their way toward Canada just ahead of the winter storms. She didn't want to think about her sister or her grandmother. How missing them was a physical pain that took her breath away. She didn't want to think about anything. She swiped a tear roughly from her face.

And David Henry. She prayed to the Virgin that he was safe and successful.

Margot shook her head, trying to dislodge the memory of her hand over his heart, his thumb caressing her wrist. She touched the knife in her pocket.

"Didn't I tell you? Women's always workin'." Petal appeared at her side. Her face was flushed, and when Margot touched her wrist, she could feel the girl's heart fluttering like a trapped bird.

"You need to rest," she said.

Petal threw back her head and laughed. "Rest when I'm dead," she said. "That's about the only rest I'm-a . . ."

The rest of her sentence died on her lips as a little white boy emerged from the woods from the direction of the creek. He looked to be nine or ten years old and carried a string of fish on a stick over his shoulder. He saw them and smiled.

"Mornin'," he said with a slight wave. "Fish bitin' good."

Wordlessly, the two women watched him move off through the tall grass, the only sound Petal's ragged breathing. They stared after him until he disappeared into the shadow of a thin grove of birch trees.

"Sweet Jesus on a horse," whispered Petal, sagging against the table where Margot had been rolling the beeswax. "We really are out in the world."

Margot said nothing. As much as she had doubted what Mother Abigail and Winter and the other settlers had said about Remembrance being apart from the Outside, she realized that some part of her had hoped that it could be true. She laid a hand against the other woman's back.

"May be . . ." Petal was trembling. "May be that these babies needs a bit of peace and quiet though," she said, finally.

The two young women locked eyes in a silent agreement to not speak of the tiny stranger who'd just wandered through Remembrance. There would be time enough for that. And he was unlikely to be the last.

Back at the Central Fire, Margot sat and watched as Petal absently pushed her soup around in the bowl.

"It feels wrong, Mother Abigail not here," said Petal, breaking the silence. "Somebody needs to be in charge. Without a head, everything dies."

Margot laughed softly. "My *grand-mère* used to say that, too. But she was usually talking about snakes."

"Snakes, people, Remembrance." Petal grinned, but she was clearly wilting on her log perch. "It's all the same. Gotta have a head."

"*Oui*. That is true."

"David Henry could have convinced those folks to stay."

At the mention of his name Margot flushed. Petal noticed and perked up.

"You sweet on David Henry, Margot? That didn't take long now, did it?"

Margot felt heat rise up her neck and bloom in her face. "Of course not. But he is a strong man, *non*? A leader?"

Petal giggled. "Well, Miss Margot, if I didn't already have me a man I'd surely follow where he led. I'd—" She gasped, the words cut off as her face contorted in pain.

"Petal!" Margot reached for the girl as she doubled over, clutching at her middle. She felt a sharp spasm low in her own stomach as a contraction gripped the pregnant girl. Her heart found and tripped over the babies' heartbeats. "Petal!"

"Oh, Lord" cried Petal. "Oh, Lord. Margot, these babies comin' and Louisa ain't here."

Margot helped the moaning woman to her feet. "Babies know what to do, and if yours do not, I will help."

Help.

Veronique's voice sounded in her ear. *Help!* The word from her dream.

"*Merde!*" Margot swore. Would these ghosts never stop tormenting her?

"What?"

"It is nothing." She placed a firm hand on Petal's back. "But you must walk or your babies will be born in the dirt."

By the time they managed to stagger to Petal's small cabin, Remembrance had mobilized. One of the men ran to get Petal's husband. Two women went to get hot water.

Petal's cabin was not large but it was clean and airy. Margot laid the moaning woman on the low bed and closed the shutters against the cold.

"Petal?"

A young man, as fair as Margot, with a shock of rust-colored freckles covering his face burst through the door. He tried to go to his wife but Margot blocked his way.

"Kiss your wife, then you must leave," she said gently. "There is much work to be done here."

The man went to Petal's side and knelt, murmuring in her ear, just as Belle and her twins appeared at the door. Hannah and Esther each carried candles, identical to the ones Margot had been working on. The mother carried the hot water and a broad white cloth, which she'd draped around her shoulders.

"Time to go, Daniel. Let your wife labor for your children," declared Belle. He looked at her, then back at Petal, who smiled wanly and nodded. With a last glance over his shoulder, he did as he was told.

The little girls moved around the cottage lighting the candles, then Esther came and stood in front of Margot.

"It will be fine, *chérie,*" said Margot, touching her face softly. "Soon there will be new *bébés* for you and your sister to play with."

Esther nodded and glanced at Petal moaning in the bed.

"*Bébés*," she said, imitating Margot's pronunciation, then she grabbed her sister's hand and ran from the cabin.

"You can do this?" asked Belle, still holding the white cloth. "You know something about birthin'?"

Margot nodded. "I do."

"Good."

Belle studied her for a moment, eyes narrowed, then bent over Petal. She smoothed the white cloth across the girl's pregnant belly and touched her hand. "Well, then," she said, "we're gon' have us some babies."

The cabin filled with the sweet smell of honey and lavender and another more ancient smell, the smell of new life coming. Margot knelt beside the frightened girl. Petal stared at her, her eyes wide.

"Babies know how to be born," said Margot, repeating what she'd told Petal earlier. She laid one hand across Petal's belly. The cloth Belle had placed there was virgin wool, slick with lanolin. She moved her hand over Petal, stroking her. Pain—Petal's pain—suddenly gripped Margot and she gasped. She inhaled, then breathed it out, watched it hover before her like a purple flower. With each contraction, that flower pulsed but the pain stayed distant, like the memory of pain.

All through the afternoon, she labored with Petal, absorbing her contractions, her fear, calming her. Belle rubbed Petal's forehead, wet her lips with a cool cloth. When it was finally time, Margot rested her hands lightly on Petal's upraised knees and looked into her eyes.

"I ain't scared," Petal whispered. "These babies know what to do. Right, Margot? They know how to get born?"

The boy came first, followed by his sister, toffee-colored with a sprinkling of freckles. Both healthy, both angry at being thrust from the warmth of their mother's womb.

Spent, Margot let Belle wash and wrap the twins in the warmth of the wool covering. She handed them to Petal, and mother and babies promptly fell asleep. Margot stared down at them and felt as if her heart would break.

In this very first moment of their lives, they had never known sorrow.

Laughter whispered to her from the ceiling, from the corners, from everywhere. Her sister's sound.

"Veronique?" murmured Margot. The girl baby opened her eyes and stared at her.

Imbecile! Babies cannot see.

But even as she thought this, she placed one finger in the infant's hand. The baby grasped her finger and yawned, toothless and large. Margot felt the little one's life pulse in her hand, smelled her yeasty, new-baby smell.

"Tell me," she whispered. Tears ran down her face and disappeared into the brilliant fibers of the sweet, new wool. "Do you know? Do you know where I belong?"

From all around her came the sound of her sister's laughter.

39

Winter

Rain.

Day after day: hard, brittle drops just this side of ice, roaring in from the northeast, churning the ground into a soggy, impassable mess, splintering tree limbs, overfilling creek beds.

Colm didn't come back to the barn, nor did his brother Frank. It was as if they had decided their business with the captured girls was concluded, at least until the roads were reopened. Winter and Louisa's world became the damp straw and the cold, murky barn. They ate the increasingly pitiful meals that Dix brought them, and when they were alone, walked around the perimeter of the barn to strengthen their muscles. Louisa was weak but growing stronger. But mostly they sat shivering in silence and listened as the storm raged up and down the Western Reserve.

One evening, just after supper, Louisa spoke up: "It's time," she said.

Winter stopped poking at her food. Tonight it was a mysterious gray-brown goo, lukewarm and tasteless. The hardtack biscuit lay like a brick on the surface, refusing to transform into anything edible. She squinted at Louisa.

"What?"

Instead of answering, Louisa gave her a sour look and struggled to her feet. She wobbled a bit, but managed to stay upright. Slowly, she began moving around the barn, stuffing straw into her blouse, down her bloomers. Every so often, she stopped and held on to the wall for support, winded.

Winter watched, fascinated, silently waiting for an explanation. If she'd thought that freeing Louisa from her chains and helping to nurse her back to health would improve the other girl's disposition, she'd been badly mistaken. Other than their brief barn walks—during which Louisa seemed to barely tolerate her help—Louisa sat in her corner and stared into space. Winter had tried—if they couldn't be friends now, when could they ever?—but Louisa rebuffed her every effort, answering questions with one or two words or not at all, until she gave it up, resigned to sit in silence. Now Louisa wordlessly made her way around the barn, as if it were the most natural thing in the world to stuff straw down her drawers.

"What the devil," asked Winter finally, "are you doing?"

"Time to go," Louisa said.

Winter pressed her lips together but there was no help for it. She began to laugh. Louisa was now nearly as round as she was tall, a human hay bale. Straw jutted from her sleeves, her collar, fell from the hem of her skirt, leaving a prickly trail behind her as she walked.

"You ought to see yourself," she said. "You're more scarecrow than human."

Louisa shot her a murderous look.

"I'm sorry, Louisa, but my . . . you really should just see yourself. You're a perfect fright," said Winter. She took great gulps of the cold air, struggling for control. "And where is it we're going exactly? To scare the daylights out of some poor birds?" She flapped her arms around her head, then dissolved in another fit of giggles.

Louisa scowled and crossed her arms over her now heavily padded chest. Her blouse made a shushing noise as straw fluttered to the floor around her. Winter snorted, clamping down on a fresh peal of laughter.

"Tonight's the night," snapped Louisa, ignoring Winter's amusement. "We need to—"

A gust of wind rattled the barn, cutting off her words. Winter sat up, suddenly sober.

"Tonight? You want to go tonight?" she asked. Her voice cracked. "In this?"

Louisa turned away and began pulling at a small bundle hidden in one of the horse stalls. They'd been stashing away bits of food for days, a potato here, a biscuit there, hiding it for the time when they'd make their run. Now was that time.

"Bad as it is for us to get around, be worser for them," said Louisa. She glanced at Winter's stunned face, and her expression softened—a little. "You best start stuffin' that straw. Find the driest bits you can. Bunch it tight."

Winter picked up a handful of the straw and peered at it, bewildered. The older girl stopped bundling their meager foodstuffs and rooted around the back of the horse stall until she found what she was looking for. Waddling over, Louisa yanked out the top of Winter's blouse and roughly thrust a handful of straw down her chest. Winter yelped. The stalks were rough and bit at the soft skin of her breasts and stomach.

"Ain't as good as a store-bought overcoat," said Louisa. "But it'll cut the wind and buy you a penny's worth a' warm. You'll be glad of it. Even if you do scare off some birds."

Her lips twitched upward as she turned away. Winter took a deep breath and began to follow Louisa's example, reluctantly padding herself with straw, filling her clothes to near bursting. She gritted her teeth and tried to ignore the musty smell, the razorlike jabs against her skin.

"Your boyfriend happen to tell you where we at?" asked Louisa, coming to stand near her.

Winter bit back a retort.

"Dix says we're just north of someplace called Cuyahoga Falls. That mean anything to you?"

Louisa's mouth puckered at the mention of the boy's name. She shook her head. "How long we travel? You notice that?"

Winter inhaled through her mouth. "One day . . . I think." For some of that time she had been insensible, thrown across the back of Paddy's horse like an old saddlebag. She twisted her face, trying to remember. She had woken to pain and light, too frightened to register many details.

"From late morning until maybe four. The sun was just falling behind the trees, at our backs. They were going to set up camp for just one day so they could get supplies, then this storm moved in."

Louisa nodded. "On horseback," she said, quietly. "Won't be that far from Remembrance then. Two days walk if we move fast, maybe a bit longer with this weather."

Winter swallowed hard. A trill of anxiety rippled through her. "We're leaving now?"

Louisa shook her head. "We gon' wait 'til the deepest night. Then you gon' do what you do and I'm-a do what I do."

Winter frowned and Louisa rolled her eyes.

"I got the gift of readin' nature. I look at a tree, rub my hand over it a little bit, see how water puddles at the roots, and I can tell you north from south, east from west. Tell you which way the wind comin' from. Whether a storm just workin' itself up or blowin' itself out. I can tell you which berries to eat and which ones gon' make you shit yourself to death. I got that knowledge in me."

She picked up a bowl of the brown goo that was their dinner. Frowning, she fished out the hard tack and added it to their food bundle.

"Now you gots a different kinda gift," she went on, not looking at Winter. "You got a way of gettin' all up inside a thing and movin' things that don't want to be moved." She brought her eyes up to meet Winter's. "I recollect you done that to me once."

It was the most Louisa had ever said to her.

Winter flushed at the memory of their argument up at the hives, her anger at Louisa, the healer falling.

"I—" she began.

Louisa cut her off with a flick of her hand. She looked away. "Don't matter. Don't know what you are. Don't much care. But I know you got somethin' in you that's gon' prove useful in our particular situation. At least it better. You did something to that slaver man, too. Did it worse to him than me. I saw his face, but mostly I saw yours. You made him bleed." She smiled, a bitter, twisted-looking thing. "You could have killed him. Wish you had.

"We gon' wait just a bit, 'til night full on," she said, ignoring Winter's sounds of protest. "Wind dies down then. Always does. Moon be behind the clouds. Least they ain't got no dogs."

Winter hardly heard her. A certainty had begun to fill her up, hard, cruel.

I could have killed him. I could have killed that pattyroller.

And she knew that it was true. And what was worse, she wished she had.

"Time to go."

Winter started. She had been dreaming of fried trout and new potatoes. She blinked.

"Time to go," Louisa said again. She was crouched by the barn door peering through a slit at the wet darkness. She turned her head toward Winter and frowned. "Girl, get yourself on over here."

It was too dark to read her expression, but the impatience in her voice was clear enough. Heart pounding, Winter scuttled to Louisa's side.

"No lookout. Guess they didn't think they needed one with just two broke-down nigger gals chained up in the barn." Louisa raised an eyebrow and grinned. The ruined side of her face twisted horribly.

"Ready?"

"Wait!" Winter couldn't breathe. She felt as if she might suffocate. "Just wait."

Louisa looked at her, waiting.

"What if they do come for us? From Remembrance?" Winter could read the expression on Louisa's face now. "But what if they do?" she insisted. "Are you sure you know how to get us home? We could end up just be wandering around out there forever."

Louisa grabbed Winter's chin and yanked her close. "Ain't nobody comin', you twit! Nobody! The only way we gon' get saved is if we save ourself. You hearin' me?"

She pushed Winter . . . hard . . . and then they were outside the barn, rain pelting their faces as they pressed against the side. The wind twisted their skirts around their ankles and blew the stink from their bodies up their noses. Winter stood trembling in the shadows, wincing as she caught her own smell.

Dogs? They wouldn't need dogs to find them, not as bad as they smelled.

She held her face up to the weather and closed her eyes. There was the slow, low-pitched creaking of tree limbs, the shuddering whisper of rain high in the branches, and from somewhere beyond the farmhouse, the clanging of metal against metal. The world smelled fresh, like new mud, damp wood, and snow. And then she smiled. She was free! She felt light enough to sail away on the wind.

Pain ricocheted through her shoulder. She stifled a cry as her eyes snapped open. Louisa stood glowering, her arm cocked back to take another shot at her.

"Wake up!" Louisa hissed, leaning so that her mouth was close to Winter's ear. "This not the time for your mind to go wanderin' off!"

Winter glared. Louisa pointed to a skimpy grove of trees on the far side of the property. She nodded and they ran for it, any sound they made disappearing into the lifting storm. A few yards in, Louisa yanked at Winter and pulled her down hard, scanning the open ground they'd just crossed. The darkness was nearly complete and Winter could just make out the whites of Louisa's eyes.

"This way," said Louisa. "We got to go east and then north. We got to go this way."

Winter squinted. She could only barely make out the direction that Louisa was pointing. She squinched her eyes closed, then opened them, but the world was still made all of black: black sky, black trees, black everywhere.

"How . . . ?"

"We got to go. Put as much distance between them pattyrollers and us as we can 'fore daybreak. Storm breakin'."

Winter saw that it was true. The wind was dying down so that she could clearly hear the sound of rain falling on the leaves above, the trails below. She nodded, though she doubted that Louisa could see it.

They ran, Winter following Louisa as closely as she could, trusting, hoping, that what the herbalist said was true: that she could tell north from south, east from west.

She had no idea how long they ran. The lightness she'd felt when she'd first stepped out of the barn was long gone. Her chest burned. The muscles in her legs were doughy with fatigue, her hands raw from falling again and again. And she could feel the bruise growing in the middle of her forehead from crashing into a tree what seemed like hours before. She thought she might vomit.

"Louisa," she pleaded. "Louisa . . . wait!"

When Louisa stopped, Winter barely had time to register the fact before barreling into her, bringing them both to the ground. She lay on top of the older girl, panting, until Louisa pushed her roughly off. Winter rolled on her back and lay sprawled in the mud, too exhausted to move. Straw dug into her body, scraping away at tender places: the backs of her knees, her neck, her armpits.

"Where are we?" she asked finally, when she'd regained her breath. When Louisa didn't answer, she pushed herself to sitting. "How much longer?"

"Not so much. It'll be daybreak soon," said Louisa. "Need to keep putting ground between them and us while we can. Then gotta find a place to hide out." She jerked her head in the direction they'd just come.

Winter looked around. It still seemed dark night to her. Daybreak felt a long way off. She hurt in a thousand places and her head pounded. Louisa was studying her, her eyes dark in the faint moonlight.

"What you got?" she asked quietly.

Winter frowned. "What?" It was hard to talk. She had never been so tired. And any minute she expected to hear the sound of horses behind them, Colm's voice raging through the gloom.

"Can you do the thing you do? That hoodoo spell thing?" said Louisa. "Can you do it now? Protect us . . . or something?"

Winter shook her head slowly, her eyes narrowed.

"They not sayin' nothin' to you now?"

"Who?" cried Winter. "Who're you talking about?"

"The spirits . . . or ghosts . . . or God . . . or whoever it is you get your magic from! They not talkin'? 'Cause let me tell you, girl. Now would be a real good time for y'all to be workin' up some juju!"

As the world drifted closer to dawn, Louisa's voice echoed off the trees and the gray mist that was rising from the forest floor. Winter clenched and unclenched her fists, her head swinging back and forth in a silent "no." *That's not how it works,* she wanted to say. A tear ran down her cheek.

She tried to calm herself, to listen, but every twig snap, every leaf rustle caused her to jerk. Her eyes wildly searched the shadows. The only sound she heard clearly was that of her own ragged breathing.

Louisa leaned against a spindly pine. Winter could see the hard set of her mouth—it was getting definitely lighter—the fear, and rage, glittering in her eyes. The herbalist stared at her a long time before turning away. "Not much night left. Can't afford to waste it."

She straightened and began to walk again, quickly disappearing into the mist. After a moment, Winter stood and followed.

40

Mother Abigail

The soft ground sucked at her walking stick, slowing her. Still weak from her illness, she tired quickly. Mother Abigail stopped frequently to catch her breath and wait for the spasms in her back and legs to pass. By the time she reached the crest of the ridge high above Remembrance, she was drenched in sweat and pain had wrapped itself around her chest like a steel band. Below her, the trees were disappearing in shadow. It would be dark soon. This time of year, night seemed to fall from the heavens without warning. The sky glowed a deep orange.

Mango!

The sky was the color of mangoes. The thought caught her by surprise.

Mangoes.

She had not thought of mangos since fleeing the fires of Saint-Domingue with Madame Rousse and her baby. The old woman frowned. The new girl, Margot, she had belonged to the Rousse family. Not to the madame but to her . . . what was it . . . the granddaughter?

She shivered. There was no such thing as coincidence. It meant something, this girl showing up like this. Coming from the same family from which she'd walked away, the same family that had stolen her boys from her life, appearing at the exact time that the Edge should start to fail. It meant something. But what? The old priestess massaged the ache at the back of her neck. She breathed cold air in through her nose and gazed up at the blushing sky. She was so tired.

She eased herself to the ground and closed her eyes. Even now, all these years later, the thought of her boys was both a sweetness and an agony. But the fruit. Ah . . . the fruit of Saint-Domingue, that was all sweetness—oranges, limes, coconuts—as if the island had been determined to dilute all the blood spilled on its soil, all the suffering of its slaves, with the sweetness of its own bounty.

Mangoes.

She remembered sucking the juice through a stalk of sugarcane, the stickiness on her lips that lingered long after the fruit had been sucked dry. Laying there, eyes closed, she could almost feel Henri and Claude pressed hard against her, their mouths open wide, like two baby birds as she dribbled the juice onto their tongues. She had been so young. How was it possible that she had ever been that young?

She sat on the crest of the ridge, savoring the memory of that long-ago time, when her limbs had obeyed her, when she could run for hours through the forest, bundles of firewood tied across her shoulders.

Mother Abigail licked her lips and opened her eyes. The yellow and orange sky had been swallowed by deep purple. She struggled to her feet.

She could feel them out there.

All those people of Remembrance.

Trembling in the shadows.

Waiting . . . waiting for her—the great priestess, Mother Abigail—to tell them what to do, tell them where to go.

"Cowards!" she growled. "Mother Abigail protectin' you all these years. Keepin' you safe. And still it's not enough. Never, ever enough!"

She knew that Willie had led his group off to the Canada land. Knew Petal had birthed her twins.

And she knew David Henry was gone, off to search for Winter.

Remembrance was still hers, and she knew every breath it took, every beat of its heart, but this knowing gave her no joy. There was no more joy to be had for her in Remembrance. She had the power of seeing, but her power for doing had shriveled up, her skills laying like a hard brown turd in her gut, taunting her, poisoning her.

"What do you want from me?" she screamed into the darkness. She wasn't sure who the question was meant for. The ancestors? The settlers?

The priestess stood trembling in the cold and dark, as slowly another memory came to her. A memory from long after she'd left the shores of Saint-Domingue.

Brown water. Thick, chocolate-colored. So different from the navy-blue water that rolled up onto the sands of Saint-Domingue. She had been tired then, too, so tired. Simona and Josiah had led her from the docks. They had been waiting there for her in New Orleans, waiting as if they knew she was coming. Perhaps they had. They had taken her deep into the marshlands, taught her the Art, filling her heart, her soul with the sounds, the names of the saints, the spirits. Far back in the bayou, where the sun seemed to be strained through tea-colored lace, she was surrounded by the mystery, by the magic. It covered her up, until the world appeared to slide around her, shifting colors and shapes like a child's kaleidoscope. She studied and she learned because she wanted revenge. For her babies, for her Hercule's murder at the edge of that fat pig's coffee grove. She wanted revenge, for herself and for her sister, snatched from a village that grew dimmer in her memory with each passing year.

She studied and learned and plotted. And then she was alone. She left Simona, left Josiah. She didn't need them anymore. They had nothing left to teach her.

She'd wandered the Crescent City and the nearby river towns for years.

Paid in coin to find true love for the *gens de couleur*—the free people of color—working roots to bring healthy babies to barren couples or return unfaithful husbands to their wives. Abigail drifted along like a ghost and was left to herself. Hating them, planning her vengeance.

But there were so many of them. Too many. She wanted to kill them all. But what she wanted even more—her man, her babies back in her arms—remained out of her reach. Even her powerful magic could not bring them back.

But the whites feared her, even as they sent for her to cure their ills, erase their gambling debts, or predict the vagaries of the sea where their ships sailed. And she extracted what vengeance she could: poisoning their animals, sabotaging their businesses. Not enough that they ever suspected her, but enough to inflict pain.

And then there was the girl. The baker's girl. A tiny slave girl with pale skin and red hair. A child, perhaps seven or eight. She was tied at the ankle every morning to a hitching post at the side of the shop. Her face so thin, bruises up and down her bony arms. Every morning she followed Abigail with her eyes as she walked past, staring hungrily at the bread basket she carried.

One morning Abigail stopped.

"Quel est votre nom, enfant?" The girl frowned. "What is your name, child?" Abigail repeated in English.

The girl blinked at her.

"You would like a biscuit, *wi*?" Abigail held out a sweet roll to the girl, who snatched it from her. The little girl looked furtively over her shoulder, then took a bite.

"Dorcas," she murmured.

The baker materialized in the shop door, swearing in a language Abigail didn't understand. He was fat and sweaty, with greasy, gray hair. He drew back a beefy hand and struck the little girl across the face, knocking the sweet into the dirt. Dorcas sprawled on the ground, arms up to protect her face, whimpering.

The baker turned toward Abigail, ready to strike again. She raised her chin and stared into his eyes.

A mistake, blanc. The last you will make.

The man froze, arm upraised. He saw the look in her eye, seemed to sense the danger. His Adam's apple bobbed in his thick throat.

"Get away from here, Negress," he snarled. "Get!"

Abigail smiled and the white man flinched. A bead of sweat formed on his forehead. His eyes spun wildly in their sockets. She bent and righted the girl, handed her the sweet roll. The baker made a noise in the back of his throat, and Abigail fixed him with a hard look, a warning, then bowed and walked away.

Late into that night, in her small shack at the far edge of the city, she saw in her mind the baker strike the child again and again. And her anger fermented in the stifling heat. If she could not get back to Saint-Domingue—they called it Haiti now—then she could still have her revenge.

For three mornings she walked past the baker's shop, but the little girl was not there. On the fourth morning, the child was tied once more to the hitching post. She did not look up as Abigail approached, but it was impossible to miss the new bruises that covered her face, her neck.

Abigail ground her teeth but did not go to her. Instead, she stood at the edge of the street facing the bakery door. All through the morning, patrons drew near, then, seeing her standing there, beat a hasty retreat. At first the baker only glared at her through the shop window, his face growing redder and redder as the hours ticked by without customers. Finally, he stormed from the door.

"You go now," he cried. "Before I call the police."

She smiled. "The police do not answer calls from the dead, *Monsieur.*"

The baker blanched. "Get away now," he screamed. He threw his baker's hat at her. She bent to pick it up. "Get away from me."

Abigail nodded and walked away.

That night, under a full moon, she took the cap—pleased to see that there were two gray hairs still inside—and placed it on the ground behind her shack. She pricked her finger with a sharp knife, then held her hand over the cap as she bled. Seven drops, in the shape of an eye. She covered the cap with rosemary, lavender, saltpeter, and cinnamon, then set it afire with the flame from a black candle.

She smiled as the flames beat back the darkness. The baker would never beat the child again. Seven days later the baker, his wife, and their four children were dead, found dead in their beds from no cause the doctors were able to figure. It was two more days before she heard that the same mysterious illness had taken the slave, Dorcas, as well.

Several days later, the decapitated heads of the slaves who'd revolted against the sugarcane plantation owners lined the Mississippi on spikes from the Place d'Armes to the plantations far out into the countryside.

And Abigail was finally broken.

Despair and hate filled her, souring her magic. She retreated deep into the swamplands, with their thick, dark water and impenetrable shadows, and built a shelter among the roots of a cedar tree, a rude, stick shelter, not much different than a beaver's den. From its opening, she could look out at the brilliant white egrets high-stepping among the cattails and water lilies, could hear the growl of panthers. She huddled in her stick shelter and waited to die. It seemed all that was left for her.

And then he appeared.

Josiah.

He had come looking for her, appearing out of the mist during low tide. He'd been barely recognizable, his hair nearly pure white, his spine bent.

"I was sent," he said.

She didn't ask who'd sent him, what'd sent him. Simona, he said, was gone.

He forced her back to the land of the living, led her from the bayou, led her to this place. Or they'd led each other. Not for revenge, but for redemption.

"To make things right," whispered Mother Abigail. And now it wasn't.

"Abigail?"

She looked up and smiled bitterly. As she'd grown stronger, so had he, the years dropping from him like autumn leaves. He was always there, wasn't he? They were bound to each other, their magic intertwined. His magic, his life, was braided into hers, just as before her it had been to Simona's.

"Abigail?" Josiah said again. He held a hand out to her and she allowed herself to be pulled to her feet.

"Come, Abigail," said the old man.

"I see them," she whispered. "They out there."

"Yes." He wrapped a strong hand around her elbow, and they began to make their way down from the ridge, him guiding her, moving as surely in the dark as she did at high noon.

"I see them, Josiah," she said again. "I see my girl, and Louisa with her." And she did, as clearly as if they stood in front of her. She saw Winter and Louisa by the side of a leaning, broken barn, shivering in icy rain. And she saw the *blancs*. Out there in the world that Remembrance was now a part of, like pale shadows darting through the mist, the smell of blood and death drifting behind them like smoke.

Josiah stopped and held his face to the sky. There was anger in him. She could feel it. "I know, Abigail. And they not the only ones out there."

When he turned his face to her, her blood ran cold. "No," she whispered. "No, they not."

Gaelle

She felt as if she were made of wood, slow and thick, the air suddenly turned to molasses.

She was proud of Rose, had been terrified, but thrilled, when her baby sister had gotten a scholarship to that fancy college in California. In the pictures, ragged, snow-capped mountains reached to a clear sky the color of a robin's egg; perfect green grass flowed between leaning palm trees. In tiny ways, it reminded her of home, of Haiti, and she understood why Rose wouldn't want to come back to this gray, cold, decaying place.

But she was family and *fanmi se tout.*

Gaelle could never have imagined how empty, how imbalanced she could feel being separated from her sister. It was if a limb had been cut off. Only the thought of seeing her at Christmas had made the past months bearable.

She held her face to the dark sky. It had stopped snowing for the most part, but an occasional flake drifted onto her face, where it instantly melted.

She'd already picked out their tree, the biggest one that would fit in their tiny living room, and the aniseed was soaking in rum in the cupboard, in preparation for the traditional anisette. Eyes closed, she smiled slightly. Toya loved the anisette she made each Christmas.

The year before, Kevin, her youngest, had gotten slightly tipsy off of it. Toya had teased him for weeks.

Gaelle swallowed hard, then slid heavily into the car.

As soon as she pulled into the parking lot, she saw him, standing just outside the circle of light by the entrance. And she realized that, on some level, she'd been half expecting him. As she stepped from the car, there was a crackle of electricity in the air, like the feeling of anticipation when you open the door to see what gifts Tonton Nwèl has left in your shoe on Christmas morning.

Swearing softly, she walked toward the door. He was smoking his pipe, and despite the fact that the sun had not yet risen, he still wore the dark glasses. He looked somehow different, younger. She guessed it was a trick of the light.

"Good morning," he said as she drew near. "Gaelle, isn't it?"

She jerked, then turned slowly to face him. She hadn't been wearing her badge when she'd seen him that first evening in Winter's room. And she definitely hadn't introduced herself. She shot a glance through the glass entry door. It was the middle of shift change and the hallway was empty.

"You need to go away. I will call security."

He cocked his head, but made no move to leave.

She eased toward the door and tugged on the handle. A mound of half-frozen slush was piled near the bottom, preventing it from opening. She felt him there, watching her, and pulled harder.

"*Bondye ede mwen,*" she muttered.

Behind her, the strange man chuckled. "Oh, child, there is no god."

Gaelle whirled. "*Ou pale kreyòl?*"

"Only a little," he answered in English. "A long time ago."

"Who are you?"

She was breathing hard, her breath crystallizing in the predawn air.

They stared at each other for a long moment. "I am a friend," he said, finally.

A friend? Whose friend?

"You do not work for Joint Commission."

"No."

"Then who are you?" she demanded once again. "What do you want?"

He looked away and relit his pipe before answering. "You are special," he said.

She felt a zip of heat spiral between her shoulder blades.

"Special," he said again, his voice hard. "How much more will you allow this world to take from you? From us? You feel it, don't you? Your power."

The heat had spread to her shoulders and down into her hands. Inside her coat, she was shaking. He leaned close.

"The world has been waiting. I have been waiting. You help those people in there? How many? One person? Five? This . . ." He waved a dismissive hand at the building behind him. "This is small. This is nothing. You are so much more."

"Go away," she whispered, her voice pitched high with fear. "Go away and leave me alone, or I will call security."

Josiah bowed his head and stepped aside. She turned and fled into the brightly lit nursing home.

42

Winter

Winter could just barely make out Louisa's shape ahead of her as they crashed through the darkness. If anyone had been following them, they would have been easy enough to find as they stumbled through the trees and thickly tangled brush, falling again and again over invisible obstacles on the ground.

"Christ and damnation!" swore Louisa for the thousandth time.

The escape seemed to have fired her, burning away the remaining effects of her injuries. Numb with exhaustion, Winter kept up as best she could. She cried out as a branch snapped back into her face, narrowly missing her eyes.

When Louisa finally stopped, hands on her knees, her breath coming in short, ragged bursts, Winter slid gratefully to the ground beside her.

"Need to stop," panted Louisa. "Got to build us a shelter. Got to be hid by the time the sun comes up."

Winter raised her head. Louisa was right. Dawn was not far off.

"Where . . . ?" she asked, too tired to finish the sentence. All around them, there were only trees and trees and more trees, nothing that looked like a safe hiding place.

Louisa straightened, and despite the low light, Winter could make out the tightness around her mouth, the hollowness of her eyes. She was done in. They both were. Without rest, they were going no farther. The healer looked slowly around.

"This a good place," she said. "Lotta trees. Lotta brush. Land uneven. Fools the eye, makes it hard for the slavers to see everything they should. It be good cover . . . least the best we gon' hope to find out here."

Winter blinked. The route they'd been following for hours was hilly and rock-strewn. Since their escape from the barn, she'd barely noticed anything, except how tired she was and how cold. It had been enough just to stay on her feet and not become separated from Louisa. But now, in the bit of light leaking through the treetops, she could make out darker shadows, there off to their left. She squinted and saw that the shadows were, in fact, shallow gullies rising and falling along the forest floor.

Louisa moved slightly uphill and dropped to her knees. As Winter watched, she began pushing aside the soggy debris at the base of a broad maple tree.

"What're you doing?"

"You need to go find us a couple of rocks. Something big. Flat like. With sharp edges to cut with," said Louisa without turning around. Winter waited for something more, an explanation, but Louisa ignored her as she frantically dug through the dirt, with sticks, leaves, and mud piling up quickly beside her.

"Easy as pie," muttered Winter. "Sharp ones. In the dark. In all this mud."

She stomped off to look for the rocks Louisa had demanded. Slogging through sodden, ankle-deep leaves and mud, it took nearly a quarter of an hour. Every shadow made her heart race, every twig snap made her bite back a scream. She was shaking with exhaustion and terror by the time she'd found what she needed, her hands bloodied and raw from scrabbling through the stone-pocked mud. Struggling up the short incline, back toward the maple, she stopped short, her head whipping back and forth. Louisa was gone!

"Louisa?" she hissed, panic clawing its way up her throat.

"Did you find them?"

Winter screamed. She tumbled backward, slipping on the muddy ground and dropping her handful of rocks as Louisa seemed to rise from the ground like a spirit.

"Shush that noise!" she hissed. "What's the matter with you, girl? You git them rocks I tol' you to git, or not?"

Heart thudding loudly in her chest, Winter nodded. She picked them off the forest floor and held them out toward Louisa who sucked her teeth and snatched them from her. She turned, took two steps, and vanished again, the earth seeming to suck her down into itself. Winter bit her lip hard to keep from screaming again; she thought she saw slavers hiding behind every tree and bush now. Hardly daring to breathe, she crept forward.

Her mouth dropped open in amazement as she saw the reason the healer had seemed to disappear before her very eyes. Louisa was crouched in a shallow hole, maybe two feet deep by three feet wide, dug into the hillside.

"What . . . ?" she asked. "What is this?"

"It's gon' be our hidin' place," said Louisa. She glanced around nervously. It was much lighter now. "And we got to get a hurry on, too."

She quickly showed Winter how to cut branches with the knife she fashioned from one of the sharp rocks; how to poke the pointy ends of the branches in the ground on either side of the hole until they had a sort of roof. Then together they covered the roof with mud, followed by a thick layering of damp leaves, until the shelter resembled just another small rise on the landscape. Even just a very few feet away, it was completely invisible.

Winter stared in amazement, first at the shelter, then at Louisa, who flicked her hand dismissively and turned away.

"We best be gettin' in there then," she said. "They sure to find we gone at first light if they ain't already, and they be comin' for us."

She crawled into the hiding space and Winter scrambled in after. There was barely enough room for the both of them as they lay pressed shoulder to shoulder against each other, trembling in silence. Insulated with pine needles and tree moss, and warmed by their own body heat, Louisa's shelter was surprisingly cozy.

Winter felt almost safe, and that thought made her nearly laugh aloud. Stuffed with straw, laying in a hole in the ground, hiding from men who wanted to take her to God-only-knew-where and make her do God-only-knew-what . . . she felt safe. At least safer than she had in many days.

She was drifting off to sleep when Louisa poked her in the side and pushed a ragged square of something toward her.

"Drink," she whispered.

Winter reached for it, then yanked her hand back, startled. The thing in Louisa's hand was cold . . . and furry.

"What is that?" Winter squinted at it. Pale light was oozing through their mud roof. Dawn had broken.

"Moss. Drink."

Winter stared in bewilderment. She could feel Louisa rolling her eyes.

"Gotta drink," she whispered irritably. "Bad for your muscles, all this runnin' and no water. Didn't have time to pack no fancy silver or fine china, so just open up your damn mouth."

Still, Winter hesitated, and Louisa poked her again, hard, in the soft spot just below her ribs. With a whimper, Winter opened her mouth, just barely.

"And you best not waste one drop, you hear me?" hissed Louisa as she squeezed the moss in her fist. "I ain't Mother Abigail. I ain't fixin' to spoil you. You want outa here, then you best keep this down."

Dark water ran into Winter's mouth, dark, muddy, green-tasting water. Something crawly landed on her tongue and she gagged, earning another painful blow from Louisa.

Winter closed her eyes and fought to keep the water down. She ground her teeth and breathed slowly through her nose, willing herself not to think about the slime and grit she felt inside her mouth, about the wiggly creatures she had just swallowed.

"Here."

Winter opened her eyes. Louisa held out a piece of hardtack and

Winter took it. The biscuit was tasteless, but after the gritty moss water, she was grateful for that at least. Her stomach growled angrily. The biscuit was hard as a stone but, cramped with hunger, she bit down in desperation, gasping as pain shot through her teeth. Snarling in frustration, she threw the hardtack. The biscuit hit the top of the shelter and bounced, landing back on her chest with an audible thud. Winter glared at it in silence.

"Well," she said finally. "You sure do throw one fine dinner party, Louisa." She sniffled. "I sure hope that was a piece of hardtack I just swallowed, not a tooth."

At first, in the silence of their little shelter, there was only the sound of their breathing. Then Louisa snorted, and snorted again. Winter turned her head and the two girls locked eyes.

Louisa let out a soft whoop and then they were laughing, both of them, struggling to muffle the sound, laughing until tears ran down their faces, mixing with the mud.

When they could catch their breath again, Louisa said, "I still hate you."

Winter wiped her face and struggled onto her side, her back pressed against Louisa's in the small space. "I know. I hate you, too."

And then she was asleep, dreaming of warmer places and happier times.

Winter was dreaming of the spring that ran high up near the smoke-house in early summer. The water there was so cold that if you gulped it, it caused a pain like a hammer between your eyes and chilled you to your toes. Bright jays flitted high in the branches of an old buck-eye, and the whole world smelled like apples, the apples that had fermented the whole winter in the root cellar. She heard voices, but when she turned toward them, the figures approaching her were lost in the sun. They were familiar, those voices, familiar and wrong. They didn't belong in Remembrance.

Winter jerked awake.

Her body hurt and there was a weird, moldy taste in her mouth. She blinked and it all came rushing back, the pattyrollers, the chains, the barn, Colm.

She was lying in a hole somewhere in an Ohio forest, and that odd, buzzing sound at her back was Louisa snoring. Winter squinted up at the roof of the shelter. The icy rain had finally stopped and she could hear birdsong. She thought it might be midday, but in the feathery light of their shelter it was hard to tell.

The muscles in her legs seized and Winter stretched as best she could, wincing as the now-soggy straw inside her clothes shifted across her skin. Carefully rolling over so as not to disturb Louisa, she tried to reach the sack where they'd stored the small amount of food they'd brought with them. She was hungry . . . and thirsty, but her stomach clenched at the thought of drinking water squeezed from the moss again. Her hand had just landed on the tiny food bundle when she heard them again—voices. She froze, her hand clutching the bundle.

She heard horses. Two, maybe three. And voices fading in and out.

"Damn it to hell!" she heard, then laughter.

Frank!

She recognized the big pattyroller's voice and pictured him: tall and broad and covered all over with coarse black hair. She could almost smell his hot breath inside the shelter and tried to push herself deeper into the pine-needle-covered dirt.

"Well, ain't we just between shit and sweat!"

Frank's voice again. Winter couldn't tell where it was coming from. He could have been far down the hill, across a gully. Or standing right above them. His voice seemed to bounce off the pine-and-leaf covering of their hiding place. Were Colm and Paddy with him? Was Dix? Beside her, Louisa stirred, and Winter clasped a hand over her mouth. She felt Louisa's eyes on her, but it was the sounds outside their makeshift shelter that gripped her attention. She listened so hard that she trembled, but the voices finally disappeared.

"They gone?" Louisa whispered next to her ear when Winter moved her hand.

Winter nodded. Yes, they had moved on. All around her, she could feel the forest settling back into its quiet murmuring. They were alone again.

"Then they not comin' back this way. Best get some sleep."

Winter pulled a wedge of potato from their pack, cold now and sickly gray, and popped it into her mouth. She chewed for a minute, then closed her eyes. As soon as the slavers had moved away, Louisa had dropped immediately back to sleep, but Winter, tired as she was, was wide awake. She huddled under the roof of mud and branches, straining to hear, worried that Frank and Colm might find their trail at any minute and double back.

Winter opened her eyes and peered at the herbalist. The swelling was nearly all gone from Louisa's face, and most of the bruising as well. All that was left were the horrific scars, the first thing Winter had noticed on the day Louisa arrived in Remembrance, the deep, shiny furrows that ran from one eye to the corner of where her top lip should have been . . . and wasn't.

"Louisa? How . . . ? Where did those scars come from?"

Louisa's eyes flickered open. Winter realized that she had never really looked at the other girl before, not really. And as she examined her, she was astonished to realize that except for her horrific wounds, Louisa would have been beautiful.

"Back on the . . . plantation, I forgot my place," said Louisa finally, her voice barely above a whisper. "My master reminded me with a sledgehammer upside a' my face."

Winter felt the spit curdle in her mouth and tried to swallow.

She stared at the other girl, horrified. "He . . . hit you with . . . ?" The thought was too unspeakable to complete.

Louisa closed her eyes again and turned her face away. "Go to sleep. We can't go nowhere 'til it gets dark again, so you best get rested up."

"What if they come back?" She could almost see it, the arc of the sledgehammer as it whistled through the air, hear the muffled crunch of bone as the sledgehammer connected. She could see the spray of blood as it flew from Louisa's face. Her mind began to fill with the images of things that might happen to them if they were caught, shocking things that had never occurred to her before.

Louisa sighed irritably. "Then they come back. But they ain't here now, so may as well wait 'til if and when they shows up to fight that fight."

Reluctantly, Winter closed her eyes, but every fiber, every inch of her skin was tuned to the outside, listening, waiting. She tried to focus, to calm herself, but after just a few minutes would forget and start to panic, her breath coming so fast she made herself dizzy.

They hit her in the face with a sledgehammer.

If they found them . . . what would they do if they found them?

"Louisa?"

Winter struggled to turn in the cramped space. She had to get out of there. She couldn't breathe. The shallow hole was like lying in her own grave. And the slavers. Where were the slavers?

"Louisa?"

The only response was Louisa's soft snoring.

43

Winter

She fought the urge to kick Louisa awake.

Squinching her eyes closed, she tried to sleep. Louisa was right. She had to get some rest. She was so tired even her eyes ached.

Time dragged on, and the light inside their shelter turned the color of scorched butter as sunlight filtered through the makeshift roof. And still she found herself fidgeting this way and that, trying to turn her thoughts to something, anything but the small space, the cold, the slavers that were somewhere in the woods hunting them down. But there was just no sleep to be had.

The ground beneath her was lumpy, damp. And there were things, biting, crawling things, moving around inside her clothes, feeding on her, tormenting her. The straw they'd stuffed inside their blouses and drawers to fight off the chill had come alive in the night, and now every inch of her skin was itching to drive her mad.

Breathe. It's just fleas . . . or lice. Just breathe.

She took slow, deep breaths through her nose. She ground her teeth. She counted slowly backward from fifty once and then again. But sleep moved further away, as the mud walls moved closer.

She couldn't breathe. She was going to die in that mud hole. Only Louisa knew she was there and she was probably going to die, too.

With surging panic she began to claw her way out of the shelter. But getting out proved to be much more difficult than getting in. In the tight space there was little room to move, nothing to grab hold of for traction save the bent twigs of the roof, which would have brought the shelter crashing down on their heads.

Grunting, groaning, she twisted and bucked her way free, sweating with the effort, praying that when she popped out of the ground, it wouldn't be right under Colm or his brother.

Finally free, she sprawled on her stomach, gasping for breath. As her breathing slowed, she pushed herself up and crawled to a maple tree, collapsing against it. The sharp air felt clean and fresh, heaven against her sweaty face.

It was warmer than the night before, and though the ground was soggy, the rain had finally stopped. Winter peered into the trees. The late-afternoon sun was low against the horizon and sparkled through the branches like jewels.

She must have slept some, though she felt no better for it.

Winter clawed at her skin. The itching was worse and she yanked at the straw poking from the cuffs of her blouse. It was damp and had begun to rot. She pushed up one sleeve, sucking her teeth at the sight of the angry red welts that ran from her wrist to her elbow. She considered pulling the rest of the straw from her clothes—being cold had to be better than being bitten to death by vermin—but where would she put it all? She settled on emptying most of it from her sleeves and a bit more from her bloomers, sighing with relief at the little speck of comfort that brought her, then buried the moldering straw beneath a thick mound of leaves, out of sight of those who were tracking them . . . she hoped.

The sun was setting fast, as it always did at that time of year, and Winter's stomach growled. She glanced toward the shelter, but even this close by, even knowing that it was there, it was hard to see. It blended seamlessly into the steep, leaf-strewn hillside, and Winter marveled once again at Louisa's cleverness.

It would soon be time to wake Louisa, but not yet. She would let her sleep as long as possible. It was going to be a long night, and at least one of them needed a clear head.

She folded her legs up under her chin and watched the setting sun turn the forest a golden yellow, then brilliant orange. She was tucked in the space between the wide maple tree and the mounded shelter, and it was growing colder. A small herd of deer made its way along the gully a short distance downhill from where she sat. A black squirrel materialized from beneath a wild rosebush and sat up on its hind legs, studying her before dashing up the maple and vanishing into shadow. Everything seemed so . . . normal.

Sitting quietly against the tree, as the world began to fall asleep, Winter felt her heart slowing into a calm, steady rhythm. She unfolded her hands and placed them flat on the cool, wet ground. She closed her eyes.

She felt the ground vibrating beneath her palm, the individual particles of dirt spinning around each other, the slight change in speed when an animal skittered in the underbrush nearby.

The itching faded away, and the bone-crushing exhaustion. She was warm. She felt herself sinking and she was warm and safe.

Suddenly she felt a shift in the vibration against her palm, something moving against the earth. Not a deer. She knew that sensation from her hunts with David Henry. This was different. This was . . .

The slavers.

She felt it with absolute certainty.

They were moving away, but they were still out there, hunting for her and Louisa.

And there was someone else too, coming from a different direction.

She felt a touch on her shoulder, and her link with the world abruptly vanished, the sense of falling into the spaces inside the earth jerked away. Louisa, her face pinched with anger, or maybe it was fear, was squatting beside her.

"What the devil you doin' out here?" she asked.

Winter tried to swallow. Her tongue felt thick. She was dizzy, and it took a moment to orient herself back to the cold forest floor. "The slavers have moved off, just like you said."

"How you know that?"

Winter pressed her lips together and met Louisa's gaze.

"Lord have mercy," cried Louisa. She crossed herself. "You work some of your juju finally? Is that it? You have a vision? You had a vision, didn't you?"

"Sssh!" Winter was shaking her head trying to stop Louisa's questions. It wasn't a vision at all. It was more like falling into the world and being a part of everything.

"Yes," Winter said finally. She sighed. "I had a vision. And there's somebody else out there, too."

"Who?"

Winter rubbed her eyes, light-headed with hunger. "I don't know."

Louisa stared at her, the light from the three-quarter moon reflected in her eyes. She sighed. "We'll wait for the deepest part of night to move."

Silently, she divided a potato and half a shriveled apple. When she offered Winter a chunk of moss to drink from, Winter managed, this time, to not retch on the thick, brackish water. Still hungry and aching with exhaustion, she dropped her head onto her knees.

"What's it like?"

Winter raised her head. Louisa was staring at her, her expression unreadable.

"What's what like?" asked Winter.

Louisa waved a hand back and forth between them, as if trying to feel for the right words. "That thing you do. That thing you and Mother Abigail do. Workin' magic." She waved away Winter's protest. "What's it like?"

Winter twisted a tangled, gritty strand of hair around her finger. What was it like? She didn't know what it was like for Mother Abigail, wasn't sure she could explain what it was like for her.

"It's like . . . ," she said slowly, "just paying attention."

Louisa frowned.

Winter thought for a minute. "Like a leaf. You pick it up but stop looking at it as a leaf. You start seeing the things that make it a leaf. The veins, the stem. And then you look closer and you see all the shapes inside the veins. And the shapes inside those, until what you're looking at's not even a leaf anymore."

She shrugged, not sure she was making any sense. But Louisa was watching her intently, listening.

Winter was quiet for a moment. "It feels like . . . like something anybody could do if they just concentrated hard enough."

Louisa made a face.

"No, listen." Winter waved her hands, trying to get her to understand. "Like you and your plants. Your bees. How you know just what they want and need. How you know which plants'll cure a cough and which will kill you."

Louisa seemed to think this over. "When'd you know you could do it?"

Winter shrugged again. "When'd you know you could breathe?"

Louisa's lip twitched upward. "Humph."

The two girls sat in the deepening night listening to the forest. High up in the trees, an owl hooted. Now and then, flying shadows crisscrossed the face of the moon, dropping low to search for mice in the underbrush.

"And when you do . . . that other thing. That thing you did to the slaver . . . and . . . me, is that like breathing, too?"

Winter looked away, ashamed again, not for what she'd done to Colm—she would have turned him inside out if she'd known how—but because of the horrible things she'd said to Louisa back in Remembrance, and the "touch" that had sent the girl flying. That felt like a dozen lifetimes ago. She could barely remember now what she'd even been so angry about.

She shook her head. "No," she whispered. "That's feels like something different. Like a kettle set to boil. The steam just building and building until I feel like I'm going to bust. I see the little bits that make up something and they're all spinning and everything. And somehow, I can touch them, make them spin faster or slower or let go of each other altogether and then . . ."

She swallowed hard. "A thing becomes a different thing. Not what it was before."

"The leaf becomes . . ."

"Not a leaf."

"Like the chain," said Louisa.

Winter nodded. Yes, like the chain.

The two girls stared at each other a long moment.

"And does it feel . . . good?" asked Louisa, finally.

"It doesn't," said Winter. She looked into the trees. "And it does. Like nothin' in the world could stand in your way."

She thought about Mother Abigail's chickens and chuckled mirthlessly. "Course, I don't always get it right."

"People scared a' you." Not a question.

Winter looked at her sharply. "Some," she acknowledged, surprised at how hurtful the admission was.

"Folks can be funny. Judgy." Louisa stroked the scars on her face with one finger and met her gaze. "In any case, magic or whatever you call it seems like a useful thing to have."

Winter snorted. "Not so useful." Louisa frowned and Winter grinned crookedly. "I'm still stuck out here with you, sucking mud out of moss."

To Winter's surprise, Louisa returned the grin. "Yeah, you are, aren't ya?"

The light from the moon helped them move more quickly than the night before, if not more quietly. The two girls hurried through the forest, stumbling over tree roots and fallen trees, pushing their way through thick brush. Louisa seemed to be following some sort of trail, but, for the life of her, Winter could see no trace of it. Every tree looked like every other tree, every hill like the one they'd climbed the hour before and the hour before that. With the sun down, the air had become frigid again and each breath formed a cloud in front of their lips. Winter's lack of sleep soon caught up with her. Her head pounded and her chest burned. There were long chunks of time when she thought she must have fallen asleep while still running.

The ground slid beneath her feet and something sharp punctured her heel.

"Wait," she cried out hoarsely. "Louisa, wait! Please!"

She sank to her knees. The fire in her chest burned away her breath. She just wanted to be home, to be sitting by the Central Fire.

The weight of her exhaustion pushed her down until she rolled forward, her forehead resting on the cold ground, her fingers digging into the soil. She sobbed softly. Louisa squatted down beside her. The other girl said nothing, and finally Winter turned her face so that she was looking up at her. Louisa was gazing out into the dark woods.

Around them were the night sounds of the forest, a sound that until now Winter had loved: the rustling in the forest understory, the hoot of an owl, the distant call of a coyote, all sounds that should have made her feel safe but had now turned into the background noise of her own personal hell.

"This is when you decide," said Louisa finally. Her voice was barely audible.

Winter whimpered. Her tears were cold on her face. It hurt to breathe. "Decide what?" She was so tired.

"What you is," said Louisa. "How your life gets run out."

Winter forced herself slowly upright. The world spun and she swallowed, tasting vomit in the back of her throat. "What in the devil's name're you talking about, Louisa?" she asked listlessly.

Louisa turned her head. In the moonlight the scars on her face seemed to glow. "Whatever you was before don't matter, girl. You a slave now. Until you reach Remembrance, you a slave. A runaway slave. So now you got to decide."

She turned back to stare up into the trees. "I know it feels like you dyin'. Like you can't take not one more single step. But when you a runaway you already done made the decision that you can live with dyin'. Only thing left to decide is whether you gonna die a slave or free. If we manage to get to Remembrance, that just be butter on the biscuit."

"I don't . . ." Winter shook her head. "What're you saying? That when you ran that first time you didn't actually expect to get to freedom?"

Louisa shrugged, not looking at her. "I learned a long time ago not to expect nothin'. That part almost always out my hands. Just mattered what I accepted."

She stood. "And I accepted I might die, but I wasn't dyin' no slave. That's what I decided."

Kneeling there, Winter smelled the filth on herself—the rotting hay and old sweat, the stink of the barn—felt pain through every muscle of her body. She wanted to be brave, she did. She wanted to scream out: I will die before I am a slave!

But she didn't feel brave. Or strong. Or sure of anything . . . especially death. She wanted a warm bath, warm food, and warm clothes. She wanted to be sitting by the fire listening to Old Peter play his harmonica while Sir Galahad chased his stupid goats through the settlement. She wanted to sleep on a real straw mattress with a brick to heat her toes.

Louisa was watching her. Slowly, she dragged herself to her feet, wincing at the sore spot on her heel. She roughly swiped at her tears. She wasn't brave enough to accept her own death and she wasn't brave enough to stay in the woods alone. She got up from the ground only because she couldn't think of anything else to do. With another whimper, she fell in behind Louisa, who nodded and began to move, once again, down a forest trail that only she could see.

They hadn't gone far when Winter thought she heard something. She grabbed at Louisa's skirt.

"What now, girl?"

Winter shook her head, listening. High above them, tree branches creaked in the faint wind.

"What?" whispered Louisa. "What is it?"

Winter held up her hand and shook her head again. There was something . . . someone . . . out there. "I . . . don't know. I thought . . . I thought I heard . . ."

She began to walk quickly, forcing Louisa to follow her now, throwing worried glances over her shoulders. "Let's just go."

There!

There it was again. Winter stopped short and Louisa crashed into her.

"What is it, Winter?" Winter heard panic in Louisa's voice.

There was something—someone—moving in the woods, coming toward them, coming fast. Whipping her head around, she searched for some place to hide.

"You hear something out there?" cried Louisa. "Is it—" She spun toward a sound, the question cut off. Slowly, she began to back toward a deep shadow, pulling Winter with her.

The two girls crouched between the raised roots of an oak and listened, barely daring to breathe. As they waited, straining to hear, to see, time stretched, slowed. The only sounds were the normal night sounds of the forest.

"It was just an animal," Louisa whispered into Winter's ear. "It could have just been an animal, couldn't it?"

Winter nodded. But it hadn't been an animal. She was absolutely sure of that. She stood. Her throat hurt. She had no spit to swallow.

"Let's just go!" she murmured again.

She stepped away from the oak and the woods exploded. A figure as dark as the shadows themselves dropped down from the trees, raining rainwater and leaves and small branches on their heads. Louisa, a few steps behind Winter, let out a strangled scream and then was silent. In the moonlight, Winter could see a man on top of Louisa, holding her down. Pinned, Louisa wrestled in desperate silence with her attacker. With a snarl, Winter launched herself at the man, landing squarely on his back. He flicked her off as easily as if she were a tick on a dog. She landed painfully on her side. Gritting her teeth, she whirled, preparing to attack again . . . and froze.

There, kneeling with his hand over Louisa's mouth, his brown face illuminated by moonlight, was David Henry. The two girls gaped at him as he stood, breathing heavily.

"Doggone! What'd I even come out here lookin' for y'all for? Y'all act like y'all can take care of yourselves." He grinned.

Winter looked down at Louisa, who was sitting on the ground, her eyes as round as skillets, staring up at David Henry. When David Henry winked at Winter, something inside her chest ripped open, some fragile thing that had been holding her together through the whole terrible ordeal. She flung herself at him, nearly knocking him off his feet.

"You came for us," she sobbed. And she held on to him as tightly as she could, afraid that if she let go, even for a single minute, she would be back in the middle of the nightmare again. "You came. I knew someone would come for us. I knew it!"

"Course I came, li'l bit," he said into the tangle of her hair. "Come on, girl, turn me loose. You a bit ripe. Come on now. Time to go home." He laughed, then stopped.

She felt him tense against her, heard Louisa's sharp intake of breath, and she knew, knew with every cell, every hair, every drop of blood that flowed in her veins they weren't going home.

In slow motion, David Henry pried her arms from his neck and stepped away from her, his hands held loosely away from his sides.

She swallowed hard. If she didn't turn—if she stayed just like this—it would be alright. Everything will be alright.

But she did turn, the motion painful, as if her bones were breaking, though she imagined it was probably just her heart.

In the moonlight, Dix's gaunt, white face shone pale and smooth as candle wax. But Winter noticed only the gun, the gun pointed directly at David Henry's heart.

Gaelle

Gaelle glanced at her watch, her hands still shaking after the bizarre confrontation with the old man in the parking lot. His words had made no sense.

She was so much more than what?

He didn't know her. Shouldn't have even known her name. And the power he spoke of? Once again she felt a prickle of heat between her shoulder blades. Everything about him seemed wrong. Crazy stalker, as Toya would say. He seemed to know things about her. He spoke Creole.

And . . . it hadn't just been the effect of the lights. He *had* looked younger.

She ground her teeth and tried to put him out of her mind. He wasn't dangerous . . . she didn't think . . . but the DON would be in in a few hours and Gaelle would tell her about what had happened, have security walk her to her car for the next few days.

She glanced up and frowned. The facility was eerily quiet, even for shift change. Usually nurses and aides huddled at the front desk or the work stations at the end of the hall getting signed out, going over the day's assignments, joking with each other, but there was no one.

The hair stood up on the back of Gaelle's neck, and she hurried toward the staff lounge, peeling her coat off as she went. Was there a meeting she'd forgotten? Could they all be in there?

She passed Winter's room and out of force of habit she glanced in. She cried out in surprise, skidding to a stop, her coat falling unheeded to the floor.

The television was turned to the news station as usual, the faded comforter crumpled in the chair.

But the old woman was gone.

Despite the fact that Winter had never moved a single foot without assistance, Gaelle quickly searched the small room, but the old woman had vanished.

She dashed into the hall. There was an alarm near every door that automatically locked the facility down and blared an ear-piercing sound to alert everyone that a resident was missing.

As she reached to push the button, she heard a commotion coming from the staff lounge. A low, distressed sound. She hurried toward it. The door was ajar and she pushed it open, inhaling in surprise. The entire day shift and most of the night shift were crowded around the few tables. A tiny nurse who only worked part-time, named Mae, stood in the corner scrolling frantically through her phone, as everyone stared expectantly at her.

"That's all there is. I just can't believe it," said Mae. "It's so horrible. Someone should . . ."

She looked up, her eyes widening as she caught sight of Gaelle. "Oh," she said.

The others turned and stared at her in silence, exchanging nervous glances, and her heart thudded hard in her chest.

"What is it?" she asked, the old woman forgotten for the moment.

"Have you spoken to Toya?" asked Mae.

She glanced around the lounge, realizing for the first time that her friend was not there. She stood frozen, not answering, as Mae slowly made her way across the room to her.

Gaelle was still holding her keys in her hand and she gripped them hard, feeling them bite into the soft skin of her palm. Mae held the phone out to her.

There on the screen was Kevin, Toya's youngest son, wearing a broad smile and the gold-and-burgundy Cleveland Cavalier jersey he never took off. She shook her head, confused. Why was there a picture of Kevin on Mae's phone?

"Gaelle, something happened."

She looked up, frowning, still not understanding. Her coworkers stared fixedly at the floor. A few wiped away tears.

"I do not . . ."

"He was . . . shot, Gaelle."

"What?"

"He went out to warm up the car for Toya, and someone . . . shot him. They killed him."

"No," she screamed. There was a roaring sound in her head. "That is not the truth. No."

She thrust the phone back into Mae's chest.

"*Ou se manti,*" she cried. "You lie! God would not do this."

Josiah's words echoed in her head, mocking her. *There is no god.*

She spun and raced down the hall. She couldn't tell if the howling was only in her head or not. She didn't care. As she passed the front door she punched the alarm and the sound braided itself into her own agonized wail.

In the car, she gripped the steering wheel, holding on even as it went from cold to warm and then to hot. She held on as the windows fogged with heat, then cracked. She held on and she screamed.

The world would not take another thing from her.

45

Margot

Margot stepped from her little lean-to out into the night. Remembrance was quiet, but the world seemed filled with ghosts. She couldn't sleep. It was the coldest it had been in days and the air felt heavy.

Three days. It had been three days since David Henry had slipped away with a promise to bring Winter and Louisa back, and more than a week since the five slavers had burst through the Edge bringing fear and death with them into the settlement. One of the slavers and his horse had died for their efforts. Margot had seen the bodies. Both were unmarked. The loss of the horse had been a waste; it had been a fine bay. Not so the slaver. The men had taken the dead pattyroller's body deep into the woods and buried it in a shallow grave, paying him more respect than Margot felt he deserved.

She clenched her cloak tightly and moved aimlessly around the settlement. The Central Fire had burned low but the aromas from dinner still drifted above it. Lighting one of the lanterns that sat at the fire's edge, she straightened and squinted into the shadows ringing the clearing. The small settler's cottages were all but invisible in the darkness. She felt completely alone in the world.

Earlier, she had checked on the newborn twins, who Petal had named Delilah and Aron. It hadn't been necessary to go to the cottage to do that. Their bodies were linked, would stay that way for the next few days. She could sense every breath they took, feel the beating of their tiny hearts beneath her ribs, but she had wanted to see them, to look into their bright, innocent eyes. And because Petal made her smile. *If I had two more tits, I could rent myself out,* Petal had said as soon as Margot had stepped into the cottage.

Now she stood quietly, feeling the isolation, trying it on for size. The night grew bigger, heavier, cutting off her wind. She shuddered and began to move again, skirting around the Central Fire and the bakehouse. She inhaled as the aroma of beans and butter wafted over her. The night nearly overwhelmed the lantern light and she stumbled once, then again. She was so preoccupied with keeping her footing, and with thoughts of David Henry, that it was only when she tripped over the knobby roots of the hollow tree and fell to her knees that she realized that she had walked all the way to the clearing.

Margot scooted toward the tree and leaned her back against it, feeling the worn bark through her cloak. Her heart thudded heavily in her chest and she reached to pull the lantern close, relieved that it had not gone out when she fell. She'd not been here, to this place, since the day she'd arrived in Remembrance.

She drew slow breaths in through her nose, and the damp air stung as it filled her nose. She rubbed the space between her eyebrows.

Her life had changed, then changed again since that night they'd fled that rocky tobacco farm. A lifetime ago.

"Veronique," she whispered into the stillness.

She dropped her head to her chest and sobbed. She missed her sister. Her sister and so many other things. The smell of chicory roasting in the yard. The whistle of the boats moving up the muddy Mississippi. The clip-clop of horse hooves on cobblestone, and Grandmere's low-pitched hum as she beat the flour for morning beignets.

All those things she ached for, and more, but she had picked through her memories so many times that they'd grown hazy, leaving her not with joy but with a terrible stinging in her soul.

Mon couer est brisé. *My heart is broken!*

She sat like that for a long time, until the pain died down a little and the muscles in her legs began to knot up. Slowly, Margot became aware of a sense of wrongness around her, something that had nothing to do with her sad memories. She raised her head and frowned, concentrating, struggling to find the source of her unease.

It was so quiet.

That was it: the quiet, the complete, unnatural silence of the clearing and the surrounding woods. There was no rustling of mice beneath the leaves, no owls high in the trees, even the wind was still as death.

Swallowing a growing sense of alarm, she got slowly to her feet and scanned the tree line before her. She saw nothing, heard nothing, and yet . . .

Margot picked up her lantern, and as she did so, her wrist brushed against something hard in the pocket of her skirt. Hands shaking, she felt around until her fingers touched the knife David Henry had given her just before disappearing into the countryside in search of Winter and Louisa. Her fingers closed around the cool, rough hilt, and some of her anxiety leached away. She didn't think the slavers would be foolish enough to return to Remembrance. Hadn't she said so to David Henry? Petal?

But if they are so stupid, then let them come! Imbeciles! I will be happy to stick them like the cochons *they are.*

Somewhere in the darkness, unseen, were David Henry's men, full of rage and armed, watching, waiting. She hoped.

Margot listened, every fiber tensed and ready, some part of her almost hoping that the slave catchers had returned. But the forest remained eerily still. Finally, sagging with exhaustion, she relaxed her grip on the knife and raised the lantern again. It would be morning soon, and though she doubted that she would sleep at all, she longed for the thick coverings, the straw mattress of her lean-to. The woods were spooking her, scraping at her already raw nerves.

Je suis imbécile. *What was it I was thinking, to come out here in the dead of night?*

The moon came from behind the clouds, turning the clearing a deep gold. Thick mist floated just above the dry grass, which seemed to glow in the moonlight.

She had just turned away, just begun the trek back to the settlement, determined that if she couldn't sleep, then at least she would force herself to stay in the lean-to until dawn, when something moved at the corner of her eye. She froze, the lantern held waist-high.

Margot stared across the clearing, squinting into the mist. There was nothing, just the silence.

Nothing! There is nothing there, you goose. Just fantômes. *Nothing but the ghosts that live in your heart.*

But it was more than ghosts. Something very real was moving around out there in the moonlit mist. Stepping off the narrow track that would take her back into the heart of Remembrance, Margot doused her lantern with one swift movement, then pressed herself into the shadows.

There!

There it was again! Across the clearing, moving in and out of the golden haze. She strained to see.

No one should be out here.

She smiled bitterly. *She* shouldn't be out here. Only David Henry's men had been back to the Edge, as far as she knew; everyone else in Remembrance avoided it as a cursed place.

Across the clearing came the snapping of twigs, the sound exaggerated in the queer floating fog. A shape—large, human—appeared between the trees, before fading back into darkness.

Margot tried to swallow. She gripped the lantern with such force that the handle bit into her palm, but fear had pushed her far beyond pain. Whipping her head around, she contemplated making a run for it, dashing back up the small trail, but there was no way to relight the lantern, and in the dark she would be crashing around blindly, lost and loud.

Mère douce, *sweet Mother, what should I do?*

She broke out in a cold sweat as she crouched low, the darkened lantern pulled tight against her chest. She searched with her free hand until she again felt the knife through the fabric of her skirt.

If they come . . . if they are so stupid that they come back . . . then I will stand against them. I will fight! I will run no more. Sweet Lord, I sound like Petal.

She stared across the clearing, holding her breath until her vision blurred. And then, someone crashed through the trees, out into the open. Margot clapped a hand over her mouth.

Mother Abigail lurched into the high grass of the clearing, arms held above her head, staggering from side to side. She shook her fists at the inky sky, crying out in a language that was familiar to Margot. Like French seasoned by another place, another time: the words and rhythms thick and exotic. The streets of New Orleans were filled with Negroes, both free and slave, who spoke it. It was the language of vodun.

The fog roiled around Mother Abigail like a wide, shimmering river, rendering the priestess nearly unrecognizable.

"*Fantôme*," whispered Margot.

She strained to hear as Mother Abigail wobbled in the center of the small clearing, head thrown back.

"Why?" cried the old woman. "Why? Have I not been a loyal servant? For the *loa* did I not forsake vengeance? For the spirits did I not swallow my wrath like a stone? And for this I end my days the way I started? Hiding in my home like *akrochaj tóti*, a snapping turtle."

The hair on Margot's neck stood on end. Vengeance? Against whom? The slavers? She watched as the old woman staggered about the clearing, crying out, pleading. And it was not necessary to touch her to know that something was badly wrong.

46

Winter

"You gon' shoot me, boy?" David Henry's voice was quiet, barely a whisper. At first Winter wasn't sure that Dix even heard, but after a pause that seemed to stretch forever out into the cold night, she saw the boy shake his head, saw his Adam's apple bobbing wildly in his throat.

"N-n-no," said Dix. The barrel of the gun wavered but then steadied so that once again it was aimed at the dead center of David Henry's chest. "Not if I don't got to . . . no."

David Henry took a step toward the white boy. Winter's gut clenched and she shot out a hand to stop him, but he pushed past her.

"Do something," hissed Louisa.

She had nearly forgotten Louisa, forgotten everything except the icy pain in the center of herself, the pain that was actually horror, as she stared at the gun leveled at David Henry's heart.

"Do something, girl. Work a spell on him or something!"

She felt, rather than saw, Louisa move closer.

"Stay right where you are." Dix swung the gun toward them, then back toward David Henry. "I ain't tryin' . . . I ain't wantin' to hurt nobody but . . . but I'll shoot . . . I'll shoot every one a' y'all dead where you stand. Y'all hear me?"

David Henry nodded. "We hear ya, son." He took another step. "But we not gon' be much use to you dead, ain't that right?"

"Mister, I gotta take these girls. They run off from us. I gotta take them. They worth nearly half a year's wage. That's a fact. And I don't bring 'em back . . . if I just let y'all run off, then Colm and Frank . . . then they say they gon' go back to your place . . . they gonna . . ." Dix took a step back as David Henry took another step toward him, and then another.

"Don't come no closer. I'll shoot. I swear it!"

Inch by slow inch, David Henry moved closer, and closer still, until the barrel of the gun was pressed hard into the fabric of his overcoat.

"I'm sorry, son."

But he didn't look sorry, he looked . . . crazed. As if any minute he might knock Dixon McHugh to the ground and beat him to death. Everyone in Remembrance had seen this look on him, this streak of madness that surfaced unexpectedly in him from time to time, and they knew that when he was in that, when it came, it was best to stay away. He stood, pressing his weight against the barrel of the gun. Dix stood there, too, blinking, as if unsure what to do.

"What they gon' do to Remembrance, boy?" snarled David Henry into Dix's face. "They goin' back there? Your pattyroller brothers stupid enough to go back there and try again? That what you sayin'?"

The Adam's apple jiggled in Dix's throat. "They not my brothers," croaked Dix. "They just . . . some men I met on the road. Had food and a fire. Said I could make good money if I stayed on with 'em."

He looked at Winter as he said this, his pale eyes wide in his pale face, as if trying to explain himself to her. And for a moment, a heartbeat, she felt a flicker of pity for the skinny, ragged boy, even as he stood there trembling, his gun pressed over David Henry's heart.

David Henry pressed forward and Dix stumbled, then righted himself. David Henry was shorter than Dix but thickly muscled and nearly twice as wide. She saw Dix tense, saw him go rigid as his backbone tightened against the weight of the older man.

Oh, god. Please don't shoot. Please, please, please don't shoot.

"Sorry, young son," said David Henry again. "But these girls don't belong to you and they ain't goin' with you."

Dix's eyes flicked toward Winter again. She read the confusion, the panic there, and something else too, something sadder.

"Shoot me," said David Henry.

She jerked at the words. So did the white boy.

"I . . ."

"Shoot me! Shoot. Me."

The boy said nothing. His pale eyes looked wet in the moonlight as they spun wildly from David Henry to Winter and back again, his mouth a round O.

"Shoot me!" screamed David Henry. "Shoot me, damn you! Shoot me!"

His voice bounced off the trees, echoing in the brittle air, and Winter wondered if she was the one that had gone crazy.

"Do something," Louisa said again.

"What?" Winter hissed under her breath, her eyes never leaving the gun pointed at David Henry. "What do you want me to do?"

"Shoot me."

And then Dix was facedown on the ground, the gun flung deep into the woods, David Henry with a knee pressed between the boy's shoulder blades. He yanked the boy around and punched him in the face again and again. Dix brought up his hands, vainly trying to protect his face.

"No," screamed Winter. She threw herself at David Henry. "Stop!"

David Henry stopped, his arm cocked for another blow. He was breathing hard and she felt him trembling as he battled for self-control. With a growl, he shook himself and yanked Dix to his feet. Without a word he quickly bound the boy's hands.

He jerked him around and peered into his face. "You shoulda shot me, boy," he hissed. "'Cause brothers or not, you gon' curse the day you ever broke bread with them slavers. And if they even think the name Remembrance . . ."

David Henry laughed, a harsh, barking sound. ". . . Then I guess it falls to me to end their slave-catchin' days forever."

Dix stumbled as David Henry pushed him roughly before him into the darkness.

"Let's go, ladies," said David Henry.

Louisa appeared at Winter's side. "Good for nothin'," she snarled. She glared, her hatred for Winter obvious even in the dim light. "He coulda shot him while you just stood there like a lump. You like tits on a rooster. Just plain ol' good for nothin'."

She spat at Winter's feet then turned to follow David Henry into the night. Winter stood frozen on the invisible path. In the yellow light from the moon, the three—Louisa, David Henry, and the hapless Dix—looked like ghosts as they moved between the trees.

Louisa's words rolled round and round in her head like a wooden marble, hurting all the places it hit. The icy pain in her gut had turned solid, as if she'd swallowed some terrible thing. She saw David Henry turn, heard him call her name. He was still angry. She couldn't see his face in the shadows but she could hear it.

Louisa had stopped a half-dozen yards away and was watching her, a shaft of moonlight lighting her ruined face. It may have just been the scars that made it seem that way, but she was sure Louisa was silently laughing at her, taunting her.

Winter felt the air vibrating against her skin, felt the minute shifts in the ground beneath her feet as unseen animals scurried along the forest floor. She felt a thrum of anger building inside.

She had nursed her. Fed her. Cleaned her wounds. She had saved her life.

With no memory of moving at all, she was in front of Louisa. What would it feel like, she wondered, to reach inside of her. To send her particles spinning around each other in confusion. To make that hatred melt from her face the way she'd melted the chains back in the barn. She stared at Louisa, and the herbalist was no more solid to her than smoke. Winter could see through and inside the other girl, see every single cell that made Louisa Louisa. She could see the other girl's heart beating beneath her clothes, see blood flowing like a stream through her veins.

"Good for nothing?" Winter hissed. Her voice sounded too deep, strangled, not her voice at all. She reached out one hand to feel the beating heart. Just one breath.

One.

She spread her fingers wide, reaching.

Two.

Louisa's skin, so solid, so brown, was millions upon millions of octagonal cells overlapping each other. And where those cells connected were spaces along the seams. And she could see down through the seams, down to the muscle below. The sound of her breathing filled her ears.

"Y'all girls don't settle down, I swear I'm-a make this white boy go find his gun over yonder and shoot you both!"

David Henry thrust his thick body between them and she felt something tear inside her, her connection to the healer severed. She staggered backward, gasping, one hand still stretched toward Louisa's chest.

In the shadowed light, Louisa was staring at her. There was still hatred, but now it was overshadowed by fear. Winter smiled, reveling in that terror. If she couldn't make her like her, she would make her fear her.

David Henry seemed not to notice.

"Try me, hear?" he said. "Just try me, and the only one's gon' end up back at Remembrance gon' be me and this here white boy. I don't have the time or the inclination to deal with the two a' you fightin' like cats and dogs."

He turned to Dix. "I got half a mind to just turn 'em over to you like you wanted in the first place. And heaven help you with that, boy." Dix glanced at the two girls but said nothing.

With a grunt of irritation, David Henry whirled and began moving along the trail, the others close behind. The trail seemed more clear to her now. Every branch, every tree root glowed with a faint energy.

Home! I'm going home!

She made a noise and David Henry shot her a look over his shoulder. She pressed her lips together and forced herself to follow in silence. But inside she was screaming with joy. She was going home.

47

Winter

"Best to stop. Rest up a bit. We close. Should be there by mornin'."

David Henry's words startled Winter. She wasn't tired, hadn't been tired since the confrontation with Louisa hours before. She'd barely noticed the passing of the night around her. In the cold air, her muscles sang. She could walk forever. Food, sleep—she didn't need them now. The long, terrible days of being chained in a barn, the horrible night of sleeping like a mole under the ground had evaporated, replaced by a bright, dazzling energy. She had Louisa to thank for it. Rage and hate had sharpened her focus. Around her, the night shimmered. She stopped and breathed in brittle air. Louisa crouched down at the base of a tree and glared at her. Winter caught her eye, and the healer jerked her head away and stared fixedly at the ground.

"Sit down, Winter," David Henry said quietly.

"But if we're almost there . . ." Her skin tingled with excitement. "We should just keep going. We need to . . ."

He wrapped a thick hand around her arm and guided her firmly to a mound opposite Louisa. He pointed.

"Sit! You get tired, you make mistakes. You make mistakes, you get took." He frowned and peered into her face. "What is the matter with you, girl? You twitchy as a tick."

Winter grinned. David Henry glowed in the dark, a soft blue light moving in and around his skin. He shook her slightly. "If you gon' get softheaded on me, Winter, you just better wait 'til we get back to Remembrance. Can you do that? Can you wait to go buggy 'til we get back to home?"

She nodded and bit back a laugh. "I can wait."

"Good." His face softened and he smiled. "Now sit here and watch this white boy. I'm-a walk up that trail a ways and check things out."

She folded herself onto the muddy rise and tucked her knees under her chin. David Henry strode into the darkness and quickly disappeared, seeming to melt into the forest. She leaned back and stared up into the trees. The ground thrummed beneath her, the sensation unexpectedly soothing. Things were changing and she was changing with them. Remembrance was close now.

"What y'all gonna do with me?"

Dix sat a few feet away, nearly hidden among the branches of a chokeberry bush. Head down, bound hands between his knees, his teeth chattered loudly in the dark.

"What you deserve, white boy," snarled Louisa without looking up.

Winter sensed David Henry creeping stealthily in the shadows far up the trail, could feel the tension in him as he searched the darkness for danger.

She turned toward the frightened boy. "I don't know," she said, finally.

"Y'all gonna kill me?" he asked. "That what you do with white folks?"

"Yeah," muttered Louisa. "Every chance we get. Just like you do us."

He seemed to shrink into himself.

"No," said Winter. She shot a glance at Louisa.

"That's not what we do. We don't kill people for no reason," she said pointedly. He refused to meet her eyes. "But we can't just let you go home, either. We won't let you hurt us again."

"Ain't got no home," said Dix. "Told you that before."

"Maybe we just hold on to you for a while," said Louisa. She was looking at Dix now, her eyes flashing dangerously. "Make you our slave. Maybe sell you off. Though you a bit puny to bring much."

Dix's head shot up. "Can't no white man be no slave."

"Why not?" asked Winter. She wasn't really interested in having Dix stay in Remembrance, let alone have him as her slave. But why couldn't a white man be a slave?

"It . . . ," sputtered the boy, clearly taken aback. "Well, it just ain't even natural, is all."

The two girls looked at him incredulously. Louisa gave a harsh laugh. "Boy, you got a lot to learn about what's 'natural' in Remembrance."

Winter opened her mouth to remind him that, not so long ago, he'd accused them of being witches, that he'd heard things, seen things with his own eyes he couldn't explain. In an upside-down world where they could be witches, where folks appeared and disappeared out of thin air, why couldn't he be a slave? In that sort of world, she knew anything was possible. The words were there, almost out of her mouth, to ask him that, when she felt the night shift around her. Her head whipped around. Had someone called her name out of the darkness?

Everything suddenly went still. The trees, the rocks, the dirt all seemed to harden, become impenetrable, and she was abruptly disconnected from everything. The particles that made up all things had suddenly seemed to stop spinning and the energy that had been pulsing around her in bright swaths of color had gone dark. The night became an ugly place of throbbing grays and blacks. She stood and squinted up the trail.

"David Henry?" she called softly.

There was no answer.

"David Henry?" she called again, her voice trembling.

"What is it?" Louisa was standing now, too. She kept her distance from Winter, but her head whipped this way and that as she tried to see into the darkness. "What you see out there?"

Dix stared wide-eyed at them. "What? I don't see nothin'."

"Something's wrong," said Winter.

Louisa's laugh was shrill. "Really? No kiddin'."

"We have to go," cried Winter. "We have to go now!"

"What?" Louisa backed away from her. "Go? Go where? We not goin' nowhere without David Henry."

"Then we need to go find him, but we can't stay here."

"He said to wait here."

"Get up."

"No. I'm not going anywhere with you!"

Dix gaped as Winter grabbed the older girl by the collar of her cloak and yanked her up, flinging her a few feet down the dark trail.

"Go!" she snapped.

Whirling, she turned to face Dix. He hesitated only a moment before getting to his feet.

"What do you think you doin'? Two days ago you couldn't find your way out the barn, now you Daniel blamin' Boone?" Louisa huffed breathlessly as Winter led them off the small, rutted trail and deeper into the woods. The land slanted slightly downhill. Vines twined like netting between the trees, tripping them up, slowing them down. Wild thorns tore at their faces until they were scratched and bloody.

She pushed on, using her own sense of the forest and the little bit she'd learned tracking with David Henry. They needed to find him. Something had shifted around them. She didn't understand it, but they had to get back to Remembrance. Now.

"You gon' get us killed, girl. We shoulda just stayed—"

"Louisa, just shut up, hear?" Winter spun. "He wouldn't have wanted us to just sit there if we were in danger. And something felt wrong."

She whirled on Dix. "You felt it, right?"

He opened his mouth but no words came out.

But Louisa wasn't done. "So what? We just wander around until we find him or stumble into Remembrance? You couldn't find Remembrance if you was standin' barefoot in the middle of the Central Fire."

"I tell you what! You sit right there and wait. Nobody cares. But I—"

"Shut it already!"

Both girls went silent and turned to face Dix. The boy was leaning against a bent sapling glaring at them. He pounded his forehead with a tied fist.

"Sweet Lord in heaven," the boy cried. "Y'all don't have to worry 'bout what to do with me. Just kill me now. Right here! Right where I stand!"

He bent and picked up a thick branch. "Here," he snapped. "Use this. Just bash my head in. I'll close my eyes. I'll even turn my back. Just please put me out my misery 'cause I can't take not one more single minute of you two blabberin' on and on. I swear on the graves of my momma and my dear dead sister, I can't."

The two girls stared at the branch, then at Dix, who stood breathing hard. Above them, the earliest rising birds began to chirp in the trees. Laughter bubbled up in Winter's chest. She gritted her teeth, trying to hold it in.

Dix shook the branch in their direction. "Come on. I mean it. I'd do it myself if I could get a good enough hold on this here stick."

Beside her, Louisa snorted. "White boy gone crazy," she muttered.

A small laugh escaped, followed by another, until Winter was doubled up with it. She pressed her fists against her mouth, trying to muffle the sound. From the corner of her eye she saw Louisa cover her mouth with her hand. A soft chuckle escaped through the older girl's fingers and sent Winter into a fresh fit of hysterics until she sank to her knees, too weak to stand.

Dix watched the two girls silently. "Y'all about done?" he asked sourly when Winter finally got a grip on herself.

"Expect so," said Louisa. Winter grinned and bit down on her bottom lip.

"Y'all won't be doin' much laughin' if Colm and them catch back up with you," he said quietly. The last of the laughter shriveled and died in Winter's throat. She glanced at Louisa, who stood watching the white boy, her expression hard.

"Y'all think Frank the one you got to be worried on, but I'm here to tell you it's Colm. Near as I can tell, the only thing he ever loved in this life besides a silver dollar in his pocket was his brother. The one he always be talkin' about. The one you all made crazy."

"We didn't make his brother crazy," snapped Winter, but she shuddered at the mention of the slaver. She could see his curly hair and narrow face, his hard black eyes as clearly as if he were standing in front of her. She glanced up. Streaks of gray and orange showed through the trees. Daylight was coming. They had to get moving.

As she turned, Dix reached out to stop her. His hands hovered near her elbow, not quite touching. "Colm's a fair tracker, but I'm better. How you think I found your boy?"

"You mean David Henry," interrupted Louisa.

"David Henry," he agreed, meeting her eyes.

"They didn't think I was good for much," he went on. "But I was good for that. I sure can track a thing." He looked away as he said this. "Cut me loose," he said after a moment.

"What? No," cried Louisa. She looked around nervously. "No," she said again more quietly. Winter said nothing.

"Y'all need to start huntin' 'stead a runnin'. We gon' need to stay behind Colm and them," said Dix. "Cut around 'em when we can. Warn your people. If they get to your place—Remembrance?—first." He shook his head. "Well, hopefully y'all's menfolk's got the stomach for a fight."

"They won't find nothing when they get to Remembrance," snapped Louisa. "The Edge will hold. They won't get in."

"They got in the last time," murmured Winter. Louisa flicked a hand, dismissing her.

"What's the Edge?" he asked. He looked from one girl to the other, but neither answered.

"Fine," he said with a sigh. "I'm just tellin' you. You don't want to get caught up by them again. Trust me when I say what they done to you before won't be nothin' like what'll happen if they catch y'all a second time."

"So now you want to help us?" said Winter.

Dix was quiet a long time.

"Don't know who I'm helpin' no more, you want to know the truth of it," he said finally. "You got no idea, you don't, what it's like to be hungry like that. So hungry it's like you got a wild animal runnin' in your insides. And alone. The nights goin' on forever."

"We ain't got no idea?" snapped Louisa, her eyes wild. "And you ain't got no idea what it's like to work from sunup to sundown like an animal. What it's like to have your baby ripped from your arms and know you ain't never gon' see that child again in this life. To be beat near to death 'cause it's a Tuesday. And we supposed to be feelin' sorry for you 'cause you was hungry?"

She stepped close and spit in his face.

Winter stared.

Dix raised his head and met her hatred face on. "No," he said softly. "It was wrong, a sin, sellin' flesh, but . . . it seemed at the time like . . . well, I got no more stomach for it, is all." He turned to face Winter. "You cut me loose, I'll help you get back to your people."

Louisa crossed her arms and glowered at the boy. "Then what?"

"Then I go on my way," he said.

"Just like that," said Louisa, rolling her eyes. "All's forgiven. No harm done? That it? Well, then that makes it alright. Go on then, Winter, cut him loose."

Winter stepped forward, pulling one of the remaining sharp-edged rocks from her skirt pocket. As she reached for Dix's wrist, Louisa snatched at her hand.

"Are you out your mind?" she cried. "What you doin', girl?"

"Cutting him loose," said Winter. She shook off Louisa's hand and sawed at the rough rope binding Dix.

"You know this white boy is either gonna run off or lead us right back where we started."

The forest around them was a misty gray, and Winter saw tears glittering in Louisa's eyes. She turned to look into Dix's face. There were deep shadows under his eyes, and the dark bruises near his mouth and around his neck where David Henry had beaten him blended into the older bruises that had not yet faded. He was worse for wear than they were.

"Dix?"

He returned her look and then stepped toward Louisa. She flinched. "I ain't got much," he said. "But I got my word and I'm givin' it to you. I'm-a help y'all get back to your place, to your Remembrance, and then you're shed of me for good."

He held out a hand to Louisa, who shrank back, horrified. He dropped his hand and turned back toward Winter.

She ignored it, sniffing at the air. An echo, just the faintest vibration came to her through the trees.

"We need to find your . . . David Henry," said Dix.

Winter hesitated.

Dix stepped to her and touched her shoulder. "He came for you," he said softly. "He won't be far off if he's scopin' the trail. It's what I would do. I can find him."

Winter nodded and, ignoring Louisa, turned to follow Dix back the way they'd come.

48

Mother Abigail

She screamed at the *loa* until her throat burned, throwing her voice again and again into the sky. This was wrong. Cruel and unforgivable. The *loa* had broken faith with her . . . again.

She screamed for everything that had been taken from her: her name, her family, her children. They'd left her with this one thing, her power. And she'd made a home. For herself. And for others like her. And now they'd taken that, too, and there was no answer, not even a murmuring in the trees.

Remembrance.

In the blink of an eye it had become just another small, poor settlement of runaway slaves who would, from now on, be forever looking over their shoulders.

She closed her eyes and could see her powers, smoldering like spent coals, there at the bottom of her soul. She needed to save Remembrance. To save her people.

She gave a bitter laugh. Save her people. She couldn't even save herself.

She heard someone approach and the laughter died. Squinting, she tried to see, but the moonlight bounced off the drifting fog, confusing her. She saw shapes moving about in the mist. One? Two? Had the *loa* decided to answer her then? Or perhaps the slavers had come back for a second helping. She ground her teeth.

She wasn't afraid for herself. She'd lost all there was to lose. But they would steal no one else. She was weak but . . . *yon kaiman avék yon dan ka toujou móde.* An alligator with one tooth could still bite.

The priestess's eyes widened as Margot stepped from the shadows. The new girl. The one who bore the Rousse stench on her. She spit in disgust and turned her back on the girl. Had it been her that brought this terrible luck down on them? There was no such thing as coincidence.

"We have to go," said the girl. "It is not safe here."

"Not safe?" The old woman peered into the mist. Were they out there? The *loa?* Watching? Were they simply creatures created for their amusement? She gave a bitter laugh.

"Where should we go then that is safe, *petite?*"

What did it matter? Time was rushing past, washing over her like a river, moving her toward the end. And it was right that she should be here, on this very spot when the end came, whatever it was.

"On this very spot," whispered Mother Abigail. "It started here on this spot."

"*Ce qui?*" asked Margot. "What did?"

Mother Abigail turned and peered up at the girl. With her angular, near-white face and strong jaw, her long, softly curling hair, she truly was striking. Not pretty, but handsome. In another time, another place, Mother Abigail could have made her appear in a gown of smooth satin, even created the sounds of New Orleans's church bells and steamships all around them, if only for a bit. But that time was gone now, and Margot stood before her in a tattered cloak inches too short for her, her dirty hair a tangled knot at the nape of her neck. And the only sound around them was the rustling of the dry grass, the squeal of fruit bats searching the bare trees.

"Remembrance." The priestess thought she spoke this aloud but she wasn't sure. The mist and the moonlight were playing tricks on her eyes, and the sounds of the night seemed to come from nowhere and everywhere.

Daylight was coming.

Even as she thought this, the clearing seemed to brighten, to warm. She smelled thick, dark earth, wet leaves and sunlight. A fawn stood just at the edge of the greening grass, and she knew she was seeing the clearing the way it had been on that day so many years before, when she and Josiah had stood on this very spot and created Remembrance, a sanctuary of hope for them, a safe haven for runaway slaves.

"Mother Abigail?"

Margot's voice seemed to fall from the pale blue sky, and the priestess laughed.

"It's time," the priestess whispered. She felt them then, the spirits, the ancestors, sensed how thin the veil really was between past and present, living and dead.

Mother Abigail looked around, taking in everything: the hollow tree, the wild mulberry, trying to memorize every blade of grass, every bush, how the sky touched the horizon, knowing she was seeing it all for the last time.

"Thank you," she whispered.

"Mother Abigail?" Margot's voice was closer, more urgent.

The old priestess closed her eyes, and when she opened them, it was cold and dark again, though not nearly as dark as before, and Margot was standing close, her face pinched in confusion.

"Chére?"

Margot straightened, relieved. "We need to go back to the settlement. It feels . . . wrong here." She cast a quick look over her shoulder and shuddered.

Mother Abigail took a deep breath, nearly laughed again. She could still smell the sunshine in her nostrils. But the *ti fi* was right: the end was coming and it was bringing something with it. The old priestess tried with everything she had left to push her senses out into the breaking dawn, but there were no seams, no spaces for her to bend. The world had become flat, all the hidden places exposed.

She sniffed at the air. The world seemed to ripple, and for the briefest moment, she could see that other time, when Remembrance was new and bright and full of hope. Like a reflection in a pond, she saw that warm, green Remembrance hovering just beneath the gray, icy one where they stood.

The end was coming. For her. Perhaps for Remembrance.

And she had a sense that neither would go gentle.

She motioned to Margot. "Come along, *ti fi*. I can die as easy by a warm fire as out here in the cold."

With an apprehensive glance at the old priestess, Margot moved toward the path tucked just beyond the hollow tree, not waiting to see if the priestess followed. Once on the narrow trail, the old woman turned and bowed her head.

"*Mèsi*," she whispered. She thanked the spirits of all the slaves that had come to her looking for freedom, for as surely as she had saved them, so had they saved her.

She felt them around her, could see the hundreds of faces that she'd come to know in the more than four decades since she and Josiah had stood staring out over this very clearing. All the saints and *loa* were there, too. They may have stopped talking to her but they hadn't abandoned her after all.

She laid a wrinkled hand over her chest and was almost surprised to feel the reluctant thrum of her heart beneath her palm. She stood a moment longer, watching the mist rising into the lightening sky.

"*Il es fait*," she said. "Enough." Squaring her shoulders, she turned to follow Margot back toward the settlement. She stumbled and Margot returned to her side. She took the girl's arm without complaint.

"Enough," she murmured. "This life has been enough."

49

Margot

The narrow path leading back to the center of the settlement was slick and uneven, and the old woman leaned heavily against her. They were forced to stop frequently so Mother Abigail could rest. They were only a few hundred yards up the trail when it became clear that the priestess would never make it back to the center of the settlement. Margot wondered how she'd managed to get so far alone in the first place.

The farther they walked, the more of the old woman's weight she supported. Feeling the woman's fragility, Margot tried to hold her gently, but she could do nothing about the swell of sensations bombarding her as she propped up the priestess. She felt a pressure in her head, a wet, sliding sensation, pulses of red and pink. The old woman was bleeding inside her head again, the leak slow but persistent.

Mother Abigail was dying.

Margot felt the effort each step cost the old woman, felt how hard the old woman's heart was pumping in her chest, every agony mirrored in her own head and heart.

They were close, had passed the cemetery, when the priestess sagged against her. The muscles in Margot's shoulders seized and she managed, just barely, to ease the priestess to the ground. Breathless, she rubbed her aching muscles and stared at Mother Abigail.

The old woman lay on the cold ground smiling vaguely into the treetops. In the growing light, her broad face was skeletal. The clarity that she'd shown just a short time before had faded, and her eyes, sunken deep in her face, were dull, blank.

"Madame," said Margot finally. "We are nearly there. We must go or you will surely catch your death here." She heard the irony in her own words and winced.

"My death, yes." And the old woman chuckled, her eyes never leaving the latticework of branches overhead. "Oh, child."

She laughed again and the sound turned into a wet, sputtering cough. She stared up into the branches. Margot frowned and glanced up. The trees formed a dark pattern against the sky, which had turned the color of an egg, but otherwise there was nothing to see there. She shivered as goosebumps prickled her arms.

The old woman lay motionless.

"Please, you must get up now," she said, squatting beside her.

She leaned closer, and a loud snore, carried on a wave of sour breath blasted her face.

"*Merde! Jesus doux!*" she cried, jerking back.

The old woman had fallen asleep.

How was that even possible?

"Mother Abigail, Madame, wake up." She poked the old woman hard. "Madame!"

But Mother Abigail snorted and rolled onto her side. She could have been in a feather bed, covered in satin quilts. The hair on Margot's arms stood up and she shivered again.

"*Enchantée,* bewitched," Margot whispered. She looked uneasily down the trail in the direction they'd just come. She could just make out the headstones through the trees. She quickly crossed herself.

Ghosts, slavers, it didn't matter, she had to get the old woman off the ground and back to the settlement. But try as she might, Mother Abigail could not be wakened. Grunting, Margot pulled her as far off the trail as she could. She hesitated, uncertain of leaving the old woman out in the open alone, but she needed help, and surely someone would be up by now. With a final look over her shoulder, she hurried toward the settlement.

"Sweet Sadie! Margot?" cried Petal. "You just scared ten years off my body. Wherever did you pop up from, girl? And what is the matter with you? You look like death warmed twice in a skillet. And I'm the one that just pushed two giant babies out my lady parts."

Despite the blanket of dread that seemed to lay over everything, Margot smiled.

"It is the priestess. Mother Abigail. I found her in the woods. She has fallen asleep. I cannot get her up."

"Sleeping?" Petal's face twisted in confusion. "In the woods?"

Margot nodded.

Petal stared at her, eyes narrowed. "Alright, then," she said slowly. "But why you look like someone just danced over your grave?"

Margot rubbed her forehead and looked away. In her mind she saw once again Mother Abigail on her hands and knees, screaming at the spirits, pawing at the frozen grass like a wild animal. Heard Mother Abigail predicting her own death. And she could not shake the feeling that, despite everything that had already happened, something even more terrible was upon them.

"It is . . . We must get her up and by a warm fire," she said finally, not answering the other woman's question. "We must find someone to help."

She felt Petal's questioning eyes on her a moment more.

"Well." Petal took a deep breath. "Let's shake a tail feather then. Those babies of mine sleepin' now, but that ain't gon' last, and when they open they eyes, they gon' be ready for breakfast."

Margot tried to restrain her. "Wait! No. You cannot," she cried. "It is too soon after the birth. You need to rest."

Petal looked up at her, her mouth twisted in amusement. "What colored woman you know got time to rest?"

She tugged at Margot's cloak. "Come on, fancy lady. 'Fore I change my mind."

Margot chuckled and reluctantly allowed herself to be dragged along. "You are a funny girl, Petal."

Petal scrunched her face. "You got no idea."

Mother Abigail lay in the exact spot where Margot had dropped her. If there'd been any leaves left on the trees, her snoring would have shaken them loose. Petal stood over the old woman and frowned.

"This don't seem peculiar to you?" she asked, locking eyes with Margot.

"Yes," answered Margot simply.

Petal looked at her, questions playing across her face. "Well . . . she looks peaceful enough," she said, finally.

"Yes," she agreed again.

"And you tried wakin' her up?"

Margot twisted her lips and waved an impatient hand, not bothering to reply.

"Yeah, guess you did that or you wouldn'a bothered to come lookin' for help, would you?" Petal sighed. "Okay then, you're a big girl and I'm stronger than I look." She flexed a tiny muscle. "And she's an old thing. Between the two of us we ought a be able to get her back to her place and tucked in."

It proved much more difficult than that. Mother Abigail was dead weight. Petal grabbed the old woman under the arms while Margot gripped the ankles. But Margot was nearly half a foot taller than Petal, and this threw the old woman's weight off-balance. As she lifted the priestess's legs, Mother Abigail's head fell back, striking Petal in the teeth. The girl's mouth snapped shut with an audible click.

"Sweet Sadie!" Petal cried. Staggering, she fell, landing on her back, hands clasped over her mouth. The top half of Mother Abigail landed on Petal's stomach with a soft thump, the sudden weight pulling Margot forward. She tripped over the priestess's feet, landing on her knees in the wet dirt. The old priestess gave one loud snort and then resumed her deep, rhythmic snoring.

"Well, goddamn, and 'scuse me for taken the Lord's name in vain, but guess this my reward for gettin' up early. Mother Abigail is dead to the world," said Petal through her fingers.

"Yes," said Margot. She smiled grimly. "And she may well be dead in fact if we cannot get her back."

The sky had lightened and birdsong was beginning to fill the air, but there, in the shadows of the trail, it was still bitterly cold.

"Perhaps we should get one of the men to help us. Surely someone will be up by now," Margot said.

"Let's just get this thing done."

Margot clutched at the old woman's cloak, dragging her partially upright. Grunting with the effort, the two women managed, finally, to half carry, half drag Mother Abigail into the still-quiet settlement.

"We got to stop. Let's just prop her up over here by the Central Fire for a minute. It's warm and folks'll be up soon. Then we can get one of the men to help us get her to her cabin." Petal was panting and her bottom lip had started to swell. "Thomas's boy. He always one of the first up looking for coffee. He'll help."

"What about Josiah?" The spit soured in Margot's mouth as the old man's name passed her lips.

A shadow passed across Petal's face. "You wanna know somethin'?" she said, leaning toward Margot. "He Mother Abigail's friend and all, but he the most peculiar person, don't you think? With those weird, unnatural eyes a' his. Between you and me, he just gives me the heebie-jeebies."

Margot smiled slightly. "He gives me the . . . heebie-jeebies as well."

They positioned the old woman close to one of the woodpiles next to the bakehouse. Petal went to the fire and stirred the coals that smoldered in the gray ash, feeding in dry kindling until there was a fine fire crackling inside the circle of stones. Margot brought Petal water to start the coffee, then they both slumped near Mother Abigail to warm themselves and rest.

Margot eyed the old woman uneasily.

A bit peculiar.

She turned to Petal, who sat with her eyes closed, her face jutted toward the heat of the now-roaring fire.

"You'll want to put something cool on that," she said, touching Petal's bruised lip gently with her finger.

Without opening her eyes, Petal waved her off. "No, no, it'll be fine. Had way worse."

Her hand hovered near Petal's face a moment longer before she let it drop to her lap. She glanced at Mother Abigail, feeling the wrongness of the old woman's deep, impenetrable sleep.

Day had finally broken, and around them Remembrance was stirring to life. Soon the women would be heading to the Central Fire to start breakfast for their families and get water from the nearby well to wash. Petal pushed a metal cup half filled with scalding coffee into Margot's hand.

"I gotta go check on my babies," she said. She stood and looked down at the snoring priestess, a frown creasing her tiny face. "You sure ain't nothin' else wrong with her? I ain't never seen nobody sleep like this before—never in my whole life. And I seen me some tired colored folks."

Margot stared into her coffee cup. She shrugged. "As you say, she is very old."

"Old or not, this just don't seem right at all."

She looked up and met Petal's eyes. They gazed at each other, an uneasy, silent conversation taking place. One more secret between them. Petal looked away first.

"Well, what I know?" she said. "I just an old field hand. Lots of things past my understandin'."

She stood for a minute longer looking down at the insensible priestess, then yawned. "Time will tell. Always does." She winced and touched her swollen lip. "And right now the time is for them greedy babies to suckle."

She started across the clearing, skirting the now-white-hot fire. She stopped and turned around.

"You gon' watch—?" The unfinished question hung in the air as her head jerked up.

Margot was on her feet in an instant. She'd heard it, too—the sound of horses moving through the brush, and there were no horses in Remembrance. Their eyes met across the fire. She saw Petal trembling beneath her thin cloak, her tiny fists clenched at her side.

Margot tried to follow the sound. One horse? Two? She couldn't tell. Petal began to back away, moving toward her cabin, her eyes wide and frightened.

She sensed movement behind her, heard Petal cry out a warning. She spun and found herself face-to-face with a tall white man—broad shouldered, with curly, dark hair and dimples—and he was holding a rifle.

"Well, now," he said cheerfully. "Coffee's on, fire's made. A lovely start to a lovely day all around, I'd say, wouldn't you, Frank?"

A huge white man stepped from the trees near the river path, leading a horse. He swung his gaze between Petal and Margot, looking them up and down, as if silently daring them to try to run, to scream. He folded his arms across his wide chest and watched them wordlessly, his expression dark, dangerous.

The first slaver grinned and turned to Margot. "Be a good girl and fetch us some coffee, lass."

Never, porc!

She stared at him, not moving, watched how his breath hung in the frigid morning air. She could smell him . . . and the other one. They smelled like death. The slaver took a step toward her. She cringed involuntarily. He saw it and his smile widened.

He leaned down until he was gazing into her eyes. Only with great will was she able to make herself stand and meet his look.

"Ah," he said. "You're not feeling hospitable then. Pity, that."

The false smile vanished, and she felt a bloom of bright pain across her face, her vision blurring. It took her a moment to register the blow. In all her life, no one had ever struck her. She stood blinking at the slaver, more shocked than afraid. He smiled and Margot saw the full killer in his soul.

She looked into his eyes and moved her fingers inside her skirt pocket, searching for the knife David Henry had given her days before. At her feet, Mother Abigail snored softly.

50

Winter

Dix led the way, weaving in and among the trees, following a route that once again was invisible to Winter. Meanwhile, behind her, Louisa kept up a steady stream of complaint.

"I must be the stupidest colored girl on the planet. Followin' a white pattyroller boy and a half-brained nigra girl through the middle of the forest in broad daylight," groused Louisa. "Might as well go stand out in the middle of the post road and wait for a pack of slavers to just come by and invite me in their wagon. Might as well—"

"Shut up, Louisa!" cried Dix and Winter in unison. Dix looked over his shoulder and caught Winter's eye. He gave her a weak smile. Louisa was quiet for nearly a full minute before the grumbling started once again. Dix groaned, but Winter simply shook her head and tried to tune her out as they struggled uphill through the dense growth.

The ground gradually leveled off and the tangle of brush thinned. It was fully morning now, and sunlight, the color of churned butter, reached them through the bare branches. The air crackled with the cold. A stray snowflake landed on her face, where it quickly disappeared, leaving only a trace of dampness. As the cover of trees thinned, Dix slowed, then stopped, crouching next to an uprooted tree.

"Your David Henry's a mighty fine woodsman. Makes himself invisible out here," he said. "He's not far, though. He wouldn't have gone too far from y'all. Once we meet back up, I figure we got another five, maybe six miles before we get to your home place." He smiled. "If we're lucky, might make it in time for breakfast."

At the mention of breakfast, Winter's stomach growled loudly and Louisa's responded in sympathy.

"Best be gettin' on," he said. Something in his tone snapped Winter to attention. She peered into the trees uneasily.

"What is it?" she asked.

"Nothin', but we best find your man quick. We burnin' up good travelin' time, and Colm and them gonna be movin' faster than us."

She watched as he studied the shadows around them. Was Louisa right? Was he leading them into a trap?

They had only taken a few steps when they heard the sharp report of twigs breaking behind them. They froze, listening. For an instant there was no sound. Even the birds had gone silent.

Dix moved slowly, silently, pushing both girls until they were behind him. She thought she saw a shadow moving in the trees. Behind her, Louisa's breathing was loud, ragged.

"Move," whispered Dix.

Winter took a step back, forcing Louisa to move with her. She could run. All the way to Remembrance if she had to.

Louisa seemed rooted to the spot, her eyes so wide they seemed about to pop from her skull. Winter tugged at her sleeve just as the rustling in front of them grew louder.

"Come on," she hissed.

And then David Henry stepped from the shadows. Louisa made a strangled, high-pitched sound and covered her face.

"Are y'all just cockeyed stupid or what?" he hissed.

"David Henry!" Winter smiled and started to explain why they were out there, but the words died on her lips. David Henry was shaking with rage, his rifle gripped tight in his hands.

"We had to move, David Henry," she began again, speaking softly. "Something—"

He shot her a withering look, and she looked down at her feet. Slowly, he swiveled toward Dix, looking him up and down, his finger still on the trigger. "And what in the name of God is your story, boy? How come you ain't just run off when these two simple-headed girls cut you loose?"

Dix returned David Henry's gaze, his face blank, unreadable.

"They been through here already," he said, quietly.

In an instant, David Henry's demeanor changed. His body tensed. He seemed to sniff at the air, his narrowed eyes taking in every detail of the area around them.

"What?" He leaned toward Dix, who blinked but held his ground. "What you mean?"

"I mean Colm and them. They been through here already. I think they headin' to your Remembrance."

"I been all up in these hills. I ain't seen no tracks." David Henry's voice was harsh.

"No." Dix shook his head. "It's what they do. They get off their horses and then they split up. Circle wide around what they huntin'. If you see any signs of them at all, it just looks like one man huntin' maybe. Some a' that they figured out on their own. Some a' that"—he swallowed hard—"I taught 'em. They ain't never lost a slave they had their mind set to."

He locked eyes with David Henry as he said this last, his mouth a hard line.

The muscles in David Henry's jaw worked. "Show me," he said, after a long moment.

Dix nodded and began to move stealthily through the trees. David Henry started to follow but stopped. He turned and glared at the two girls.

"You two go wanderin' off this time and you on your own. I'll just tell Mother Abigail you got ate by bears. You hear me?"

"David Henry . . . ," began Winter.

David Henry growled and leaned close, his nose nearly touching hers. "Do . . . you . . . hear . . . me, Winter?"

Winter gritted her teeth and nodded, and then Dix and David Henry disappeared into the shadow of the trees. Left alone, the two girls sat in silence, not looking at each other.

"So what if they headed back to Remembrance?" muttered Louisa finally. "Either they'll find the business end of a gun or nothing at all. Mother Abigail must a' been outside the Edge hangin' the quilt to signal the exchange or something, otherwise don't know how those 'rollers got past the Edge in the first place."

But Winter knew how.

The Edge was broken.

Mother Abigail was broken.

But she'd fixed it. They'd fixed it. Right before . . .

She dug her nails into the soft earth, feeling the faint vibration there. In her mind's eye, she saw it all again and whimpered. The slavers bursting through the bushes. Mother Abigail sprawled on the ground. She could still feel the heat from the priestess's hands, the way the ground shifted under them, the weight of Mother Abigail's limp body weighing her down. She could hear the gunshots, the screaming horses. And Thomas? Thomas had been running from the woods to protect them, to protect Mother Abigail, but he had disappeared in a haze of mud and smoke.

"I hope you're right," whispered Winter.

Louisa stared at her sullenly. "Course I'm right! You think those crackers gon' be able to get into Remembrance more than once? The men's just probably sittin' there waitin', prayin' those pattyrollers come back again."

She looked at Louisa, surprised by the other girl's sudden bravado. Louisa glared.

"What you lookin' at me for?"

She dropped her chin onto her knees and wordlessly twirled a damp, gritty strand of hair round and round her finger.

Dix and David Henry reappeared from the shadow of the forest.

"This boy's right," said David Henry. He looked at Dix with grudging respect. Glancing up at the now-blue sky visible through the trees, he said, "Got to get a hurry on. Remembrance is close and I got a bad feelin' about those slavers." He glanced at Dix, who nodded. "We goin' home," said David Henry.

He raised an eyebrow at the girls, who had jumped to their feet. "And we goin' quiet."

"Come on, ladies," said Dix. "It's gonna be okay. You almost home."

He turned to follow David Henry into the thick brush. Louisa followed, careful to give the white boy a wide berth as she passed.

Winter shot a look at Dix as she passed. His pale, angular face was drawn, the circles under his eyes violet, blending into the deep purple bruises on his cheek. His hair stood up in stiff, pale spikes behind his ears. He reminded her of a half-starved rabbit, exhausted and scared.

He patted her roughly on the shoulder and she jerked away

"It's gonna be just fine, Winter," he said, pulling his hand back. "You'll see. Just fine."

51

Winter

Winter stumbled. Dix was at her side in an instant, and she shot him a look as she regained her footing and brushed past.

The sun was high in the sky, producing light but not warmth, and the snow had begun to fall in earnest. Fat, wet flakes collected in Winter's hair, melted inside her collar, the snow only adding to her misery. She slogged gloomily behind David Henry and Louisa and Dix, with no thought in her head except putting one foot in front of the other.

Louisa stopped suddenly, and Winter, her eyes glued to the ground at her feet, her mind numb from cold and hunger and exhaustion, lurched hard into her back. Stumbling backward, she lost her balance and fell, spread-eagle, into a shallow hollow between the trees. She lay there staring at the sky, fat snowflakes covering her face, unmoving.

"Winter?" cried Dix. He reached a hand to pull her up but she ignored it.

"You alright?" David Henry's face appeared next to Dix's.

Winter turned her head and blinked slowly. "I would sell my body and my soul to the first person that came along with some hot food and a warm fire." She tried to laugh but it came out as a sob. She swiped at her eyes with a muddy fist.

David Henry grinned crookedly. "I'll be sure to keep an eye out. Someone like that sure to be around directly."

"Wait," cried Louisa, cutting them off. "I know this place. I know it."
David Henry and Dix turned toward her.

"I know this place," she said again. She stepped around a moldering log and pointed. "My first night of true freedom, the night Mother
Abigail found me, I stood right there." Her voice cracked.

David Henry went to her side.

"Yes," he said quietly. "I remember this place too. It was dark and
I was near starved. Don't know how many days I been runnin'. Hidin'
in ditches and up in trees. Then Mother Abigail appeared like some
kind of guardian angel, right over yonder."

The two ex-slaves stood side by side, gazing in silence out over the
countryside that rose before them. Winter struggled to her feet and
followed their gaze, but this part of the forest looked like all the other
parts they'd come through over the past few hours.

This place held no memories for her. Her freedom had been bought
with the last of her mother's body heat, and all her memories began
and ended in Remembrance.

"We need to get movin'," Dix said, breaking the silence.

David Henry turned to him, his expression cold. "Last time I came
through here, I vowed wouldn't no white man ever give me another
order."

Dix met his look without comment. After a long moment, David
Henry smiled tightly. "Who'd-a ever thought one day I'd be bringin' a
white boy into the heart of Remembrance."

Dix shook his head and sighed. "Let's just finish this."

A short time later they were half walking, half sliding down a hill,
the mulberry and the clearing beyond in sight.

"How do we get past the Edge?" asked Louisa.

But David Henry was not listening. He was staring down a wagon track
that curved off into the distance. "This ain't right," he said, frowning.

"What isn't?" asked Winter.

"This. This road," he said, still frowning. "There's no road at the
Edge of Remembrance."

David Henry, Winter, and Louisa exchanged a look. Dix looked
from one to the other, his eyes narrowed in confusion.

"There is no more Edge," said Winter.

A wave of nausea washed over her. They were in Remembrance but it felt wrong, out of tune. She felt the air pulse around her, filled with strands of energy, bits of things that didn't belong. She swayed slightly.

"Winter?"

"What she mean there ain't no Edge?"

"You okay?"

They were all talking at once, their voices coming from far away.

She sank slowly to her knees and pressed her hands against the snowy ground. Remembrance was not one thing. It was the trees and the water. It was Thomas's ironworks, Sir Galahad's goats, and Old Peter's harmonica. It was the cabins and the fire and the cemetery. And it was the people. And all those things, small and large, gave off energy, their little pieces spinning and spinning. Connected. And the energy of Remembrance was not right.

"What she talkin' about, David Henry? What's this idiot girl mean about Remembrance? What she mean ain't no Edge?

"Is she sick? She looks sick?"

"Winter, stop it! What's wrong with you, girl?"

Winter dug her fingers into the icy dirt, feeling the spaces, all the spinning parts that connected Remembrance.

"They're here," Winter croaked. "Colm and the others—they're here. They're inside Remembrance."

"How can she know that?" said Dix. "She can't know that!"

"She knows," muttered David Henry

He knelt a few feet away, his proud, dark face worried. Louisa, shivering in the cold, looked terrified.

Winter felt herself fall into the spaces beneath her, felt the earth moving slowly in the cold. They were here, and the thought almost suffocated her with fear. They had hurt her, and now they were here and going to hurt other people, her people.

She clenched her fists and touched the closest speck of soil, felt it shudder, slowly, felt its energy move into the tip of her finger. And she touched another, then another.

Decide.

Louisa said she had to decide.

With each piece she touched, she felt her fear get smaller, felt it changing, like she was changing the soil. Turning it into something else. Turning it into fury.

She opened her eyes and stood. Her companions were staring at her, a mix of alarm and confusion in their eyes. Around her, the snow had melted and the trees were blackened as if by fire. What had been snow-covered dirt was now a smooth circle of white-streaked marble. She smiled. The slavers would never hurt anyone again.

"We need to go," she said. "We need to save Remembrance."

David Henry held up a hand once more, and they all settled in silently behind him, hiding in the thick brush surrounding the cemetery. Voices came to them through the trees, frightened, confused voices.

David Henry swore. He held up three fingers indicating that the three slavers were already there. Dix nodded. Beside her, Louisa was trembling, and Winter reached to touch her shoulder. The other girl jerked away.

David Henry and Dix knelt with their heads close together, speaking in hurried, frantic whispers. Winter couldn't hear their words but it didn't matter. She stood, and the two men turned to look at her. Without a word, she pushed her way from the shadow of the trees.

"Winter, no. Wait!" hissed David Henry. He grabbed for her but she dodged him, darting around the grave markers—one looked fresh— and onto the trail that would take her into the main settlement, moving fast on the snowy ground. The snow was falling thickly now, draping everything in a veil of white. Her breath crystallized in front of her face as she ran.

At the top of the trail she glanced over her shoulder. She could just barely make out the figures of David Henry, Dix, and Louisa crouched among the trees in the graveyard. David Henry waved his arm frantically, beckoning her back, but she turned her back to him and dashed up the narrow, rocky trail that would take her to the Central Fire— into the heart of Remembrance.

Remembrance.

Home.

No matter that the Edge had collapsed. No matter that the patty-rollers had come back, fouling the place, her place, Remembrance. She was home.

At the top of the rise, just inside the tree line behind the bakehouse, she stopped and squatted at the base of a tree. From there, she had a clear view of the area around the Central Fire.

Mother Abigail lay sprawled near the Central Fire. She looked dead. Frank stood a few feet from the priestess, holding Petal by the hair. The tiny woman's toes barely scraped the ground as she swung wildly at the big slaver, cursing him. Frank merely laughed, holding his face back to avoid her blows. Winter felt the terror of the settlers like a snail oozing across her skin. She took it all in, felt her power flare up, feeding on her rage. She forced herself to focus on the slavers.

All around the settlement, everyone was moving sluggishly, as if wading through molasses, toward the Central Fire. Except for Petal's curses and Frank's laughter, it was eerily quiet. No one noticed Winter hunched there just inside the tree line.

Where were the men with guns? Where was Josiah?

She heard the others creeping up behind her and turned just as David Henry slid down beside her.

"They're by the Central Fire," said Winter in response to David Henry's silent question. "Mother Abigail is just laying there. Sick. Worse. I can't tell."

David Henry's eyes flicked in the direction of the Central Fire. He pushed past her to see for himself, and his face contorted in fury at the sight before him.

Dix reached a hand to restrain David Henry. "Don't know what you thinkin' you can do," he said, speaking to both the man and Winter. "I don't know nothin' about this power, this Edge, whatever it is all y'all talkin', but I need to tell you, goin' up against them boys without a plan and a whole lotta guns is just plain foolhardy."

"I got a gun," said David Henry.

Winter smiled grimly. "I won't need a gun."

Dix shook his head. His light hair was plastered against his forehead. "Look, we can't just go up in there and start shootin' up—"

She stood suddenly, cutting off his words. "It's alright," she said. "It's all going to be alright."

She brushed his hand aside and stepped from the cover of the trees.

52

Mother Abigail

So beautiful! It is so beautiful here!

The air was warm and smelled of freshly mowed grass. Early morning sun filtered through the leaves of the trees, loosening her limbs, feeding her tired, worn muscles. Her heart was full. So very full.

She thought she might float with joy!

They were back! On the other side of a narrow river that seemed filled with golden light instead of water. There was her brother, Ajani, and the other half of her heart, Hercule. And her parents, and Ama, her sister! She didn't know this place, but it felt like the only place she would ever want to be again.

"Mama!" she cried.

The faces of her loved ones were shrouded in a brilliant yellow glow, blurring their features, but she felt her mother's smile. The priestess tried to stand and found that every one of her pains had disappeared. Delighted, she jumped up and down, laughing like she hadn't since childhood, when her body obeyed her commands easily and her whole world was the tiny village tucked in the bend of the river.

Mother Abigail took a step toward the river's edge, toward her family, but from the other side of the rippling light, her brother held out a hand to stop her. A wave of anger rolled through her.

No! This is the time! I come with you now. You promised me this.

"One moment more," said her brother. But it was not Ajani's voice that came

from his lips. The voice was that of many, and ancient. It was the voice of the spirits, the voice of the old gods and goddesses.

"One moment more," said the spirits with her brother's lips.

Grinding her teeth, the old woman turned reluctantly away from the lake of golden light to face all that she had created.

Remembrance.

She gasped, and another wave of anger rolled through her, this one so strong that she staggered. There, in the very midst of Remembrance, like manure steaming in a farmyard, stood three slavers. The very same ones from before.

One of the dark-haired devils stood on the far side of the Central Fire, the barrel of a rifle pointing at Margot's throat.

Tiny Petal was barely an arm's length away. She screeched curses and clawed at the face of a massive slaver, who scowled in annoyance as he held her by the hair and shook her. The priestess reached for the girl, but her hands seemed to glide off an unseen barrier. Frowning, she glanced over her shoulder. The golden lake still glimmered among the trees. Her loved ones stood in silence, their faces radiating light from within and without. She could feel them watching, waiting for her. She could feel their love.

She turned back to Remembrance and tried once again to move toward the Central Fire, to move against the slavers that had dared to enter Remembrance, her Remembrance, for the second time. But once again, she found herself unable to go to her people, unable to save them from the slavers. It was like watching through window glass.

"What you going to have me do then?" she cried to the ancestors who stood behind her watching. "Stand here and watch Remembrance die?"

That couldn't be it, she thought. The spirits would not be so cruel. A sudden movement at the edge of the trees caught her eye.

Winter.

Her heart sang. Her girl was alive.

The girl stepped from the shadow of the forest and stood, unnoticed for the moment, watching the tableau in front of her. The priestess saw her start, saw her mouth the words "Mother Abigail." The girl was not looking at her but at a point several feet away. Mother Abigail followed Winter's gaze and saw, propped against a low pile of logs, head thrown back, mouth open, her own body slumped carelessly on the ground.

"Well . . . *merde!*" she said. She frowned as understanding suddenly came to her.

Caught.

She was stranded in that ancient place, between the living and dead. A shiver of fear rippled through her, but she pushed it away.

"I am Mother Abigail," she whispered. "I am Babalawa."

She closed her eyes. "I am Babalawa."

She felt inside herself, reaching for the last bit of power. As long as she drew breath, she knew it was there, always there.

Tired. So tired.

But it was there waiting, just waiting to be released. Those patty-rollers would not desecrate Remembrance again. Her chest burned as she tried to force herself forward, tried to break through the invisible seam of time and space that held her trapped. The burning grew worse, eating up her breath, squeezing her lungs in a fiery fist. Something tore inside her head, and the pain seemed to settle behind her eyes, causing them to water, but when she touched her face, it was blood on her fingertips and not tears. Mother Abigail moaned.

At the edge of the settlement, Winter was still standing, watching the curly-haired slaver that had dragged Margot to the far side of the fire circle.

Winter looked as if the earth had chewed her up, then spit her back out. Her clothes were rags, her hair a tangled mess. She was covered in mud and her face was scratched and swollen.

But it wasn't the bruising or the girl's battered appearance that gripped Mother Abigail's attention. There was something else—something wild and strong—something the priestess had only seen two other times in her very long life.

The air around Winter pulsed with energy.

Her girl had found the key to her power.

53

Winter

She took in everything with a glance: Petal screaming and slashing at the giant Frank's face with her nails; Colm, his hand wrapped around Margot's arm, his gun dangerously close to her face. His back was to Winter, but she didn't need to see his face to recognize him.

She dug her fingernails into her hand. She wanted them gone. These white men, these slavers. They were a disease, rotting flesh in the midst of Remembrance, poisoning everything around them.

"Winter," hissed David Henry from the shadows behind her. She hunched her shoulders, shrugging him off.

"No, child! No, *petite!*"

Winter's head jerked up. Mother Abigail's voice seemed to come to her in the air, as soft as the snowflakes clinging to her lashes. She scanned the area around the Central Fire, squinting to see through the worsening snow. She pressed her lips together at the sight of the priestess, slumped against a low rise of stacked timbers like a pile of discarded rags on the opposite side of the fire from the slavers.

"Mother Abigail," she whispered.

In a flash she was at the old woman's side. The priestess was not dead, but Winter felt how faint her life force was.

"Mother Abigail," she whispered. "I'm here."

She touched her face. It was cold as ice. She pressed her cheek against the priestess's to warm her.

"I'm here," she said again. "Can you hear me? I'm right here."

But Mother Abigail seemed not to hear. Winter stroked the snow from her lashes and squeezed her hand.

Suddenly, the old woman shuddered. She turned her head and her eyes lit with recognition. Winter gripped her hand and pressed it to her heart.

"It's going to be okay, Mother Abigail. I promise. It's going to be okay."

She felt a current pass into her chest, through her. It was painful, powerful, but still she held on, staring into Mother Abigail's eyes until the light there faded.

She felt a howl of rage and grief rise up inside, and she turned slowly, still gripping Mother Abigail's hand, taking it all in, the chaos the slavers had brought into her home. As her eyes fell on the trail leading up to the cottages, she inhaled sharply.

Josiah stood half hidden in the trees at the head of the trail. But it was not Josiah as she had known him all of her life. This Josiah was bent, frail, with rivers of white running through his thick hair. He met her eye and shrank into the shadows.

With a last look at Mother Abigail, she stood. She had never truly felt a part of Remembrance, but Remembrance was part of her.

She had decided.

She took a deep breath and turned reluctantly back toward Colm. At the periphery of the Central Fire, coming down from the grazing pastures, from the doors of their cottages, the settlers of Remembrance were trickling toward the slavers, toward the screaming Petal. They carried sticks, knives, and axes, the everyday tools of farming, cooking, and tending their animals. Only a handful of the men had real weapons. Despite Louisa's boast, there were few guns in Remembrance. Mother Abigail and the Edge had given them more than enough protection, had kept them safer than a hundred guns—until now.

Margot saw her first. Her eyes flicked over the slaver's shoulders, widening for just a fraction of a second, before going blank again. But

Colm had caught the look. Winter saw his shoulders tighten, felt his awareness shift from Margot to her.

"Well, if it isn't the prodigal daughter." He turned slightly, pulling Margot with him as he raised his gun. "Welcome to the party."

Winter stared narrow-eyed at him. She felt as if she'd been planted, as if she'd taken root where she stood. Swirling snow blew across her face in the frigid air, but she was beyond feeling it. Colm's voice came to her as if from very far away. She pulled her lips back from her teeth in a snarl and saw him flinch, a fleeting shadow of fear crossing his face, the hunter sensing danger.

Across the fire, Petal had gone silent. All of Remembrance had gone silent. The only sounds were the crackling of the fire and the soft murmuring of the snow as it fell to the ground.

Colm's mouth turned up, his eyes dark holes in his pale face. "Our feelings have been deeply hurt, haven't they, Frank?"

The big slaver grunted but said nothing.

"Well," Colm went on, his smile wide. "You and that other one, the ugly one, didn't seem to much appreciate our hospitality. And that cuts me deeply. To the quick, in point of fact."

He took a step toward Winter.

She stared at him, feeling her power churning. She saw him. Saw his dirty green jacket. Saw the suspenders that bit into the frayed wool of his pants. She saw him. All of him. And she held herself motionless, breathing frost-laden air into her lungs.

"I'm not used to having to chase my bounty twice," said Colm. The smile vanished as his face contorted into a mask of rage. "And just how am I to be paid back for that, do you think?"

He waited. Winter cocked her head and regarded him silently. The slaver's face twisted. "How?" he screamed. "How do you plan to make that up to me? To us?"

He leaned toward her, breathing hard, his breath sour on her face. He wiped the back of one hand across his lips, then straightened. And then he smiled.

The few armed black men, David Henry's men, inched closer, but the slavers were careful to not give them a chance at a clear shot.

"I know, Frank," he said, his eyes never leaving Winter's. "We came here looking for the witch that broke our brother's mind. First, we just got you and the ugly one, but now, it looks like we're too late for the witch." He jerked his head toward the fallen priestess.

Winter breathed in slowly through her nose but held Colm's gaze. "You're going to leave this place," she said quietly.

Surprise flared in Colm's eyes before he could hide it.

"Leave?" Frank's voice cut through the stunned quiet. "Oh, we'll be leaving alright. And we'll be taking way more than we came with. All you niggers up there, throw down those damn guns and get down here."

No one moved. The men kept their guns raised, waiting for the moment when they could fire on the slavers without hitting one of their own, their wrath a low thrum against Winter's skin.

"Don't make me ask you all again," growled Frank.

"My brother's not known for his patience or goodwill toward his fellow man," said Colm. He grinned at Winter. "Why don't you tell them, lass? You yourself have been on the receiving end of our Frank's bad temperament. Now tell them to be good boys and throw down those guns before somebody gets hurt."

She stared, unblinking. She felt nothing, not the cold, not fear. Even her anger felt like a distant echo. Colm was nothing. His brother Frank and the taciturn Paddy, they were nothing. Millions and millions of spinning particles, held together in the shape of men.

"Tell them," screamed Colm. Spittle flew from his lips, mixing with the blowing snow. When she remained silent, the slaver signaled with his free hand.

"Paddy!" called Frank. "Bring your ass out here. Tired of playin' with these niggers."

The third slaver stepped from between two cottages. Knife-thin and silent, Paddy held a small bundle carelessly in each hand. Petal's scream ripped through the settlement, the sound of pure agony.

"My babies! Not my babies!"

Ripping free of Frank, she dashed, screaming, toward Paddy. The skeletal slaver made as if to toss the infants into the fire, and Petal froze. She stood rigid in front of Paddy, her arms outstretched, reaching for her twins, then collapsed at the slaver's feet.

"Please," she begged. "Please. I'll go with you. Just give me my babies. Please give me my babies."

The three slavers laughed as the freed slaves of Remembrance looked on in horror.

Winter had turned to fire inside. Snowflakes sizzled to steam the instant they touched her skin. The world around her pulsed red with each beat of her heart. Petal screamed and screamed, and the screams braided themselves through Winter's soul like barbed wire.

One ex-slave, then another, threw his gun down then stepped forward as requested, but it was fury, not defeat in their eyes. All except for one, Daniel, who stepped forward, his rifle shouldered. Paddy shook the babies again, taunting him as Petal cowered at his feet, each shake of her children sending a ripple of anguish through her tiny body.

Paddy held one of the twins, Aron, over the open flame of the Central Fire. The child's cries became frantic as the swaddling cloth that wrapped him began to steam.

Margot moved.

She spun away from the gun, and a knife appeared as if out of nowhere. Sunlight flashed on metal as it arced through the air, slashing toward Colm's throat. It caught in the collar of the pattyroller's jacket, slowing the blade as it sliced through the taut skin at the edge of Colm's jaw. Screaming, she whirled, preparing to come at him again.

But the slaver was faster. Cursing, he backpedaled, deflecting the second blow with the butt of his gun, knocking the knife from her hand. Hissing in fury, Margot clawed at Colm's face with her nails, but she was off-balance and fell.

"Bitch!" screeched Colm. Blood ran into his collar, turning it black. "You nigger bitch!"

Winter could see him, through him. The structure of his skin, the pale, thin octagons layered atop each other like fallen leaves, and the spaces beneath that. His muscles, the long, thin fibers lying side by side. She could see into him. Deeper and deeper. The skin and muscles that made him, and the particles that made the skin and muscle, all spinning, round and round, holding him together. There, in that space, the blood in his veins, his bones fine as ash.

Colm raised the gun again, and Winter breathed in a fiery breath, leaned in to touch the pieces of him and pull them apart.

Ready.

But in that half beat of time between one breath and the next, in the instant just before she could release the power that would turn Colm into not-Colm, Dix erupted from the shadow of the trees.

"No," he shouted. "No, Colm."

Colm whirled on the boy.

"Wait!" Dix held his arms away from his body to show he was unarmed.

The slaver stared at the boy, the rifle in his hands trembling. He looked Dix up and down, his eyes wild with fury. "What do you think you're doing?"

"These ain't slaves, Colm. You said we was gonna be trackin' slaves."

Colm threw back his head and laughed, the sound brittle. "What the hell difference does that make, boy? A nigger is a nigger. Now get over here and start tying up some of these young bucks."

Dix was shaking his head. "No. This ain't right."

The slaver stared at him, his face red. "You are a disgrace of a white man. We should have left you to freeze to death in that ditch where we found you. You are worse than a nigger. Least they know what they are."

He spit out the words, each one thick with loathing, then spit on the ground at Dix's feet. He turned back to Margot.

"We got no use for a nigger that attacks a white man, no matter how lovely the face." He raised the rifle and rammed the barrel against her throat. "And get rid of those mewling brats, Paddy. They're less than useless. Will not waste a crust of bread on a nigger that can't do a day's work."

"No!" Dix's scream fused with Petal's in the cold morning, seeming to whip the snow into a miniature cyclone.

Winter saw Paddy fling Petal's baby boy toward the fire. Heard the sharp report of a gunshot. In that last instant, she saw a flash of movement as Dix lunged past her.

And then she could hold it no more.

She saw only Paddy, smiling, his rotted teeth, black stubs in his mouth. She saw the rot that was his mind. It was easy. So easy. His brain was like a ripe blackberry, the ridges smooth and wet in her hand. She leaned in and fell into the spaces between the spaces, touching the thing that was his brain. Even his fear in those last moments was a thing she could push, change. And she did, laughing as his brain tore itself apart.

And now Frank.

Did he think he could run from her?

Skin.

He was only skin and bones and blood and sinew. Particles strung together, just like the cold dirt on which they stood. Dust to dust. A quote Belle always said at Sunday supper. He tried to run, but Winter could see inside him, see the millions and millions of pieces that held him together, and she pushed them apart, pushed them as hard as she could. From very far away, she heard a man screaming.

They could not touch her.

They could not stop her. They were nothing but insignificant particles that she had the power to twist and bend any way she wanted.

"Winter."

Mother Abigail whispered her name in the wind.

But there was one more.

She locked eyes with Colm. He gaped at her, his eyes wild, the gun pointed at her chest. She pushed at the pieces that formed the metal of the gun, forced them to speed up until they were rotating at the same speed as the finger that gripped the trigger, pushed until the gun and the hand were indistinguishable.

He screamed. She stared into his eyes, feeling the power roar from her, pushing it toward him, into him, as Colm became not-Colm, losing his man shape. Becoming . . . something else.

The ground seemed to vanish beneath her feet, and the air burned her face, her lungs. And she could feel herself starting to come apart, feel herself becoming not-Winter.

"Stop, *petite*! Stop now, child!"

She felt the priestess's breath soft on her face, a faint wind cooling her, bringing her back to a memory of herself. She fell. And fell some more. Until she fell back into Remembrance.

54

Margot

She stepped out onto the tiny stoop and inhaled. The air smelled fresh and green. After a long, harsh winter, Remembrance was coming alive. Even now, all these months later, it still felt odd to think of the tiny cabin as home. Perched between two birch trees, it was slightly uphill from Petal and Daniel's cabin. Nearly every morning on her way down to the Central Fire, she made a point to stop in and see their babies, her babies.

It surprised her how much joy she got from cuddling the fat, warm twins in her arms, inhaling their yeasty, baby smell. They trilled slobbery laughter whenever she pressed her nose to theirs, and in just the past week, both of them, Aron and Delilah, had produced teeth. This thrilled her beyond measure. She stepped from the stoop, stopping as she saw a familiar figure making his way up the trail in the early morning light.

"Bonjour."

"Mornin'," said David Henry, grinning. He liked it when she spoke French.

"When did you return?" she asked.

"Just now. Rode out before sunrise."

David Henry and two other men had gone to Ashtabula to sell Remembrance's iron, honey, and flour, and Sir Galahad's goat cheese.

Now that they were out in the world, their reputation, and the Outsider's appetite, for these things had only grown.

"Got you somethin'."

Her eyes widened as he pulled a delicate mother-of-pearl hair comb from his jacket pocket.

"It is beautiful," she exclaimed. She turned so that he could slip it into her hair.

He took her hand and they smiled at each other.

"Have you eaten?"

He shook his head, and she turned to lead him down the trail to the Central Fire. She would see the babies later. Margot had only taken a few steps when she felt resistance. Turning, she found David Henry gazing up the trail into the trees.

"You miss her," she said, following his gaze toward Mother Abigail's now-empty cabin.

"I do." He sighed. "She was everything. If she hadn'a been, wouldn't none a' this have been."

He tried to smile. "It's good now, though, right? Different, but good."

She nodded as he reached to caress her cheek.

They had buried Mother Abigail at the foot of the giant mulberry, where her spirit could watch over Remembrance for always.

"Come," she said.

He exhaled and turned to follow her. At the bottom of the hill, Dixon McHugh stood holding a cup of coffee in one hand, a rifle in the other.

Since the day Winter had destroyed the other slavers, Dix had chosen to remain in Remembrance. It had taken the settlers a while to accept him. Some still didn't. They blamed him for what had happened to Mother Abigail, to Winter. Blamed him for the fact that Remembrance was now visible to the world. Most couldn't understand why he would want to stay, but Margot understood the need to belong to something.

Those first few weeks he'd been skinny, bruised, jumping at every sound, sleeping alone in the woods. Now the circles under his eyes were gone and his lean frame had filled out. He still preferred to sleep in one of the lean-to shelters at the edge of the settlement, but he seemed happy. He stood now at the head of the trail, sipping a cup of coffee. His face was turned away from them, and she could see the thick scar, shiny and twisted, that ran down the side of his face and into his shirt collar, a permanent reminder of that morning when he'd leaped into the fire to catch baby Aron in those last few seconds.

"Good morning," she called.

Dix turned, and they saw that his pale hair had been pulled back from his face into pigtails and tied with red string. David Henry laughed out loud at the sight of him.

Dix grinned. "Mornin'."

Margot eyed his hair. "This is . . . *inhabituel!* Unusual."

"Esther," he said, rolling his eyes.

"Ah," she answered, exchanging knowing looks with David Henry.

"Goin' huntin' for boar," said Dix to David Henry. "Welcome to join."

David Henry shook his head. "Nah, still got work to do on the reverend's school. It seem like we got new kids showin' up every day. Definitely next time."

Dix saluted him with his cup and headed up the trail. David Henry watched him go. "Catches me by surprise every time I see him walkin' around. But he a alright white boy."

"He appears to have stolen Esther's heart."

"Maybe we can have a double weddin'. That is, if Hannah still fancy's me." He grinned.

She laughed.

"Heard we expectin' more folks runnin' north," he said, turning serious.

"Yes, soon."

There were rumblings of a coming war, and every day more and more slaves found their way to them.

"Then I best get busy on that schoolhouse."

She watched him walk away and then made her way slowly around the Central Fire. Even now, nearly six months after those hideous men had come into Remembrance, the settlement bore the scars of that day.

Around the Central Fire itself, the ground was hard and nearly transparent. Nothing could grow anywhere near it, no shovel or ax could pierce it. To Margot, it looked uncannily like a massive diamond, but that was impossible. Nearby, trees were bent and blackened. But the most unnerving thing for her, the thing she could not bear to look at, even now, was the huge stone at the edge of the Central Fire.

It was there that the slaver had rammed a gun against her throat; in her dreams she still felt the metal between her collarbones. It was there that she'd tried to stab him before he struck her to the ground.

And then Winter had been there.

She remembered the swirling snow, and the heat. So hot it burned her throat.

She remembered the sound. The wind and screaming.

And then silence.

When she opened her eyes, the slaver was gone. There was only this mound of stone in the exact place he'd been standing.

Margot shuddered. She poured herself a cup of coffee, then cornered one of the younger children to run a basket of food up to Louisa. Except when someone was ill, the healer almost never left her gardens.

It was late afternoon and the sun had disappeared behind the clouds before she had another quiet moment. So many new people meant so much to do. She walked the now-familiar path through the cemetery and out to the edge of the clearing. Across the greening grass, the giant mulberry was coming into bud. She hunched her shoulders against the growing chill.

Mother Abigail was gone. From where she stood, she could see the tiny marker that showed where the old priestess had been laid to rest.

Josiah was gone. No one had seen him since the night the slavers tore through Remembrance.

And Winter was gone.

After that day, she'd moved through Remembrance like a wound, scarred, silent, no one except Dix daring to approach her.

And then she was gone, too.

Margot glanced at the sky. Tonight more would come seeking sanctuary. Or tomorrow night or the night after. And they were still here.

Remembrance was still here.

Winter

She stood on the top of a ridge. The sun was rising and the fog rolled like a river across the countryside below her. She didn't know where she was going, only that she would know it when she got there. Remembrance no longer belonged to her. She no longer belonged to Remembrance.

She ran a hand across her scalp. Still tender, the smoothness of it was still so strange.

She'd woken in her cabin, confused, her scalp, her skin burning, images playing in her head.

Colm. Paddy.

David Henry had been standing over her. And the new girl, Margot, one eye swollen shut.

"The baby," she croaked. Petal's baby. She had seen it go into the fire. Just before . . .

"The baby is fine," answered Margot.

And then she slept, waking from time to time with a scream, fighting her way back from a nightmare. It took a week for her to regain her strength, before she was well enough to step back out into Remembrance. And then she saw that everything had changed.

She saw the burned places, the ground where nothing would grow. She saw the odd-shaped stone at the edge of the Central Fire. And she saw the fear. For the most part, everyone in Remembrance steered clear of her, edging past her on the trails, refusing to meet her eye. On the rare occasion when she couldn't be avoided, they would stutter a greeting, their eyes jittery with terror. All except Dix. With his ugly new scar puckering the side of his face.

They were grateful, said David Henry, truly they were, but it was all a bit much. Everybody just needed time.

She'd nodded, and on the night of the winter solstice, she'd walked away from the only home she'd ever known.

She didn't turn when he came up behind her. She stared out across the rolling, frost-covered landscape.

"Bad times comin'," he said.

"Yes."

"Best be gettin' on, then. Folks gon' be needin' a safe place against the storm."

Josiah walked past, the sweet cherry from his tobacco borne on the wind. He was young again. Or younger. Looking the way he had always looked.

She pulled her cloak around her shoulders and followed him into the misty Ohio dawn.

Gaelle

The phone buzzed from somewhere inside the tree.

Eleven.

She'd stopped counting the texts from Rose after they'd reached eleven, stopped reading them long before that. The first had come in at midnight.

Jwaye Nwel, sè.

Then: *Gaelle?*

Are you angry with me?

Gaelle, please.

Sè, answer me, tanpri.

Until finally, she'd thrown the phone deep into the branches of the Christmas tree. The phone buzzed again and she sat up with a groan. The tree lay on its side in the corner, where she'd dropped it three days before. Taking up nearly every square inch of the tiny living room, its branches obscured the television, the coffee table, most of the couch. She had no idea how she'd managed to get it home and then into the house. And no idea why she'd bothered.

She remembered Toya, sitting on the couch at the funeral home, her face blank, her two remaining sons sitting mute beside her. She'd not spoken a word since the morning she'd found Kevin bleeding to death in the snow, her car still running. When Gaelle bent to wrap her arms around her friend, Toya was as hard and cold as marble. She'd held on tight, forcing the heat from her body into Toya's, warming her, sensing her soften in her embrace, just a little.

"It will be alright, *chè zanmi*. I promise," she whispered. "We will survive."

But in that moment she was not sure this was true. Not everything could be survived. One could be broken just so many times, *wi?*

She hugged the boys and fled. She drove aimlessly through the icy streets of Cleveland for hours, getting lost in unfamiliar neighbor-hoods, then doubling back only to get lost again. The sun was setting when she stumbled on the tree lot. This close to Christmas, there were only a few trees left, all too big for her little carriage house. She bought the biggest one. It had taken the tree man nearly half an hour to lash it to the roof of her tiny car, and now it lay bare and crammed into her living room. This was her Christmas.

A naked tree.

Alone.

In a cold apartment. That would not belong to her in just a few short weeks.

She leaned and pressed her face into a branch. The clean, fresh smell soothed her. From its hiding place inside the tree, the phone buzzed again.

"*Ase,*" she hissed, jerking upright.

She clutched a handful of pine needles in her fist, relishing the cool, prickly texture.

Grann was gone. Rose was gone.

In her hand the needles began to smolder, a wisp of earth-scented smoke wafting into the air.

Kevin was gone and Toya, his mother, her only real friend, shat-tered.

The needles glowed a soft orange.

And soon they would try to take her home away.

There was a faint sound, like paper crinkling, and the pine needles burst into flame. She threw them on the floor, smiling in satisfaction as they scorched the old rug before quickly burning out.

She pushed herself to her feet, and the room spun for a moment. She tried to remember when she'd last eaten. Yesterday? The day before? She still wore the clothes from Kevin's funeral, the black skirt wrinkled and sticky with sap. She took a deep breath and grinned, feeling clear and focused, despite the wave of dizziness.

Pushing past the tree, she pulled her backpack from a hook on the closet door. She had few valuables. Pictures of the three of them—Rose, Grann, and her—at a wedding, a bracelet of her mother's, a tiny jade heart Toya and the boys had given her for her birthday the year before. She stuffed it all into the backpack.

She didn't know where she was going, but she'd promised Toya it was going to be alright. There had to be a way to make it alright. The old man's voice echoed in her head. "How much more will you allow this world to take from you?"

"No more," she whispered.

At the door she turned and broke a small branch from the tree and placed it in the backpack. For a long moment she stared at her hand, the brown skin, dry from the frequent washings at work, the nails short and ragged; then, squatting, she grabbed hold of the tree's trunk.

Special.

She wasn't just a survivor. She was special.

Heat trickled down her spine, filling her. But even as the room grew hotter and the water inside the trunk turned to steam and hissed away into the air, she felt cool, calm.

With a *whoosh,* the tree caught fire, the trunk turning a deep orange, the needles a bright yellow. She waited, watching as the old rug, then the fabric of her secondhand couch ignited. She straightened and backed away. She gave a soft whoop of joy and stepped from the house, closing the door behind her.

He was there. Standing at the end of the alley under the broken streetlight. Christmas Eve. It was Christmas Eve, she remembered.

He was no longer old. Still wearing the expensive jacket, he stood straight, his hair now completely black. They stood staring at each other as smoke began to fill the small living-room window.

She stepped closer. The dark glasses were gone, and she saw that his eyes were the color of oyster shells, reflecting light like polished glass.

"Who are you?"

"Josiah."

"The old woman, Winter, is gone."

"Yes."

"Where?"

Josiah looked up at the lightening sky. Streaks of pink and lavender announced the coming day. "It is no longer her time."

She sighed, the euphoria of just moments before beginning to fade. She felt the emptiness seeping back into her soul. "What do you want from me?"

"The world has been waiting for you," he said, an echo of what he'd said to her in the parking lot days before.

"Poukisa?"

"The world needs a protector."

She blinked. "Protector?"

She laughed, the sound harsh to her own ears. Tears pricked her eyes.

"I can protect no one."

Josiah raised an eyebrow and cocked his head back toward the carriage house. They could see the reflection of flames dancing in the smoky window. He smiled and held out a hand. With a glance at the burning building, she laid her hand in his, gasping in surprise as she felt a surge of electricity engulf her.

"You are so much more," he said.

"Wi," she said.

Acknowledgments

It is nearly impossible to express my thanks and appreciation for my amazing agent, Joanna Volpe at New Leaf Literary Agency. From the moment we met at the Midwest Writers Conference in Muncie, Indiana, all those years ago, until now, she has been a tireless advocate for and an enthusiastic champion of *Remembrance*. She never lost faith in me or the story. Her unflagging efforts led *Remembrance* to the perfect home with Diana Gill at Forge.

I owe a debt of gratitude to Diana and the Forge team. Diana was relentless in her drive to make *Remembrance* the best that it could be, and her critical editorial eye was unparalleled.

I am forever grateful for the friendship and unflagging support of the Scribes, a group of women who have had my back both personally and creatively. Diana Hurwitz, Cy Adams, Sharon Pielemeier, Cameron Steiman, thank you for everything you do and everything you are.

And to Kym Gotches, Jennifer Bethmann, Julie Augustinas, Anke Schulte, my storytelling friends, I miss you.